"STAY," SHE WHISPERED.
"STAY WITH ME, QUINT. . . ."

He leapt to his feet, grasping the edge of the bunk, cracking his head on the low ceiling. "I cannot! Damn me to hell, Rosa, you know I can't. . . . I must be fair to you. Stop tempting me!"

He was gone across the rocking cabin; the door slammed hard. She stared after him, shocked and hurt at first; then suddenly she felt wonderful. *Stop tempting me?* She smiled and lay back in the bunk, ignoring the rolling and creaking of the ship, which seemed to be moderating now. Surely any woman could learn to tempt a man past control . . . once she knew he wanted her that much. . . .

"Ms. McGauran has created a memorable love story, one that crackles with tension and sizzles with passion . . . sharp, often witty dialogue makes their verbal sparring an exciting match of wits. This one is too good to miss!"

—*Affaire de Coeur*

To Tempt a Man

Joanna McGauran

A DELL BOOK

Published by
Dell Publishing
a division of
Bantam Doubleday Dell Publishing Group, Inc.
1540 Broadway
New York, New York 10036

ISBN: 0-440-21875-6

Printed in the United States of America

Published simultaneously in Canada

July 1995

10 9 8 7 6 5 4 3 2 1

OPM

*To Denny, who taught me all
I know, or wanted to know, about boats.*

Chapter One

— ❦ —

At first Rosamunde didn't know what wakened her. After a spring day spent outdoors riding her horse on the greening hills of Devonshire, picnicking in the unkempt meadows of Squire Cedric Brownley's ruined estate, she'd dropped into dreamless sleep as soon as she crawled into bed. But now there was pressure and movement against her slim body, an odor in the darkness that was both familiar and abhorrent, a hot stink of decayed teeth and soured whiskey . . . oh, God! She screamed out, suddenly knowing what it was—*who* it was.

"Anna! Anna, come qui—" A hand clapped over her mouth and squeezed cruelly.

"Silence, you pretty little bitch! I've sold you for a harlot and it is my right to have you first."

Struggling, Rosa bit the hand fiercely, gagging at the taste. His scrawny body was naked; she could feel his manhood thrusting against her thighs. She jabbed upward with a knee and felt him jerk away, heard the door flung open, heard big Anna's hoarse yell of sudden fury.

"Get off her! Damn you, you blithering, drunken cur, I'll break your back!"

Tall Anna shone in the darkness like an avenging angel, her wide body and thick arms clothed in a white nightdress. Rosa twisted away as the weight left her, saw her half-naked stepfather lifted up in the air kicking and screeching, heard his high, furious voice berating his captor.

"By God, I'll have you jailed for life, you fat fool! You'll not have Beatrice to get you out this time." The voice stopped as Anna slammed his feet hard onto the floor, grabbed his scrawny throat with both hands and squeezed.

Panting and fearful, Rosa stared at the shadowy figures, watching Cedric's frantic attempts to pull Anna's hands away from his neck. She despised her stepfather, even more now than she had before her mother died, and the touch of his body against hers had made her want to vomit, but . . . She gasped and cried out in terror. Cedric's hands dropped; he was sagging helplessly in Anna's grasp.

"Anna! For God's sake be careful! You'll be had up for murder!"

"The time is past for care," Anna said, panting. She dropped the body, pushing it aside with one big foot. "He's dead, and good riddance. I've watched him this past year, and I suspected that he would try something like this." She stepped to the side of the bed and lit the lamp. Her broad red face was sweating from her efforts, but angrily determined. "I'll get Thomas up, and we'll bury him in the garden."

Rosa stared at her, at first unable to take it in, and then knowing—knowing the squire was actually dead. She burst into tears, crumpling forward to bury her face in her hands, moaning in terror, "Anna, you've *killed* him!"

Anna snorted. "True. He wasn't worth spending the

rest of my life in prison for, Rosa. That wasn't just a threat, you know. He would have turned me in, and as he said, there'd be no Lady Beatrice Gilbert to get me out again."

Rosa looked at the body, fighting nausea. "But it's bound to come out! Oh, Anna, I fear for you! It's true he has no friends, but he does have creditors who will want to find him. Even his brother Lionel is planning to sue for what Cedric owes him. Lionel will be looking everywhere for him."

"Lionel will be the first to say he ran away rather than pay his debts. Thomas and I will get rid of his decent clothes and whatever else is of value. Then we'll say he took what he could and left. Don't you mind, Rosamunde. You're rid of a burden."

Rosa slid from the bed on the side opposite the body and came around to hug Anna tightly.

"All right, if we must. Don't you mind, either. I know you did it for me. If his body is ever found, *I* shall confess to killing him myself. I'll not have anyone blaming you."

"No one will find him, love. We'll bury him deep."

Thomas, Anna's big, hulking son, came white-faced and nervous to Rosa's bedroom and wrapped the body in the old rug it lay upon. And in the end Rosa flung a dark cloak around her nightdress and went with them, carrying a hooded lantern to guide them in the darkness. Thomas chose the spot, beside the garden wall where the earth was easy to turn, easy to pat back into place. When they were done he pulled the new spring shoots of a briar rose across the disturbed earth.

" 'Twill make a thorny barrier long afore someone comes lookin' for Squire Cedric," Thomas said, shouldering his spade. " 'Tis near spring, and growin' weather." He looked at the lightening sky, and then at

Anna. "We've little time to get rid of his clothes an' valuables, Ma. Make up some tea an' we'll get at it."

"Bring down the old trunk from the attic, then," Anna said, heading for the kitchen. "Put it in that hog wallow he called his suite. I'll bring up the tea."

Thomas ran up the stairs, and Rosa, still weeping but more frightened than ever for Anna, ran up after him and went into her room to look for telltale stains. Later, pale but more composed, she came out dressed in her peach morning gown, her black hair loose on her shoulders, and met Thomas coming down empty-handed.

"The trunk is gone, Lady Rosa! What will we do now?"

She looked up at his broad, worried face and saw his deep concern for his mother, and her eyes filled again. For the past seven and a half years, ever since her own mother died, Anna and Thomas had been her family. She put an arm around his thick waist and gave him a squeeze.

"We'll keep her safe, Tom. Gather up his things and look for something to hide them in." She flung open the door to Brownley's rooms and saw the trunk sitting in the middle of the anteroom, strapped shut for a journey.

"Perhaps," she said slowly, "my stepfather has saved us the trouble."

There was a small carrying bag on the grimy desk, locked and ready. Anna pushed it aside when she came in and put the tea tray down beside it. Looking from the bag to the strapped trunk, she shook her head, her pale eyes regretful.

"Had he let you alone last night," she said, "he'd be off on his travels today, and I'd not have his blood on my hands."

"He got what was comin' to him," Thomas said

gruffly. "Don't you fret, Ma. We'll hide this plunder an' that'll be an end to it."

"We'll not hide it till we've searched it," Anna said, and cocked an eye at him. "There may be something we can use. The small bag feels heavy."

Steadied by a cup of tea, Rosa found the key to the bag next to an empty bottle of whiskey on a small table. Inside the bag were Cedric's personal effects, a pistol, and a hoard of gold guineas, enough to keep a careful family for years. Anna counted them in awe.

"Enough," she said, "to pay every bill he has and leave a good sum over. But he was going to run away. Now, what's this?" She picked out a roll of parchment and unrolled it. It was covered with black script and marked with a seal beside two signatures. She handed it to Rosa. "Read it, then. We'd best know what crime he committed to get that much gold."

The document was couched in fine language and written in a careful hand Rosa didn't recognize. She skipped to the bottom, finding the scrawled signature of Cedric Brownley of Bideford and the countersignature of a Lord Quinton Spencer, Vis., of Marisco Castle on Lundy Island. Starting again, she read only a few lines before she gasped and sat down, hard, in a filthy chair.

"So that's what he meant when he said he'd sold me for a harlot! Anna, he's as much as sold us all! Listen to this:

" 'As legal guardian of Rosamunde Gilbert, daughter of Lady Beatrice Gilbert Brownley, deceased, I hereby agree to give her in marriage to Viscount Quinton Spencer of Lundy Island. The bride price of one hundred gold guineas includes the purchase of Lady Rosamunde's two bond servants, Anna Castner and her son, Thomas Castner. I also agree to give them all into

Viscount Spencer's custody on Tuesday, March 6, 1838, at my home near . . .' "

Breath failed Rosa; her trembling voice went mute, only to come back in an anguished yelp.

"Anna! That's *today*!"

An hour and a half later the trunk had been emptied; its contents hidden in the moldy eaves of the attic, it was filled again with the clothes and effects of Rosa and her two servants. Anna was dressed in her dark traveling clothes; Thomas, standing guard downstairs, wore his best trousers and coat. Rosa was pulling an old lace-trimmed ivory silk gown of her mother's over a camisole and a huge crinoline. She went right on talking inside the heavy folds, her muffled voice trembling, leaving Anna to wonder if it was anger or fear that caused it. Or both.

"Don't you see that I *must* marry him?" Tangled black hair poked through the delicate lace neckline, followed by a pale face with huge, burning blue eyes. "Don't you know what he would do if I refused? He would demand to see Cedric immediately!"

"We could manage that," Anna said dourly. "Thomas could open the grave while I stood behind the man with Cedric's pistol. One shot and he'd join his friend in silence."

"Anna!"

Anna shrugged, giving the gesture a bit of bravado. "In for a penny, in for a pound. I can only hang once."

Rosa dashed tears from her eyes. "You'll not hang at all if I can help it. Stop being foolish and do my hair. I warrant the old fool will be here by noon, wanting a meal as well as a wife. I intend to marry him, distract him, and tell him as many lies as needed. Later I'll think of how to get away."

Grabbing a brush, Anna began making tangles into waves, adding shine with vigorous strokes. "See that the marriage vows are made before the marriage bed is turned down," she advised. "Once he's your legal husband he'll have good reason to keep his doubts to himself."

"Is the load from the trunk hidden? The small bag too?"

"Yes. And half the gold in the small bag transferred to your baggage."

"Half?"

"If he knew the squire, you'll never convince him that the old sot gave all of it to you."

"I don't care about that! But you'll need it all, Anna, if you're forced to run."

"The other half is sewn into the hem of my cloak."

"Oh." After a moment, Rosa nodded. "If we are somehow separated, neither of us will be penniless. You think of everything."

"No, I do not. For instance . . ." Anna swept the mass of satiny black hair to the top of Rosa's head, pinned it neatly, and then drew forth several long, curling locks to lie against the curve of white neck and shoulder. Standing back, her head cocked, to see the effect, she went on. "For instance, I have yet to think of an easy way to get rid of Lord Quinton Spencer without arousing suspicion."

"Never mind," Rosa said. "Who knows? We may be glad to have his protection for a time." She turned her head toward the front windows and listened. "Could that be him?"

Anna strode to the window and looked down. " 'Tis a man younger than we thought, but I'd say he looks a nobleman. He's riding a spirited horse and handling it well. Yes, he's turning in." She looked back at Rosa and frowned. "He hasn't the look of a fool, Rosa. We may not manage him as easily as we hoped. Do you remember all that we decided?"

"I do, but let me look." Rosa ran lightly across the room and peered down. "Oh! He is very tall and strong-looking, isn't he? And his hair as black as mine. I wonder if his eyes are blue."

There was a silence, and then Anna laughed. "If your fiancé inherited Marisco Castle because he carries Marisco blood, his eyes may be as brown as yours are blue. His family began as Turkish pirates, harassing sailors along the coast of Spain two hundred years ago. My seafaring father told me of their daring exploits. He greatly admired them. Ah, our visitor has dismounted. I'll go down and let him in."

Rosa stayed at the window, hiding herself with the ragged curtain and watching Lord Spencer take in his surroundings with a quizzical air. Anna came from a seafaring family and knew many descendants of pirates and privateers, and what she had said about this one intrigued her. His eyes, she noted, were not brown. They were green; green as grass and startlingly clear in a seafarer's strong, sun-darkened face. The expression in them was also clear. He found what he saw distasteful. Rosa would have laughed had she been sure he wouldn't hear her.

Obviously, Cedric had pulled the wool over Lord Spencer's eyes. His lordship had expected a much finer place than this hovel made of color-washed cob, with its pretentious planked second story. Undoubtedly he would expect a more fashionable bride. Perhaps it would be easier to lose him than she'd thought. Unless somehow he'd found out about her rather handsome dowry, hidden in London by her mother, who had made sure Cedric would never hear of it. She brightened. Very few people had been told—likely this Lord Spencer had no knowledge of it.

She dodged back as Thomas came out and took the reins of Spencer's horse to lead him around the house to the stable. Lord Spencer disappeared under the roof of the tiny entry, and stiffening her spine, Rosa lifted her head and went out to the head of the stairs.

Below in the hall Anna came forward and curtsied, remarkably agile for a woman who weighed over fifteen stone.

"Lady Rosamunde expects you, m'lord. If you'll have a seat in the drawing room, I will tell her of your arrival."

"That will not be necessary," Rosa said from the stair, "I am here." She came down, extending her hand when she reached them. Lord Spencer, his black brows rising as he noted the formal ivory silk and lace gown, took the hand and kissed it. Straightening, he smiled. "A distinct pleasure, my lady. Squire Brownley did not exaggerate your beauty."

Rosa's pulse leapt, her cheeks grew hot. Those green eyes had lost the chill she had noticed when he examined the house and warmed now to green fire. She knew she must be pink-faced, but from his smile he didn't mind that. She looked away, mostly because the very air between them seemed to interfere with her breathing. Trying to calm down, she allowed herself to hope. In any event, she decided, he wasn't displeased. If she read his expression correctly, he was—well, perhaps gratified.

"It was good of you to allow me to attend you at such short notice, Lady Rosamunde."

Behind her, Anna coughed warningly, and Rosa extracted her hand from his. Still, an aura of excitement shimmered between them and left her breathless. Then she remembered what Anna had told her to say and she burst out with it.

"You are welcome, Lord Spencer. I regret that Squire Brownley cannot be with us, due to a sudden change in his plans. However, I have seen the contract made between you and agreed to it." She turned to Anna. "Will you bring tea, Anna?" She glanced back at Spencer. "Or would you prefer wine?"

"Neither, my lady. I hired a coach-and-four to take all of us back to Clovelly and hence to my home on Lundy Island. It should be here soon. You will barely have time to pack."

Rosa's blush grew. "But we are packed, my lord. All three of us. Nothing remains to be done except for you to—to marry me."

Spencer frowned. "I have plans to wed in Marisco Castle, tomorrow."

Rosa reminded herself again of Anna's warning and steeled herself to carry it out. "My lord, I am a woman of good repute. I cannot leave here unwed and spend a night with you. For that reason I've sent my man Thomas to Bideford for a special license and a curate to listen to our vows."

Taken aback, Spencer stared at her. "He'll not get a special license, my lady. They are not handed out to just anyone who asks."

"Perhaps you are right, then, though I did tell him to mention that the bridegroom was Viscount Quinton Spencer of Marisco Castle and the bride the daughter of the late Lady Beatrice Gilbert."

Quinton frowned. "Oh? Did you also arrange for witnesses?"

"There can be no trouble about that. Both Anna and Thomas will be present and make their marks. The curate will vouch for them and put their names down." She trusted Anna; she needed to keep Anna safe, yet her voice faltered. She hated to go against his plan. It sounded so wonderful, marrying in an old castle.

Sir Quinton's strong face had taken on an expression of unwilling admiration. His gaze dropped farther, gliding over the top of her round breasts above the lacy décolletage, the tiny waist above the tremendous bell of crinolined skirt. "Odd," he said finally. "I would have thought a lady would wish to spend at least a bit of time getting acquainted with a man before she took him as her husband."

The small hand on his arm slipped down and folded warmly into his. "How considerate of you, my lord! Few men would be so understanding. Indeed, yes, it will be lovely to get well acquainted before we share a bed. Thank you very much."

Quinton was saved from answering by a knock on the door and the entry of the curate, followed by Thomas. The curate was visibly excited by the sight of Viscount Spencer. He bowed and grasped Quinton's offered hand, shaking it energetically.

"A rare privilege! A rare privilege, dear Lord Spencer!"

"Rare indeed," Quinton said with a wry look. "A once in a lifetime event, I hope. Has Thomas told you we are pressed for time?"

"No, No! Not in so many words, my lord, but as he came in haste, I suspected it." The curate turned, smiling, to Rosa. "Have you something to say, Lady Rosamunde?"

Rosa turned white again, struggling for words. When Anna had told her this part she hadn't realized how difficult it would be to go through with it. "Yes, Father, I do. When . . . when next you see Squire Brownley you must tell him of this day. It will ease his mind. He did so want us to wed—and soon."

Behind her, Anna turned aside and coughed, her hand over her mouth, and then turned back, attentive.

"Certainly, certainly! Was he called away?"

"Yes. Some family problem, I was told."

The curate looked mildly sympathetic. "Too bad. Too bad. I'm sure he'd be delighted to be here."

"Perhaps," Quinton broke in, wearily, "he is here in spirit. In the meantime, let us remember we have a long ride and perhaps a rough crossing back to Lundy Island."

"Of course! Of course! I have the license right here. Now, if you'll take your places in front of me . . ."

The ceremony was short, and followed by nervous toasts made with Madeira wine. In less than an hour the coach arrived, Thomas loaded the trunk and bags onto the rear platform, and the newlyweds entered the privacy of the coach interior. Thomas, having tied Lord Spencer's gelding and Rosa's mare to the rear of the coach, sat on the baggage. Anna sat with the driver. The curate, his young face rosy with pleasure, waved until they were out of sight.

Rosa, in her ivory gown, minus the crinoline but plus a bonnet and a dark cloak that covered her from chin to toe, sat up on the thickly padded seat and stared outside as they rode. The springs of the coach and the softness of the squabs offset the jarring ride on the rutted road, but Rosa was acutely uncomfortable. Now that the danger of discovery was lessened by every mile and every hour that passed, she could put aside thoughts of Anna's danger and think about her own predicament.

The questions in her mind were two: How could she secretly gain possession of the money she was to receive when she married, and how keep Lord Spencer from finding out how much money she had? Had the will specified the usual conditions? Once married and in possession of the monies left to her, would her husband manage that fund as well as the dowry? That certainly didn't sound like a plan of her mother's, for the strong-minded Lady Beatrice Gilbert had never allowed her husbands to make a decision about her money. Still, solicitors did like a male hand at the helm. She sighed soundlessly. Could they change the will? No solicitor would be likely to turn over a fortune to a woman not yet of age. . . .

"Lean back, my lady. 'Tis a long ride to Clovelly and the sailing vessel waiting there."

She leaned back obediently and felt his arm move around her and draw her closer. Sudden doubt assailed her, even as she softened and glowed. Both touch and doubt made her breathless. She wondered wildly if it was because she was unused to attractive men that she found him so compelling. He was indeed tall and seemed extremely muscular and strong. His green eyes were brilliant and hard, fierce even in repose, though when he smiled—and he was smiling now—he looked dangerously charming. Her heart leapt as he reached over and took her hand in his.

"First," he said, as if she'd asked his plans, "you'll spend some time getting acquainted with our home on Lundy Island. Then we'll make our way to London and visit the offices of Plimpton and Reuther, your late mother's solicitors. Never too early to claim our rightful share of the Gilbert fortune, now, is it?"

Rosa stared at him incredulously. His wicked smile

broadened into a white-toothed grin, his green eyes danced and invited her to laugh with him.

"Why," she gasped, "why, damn you, that pirate blood of yours must be a strong strain, indeed! You married me for that money!"

He threw back his head and laughed aloud. "And you married me to get away from old Cedric, didn't you? *And* to get the money you couldn't have until you were wed. It's six of one rascal, a half dozen t'other."

Rosa swallowed. It wasn't illegal for a man to marry for money, but she was fleeing from a possible murder charge against her beloved Anna. Of the two rascals, she thought, she was far the worse. She held back a sharp retort and stared out the window, wondering at herself and feeling as foolish as a child.

And why not? Certainly she had been thinking like a child. Actually, she'd been dreaming that somehow this man had seen her from a distance and fallen in love . . . ah, how stupid she had been!

But then what was his reason for taking such a chance? It could be nothing less than her mother's whole fortune. She thought of the astounded pleasure in his eyes when they met on the stairs and knew he couldn't have ever seen her before. Why, as far as he knew, she could have been ugly as sin and even more stupid than she felt now! If that were possible.

She shrugged, determined that no matter how profligate her new husband was, she would see that she ended up with enough money to make a home for herself, Anna, and Thomas. She groped for words to quiet any suspicion he had.

"I suppose you're right. We'd be wise to simply make the best of it, Sir Quinton."

"Precisely! But call me Quint, my angel. I'm not fond of formality."

She nodded. Offending this powerful and daring man would serve no possible use and might ruin her plans. Managing a small smile, she spoke agreeably. "As you wish, Quint."

Chapter Two

────── ❦ ──────

$\mathcal{F}$or the next twenty miles the road ran through the lush green valleys of Devon farmland, where families worked from sunup to sundown to grow fruit in their orchards and raise pigs in their pens and lambs in the fields. The small red Devon cattle were shedding their winter coats and looked moth-eaten but happy, munching fresh grass in warm sunlight. Rosa watched the scenery and tried to congratulate herself on Anna's successful escape. After all, they had managed it well, and she had a right to be proud. She straightened and held her head high while the coach rattled its way along the northeast edge of Barnstaple Bay and down into the small town of Clovelly. The afternoon had waned, and with it the strong wind. The bay had gentled into small, lapping waves.

"A night crossing to Lundy can be harrowing," Quint said as they neared the docks. "But good fortune has smiled on you. The breeze is from the right quarter, and steady. It will be an easy trip and a comfortable landing."

Never having been on a boat or ship of any kind, Rosa was nervous. Getting out of the coach and walking onto the dock, she eyed the vessel and its huge, flapping sails with misgivings.

"That boat looks as if it could turn over very easily," she said, watching Thomas wrestle the trunk and bags aboard. "A good gust of wind against those sails and there it would be, upside down."

Quint's brows shot up, the corners of his mouth tried to follow. "Possible, I suppose. Can you swim?"

Rosa paled. "I can float a little."

Anna spoke behind her. "My lady, the vessel is sturdy and safe. You could undoubtedly travel the Mediterranean Sea from end to end in such a boat. There is no reason for you to fear the trip."

Quint turned and stared at the big woman. He had been so intrigued by his new wife that he'd paid little attention to her servants.

"You sound rather knowledgeable about boats, Anna. Have you had experience on the seas?"

"I was raised in Liverpool, Lord Spencer," Anna said, "and often went out in the boats of the fishing fleet there. This is a strongly built boat for the coastal trade."

Rosa gave Quint a deliberately cool look and turned to Anna. "Thank you, Anna. I am no longer apprehensive. Perhaps we should get on the thing while it is still light enough to see." She glanced around and saw the coach disappearing toward the town, the horses still tied to the rear. "Oh! What will happen to my mare?"

"Our coachman runs the livery stable," Quint said, taking her arm to help her onto the bobbing vessel. "He'll take good care of our saddle horses. We won't need them on Lundy. We use donkeys there."

"Donkeys?" Rosa frowned. "Whyever donkeys? Such slow, plodding creatures."

"Slow, plodding, and very agile in precipitous places. Safe, in other words, on our steep island. The path to

Marisco Castle climbs a three-hundred-foot cliff over-looking a rock-strewn beach."

Rosa shuddered and drew away, sitting down amid-ships on a coil of rope. She would ask no more, say no more, until she was in surroundings that she under-stood. She shut her eyes as two ragged young boys scrambled up the masts like monkeys intent on suicide and began setting the sails. She felt the coil of rope beneath her give a little and opened her eyes. Quint smiled charmingly from his seat beside her, and from somewhere deep inside, a smile came and curled sweetly on her own mouth. He reached over and took her hand in his, holding it warmly.

"I didn't mean to interrupt your prayers."

"I wasn't praying." She would have been, if she hadn't thought it likely that God had closed his ears to her for such craven cowardice. But that was none of Lord Spencer's business. Besides, the boat beneath her tilted just then and swung its high nose northwest, away from Barnstaple Bay and toward the open sea. She lifted her face and looked at the fluttering sails. They were white and lovely against the sunset sky, billowing out and giving a sharp snap when the breeze filled each one to the last inch. Glancing around, she saw Anna leaning against the rail, looking forward as her straw-colored hair blew around her broad face. Thomas had taken up a position a few feet away from the helmsman and was watching every move the man made. After a few mo-ments, Rosa forced herself to let go of Quint's hand, found her balance on the slanting deck, and went care-fully across to the rail. Leaning there, she saw that Anna looked contented.

"You like this, don't you?"

Anna looked down at her and smiled. "I do. I came

up as a child of a waterman, and my first memories have to do with boats. This is a fair treat for me."

Rosa laughed, looking down at the foam sweeping along the hull. "And for me. I had no idea how pleasant it could be."

For a time they simply watched the sky and water, enjoying it. Then Anna spoke again.

"I like your Lord Spencer, though he may pose us a problem later."

Rosa gasped. "You *like* him? I thought you'd hate him. He told me he married me for my dowry!"

Anna laughed. "I thought he must know of the money. He's not the kind to buy a pig in a poke. I suspect he needs it."

"He had a hundred gold guineas, Anna."

"Likely 'twas all he had, and now he stands repaid many times over by your dowry. He'd tell you the truth of it if you asked, I believe. He's all of a piece."

"What do you mean by that?"

"I mean," Anna said, "he's an honest man; the same all the way through. A man you can count on to be the way he appears to be. No silly pretense; no lies." Her gray eyes, often chilly but now bright with interest, moved over Rosa's puzzled face. "What he is, he is. You'll not change him."

"I don't want to change him," Rosa said, looking defiant. "I want to be rid of him. Somehow, I'm going to manage that."

Anna glanced over her shoulder. "You have your wish, at least for a while. He's gone into the captain's quarters. They will probably talk for the whole trip."

"I wonder how long that will be."

"I asked. An hour and a half, or if the wind changes, two hours."

Rosa's throat tightened. The docks of Clovelly had faded from sight. "It will be black night then."

"True. But there will be signal lights. Don't worry, dearie. Lord Spencer will look out for you."

Rosa sighed and leaned again on the rail. "He will until the dowry is paid over, in any event. I wonder what it is that he plans to do." She yawned, covering her mouth politely. "Perhaps he'll set up a place for us in London. That might be amusing."

"Not nearly so amusing as it used to be before dull William ascended the throne," Anna said. "And with our new Queen it will become even duller. Victoria is both young and unmarried, which means she'll be guided by careful old men. If you wish to enjoy yourself, you must leave London to the church and state and play in the country."

"Or on Lundy Island?" Rosa asked, and chuckled. "Perhaps we could ride to hounds on donkeys, calling out, 'Hee-haw and away!'"

Anna broke into laughter. "In our troubles I forget you're even younger than our queen," she said. "Yet, thank God, not so frigidly proper. You're seventeen now, aren't you?"

"Eighteen next month, and feel twenty-five. I wish— ah, how I wish—for something memorable to happen this spring! Something extraordinary that I could remember all my life."

"Perhaps it already has."

By the time Lundy Island loomed out of moon-silvered water Rosa felt completely at home on the big, smooth-running sailboat. She moved around in the moonlight, watching the men handling the sails; the way they trimmed them to catch the wind. It had impressed her, but now, as the dark mass of the island came nearer, she grew anxious again. Out of the corner of her eye she saw the door to the captain's quarters open. Quint came out and started toward her, and she turned to face him, hoping he'd reassure her, not tease her as he had before.

The sea breeze caught the edges of her dark cloak, sending it rising and billowing around her and molding the fine ivory silk of her gown to her slim body. She saw the glint of Quint's grin in the shadows.

"You'll distract our deckhands," he told her, and pulled the edges of her cloak together. "They need their skill here."

"They must. I see nothing of docks nor an anchorage, nothing but that sheer black wall."

He laughed and put an arm around her shoulders, pulling her close. "Where there's a wall, there's a way around it. We'll be at Marisco Castle in an hour and having dinner in the keep."

His warmth and closeness dizzied her, his clean masculine scent was pleasant, inviting. She yielded to the pressure of his arm and studied him in the wavering light of lanterns swinging on the masts. He was very good-looking. Undoubtedly he was a master at the game of love, a game she had never played, though she'd dreamed of wonderful lovers, begging her favors, stealing kisses, telling her how beautiful she was— whether she was or not. And all at once she mourned the fact that he'd been attracted to her dowry instead of her person. After a moment, she told herself that was a weakness, a childish desire to be admired. He'd laugh if he knew.

"I see lights ahead," she said, moving away from him. "Three bright ones; others that flicker and move." She glanced upward at a small noise and saw the shadowed bare legs of the young boys as they climbed up the swaying masts. Her heart clenched; whispered words tumbled swiftly from her mouth.

"Oh, Lord, guide them! Don't let them fall."

"They won't fall." Quint's reassuring voice came through the breeze; his arm reached out and spanned her shoulders again, sending warmth to her frightened heart, easing her worry. "They're young, but they've years of training behind them. Your heart is too easily touched, my lady."

She was silent, wondering what he would think if he knew how easily she'd dispatched any sympathy or guilt in the case of Cedric Brownley. Now that Anna was safe, her conscience had begun to bother her. Or *was* Anna safe? If the squire's body was found, with the throat crushed, the neighbors might well remember Anna and her strength.

The boat was in a channel protected by a smaller island lying close to Lundy on the southeast, the sails loosened and flapping; lights on a blackly silhouetted dock seeming to draw nearer. Thomas had already disappeared into the hold of the ship to bring out the trunk and bags. She looked up at Quint and noticed the lines of fatigue bracketing his wide mouth.

"A long day for you, my lord."

The green eyes came around to her, and one of them winked. "A day worth the effort. I am bringing home a lovely bride."

"Have you family here to greet me?"

He shook his head. "No family here. None, at present, in any corner of England." He smiled and drew her inside his cloak, holding her against his warmth, his eyes only inches away. "We shall be alone."

For a moment Rosa felt a shiver of excitement; a feeling of a strange future rushing toward her, of forces in this man that could change her whole life. Then, frightened, she moved away and spoke as coolly as she could manage.

"It was kind of you to buy my bond servants, Lord Spencer. I never feel alone when they are about. They are very faithful in looking out for me."

He laughed and swung her away from the main mast as the sails came rattling down.

"Then you'll have three guardians, my lady. Step aside and allow the men to lower the gangway, so we can use it."

In moments they were off, into a dark world of flaring lanterns; a curving wall of wet black rock ahead, a surge of hard running tide glistening beneath the shuddering planks they walked on. Rosa clutched Quint's arm, found it muscled in steel, and gained confidence. Behind them she heard Anna's firm tread and the sound of Thomas dragging the trunk along. She looked up into total darkness, for the stars were blocked out by the overhanging promontory above.

"Only a fly could walk that wall."

Quint's laugh rang out. "True. But there is another way."

Once on the narrow beach Rosa saw what it was. There were saddled donkeys waiting in a sheltered crevice; two more donkeys hitched to a cart. The crevice led around to a path broad enough for the cart yet steep enough for her to fear, winding upward into darkness.

"This once I must precede you, my lady. You will follow me, and after you your servants. Then the cart and driver. Take your place and wait until all is ready."

She did as she was told, mounting the donkey he indicated and settling into the saddle, which seemed comfortable enough. The donkey complained, thrusting out his nose and hee-hawing sonorously, and the others sympathized loudly. Rosa caught Anna's amused gaze and in the midst of her uncertainty was overcome by ringing laughter, swallowing the sound as she noted Quint's turn of head, his quizzical look.

The cart was loaded; the driver roped the load tight to keep it from sliding off, and the others mounted their donkeys to an increasing chorus of plaintive noises. But once Quint expertly encouraged the lead donkey to begin the climb, the complaints died away. The small animals put their surprising strength to work and scrambled upward.

"Don't try to guide your mount," Quint ordered, including them all in a sweeping look, "they know the safest way."

A half hour later, when the trail bent even more steeply upward, Rosa clenched her hands on the saddle and closed her eyes. She had no other recourse. She couldn't turn back; she couldn't guide the stubborn beast, she couldn't complain. She could hang on and ignore her surroundings. She kept her eyes shut even after she realized they were on flat ground and the donkey was trotting. When he stopped she opened her eyes and saw Quint looking down at her.

"So you shut out the sight. It's just as well; the trip is nerve-wracking to strangers even by day."

Light from a half moon showed Rosa they were in a ruined courtyard, a space paved with split stone in medieval style. Around them were dark, crumbling buildings against crumbling walls. At first glance her heart failed her. The scene was desperately poor and strange, as if nothing here were alive and the place inhabited only by ghosts. But then her gaze was attracted by light off to one side, and she turned. In the midst of the ancient ruins there was a great medieval keep, far more welcoming than the rest, for there were lights within, the broad double doors were open, and a group of smiling servants had gathered on the steps to welcome them.

"Thank God," Rosa said, and slid out of her saddle. "I'm starving." She smoothed down her wrinkled cloak and took Quint's offered arm.

"Welcome," he said dryly, "to Marisco Castle and the ghosts of my piratical ancestors. Are you superstitious, my lady?"

"Not at all." That wasn't quite true, but she kept a confident air as they walked up the broad steps together and Quint introduced her to the small staff, beginning with a plump middle-aged couple with reddish hair who stood together.

"This is Henry Trask, my majordomo, and Evaline, his sister and our cook. And this is Paul Brooks, our stableman, whose wife, Lillian, is the downstairs maid. And, last but not least, nine-year-old Robert, son of Lillian and Paul, our errand boy." He tousled the boy's silky hair affectionately.

"You will remember my lady, won't you, Rob? Whatever she asks you to do, you must do. Understand?"

The boy nodded, glancing shyly at Rosa. She stared back at him with interest. She had seen very few children since her mother died, for the squire detested them and ran them off if they came around.

"I am very happy to meet all of you," Rosa said, raising her eyes from Robert's young face. "And I'm sure we'll go along splendidly. You must help me learn the ways of Marisco Castle, so I will fit in."

They all smiled and she smiled back. Then Henry bowed and spoke.

"My lady, you must be hungry. Dinner is laid in the hall, and Lillian is ready to serve you. Take your ease while we unpack your belongings."

Anna stepped forward quickly. "Do not concern

yourself, Master Henry. The unpacking for my lady is
my duty, and my son Thomas will help me. I have cared
for Lady Rosamunde since she was an infant; I'll not
give up my privilege to continue."

A weight dropped from Rosa's shoulders. Considering the gold they had to keep hidden she was grateful
for Anna's speech. But the majordomo's face had stiffened and grown haughty. Seeing Anna and Thomas, he
had undoubtedly thought they would be under his orders. He looked angry, and for a moment it seemed he
might make an issue of it. Rosa glanced quickly at
Quint and he spoke, calming the gathering storm.

"My mistake, Henry. I should have added that both
Anna and Thomas, her son, are bond servants to the
Lady Rosamunde, who is happy to have her most familiar people near her. I am entirely in agreement. Knowing how understanding all of you are, I'm sure you will
go along smoothly together."

Smiling at the murmur of agreement, he took Rosa's
arm again and swept her into a great hall, a huge room
apparently without a ceiling; a dusky space soared past
the gallery circling it and on toward heaven, disappearing in shadow. An occasional faint moonbeam shone
through what must have been a crack in an unseen
dome. The floor was split stone, very like the courtyard,
the roaring fire in the north-facing wall was welcome in
the chilly air. There were a few ancient tapestries hanging on the wall as if forgotten, and only one dining table
where there would have been several in centuries past.
But the one table was laden with food and set along
each side with a number of chairs, crude but padded for
comfort.

"If you'd like to wash your hands," Quint said,
"there's something Henry calls a laver in the corner
there. There's water in it, soap alongside, and a towel

hung underneath. Or you can use the ancient garderobe, down that hall."

Rosa's eyes swept the well-stocked table filled with platters of roast meat, bowls of vegetables, and loaves of fresh bread. "I'll just wash my hands, m'lord. Is there company on the way? This is enough food for a banquet."

Quint laughed. "No company, I fear. The kitchen here is very small, and our servants are family people. In order to save time, they put out enough food for everyone. Once we are through, they clear away our dishes and sit down to eat at the same table."

After a moment, Rosa's puzzled expression cleared. "I see. How delightful. You've retained the old ways of castles. Which corner was it that had the laver? It's hard to see the corners in the dark."

Once seated, they were served efficiently by Lillian, with Henry bringing in a chilled wine and later brandy with a tart made of the first of the spring berries. Rosa had removed her cloak, and her low-cut gown clearly impressed Lillian, whose eyes sparkled at sight of it. Leaning down to replenish the wine in Rosa's glass, she couldn't resist a compliment.

"You're a wonderful rare sight in your silk bridegown, Lady Spencer."

Jolted, Rosa managed a smile. "Thank you, Lillian." She put down her wineglass carefully. *Lady Spencer.* She glanced at Quint, wondering if the title was as odd-sounding to him as it was to her. He was leaning back in his chair, his brandy glass between his palms and his green eyes on her, inquisitive and measuring, as if now he had time to judge his new wife.

"Now that we have privacy," he said when Lillian left. "I'd like to know why you fell in so readily with my plans. I thought I'd have to prove myself somewhat bet-

ter than a mere fortune hunter before a noblewoman
would agree to marry me. Instead, you leapt into my net
and insisted on an immediate ceremony. Surely your life
there with the squire was not so horrible as all that."

Ice filled Rosa's veins. He was watching her closely,
as if he knew something was wrong. She looked down
quickly to hide the sudden and awful fear she felt at his
question. Had he any idea her flight from Cedric's home
was connected to Cedric's disappearance? She had to
say something—anything that would sound like a be-
lievable reason. Something that would make her obvi-
ous nervousness seem logical. . . .

"He—he is not a decent man. He told me he'd sold
me as a harlot. Then I—I was able to read the contract,
and I was so—so relieved. . . ." Her voice trembled to
a stop as Quint cursed softly. Looking up, she knew he
wasn't cursing at her. His green eyes were shocked and
sympathetic. She went on. "Certainly it must have
seemed very foolish and forward of me to agree so
readily, but he had legal power over me until next
month, and . . . and the alternative was horrible."

"Of course it was! Good God, the man must be
mad."

She nodded sadly. "I do believe drink had—has the
best of him. He's changed so much since my mother
died." She looked up again and saw suspicion forming
again in Quint's steady gaze. She waited, breathless, for
what he might say now.

"On the other hand," he said, calmer after thought,
"he'd never have got a hundred gold guineas from the
crib masters, no matter your beauty. I'm sure he knew
that, for I was greeted with open arms when I mentioned the sum I'd pay for the three of you. However, he
would have had many more offers, and better offers,
once you'd appeared in London. There's been specula-

tion growing as your eighteenth birthday nears. No one knew what you were like, but all knew you'd have a handsome dowry."

She sighed. "Everyone but Cedric. My mother assured him I'd have but a pittance, and he believed her, taking for granted that others would likely think it much more, due to the fortunes of her past husbands. She had learned him well. Had he known the true amount of my dowry and inheritance, he'd have auctioned me off at twelve for a tremendous price."

"Then I do understand," Quint said briskly, and stood up. "And that's enough of dull, dishonest Cedric. You deserve a chance to forget him and the life he forced you to lead. Come along now and let me show you to your suite."

She rose and wrapped herself in her cloak again, remembering the chill of the entry. Taking his arm, she went with him up the nearest set of stairs, ignoring the cold of the stone striking through her thin shoes. At the end of the circling gallery a door showed a crack of light.

"Your faithful Anna is hard at work," Quint said, "making a cold and dreary room comfortable. You must count her a treasure."

Rosa glanced up at him. "I count her a friend. I can't remember life without Anna. She was one of my mother's most notable successes."

Quint laughed, lowering his voice as they neared the door. "I've heard many stories about the strong-minded Lady Beatrice and her enthusiasms. Someday you must tell me the ones that you like best. Ah, there you are, Anna! And the room gloriously warm and inviting."

Anna bowed slightly, giving Rosa a questioning glance, and stood aside.

"Then if you are satisfied, m'lord, I'll leave you."

"Oh, no, no, by all means stay and help Lady Rosamunde prepare herself for bed." He turned swiftly to Rosa and took her hand, raising it to his lips. "Till we meet again, my lady, and may you sleep well." And he was clattering down the stairs again, grabbing his cloak and swinging it around his broad shoulders. Then he disappeared beneath the gallery where they stood, and a door slammed. Rosa, turning away, felt her hand tingling from his kiss and rubbed it, frowning.

"So far, so good," Anna said. "Have you any idea yet of his plans?"

Rosa shook her head. She felt as if fate had robbed her of something wonderful, something other women could take for granted.

"No. But all I see about me is falling into ruin. Perhaps he means to use my money to bring it back to glory."

"I doubt it."

"Why?"

"No adventure. Repairing castles is a dull, forever kind of work. Not for your Lord Spencer."

Rosamunde gave Anna a slanted glance. "Not *my* Lord Spencer, please." She was still feeling put out because he hadn't asked to stay the night with her. Of course she would have begged off, but it would be courteous of him to act as if he found her desirable, whether he did or not. She turned away, hiding her disappointment with a bored look.

"Well then, what do you think he'll do with my dowry?"

"Something different," Anna said slowly. "Possibly something extraordinary. We'll have to wait and see."

Chapter Three

$\mathcal{V}$enturing out into sunlight and a clean, brisk wind the next day, Rosa discovered that aside from the ancient ruins—and even they were interesting—Lundy Island was a pleasant place. She could see homes in the distance; fields with men plowing for a spring planting. It made a kind of peace neither she nor Anna had ever enjoyed on the barren Brownley estate. Now, standing at the old castle gate and looking out over the rolling land to the sea far below, she and Anna noticed young Robert Brooks leaning against the crumbling wall, watching them. Rosa called him to her and asked him to be their guide to the village. He went red with pleasure and took her hand, beaming.

" 'Tis an honor, Lady Spencer. I'll look after you well. I promised Lord Spencer last night that I'd keep an eye on you until he comes back."

Startled, Rosa questioned him as they began walking down the path to the small town below. "Where did he go, Robert? To the village?"

"No, my lady. He's off to the mainland. But he said he'd return in a few days."

"I see." She glanced at Anna and grimaced, putting

on an air of indifference she didn't feel. "More scalawag than English lord, perhaps. And more secretive than I thought. But no doubt we'll learn his ways." She was careful not to show her disappointment at being left behind by her new husband. Anna would laugh at her.

For the better part of a week they explored the small village a half mile away, where Rosa was treated like royalty, and walked for hours, picnicking on the broad stone wall that overlooked the tiny harbor below. Thomas was lost to them now, his interest in the sailing ships rising to a fever pitch and pulling him down to the harbor, where the island men took him out in their boats when they fished.

The week passed, and then another few days. An evening came when Lord Quinton Spencer appeared on Clovelly's docks and took passage again for Lundy. It was midnight before he entered the castle keep. Quietly, for he had no desire to waken anyone, he went from the entrance to the steps that led up to the sleeping rooms and on past the door to Rosamunde's room. Then he hesitated and went back, wondering if the door was locked. The door opened easily.

Quint stood in the doorway for a minute, staring at the moonlit, sleeping face of his young bride. Then he went in, still making no sound, to stand beside the bed, fascinated by the beauty and young innocence of her face. He had thought of her constantly during this stealthy trip, wondering what she was hiding from him, wondering if he'd made a mistake in marrying her. His suspicions grew every day. It was nearly impossible, now that he knew all about her, not to think she had a reason she couldn't—or wouldn't—expose. She was so unexpectedly beautiful, so acquiescent to the marriage, and so soon wealthy! In a month she would have come into her inheritance from her mother, and that fortune, along with her tremendous dowry, would have let her pick and choose from all the single men in London. But she had jumped at the chance to marry a man she had never met. Something was wrong. Or perhaps he was crediting her with more intelligence than she actually had.

Rosa woke as a hand smoothed her hair and a low voice spoke her name. She opened her eyes, frightened, and saw Quint standing beside her bed in full moonlight. He was smiling, caressing her forehead with a warm palm.

"Forgive me for waking you, my lady," he whispered, and bent down to look into her wide eyes. "I am sorry to have frightened you, but I had to see if you were truly as beautiful as I remembered . . . and you are."

Rosa breathed in his lusty male scent, the tang of salt from the sea, and then, when his warm mouth touched hers and his tongue slipped between her parted lips, she tasted desire. She felt her skin flushing, her heart beginning to pound. She stared up at his shadowed, intent face. Was he here to claim his marital rights? What should she do? Surely he wouldn't come here like a thief in the night and take her without warning. Or would he? She could hardly breathe for excitement, but still she raised her arms to him.

But Quint was straightening to his full height and making no more overtures. "I have frightened you, haven't I, Rosamunde? I beg forgiveness. Go back to sleep, my angel. We'll talk tomorrow, and I will tell you of my plans."

She managed a smile. "Yes, my lord. Tomorrow." She watched him leave, his step silent, his tall figure slipping into the shadows, no sound except the faint creak of the heavy hinges on her door as he closed it behind him. Filling her starved lungs with air, she was immediately angry with herself. She sat up and pounded her pillow into shape again, pounding it harder when she thought of how she'd acted like a terrified mouse. If she had greeted him and lighted the lamp, they could have talked, and laughed, and learned more of each other. As it was, he probably thought her a fool.

Rosa dressed in her fanciest morning gown for their meeting the next day. It was completely out of style, but since she had seldom worn it, it looked new. The fabric was printed with sprays of tiny bluebells, and the low neckline trimmed with nearly transparent lace. The sleeves were enormous, sprouting like puffballs between her shoulders and her elbows. Besides that, she was further encumbered by the many petticoats and wide crinoline that went with it.

She hated the gown, which from the first had made her feel like an Arabian struggling to escape a collapsed tent. Besides, it seriously impeded her habit of swishing through narrow doors without taking the time to alter the slant of a crinoline. She wore it as penance for her foolishness the night before, but also, she admitted to herself on her way down to the great hall, because she knew the style and the colors were very becoming.

Quint rose from his seat at the dining table when she stepped from the stairs and came toward him.

"How lovely you look, my lady. Like spring itself."

She smiled and bent a knee in a quick half curtsy. "Thank you, my lord. That is good to hear. I feel in extremely good spirits."

He pulled out a chair for her. "Do you? What has set you up so well?" His green eyes were full of admiration.

She took the chair he offered, reaching for an early plum, sinking her teeth into it hungrily. "Your return," she said, after swallowing the first bite. "I have enjoyed being here, but I've been very lonely without you. Besides, I am anxious to know our plans."

Quint hid a smile as he sat down again. Not many of his female friends would admit to joy simply because he returned to them. They could be sent into ecstasies, however, if he managed to bring an expensive gift. They would laugh at Rosa's frank innocence. But he liked it in his wife. He knew she wasn't in love with him, but he hoped for at least a growing affection between them. No matter his reasons for marrying her, he meant to keep his vows. And a lifetime, if he was lucky enough to have a normal lifetime, was too long to be wed to a woman who cared nothing for him. He felt unbelievably lucky that the woman who came with the dowry he needed so badly was one of the most beautiful females he'd ever seen. He filled his cup with the newly discovered gunpowder tea and settled back.

"Why then, I will certainly tell you, at least as far as I can see ahead."

He stopped talking as Lillian came in with a rasher of bacon and hot biscuits with honey, waiting until she went back to the kitchen and began again. "I'm sure you're anxious to know everything, but I can tell you only the things that are already decided."

He went on talking while they ate, and Rosa's eyes gradually took on a look of eager anticipation. By the time he had told her all he could, or rather all he would, she was burning with a fiery desire to know more. But there were things he said must be kept from everyone else, even her trustworthy servants. And she knew by the way he looked off into the distance that he was also keeping some things from her. But it just didn't matter. It was all very wonderful, and extremely exciting. She hugged the secret. *They were going to sea!*

Later, when Quint went down into the village to inspect the livestock the villagers kept for him, Rosamunde went looking for Anna. She found her in her bedroom, sewing buttons on a shirt for young Robert Brooks. Rosa sat down.

"In a day or so, my lord tells me, we head for London. We will remain there for a while, and afterward, he said, we will, uh, travel quite a bit before we return. I asked if we would be going through Bideford. He assured me that we could go there first if I wished to stop and see Squire Brownley. Of course I said I would find such a visit extremely unpleasant."

"As would anyone," Anna said, quirking an eyebrow, "after two weeks. The squire stank even when he was alive."

"Anna!"

"Never mind. Did he say where we might travel, and how long it would be before we came home?"

"No. But from the look in his eyes I'd say it would be some little time before we climb the Lundy rocks again."

Anna stared at her. "What do you mean by that?"

Rosa laughed, flinging out her arms to take in the whole world. "You said once that something in Quint's eyes called for adventure. When he spoke to me this time I saw it myself. A look of real daring. Oh Anna, it must be some marvelously difficult thing he wants to do! And we'll be with him!"

Anna frowned. "But my child, it could be dangerous for you. Question him. Make him tell you what he has in mind."

"Indeed not! I want the surprise!" Rosa went to Anna and embraced her. "With you and Thomas along, what could happen to me?"

The next day the order went through the keep: all garments to be cleaned and pressed, ready for packing.

Food that could be carried for lunches must be prepared; word must be taken to the livery stable to have a coach made ready for a trip to London.

Rosa had seen very little of Quint except at meals; now she sought him out and questioned him again, closely. He only laughed and reminded her that he'd already given her all the information he could. "Don't fuss," he added. "I have already promised you an interesting trip."

"Any trip at all would be interesting to me, my lord. Why, I haven't been farther than Bideford since I was ten and my mother died. To think we're going to London! How long will it take?"

They were standing by the fire in the great hall of the keep; she with her hand resting on his arm, as if to keep him beside her until her curiosity was satisfied; he with his usual look of amusement.

"Several days, my lady, depending on the weather. London is at its best in the spring. We'll have a pleasant visit."

She smiled but continued to study him. She found him a fascinating subject, full of surprises and exceedingly good to look at. She was beginning to know his expressions, and the one he wore now had that shine of excitement, that look of secrets held back, that air of danger. To her mind, he was at his most charming when that devilry appeared.

"And," she said, offhandedly, "after traveling a bit on the Mediterranean Sea, we come back to Lundy?" Watching, she saw his face change, his feelings hidden under a casual expression.

"Possibly," he said, turning away. "And possibly not. Now run along and see to it that your bondwoman and her son are making ready to go with us."

She nodded and left at a sedate walk, but once out of

sight she ran up the steps to the gallery and into her room. Anna was there, packing.

"I was right, Anna! He tries to look as if it's nothing, but his eyes give him away. He's planning something extraordinary!"

Anna turned away from the trunk. "Are you sure he is taking Tom also?"

"Indeed. He asked me to see to it that both of you are ready."

"Hmm. You could be right, then. He has seen that Tom is strong and would be handy in trouble." Anna shook her head. "You must find out what his plans are, Rosa. He's a daring man, and I'll not have you in danger."

For once, Rosa looked away from Anna's stern face, setting her own chin firmly. "You haven't the say, Anna. He is my husband."

Leaving Anna, she went to find Robert Brooks and tell him good-bye. She had become very fond of Robert, and he of her. He was lonely for other children, and she knew what that was like only too well.

To make the trip down to the docks the next day they reversed the order. First the baggage on the cart, with the little old man who drove the two donkeys walking by their side; then Thomas, looking like a giant on his donkey, his feet trailing the ground. Next was Anna, who seemed impervious to fear, and then, breaking the rule of reverse, Viscount Quinton Spencer, a long leather strap fastened securely around his waist and extending backward to circle the much smaller waist of the rider of the donkey behind. Rosa had ventured a look over the wall of tumbled stones along the top of the cliff; had looked down and down and down to the huge rocks on the semicircle of narrow beach, at the waves dashing against them and roaring like lions.

Now, tied to her husband like a toddling baby, she rode down the sharp incline, stiffening as the donkey's hooves slipped, the small rocks tumbled over the precipice, the strap came tight and slackened again. Her eyes were shut and her fingers white with pressure against the hard leather of her tilted saddle.

A half hour later, on the gentler slope at the end, Rosa managed to get her eyes open and take up breathing again. Reaching level ground, Quint dismounted and came back to help her from her beast.

"For a woman with such a great urge to travel and find adventure," he said, half smiling, "you seem a trifle timid."

Rosa slipped to the ground and planted her feet firmly. "A trifle timid, my lord? It is more like utter terror. I have no faith in donkeys, nor, for that matter, any dumb beast on uncertain footing. Let me climb or descend on my own feet, and you'll not see me cringe."

He cocked a brow. "You don't believe in Fate, then. Haven't you heard our days are numbered when we're born?"

She looked up at him, thinking how black his hair was, how clear and green his eyes, like seawater. Today the aura of excitement was thick about him, almost visible in the shimmering air. She felt an answering swell of warmth deep inside and spoke quickly, to hide it.

" 'The dictates of the heart are the voice of Fate,' " she quoted. "Which I believe means we do have a measure of control over what happens to us. If, for instance, my friend here was in danger, I would risk death to save her."

For a startled moment Quint stared hard at her, a look of suspicion in his eyes. Then he seemed to relax. Glancing at Anna's broad red face, he nodded. "As she would for you, I don't doubt. But there is no time for philosophizing, my lady. The wind is fair, the tide runs hard. We must catch it at the full."

Rosa took his arm to steady herself down the incline to the docks, keeping her attention on the shifting rubble of small stones, and Anna and Thomas followed after. They were about to step onto the spray-washed planks when Quint came to an abrupt stop. Looking up, Rosa saw a fine-dressed man, close to Quint's size, coming along the wet dock toward them with a careless smile.

"So, Cousin Quinton, the gossip is true. You've found you a wife, and a pretty one at that. Accept my congratulations."

Quint's arm circled Rosa's waist smoothly. "We thank you for your good wishes. Yes, this is my wife, the former Lady Rosamunde Gilbert. Rosa, my dear, this is my cousin, Porter Ogilvie of Dorset."

Rosa offered her gloved hand; Porter Ogilvie bent over it. Straightening, he broke into a small laugh. "Don't tell me, Lady Rosamunde, that a gentle little woman like yourself is related to the fire-breathing Beatrice Gilbert, she of the iron will?"

"Indeed yes," Rosa said gravely, "Lady Beatrice was my mother. They say I am quite like her when she was young. Perhaps in time I'll make a suitable dragon myself."

Porter waved a careless hand. "I do hope not." He turned to Quint. "Don't allow it, cousin."

"I'll not. In the meantime, why are you here?"

"For the same reason that always brings me here. I grow hungry for the sight of the crumbling walls of our castle, for the feel of the wind and the smell of salt water. 'Tis a damnable shame that a gadabout like you should inherit the place. If I owned it, I'd live in it!"

Quint laughed out loud. "How long? I'd wager you'd

be back in London within three weeks. But since you're here, you can stay for a while and enjoy the wind and waves. We're just leaving."

"You mean you'll not stay and entertain me? How ungracious you've become, Quint."

Quint clapped his cousin's shoulder. "Don't take offense, Port. I have business in London, and then I plan a trip for my bride. You'll have to forgive us this time."

"Then I shall—and while you are gone, I'll search Marisco's walls for the treasure. Do you remember, Quint, how hard we all tried to find the gold your father told us lay hidden somewhere within those walls? You and I and young Jonathan. Which reminds me, where is Jon? He seems to have disappeared from the London scene."

Quint smiled tightly. "As you remember, it's often impossible to track Jon down. He does love the odd corner. Good-bye, cousin. I wish you well with your search for the Marisco treasure. But if you're back in London before we leave you'll find us with the Leightons in Mayfair."

They were no sooner in the sailboat than the lines were loosed and the sails spread to catch the north wind. It seemed they flew, the foam of their going feathering into white wings along the smooth sides of the ship. Rosa made her way to the rail, and Quint joined her, his tall body shielding her from the fine spray. Under the pretense of keeping her hat on, she held the brim firmly and peered past her hand at his face. He looked at once worried and solidly determined, staring east. He seemed to have put his cousin directly out of his mind, yet to Rosa an impression lingered, worrying her. Porter Ogilvie had a warm smile but a very cold eye, no matter whom it rested upon.

"Where are we really going, my lord?" She knew he

knew; she was tired of guessing. It had suddenly come to her that if her money was to pay for the secret trip, he should let her know every part of his plan.

"Clovelly, Exeter, Winchester, and then London," he said, frowning, naming the unimportant stops along the way to the city as if explaining to a too inquisitive child. Rosa started to argue, then turned away, biting her lip. Why should she care? The farther they went, the safer Anna would be. It very well might be best if they left not just Lundy but England itself.

"Rosa."

She turned back, surprised. "Yes, my lord?"

"I don't mean to ignore your question. When I can answer, I will."

Looking into his eyes, seeing in them his demand for patience, she nodded stiffly. Somehow, the actual beginning of the trip had brought her a few fears about it.

"We each have our secrets, Quint. We made a bargain, and we'll keep it." Startled by her own admission, which she hadn't intended, Rosa turned away, walking the slanting, rocking deck as if she'd been born at sea.

The captain, John Slater, came up from behind Quint and watched her, his grin wide.

"A real beauty, your wife, but one who walks the deck like a sailor. She must be used to sea travel."

Turning again to lean against the rail and gaze to the east, Quint shook his head. "The trip to Lundy was her first experience on the water, John. But as you see, she is quick to learn."

The coach to Exeter was waiting at the livery stable, and the Spencer party were the only fares. Handing Rosa inside, Quint turned and grasped Anna's arm and helped her in. Then he motioned to Thomas to join the women.

"I'll ride for a time with the coachman," he said. "I'd

like the air." He shut the door without waiting for an answer.

Rosa glanced at Anna. "He must have a good reason," she whispered, "to choose that hard seat. What could it be?"

" 'Tis likely," Thomas said, "he may be watchin' the road behind us." He looked at Rosa and nodded. "I see I've surprised you, m'lady. But the man is an adventurer, I'm sure, an' adventurers often have that look of a hunted man."

"Or," Anna said slowly, "the look of a man who doesn't want to be followed by an enemy. He has some plan in mind, and I believe that cold, calculating cousin of his was nagging him to disclose it."

"That may be it," Thomas agreed. "But we're away, an' the cousin is still on Lundy, waitin' for the next tide. If 'twere I who owned that island, I'd not trust Lord Ogilvie enough to let him stay there alone."

Rosa hid a smile. Thomas was becoming very possessive about Lundy and Lundy's boats. She leaned back in the corner of the broad seat and closed her eyes. They were off, and the world lay before them. In only a few days she would be in London, a wonderful city of gaiety and pleasures, of beautiful clothes and high society. She settled back to dream.

It was after midnight when the coach crossed the Exe River and came into the dark, silent streets of Exeter, which were lit by the feeble glow of gaslights and of lamplight from windows with their curtains drawn. Except for the steady hoofbeats of the horses and the rattle of the coach wheels on the cobbles, there were no sounds.

During the day they had stopped twice, once for fresh horses, once for a midday meal, and now they stopped at an inn and woke a sleepy landlord, who was pleased at the chance to make a few shillings before the day dawned. He rousted out his cook to heat food for their dinner, and they took a few hours sleep afterward, followed by a refreshing wash and change of clothes. Without comment, Quint had arranged for two rooms, sharing one with Tom, and sending Anna to stay with Lady Rosamunde.

Anna had eyed this arrangement with surprise. Alone in the room with Rosa after dinner, she spoke of it. "You are still denying Lord Spencer his marital rights?"

Caught in a yawn, Rosa snapped her jaw shut. "No! One cannot deny a man who doesn't ask." She turned away from Anna's astounded face, her own face red.

"I suppose," she went on, "I could say to him that I now know him well enough to—to share his bed. But he should ask! And I am sure he would if he wanted to. I may as well admit I am not attractive to him. It was the money he married, not the woman. Still, I must also admit he is extremely pleasant and thoughtful. I—I have no complaint."

That last part, she thought, readying herself for bed, is a damnable lie. She had no desire to end her days as a withered spinster. Still, she wondered if Quint was the right choice for her. The emotions he stirred might be stirred by any personable man. Raised the way she had been raised, she knew she needed to know more of life. She ignored the stare that Anna directed at her, but Anna spoke anyway.

"I don't believe any of that, mistress."

Rosa looked at her from under lowered brows. "Try, Anna. We'll go along better if you don't argue with me."

Discreetly, Anna was silent.

The journey from Exeter to Winchester took two days, with an uncomfortable night spent at a roadside inn where the beds and food were both lumpy. But the city of Winchester, where they had rooms in an ancient palace and enjoyed superb food, made up for it. Quint had friends there, and he met with them, going alone to meetings on what he said were matters of business. The meetings extended their stay to two nights. He was in very good spirits when they finally left for London on the third day, all of them well rested.

"Now you will begin to enjoy the best of England," he told Rosamunde, sitting across from her in the new coach he had hired in Winchester. "And the people of London will enjoy seeing you. You become more beautiful every day. Doesn't she, Anna?"

Anna gave him a sour glance. She had been thoroughly put down throughout the whole trip and considered Rosamunde's usually happy nature ruined for all time. It seemed Rosa had given her the slicing edge of a sharp tongue every day.

"My mistress," she said wryly, "prefers that I make no personal comments about her."

"It is fortunate, indeed," Rosa said icily, "that I am both blind and deaf. Otherwise, I might object to being treated as if I were merely a seated statue, with n-no f-feelings."

Quint stared at her, taking in the flushed cheeks, the damp eyes, the small, jutting jaw. Then he stuck his head through the open window and yelled up at the driver. When the coach slid to a stop, he opened the door, got out, and extended a hand to Anna.

"I believe you'll enjoy the fresh air and the spring blossoms, Anna. The driver's seat is very wide and has a comfortable back. Join the driver and Thomas for a while."

A half smile on her broad face, Anna got out and climbed to the driver's seat above. Giving the driver a signal to proceed, Quint got back inside and sat down with Rosamunde, taking her hand in his.

"I am sorry to have offended you, my lady." The look on his handsome face was humbly penitent. His hand was warm and so was he. He was sitting close, leaning over her. She could feel his heat, his male aura surrounding them. Her cheeks grew even redder.

"I spoke like a child. Think nothing of it."

"No, I cannot blame you. I married you, left you without explanation, dragged you along on this trip, and ignored your feelings. You have been much more patient than any woman should be. If nothing else, I should have thanked you for that."

She glanced up at him, seeing the faint shadow of beard on his shaven chin, noting the strong features, the hawk nose, the pleasantly wide mouth, and the regret in his green eyes. His black hair was thick and wavy and brushed the edge of his high collar, a few locks curling onto his forehead. He was, indeed, very handsome. And very courteous. She sighed and looked away.

"You need not apologize," she said finally. "We . . . we have a business arrangement."

His warm palm cupped her chin and tilted it up. "Not entirely," he said softly, and covered her mouth with his.

The kiss was like none Rosa had ever had before. It seemed to take her whole body into an embrace, send its heat through every vein. She reeled from it, tasting the male scent she associated with Quint; feeling the strength of his arms holding her, the pure fire that grew in her slim belly when his tongue slowly caressed every soft, wet corner of her mouth. She loved it, and when he finally pulled away she gave a deep sigh and leaned closer, her cheek on his warm chest, her eyes closed.

"Oh, Quint. That was . . . glorious."

Her voice was very soft, but her words were distinct. He smiled slightly, stroking her hair, holding her close, surprised and a little disturbed by his own strong reaction. He struggled to calm himself, knowing he would have to be careful not to put this woman ahead of his duty. A great deal depended on him now. It wasn't his time to fall in love.

Chapter Four

——— ❦ ———

That night they stayed again at a roadside inn and were up at dawn to finish the trip to London. They came into the southern part of the city at noon, into a crush of buildings and parks and crowds. Rosamund faintly remembered the town from her early childhood. Passing Kennington Commons and into Vauxhall Road, their coach ran on toward the northeast and the Thames, entering the maze of streets that led onto Westminister Bridge. Quint rode again with the coachman, who was unfamiliar with the city; Thomas rode with the women and spoke seldom, though once in sight of the Thames he was alert and watching.

Anna, restored to her usual good nature, gazed out eagerly. She loved the city, the masses of people, the boats on the river, and, like Thomas, the ships.

"Do you know where we're going, Rosa?"

Rosamunde smiled. She never minded Anna's informality. "I do. We are to stay with Lord Spencer's friends, Sir Henry Leighton and his wife, Lady Mara, in Berkeley Square. My lord spoke of it again yesterday, when we rode alone."

She sat back and turned to the open window, letting

rain-cooled air take the heat from her cheeks. Even speaking of that time alone in the coach made her warm again, and wishful.

Anna pursed her lips in a silent whistle. "Berkeley Square, is it? They are moneyed people, then."

"Undoubtedly."

Anna gave her a searching look. "As you will be, three short weeks from now. Have you any uncertainties about your husband's ability to manage your estate for you?"

Rosa's chin came up. "I believe I could trust him. However, I am my mother's daughter; if she managed to do what she planned, it will be my hands on the reins."

Thomas shook his massive head, looking at her with pity. "He'll not allow that," he said. "Sir Quinton is a real man. He is nothing like Squire Brownley, who was like a slave to Lady Beatrice."

"And I," Rosa said, "am a real woman. The dowry, of course, is not in question. My husband may well end up with full control of it, since it's the bride's gift to a new family. But in this case there is far more gold behind it—and all of that is mine."

Anna's face shone with admiration. "Fancy your mother standing up to those solicitors for you. She must have believed you would be as canny with your money as she was."

Rosamunde leaned back, closing the window as the rain began again. Much of her speech had been pure bravado. She wasn't at all sure her mother had managed to go against custom with her solicitors. But she intended to act as if it were so until she found out it wasn't.

"Of course. And so I shall. There will be no squandering of the fortune she left to me."

With Westminster Bridge in sight, neither Anna nor

Thomas answered. The boats on the Thames had their attention. Rosa's confidence evaporated as she looked ahead at the massive buildings of Parliament on the north shore, and the rest of the huge city stretching east in row after row of impressive buildings and wonderful parks. It made her feel too small to face up to a city person. Then they rolled onto the smooth-surfaced bridge and the sun broke from behind clouds to shine on them and strike sparkles from the swift-flowing Thames.

"There," Rosa said, and laughed. "We have been welcomed by the sun, a rare thing in London Town. Perhaps it is a good omen."

Both Anna and Thomas smiled. Then all three of them were silent, watching and hoping. . . .

Rattling down off the bridge, they proceeded east on Whitehall, bringing an exclamation from Anna: "They've torn down the King's Mews, Thomas! Who would have thought it?"

"These Londoners," Thomas said dourly, "are always at it. No doubt someone wants to put up another statue. Ah, there's Piccadilly. It won't be long, now."

The coach turned north, and Rosamunde's heart beat in double time. Questions flooded her mind. Would Lady Mara approve of her? She looked down at her undeniably out-of-fashion gown and groaned silently. The bonnet she wore had not been her choice even when it was new, and it took only a casual glance to see that the silk ribbons on it were frayed. Ah, well. If the Lady Mara based her judgment on fashion, she would not be a person one would want as a friend.

The coach slowed at Berkeley Street and turned east again, running along smoothly. Short of the middle of the narrow street it turned once more to the north, entering the square, pulling up in front of the beautifully carved marble facade of a large building. Anna turned and looked at Rosamunde.

"Straighten your bonnet, Lady Rosamunde. Otherwise, you look very well."

Rosa nodded and put on a confident smile. "Thank you, Anna." She straightened her bonnet, tucked a lock of hair behind the fluttering ribbon, and smiled again at Quint, who was opening the coach door for them. "We have arrived? What a beautiful home."

Quint grinned, reaching for her hand to help her down. She gave it to him, shaking her skirts and taking his arm to mount the steps to the wide Palladian doorway of the home. Quint lifted the gilt horseshoe knocker, and the door was opened by a silver-haired man in black and gray livery, who immediately bowed to him.

"Lord Spencer! 'Tis a pleasure to see you. And your lady." He bowed to Rosamunde, who smiled at him. He smiled back, clearly pleased, and stepped out of the doorway. "Come in, my lord and lady, come in. I'll see if one of the neighbor's men can help with the baggage."

"Don't bother, Wiggins. We have a man and woman with us who can handle everything."

"Good! Good! You'll have your usual suite, my lord, but I must tell you that Lord and Lady Leighton are not here to welcome you, though they hope to be back before you leave London. Some family matter at the country estate, I believe."

"I understand, of course," Quint said easily, and took Rosa's arm again, leading her into a marble-floored foyer. She felt odd entering a house belonging to someone who wasn't there to invite them in. Still, she thought, this must happen occasionally; plans changed, formalities forgotten. She turned, hearing a scraping sound as Tom dragged the trunk to the entry. Anna was there too and gave Rosa a searching glance over Tom's back. She looked concerned, even a little suspicious. But then Anna was always suspicious.

Looking back at Quint's smiling face, Rosa relaxed. What could possibly be wrong? This was a lovely home, and it belonged to Quint's good friends. And the butler was bowing again and motioning to her to follow him.

The upstairs suite was lovely. It had a sitting room at the rear of the house that overlooked a garden already blooming with Dutch tulips and iris. There were rose-bushes leafing out, and forsythia like fountains of gold. There was a real fountain on the greening lawn, with a small marble statue of a naiad standing in a sparkling mist. Rosa sighed with pleasure. Once this strange adventure was over and Quint ready to settle down, she'd find a place like this.

She turned, greeting Anna as the big woman hurried in. "Do look, Anna. There's a lovely garden there below."

Anna looked rather warm and upset, her mouth set in a straight line. "Aside from a cook," she said in a low voice, "there are no other servants except for the butler. I asked Wiggins why, and he said they were on holiday. There is something wrong here, my lady."

Rosa frowned. "Oh, come now, Anna. It seems sensible to me. With the family gone, the maids would have little to do. I'm sure they'd be happy to take a few days off. We can fend for ourselves, you know."

"But—" Anna closed her mouth as Quint came in, towering in the cozy sitting room. He looked at her quizzically and then at Rosa. "Is there trouble, Rosamunde?"

She hurried to deny it. "Not at all. I was just admiring the garden below. Then Anna came to tell me that I'd have to put up with her for all my needs, for the usual household maids have taken a holiday, with the Leightons gone."

Quint's eyes widened. "Is that so? How odd. Leighton will have something to say to them when he returns. But it won't disturb you, will it? We'll not be here for long."

"Oh no, it'll not disturb me. Anna is far better than any other maid for me."

"I am sure of it," Quint said, and turned toward Anna, his brows knitted. "Are you satisfied with your room, Anna? Is Thomas nearby?"

Anna gave him an incredulous glance. "My room is fine, Lord Spencer, and Thomas is more than satisfied. Is there anything either of us could do for you?"

"Nothing," Quint replied, and smiled without humor. "Except to allow my wife and me to talk for a while in privacy. We have much to discuss."

Anna's broad face flamed red. "Yes, m'lord." Two of her long strides and she was out, closing the door softly.

Rosamunde sighed. Anna would hate being reprimanded for imposing on their privacy, and the wound would be slow in healing. Still, Anna should have known not to complain about a situation that was none of her business. Anna was acting more and more like a fussy guardian instead of a maid. She turned toward Quint.

"Anna is forever suspicious of dangers lurking in cities," she said lightly. "No doubt anything unusual seems threatening to her. She's looked after me ever since my mother died, and she's very protective."

"Yes," Quint said, "I see that. I was a bit hard on her." He came and took Rosa into his arms, clasping her close. "Perhaps I was jealous. Looking after you is my privilege now."

His warmth seeped through her silk bodice and invaded her breasts. She felt them swell in response, felt a stab of heat flow down through her body and pool, throbbing, in her belly. She looked up into his eyes, now soft as new spring leaves.

"Quint . . ." She said his name for no particular reason, and then said it again in a quivering gasp. "Quint, I think—I mean, I've had enough time. . . . I know you now. We could begin our marriage."

He smiled slowly, his arms tightening. "You are sure?" He saw her nod and knew she was too emotional now to listen to him. He hugged her to him, burying his face against her neck. She was damn near irresistible. Too innocent to realize this trip was not planned as a pleasure trip. But he knew, and it wasn't fair to drag her along and perhaps leave her in the end, lost and likely pregnant, alone in the world. He had to be fair.

"I hope you'll never regret it, my darling. I want to be your husband in every way. You are so beautiful, so warm . . ." He was kissing her neck, his mouth open and hot, and she wanted it on her own mouth, as it had been in the coach, but then his arms were loosening, letting her go; he was stepping back, his face flushed.

"I must leave now," he said, "but tonight we'll have Wiggins bring our dinner up here. We will dine alone in our own suite. I am proud that you've chosen to be my wife in all ways, but . . . I'll think it through. It may be best to wait."

Rosa nodded again, still speechless, and watched him as he opened the door and slipped out. What did he mean, it may be best to wait? She felt . . . oh, Lord, how did she feel? How could she have been so bold? He'd think her too passionate for a lady. Why, she was neither as bold nor as passionate as her mother had been. Not yet. But her breasts ached; her body clamored for more touching, more thrills, more heat . . . oh, Lord, how could he *leave?*

She whirled away, stalking back to the windows to calm herself with the view of the garden. And there below was Quint, striding along the garden path to the gate letting onto the alley behind. There was a gig there, a rather shabby stanhope gig that had seen some years of use, and a man in it. The man was dark and heavyset, decently dressed, and he was clearly waiting for Quint. She saw the dark man's face, which seemed tired but patient, and stepped back behind the sheer curtain as she realized he'd see her, too, if he looked up.

Knowing she shouldn't spy on them but too curious to stop, she continued watching as the men talked: Quint leaning casually against the garden wall, the other man gesturing with abandon and leaning toward Quint as if to emphasize a point. A diamond flashed on the dark hand; white teeth lighted the dark face as both men laughed. Then Quint stepped back and the dark man picked up his reins, urging the horse forward.

Coming back along the path, Quint suddenly looked up toward the windows of the sitting room with a slight frown, as if he'd just realized someone could be watching. But Rosa had anticipated that—she was completely hidden behind the draperies, peering with one eye through a narrow slit.

Once Quint had entered the house below, Rosa pushed the draperies aside and opened the windows to allow fresh air to blow in. Then she toured the rest of the suite. Beside the cozy little sitting room there were two bedrooms, one with a large canopied double bed and one with a plain narrow bed as if arranged for a child. And there was a bath, a bath with a marble washbowl, a huge tub of porcelain piped with spigots, and one of the newest water closets, with a waterbox on the wall above and a chain to pull that let the water flush down. She was standing there contemplating this luxurious *cabinet de toilette* when Anna came to the door and looked in. Rosa glanced up and smiled.

"Isn't this wonderful? Just look at the size of the tub. Unpack one of my simple gowns and shake it out, Anna. I'm going to take a bath, right now."

Anna stared at her sourly. "Tom says we won't be here more than about ten days, according to your husband."

Rosa shrugged. "All the more reason to enjoy such luxury and convenience immediately, wouldn't you say? Go, pick out a gown. I'll want fresh clothes from the skin out. See to it."

"You are beginning to sound like your mother," Anna muttered, but left.

Stripping to her petticoats, Rosa turned on the spigots in the tub. Water gushed out, whining and gurgling in the pipes, splashing into the tub. She dipped her hand in it. The water wasn't hot, nor was it cold. What a success! She had hung her gown on a hook behind the door and now she added her petticoats and chemise to it, along with her underdrawers. She took the ribbons from her hair and leaned over, letting her long hair fall, twisting it and shaping it into a large knot, tying it tightly on the top of her head.

Looking around, she saw a cake of lavender soap lying on the edge of the basin; she picked it up and sniffed at it, shutting her eyes. So sweet, so springlike. Oh, what a lovely place this is, after all.

"The water will be cold if you stand around dreaming, my lady," Anna said, returning with the clothes. Anna's respectful use of "my lady" held a tinge of scorn, but Rosamunde only laughed and stepped into the tub, sinking down with a feeling of utter luxury.

"It has been a long time since we lived in such comfort, Anna. I wonder at you being so grumpy and cross. Don't you like the place?"

"The place is fine enough," Anna admitted, hanging up the gown and taking a sponge to Rosa's slim back. "My doubts are about the absent owners. In fact . . ." She took a moment to rinse the sponge and soap it again before she went on. "I'm beginning to wonder about Lord Spencer as well as Lord Leighton. If there truly is a Lord Leighton."

Rosa looked up at the huge woman bending over her and frowned. "But that has been explained," she said, trying to be patient. "The Leightons were called away. Wiggins said so."

"And Lord Spencer never batted an eye," Anna said. "I do believe he knew what Wiggins would say."

"Quint wouldn't lie to me!"

"Strangely enough," Anna said, straightening, "I agree. But he'd keep his mouth shut if it suited him. I think there is something going on that he doesn't want us to know."

Rosa thought of the dark man in the gig on the other side of the garden wall, the long talk Quint had with him, and knew Anna was right. But then, Quint had told her frankly that there were things he couldn't reveal to her until later. He had been honest; she had promised not to question him.

"Well, in that case," she said, taking the soap and cloth from Anna's hands, "we mustn't pry. I know you and I have always faced problems together, but now . . . now I'm married. There will be secrets between Quint and me I cannot tell you."

"That will be fine," Anna said, drying her hands. "After I learn to trust him. But I'll not have you hurt."

Rosa sighed. She had valued Anna as a guardian all through the years after her mother died. Now she felt as if she were being smothered. "Learn fast, then," she said coolly. "And be courteous. He could let you go, and I don't want to lose you."

The gown Anna had brought out was Rosamunde's favorite. It was a violet blue that matched her eyes, and very simple, trimmed with a frill of matching lace around a modest off-the-shoulder neckline. The sleeves were long, and the skirt, while full, draped from her small waist gracefully, unhindered by crinolines. Unhindered, in fact, by anything more than one silk petticoat and a fine chemise. When she could, Rosa wore clothes that allowed her to move easily.

Anna, coming in again, this time with a pot of tea and some dainty sandwiches, looked at her with reluctant admiration. "You have a good notion of what style suits you," she said, putting the tray down on a small table. "That old gown is very becoming. Here's a cup of tea and a bite or two—it'll be a while before dinner. Wiggins says Lord Spencer is out on business and asked for it at a late hour."

"That will be fine," Rosa said, feeling a leap of excitement inside. Did Quint want the others in bed and out of the way when dinner was over? "I'll just have a nap and a walk in the garden later."

It was while she was walking in the garden that evening that she thought of Cedric Brownley and felt a cold fear gather in her stomach. What could she say if the solicitors wanted him present to give his permission? After all, they knew he was her guardian until she became eighteen, and that had not yet happened. Still, she was indeed married to a nobleman, and Cedric had signed the papers allowing the marriage. But would it be enough? Solicitors were always men who wanted every *t* crossed and every *i* dotted; she remembered that from her childhood, for her mother was always enraged by their persistent questions. She went back into the house and found Anna in the kitchen with the cook.

"Come up to my sitting room," Rosa said. "I've something to ask you. It won't take long."

It didn't. Once Anna heard the question, she gave the answer. "You must tell them he left to visit his brother in Manchester on a family matter that came up unexpectedly."

"But that is an arrant lie!"

"As is anything else you can say—unless you want to tell the truth."

"You know I can't do that."

"Then you must lie well, my lady. Do it with assurance. Look the man in the eye and smile. If they ask why the squire hasn't visited you, or you him, tell them the truth—after your mother died, Squire Brownley turned to the drink and blamed his poor fortunes on you. You may even assert you were sorry for him, at least a little."

Rosa let out her breath. "That, at least, would be the truth. I was sorry for him. But in the end . . . I hated him."

"Never say it."

"I know." She rose from her chair and went to put her hands on Anna's thick shoulders. "I never will. You are my best friend, and I do not forget that."

Anna's stern face softened. "Nor I. Your mother took me and my child in, saving me from prison and Tom from an orphanage. I'll see to it that you are safe and unharmed as long as I can." She smiled suddenly. "But I do have help, now. Lord Spencer is a powerful man."

"Yes," Rosa said, and felt warmth in her cheeks. "Yes, he is." Perhaps tonight she would find out just how powerful he could be. She turned away so that Anna would not see the thought in her eyes. "Would you please brush my hair, Anna? The breeze has tangled it enough to bother me."

Chapter Five

❦

It was a quarter of ten and a black night when the old stanhope gig, its lamp dim and flaring, stopped in the alley running behind Lord Leighton's house. Quint swung down to the pavement, looking back to say a quiet word or two.

"Tomorrow will decide the stakes, Ranjit. Whether we go well-heeled and ready or go like wharf rats hiding in the hold of a ship. All I am sure of is that we will go."

Ranjit, shivering in the cold air, nodded. "And that is truly all that matters, sahib. When?"

"Within a fortnight."

"Good." Taking up the reins, Ranjit moved away toward the bright flare of gaslights on Piccadilly. Quint stood a moment watching the dark mass of gig and man disappear and then went quietly toward the gate he'd left unlocked a few hours ago. By now, he thought, Rosamunde will have gone to bed, which he had long ago decided was precisely what should happen. After what Ranjit had told him this night he knew the dangers they all would face. It was bad enough for a woman to be exposed to such terror; to expose a woman bearing a child would be criminal. There must be no lovemaking between them until this mission was finished.

Ahead of him, the gate opened and Wiggins stepped out, his silver hair and slight build identifying him in the darkness.

"My lord?"

"Yes, Wiggins?"

"A stranger came an hour ago. He asked for you, and I said I didn't know where you were or when you'd be back."

"Describe him for me." In a shaft of pale light coming from the scullery window, Quint's tired face was rock hard. "Was he English?"

"No, my lord. I believe he might be an Arab. However, he spoke English well enough. Since he didn't mention his name, I didn't ask for it. It seemed . . . wise."

Quint's jaw tensed. "You did well, Wiggins. If he comes again, tell him the same thing. But be courteous. He has tracked me down fairly, and he is not a man to insult."

Wiggins grinned. "At my age and weight, my lord, I try never to insult anyone."

"A sensible habit," Quint said wryly, "and one I often wish I had practiced. Is there supper for me?"

"Indeed. For you and your wife. She will be pleased to see you. She has been doing a bit of pacing up there."

Quint hid a frown. He had thought Rosa would be far too tired to wait up for him. "What of the others?"

"Thomas is asleep. I presume Mistress Castner is, also."

"Good. Then I'll go on up."

They had spoken too quietly for Rosa to make out the words. She stood in the darkest corner beside the wide windows, hidden, all but her eyes, in the heavy folds of the damask draperies, now pulled across the glass. From the moment Wiggins left the house for the garden wall, she had been waiting to see what would happen next. She was more than frustrated by the murmur of words she couldn't understand, but she did make out the last remark from Quint. She left the window then and went to sit in a chair in front of the small fireplace. Thomas had brought up coal and made a fire before he went to bed, and the coals were still glowing. She leaned back, pretending a peacefulness she didn't feel, until the door opened. Then she rose and went to him, smiling.

"You must be starved, my lord. Does Cook know you're here?"

Quint stared. In the simple gown Rosamunde's body was slender but lushly feminine. The smooth silk slid over her as she moved, revealing rounded breasts, a slim waist and the flare of her hips, the shape of long, slim legs. When she held out her hands to him he took them and drew her close, unable to resist; when she put up her mouth to be kissed he took her lips gently and then with sudden passion. In an instant he knew he would have to keep his hands off his lovely wife tonight. He stood back, stuttering an answer to her question.

"Ah, yes. Cook knows. Wiggins will be bringing up our food."

Rosa moved away from him, her dark mane of shining hair glistening in the fireglow. She knew Quint was trying to hide his desire for her. That kiss yesterday in the coach had taught her a great deal. Tonight there was something keeping them apart—something in his mind, not in that eager body. She knew as soon as he touched her how he felt, had felt for herself the passionate heat in his kiss, had known the moment he made himself let her go. She might be young and untried, but she already knew this man better than any other she had ever met, and she didn't want to insist . . .

"If something is wrong, my lord, and you'd rather not stay with me, I'll understand."

Quint found it impossible to agree with that. If he did, he would have to leave. "Nothing is wrong, Rosa. I am tired; and you must get your rest, too, after our trip. But my feelings for you haven't changed. Come, I think I hear Wiggins on the stairs. Open the door for him, my dear. I need to wash my hands." He headed directly toward the bath. She gazed after him, wondering. He was no stranger to any part of this house.

When Rosa opened the door Wiggins paraded into the room with a huge silver tray, so heavy with food, dishes, and utensils that it seemed too much for his thin arms. He set it on the top of a low table near the fire, bowed to Rosa, and left, saying from the door that there was more if they wanted more. She smiled and nodded as he closed the door.

"Ah!" Quint came from the bath, drying his hands on a small towel, sniffing the air and trying on a confident smile. "A joint of lamb, if I'm not mistaken."

"And a great deal more," Rosa said, waving a hand at the full tray. "Wiggins has brought us a feast. Even a bottle of wine and a decanter of brandy. Shall I pour?"

"Why, yes, thank you."

She poured wine into the two glasses on the tray and offered him one, sipping her own as she found a place to sit near the table. Quint, pulling over a footstool, sat beside her and took the carving knife and fork, serving her with a slice of the lamb, then passed a bowl of vegetable marrow and a dish of peas. He was, she thought, exceptionally friendly. And handsome. She took up her knife and fork to eat, suddenly conscious of how hungry she was and how long it had been since she had eaten those few tiny sandwiches. . . .

"More?" He was filling her wineglass for the third time. She glanced up from her nearly empty plate and saw that he was amused, smiling at her as he might at a well-fed and satisfied child. She was well fed, she thought, but not completely satisfied. She blushed and pushed her plate aside.

"You must think me greedy as a pig."

"No, indeed. I ate more. We were both hungry." Quint rose and went to the bellpull by the mantel and gave it a yank, then came back to remove the brandy and brandy glasses from the huge tray. "We'll put these aside. We may enjoy a glass as our dinner settles."

"Indeed." She tipped up her wineglass and drained it. Not for the world would she tell him that she'd never tasted brandy; that she'd been told by the squire that it wasn't for children or females. If Quint thought it proper, she told herself, then proper it was. But the thick air in the room and the heat of the fire were making her a trifle dizzy.

Rising from her chair as Wiggins came in, she went to the windows that looked out over the dark garden and opened one a crack, breathing in the cold fresh air. Behind her, she heard the door close, and then Quint's quick, soft tread coming toward her.

"Rosa."

She turned, her thick hair swinging around her slim shoulders, framing her blushing face as she looked up at him. Her adoring look was unmistakable. Quint felt his blood heating, an inevitable stirring of hot desire. It would be damned difficult to take himself down a cold hall to an empty bed when he knew she wanted him to stay. Rosa's eyes were telling him he was wonderful; her soft, tempting mouth quivered with readiness. And looking at her, he could feel that quiver as if it were already crushed beneath his lips. Suddenly, he could taste her. Feel her. In his imagination she tasted like the scent of roses; her skin was like warm silk. With an effort, he forced himself to remember the decision he had made that evening, and why he had made it. Then he turned away.

"Quint?" Her soft voice was full of doubt; there was still a warmth in it, but the warmth was fading. He saw that as he glanced back.

"I know you must be tired, Rosa. I'll not insist on my marital rights when we both need rest so badly. There will be time enough later."

Rosa didn't answer, nor did he blame her. Even to his own ears, the words sounded cold and indifferent. He saw her smile fade, her eyelids shuttering the hurt look in her eyes. He hurried to change the subject.

"We'll have a nightcap of Leighton's excellent brandy," he said, making his voice lighter, moving toward the decanter and glasses. Taking a glass, he poured a measure and held it out. "Here, take this glass, warm it with your palms, then sip it slowly."

She came, reluctant but not wishing to show her great disappointment, and took the glass, watching the brandy swirl as she rolled it back and forth between her hands. He studied her, and damned himself as a rude fool. Finally he cleared his throat and spoke again.

"We may be gone on our trip for some months, Rosa. I thought it might . . . be rather wearing for you aboard ship if you were expecting a child."

Her gaze shot up to his face. "Months? In the Mediterranean?"

"There, and very possibly in other places even more uncomfortable. Not places for an expectant mother."

"I . . . understand, I think." She was watching him

now, and seeing again that faraway look in his eyes. A challenging look, that look of daring. She moved closer, drawn now by her love of adventure. "Where?" she asked softly. "Where are we really going?"

He looked at her and smiled. "Xanadu."

She caught his arm, her hand holding him with a subtle strength, her own lips beginning to curve. "Xanadu! A place found only in a Coleridge poem. Am I cast as the woman wailing for her demon lover?"

Quint had to laugh. "Nothing so sad as that, sweet. You may wander in the pleasure domes instead." He took her into his arms but held her loosely, knowing how quickly she roused his passion. "If we succeed tomorrow with your solicitors we will leave within ten days. Perhaps less."

Rosamunde smiled. "Then we will succeed."

Chapter Six

*A*fter breakfast, Quint and Rosamunde met in the upper hall. Rosa was wearing a dark, heavy gown, as if she'd dressed for serious occasion. The gown was, of course, completely out of style. But it was made of heavy silk faille in a somber navy blue, and Rosa approved of it. She felt very businesslike in it; certainly it was properly dull, which she felt appropriate for a call on one's solicitors. Quint eyed her as they met and offered an arm down the steep stairs.

"What do you think?" she asked, resting a hand on his forearm as they went along. "Will this gown do?"

To Quint she looked like a young girl in Grandmother's funeral gown. The gown had a tiered shoulder cape that came almost to her waist, and sleeves protruded beneath it into great dark billows gathered in by delicate lace-trimmed cuffs. The high-waisted, voluminous skirt was supported by crinolines. Her bonnet was trimmed in dark feathers and bows; her black slippers, made of fine leather but very old, shone. She looked, he thought, miserably uncomfortable and astoundingly beautiful in spite of it.

"Very dignified," he said. "The solicitors will not take you lightly."

Rosa smiled, instantly cheered. "Indeed. That was my intention. I thought they might be more agreeable to the wishes of a sedate and, uh, older woman."

Quint smiled back. He was a fashion plate. He wore a tall top hat and a wrapped cravat around his neck that was tied in a wide, flat bow; his tan coat buttoned like a vest and had a widespread collar, which, along with the coat's cuffs, was a contrasting dark brown velvet. The coattails were full and hung to his knees on either side and in back, but in front the coat ended just below his waist, to reveal fine doeskin trousers. Fastened beneath his boots, the trousers fitted snugly from waist to ankles, showing off his flat belly and muscular thighs to perfection. Rosa was openly admiring of his outfit, and both Anna and Thomas stood to watch them leave in the old carriage Wiggins brought around to the door.

They set off at once, their faces washed with early sun. The visit that had been just a future event to Rosa became reality. She was suddenly sure the two old men they were going to see would not recognize her; might not believe she was the young girl they remembered. Defensively, she put on an air of confidence and sat upright, stiff as a board.

Quint recognized her defiant pose and understood her fright. He took her hand and held it as the horse trotted up Regent Street and onto Oxford, turning to the right, toward the Bank of England on Threadneedle Street at the east end of London. Quint had learned from Wiggins that clients waited for hours in the five new halls of the bank built just off Lothbury Court. And, Wiggins had added, Plimpton & Ruether likely would have offices in the new wing, for they were a well-known firm. Quint told all that to Rosa, his voice casual, and the tone of his voice soothed her into confidence again. Then, since Wiggins was to be trusted, according to Quint, they went over their hopes and intentions with each other.

"Remember," Quint said, sitting forward and looking at Rosa steadily, "there is no doubt that the solicitors would prefer having your guardian present. You are not yet of age."

"But I am married."

Quint nodded. "Indeed. And that should get us your dowry. I hope I won't sound greedy, but I may need all of it—and possibly more. In the meantime, you and your servants need clothes for our journey. The solicitors may not like handing over part of your fortune before your birthday without Squire Brownley present."

"Never mind. I shall take care of that."

Unconvinced, Quint frowned as he sat back again. "Perhaps we can send for Brownley, if they object."

Rosa turned away, feeling the awful guilt again. "I don't think so. He . . . ah, meant to travel, I believe."

"Well, tell me where he was going, then."

She looked away, hating to lie to him. "He never told us his plans. He had creditors he wished to escape."

"Good God! I was counting on him if it became necessary to find someone to vouch for me. I was leaning on a weak reed, wasn't I? Well, we'll just have to take it as it comes."

Rosa managed a smile, though her heart beat thunderously. "I'm afraid so, my lord. But look—we're nearly there."

Wiggins drove them right to the Lothbury Court entrance, tied the horse, and settled down to wait. Quint sprang from the high carriage as Rosa stood and gathered her huge skirts around her. She held them with one hand and reached out to Quint with the other. He laughed, put his warm hands around her waist, and swung her down to the pavement.

"You're as light as air, my lady, even in that heavy gown. Come, I'm beginning to think I may need your help badly."

Relieved by his sudden change of mood, Rosa laughed too, took his hand, and ran up the marble steps with him. Inside the arched doorway was an open space and then more steps, descending to a paved marble rectangle where more arched entrances led to arched passageways lined with paneled oak doors. They found a clerk hurrying down one hall and asked directions of him, Quint giving his name and explaining that they had business with Plimpton & Ruether.

The clerk beamed at them. "Just follow me, my lord. I am going there."

Rosa squeezed Quint's arm and smiled happily. "Chance is with us," she whispered. "The signs are all good."

The clerk led them to a recessed door and opened it, standing back for them to enter. "Take your seats, my lord and lady. You will be summoned into an inner office once the gentlemen are settled." He bowed politely and disappeared through another door, one of three across the rear wall.

Rosa, looking around, chose a plump settee by a fully draped window and sank into it, breathing in the pleasant odor of good leather and lemon-polished wood. Quint sat beside her, stretching long legs and looking, she thought, extremely handsome. And worried. He whispered to her, "Do you remember the men, my lady? Can you tell me something of them?"

Rosa smiled. "Oh, yes. My mother felt that Plimpton was much the more careful of the two, and that Ruether was apt to take an occasional chance. Therefore she preferred Ruether. Actually, I think she meant to marry him at one time and decided not to because they were too much alike."

Quint looked startled. "She would marry a cit?"

Rosa laughed aloud. "Of course. She did marry a cit. Her third husband was Henry Thornhill, a merchant. Most of her fortune came from him. As a matter of fact, she spoke well of him the rest of her life."

"I see. And did you like him?"

"I'm sorry to say I never met him. It was after he died that Mother married Lord Gilbert and I was born."

"Good God! Four husbands!"

"Five," Rosa said glumly, brought back to the present problem. "And as you know, the fifth was a terrible mistake. However, my mother had forethought enough to make sure Squire Brownley would never lay hands on her fortune. She left him only enough of an income to enable him to take care of me and made Anna and Thomas swear to watch over me. They were to make sure I had food and clothing." She looked away, her young face suddenly sad. "I missed her awfully, Quint. I still do."

He took her hand and held it. "I know. I wish . . ." He trailed off as the clerk came in.

"Lord Spencer," the clerk said, "Solicitor Plimpton will see you and Lady Spencer now."

Quint rose slowly, looking immensely dignified. "I'm afraid I neglected to say that our business is with Solicitor Ruether. Would it be possible . . . ?"

"Oh, indeed, my lord. They have both settled in. Please follow me."

Rosa stood and took Quint's arm, amused. It was so like Quint to want a man who took an occasional chance.

Alan Ruether's office was like the man himself: spare

but cheerful. Gray-haired, clean-shaven, and long-boned in his neat dark clothes, he stood up and smiled as the clerk introduced them. Then he came around the desk, bowed to Rosa, and shook Quint's offered hand.

"I have heard of your exploits at sea, Lord Spencer. You are a credit to England. And this is your lovely wife? I had not heard you married . . ." His voice slid to a bemused halt as he stared into Rosa's face. Then he reached out, put a hand on each caped shoulder, and laughed with startled pleasure.

"Rosamunde! My dear child, you've grown to look precisely like your mother, God bless her." He leaned down and kissed Rosa on her forehead. "So, you've found and wed an English adventurer. Lady Beatrice would be pleased."

"Yes," Rosa said with confidence, "she would. She always said life was too wonderful to spend in dull routine. But you know that, don't you? The two of you were great friends."

"True! Now, both of you come sit with me and tell me how I can serve you."

They crossed the thick Persian rug and sat near his desk in huge chairs padded for luxurious comfort. Quint brought out the papers for Ruether to read—the signed agreement from Squire Cedric Brownley; the marriage license filled in by the Bideford curate, with the curate's signature under those of the witnesses, Anna Castner and Thomas Castner. When he came to that part, Ruether looked up at Rosa.

"Anna and her son are still with you?"

Rosa nodded, smiling. "You would not know Thomas, Uncle Alan. He is even bigger than Anna, and stronger than three ordinary men."

Ruether laughed, pleased to hear the name she'd

called him when she was a child. "I am sure that is true. He was huge as a lad. They are . . . peaceable?"

Quint glanced at Rosa, surprised by the red stain mounting in her cheeks. "Yes," she answered. "They are peaceable, as Anna promised. Yet I have no doubt that they would protect me at all costs, solely for my mother's sake."

Ruether nodded and set the papers aside. "These seem all in order," he said slowly. "But I am surprised that we haven't heard of this from Cedric Brownley. He has not even applied for his quarterly stipend."

Rosa's eyes widened. "But—would he? He arranged my marriage to Lord Spencer and took a bride price of a most considerable sum in gold guineas. When he signed that contract he lost his income from my mother, didn't he?"

"Oh, no. Only half of it. He will get his half every three months until he dies."

But he *is* dead. Rosa almost said it aloud. It shocked her badly to think she had come so close to giving the awful secret away. She looked at Quint, hoping he hadn't noticed. But Quint only smiled at her and spoke to Ruether.

"No doubt the squire will be asking for his usual share once he's got rid of my gold in the grogshops he frequents. Brownley is not the man you remember, I am sure. He has gone to drink and a useless life."

"We feared that he would," Ruether said, and sighed. "He wasn't a man one would choose to bring up a young girl, but as you see, he managed it, with Anna's help. All right, what do you want from us, Lord Spencer? The dowry?"

"Indeed." Quint's face reddened beneath his sun-browned skin but his voice remained firm. "And we have a use for more, which you must take from my wife's inheritance and give to her. I'm afraid my estate is in need of repair before we can live a normal life in it. Besides, as you have undoubtedly surmised, my wife is also in need of good clothes."

Rosa looked down at her heavy, unfashionable gown and arched her brows. Of course it was true that all of her gowns were old, but this one was by far the most expensive of her outfits, bought by Cedric when his mother died and they had attended the funeral. However, she had to admit that it was truly ugly. She thought about it for a moment or so, until the silence between the two men caught her attention and she looked up. She had seen that expression on Alan Ruether's face very seldom, but even as a child it had reminded her of a closed door. She burst into frightened argument and sudden tears.

"Uncle Alan, don't you dare say no! My eighteenth birthday is less than three weeks away, but I cannot wait. I have needs right now that will take an enormous amount of money." She pulled out a lace-trimmed handkerchief and mopped her eyes. "If you had ever visited me at the squire's estate you would have known how he deprived me of everything, even of friends—and perhaps you would have helped me, then."

Alan Ruether was out of his chair and around the desk, leaning over Rosa with an arm around her slim shoulders. "I would have, indeed! I had no way of knowing you were in bad times. Please forgive me, Rosamunde. I should have done more for Beatrice's daughter."

In bad times . . . the very words reminded Rosa of that worst of all bad times at Brownley's estate. She saw in her mind the dangling body in Anna's grasp, heard his strangled cry, saw the light of the hooded lantern shining down into the deep, shadowed grave in the garden. . . .

She covered her eyes and struggled to hide her fright and tears.

Ruether groaned, his face pale with sympathy. "Poor child! Tied to a home with a worthless, drunken fool after such a happy life with your mother. Yes, we should have investigated long ago—and yes, you may have whatever funds you need now. Surely I can bend a rule to make you happy."

Before they left a damp Rosamunde thanked Alan Ruether profusely for his kindness and promised to see him again once they returned from the wedding trip they planned on the Mediterranean Sea, and in the wonderful lands about it. Quint, who listened and watched, received the monies and signed the receipts, pleasant but mostly silent. Not until they were in the carriage again and on their way back to Berkeley Square did he say anything at all to Rosamunde. And then it was in answer to a question.

"Do you think it went well?" Rosa asked him. "Or would you have asked for more?"

Quint looked at her. Her eyes were still a bit pink, but she glowed with success. "No," he answered abruptly. "I would have asked for less. Ruether must have given us every shilling your mother left."

Rosa shook her head. "Not even a quarter of it, my lord. Only near to an eighth. Besides, with Plimpton's ability in investing, the funds will be recovered by the end of a year."

"Oh." Riding west, Quint brooded for a while. Strangely, it bothered him to know that Rosa's inheritance was so large, and bothered him more because she knew it and hadn't told him. But what bothered him most was the way she had played on Ruether's emotions. Surely she had brought out those tears to get her own way. He was frowning when he spoke again.

"I shall count this affair today as a lesson. I learned how you 'take care of it' when you meet with any strong opposition. And you did it well. But to be fair I should warn you at once—women's tears have little or no effect on me. I am not a sentimental old man."

She looked at him, bewildered. "But I told the truth, Quint. Believe me, life with Squire Brownley was more than miserable. Are you angry?"

"No. You saved the day. Still, I wouldn't want you to try your childish sobs on me, for it would prove disappointing to you." Quint had been shocked by the pity he'd felt when she was crying and Ruether was comforting her. He would have given her the moon right then, had she asked for it. But God help him, he thought, if she ever found that out. He'd seen too many weepy wives controlling their husbands.

Rosamunde was turning away from him, her eyes icy. "Why then, my lord, if I feel tears coming on I shall retire to another room and shut the door. That should solve the problem."

Quint was silent, wondering why she took on so at his criticism. Those tears had to be playacting on her part—she had never cried or told him of any real cruelty on Brownley's part; only greed. Perhaps he should have a talk with her about the man and see if any of it was true. . . .

Some days later, days in which Rosa visited dressmakers and several salons where she could buy other articles of clothing, they were ready to leave for the south coast of England in a hired coach. Quint had also hired a wagon for their baggage, increased considerably by the various purchases of clothing, many of which had been made at Quint's suggestion. He had said to both Rosa and Anna that the climate was changeable and they would need clothes for both extremes of temperature. They wondered but they also bought.

Rosa had long since given up her grudge. Her new clothes, the excitement of leaving, and an air of courtesy from Quint had done away with her hurt feelings. And now she found out from Thomas that they were going to Portsmouth, where they would board a coastal tramp steamer bound for Bordeaux. But that was all Thomas knew. So while Thomas and Anna went on loading the wagon, she approached Quint.

"Thomas says we are going to Bordeaux on a paddlewheel steamer, my lord. Must we give up our Mediterranean voyage?"

Quint was strapping a small leather bag, hefting it and listening to a chinking noise inside. He turned and looked at her. The gown she was wearing was of silk in a rich dark red, with a fitted bodice that clung to the shape of high young breasts. Her hair shone, fastened in a thick knot on the back of her head. Still, a few of the silky black locks escaped as usual and gave her an air of careless beauty. He dragged his gaze away from the hair to stop on the sweet curves of hidden breasts. He sighed profoundly. Treating his wife like a young sister was becoming almost impossible. The woman was always tempting him. He thought how much easier this would be if only she'd been ugly and stupid, as he had feared.

"Indeed not, my sweet. Crossing Spain from Bordeaux is one of many ways to arrive at the Med, and shorter than most. But I must warn you—this first part of the trip can be miserable. The Bay of Biscay grows angry with only a whisper of wind. For that matter, the Med itself is often rough."

"I have heard that before. You needn't worry. Anna will take care of me. She always has."

Quint moved closer, close enough that his thighs brushed her gown. "There will come a time when I set her aside," he said in a low voice. "And then I will take care of you."

Rosa gazed into his half closed eyes and saw the look of an aroused and dominant male, wanting possession. Her breath caught in her throat, and she turned away, silent and wondering. He wanted her. It was plain enough; though she had little experience with men she could see in his eyes the same strong desire that she felt herself. A desire that she knew would pull her straight into his arms if he ever stopped fighting it. What strange conviction kept him from taking what he wanted? Of course, as he said, he might get her with child. But what of that? Anna was with them, and surely they'd never go adventuring for nine whole months before they came back to Lundy Island—or would they?

Both Anna and Thomas came through the half-open door of the house, hesitated as they saw the two together, and turned to go out again. Seeing them, Rosa spoke.

"Is the wagon loaded?"

"We have put your personal baggage in the coach," Anna answered, "and the wagon is nearly full. We came to see if there was more to be taken."

"This," Quint said, and tossed the small bag to Thomas, who caught it and nearly dropped it, surprised by the weight. Quint grinned at him. "Guard it well, Thomas. As for other things, there may be something upstairs. Please look, Anna."

Anna left, and Thomas, bag in hand, went out to the wagon. Quint turned to Rosa and offered his arm.

"Shall we go?" If he was excited he was hiding it, but

Rosa didn't even try. She grabbed her cloak from the hall rack, tucked her arm in his, and pulled him toward the door.

"Indeed, my lord! This is my first trip away from England, and I know I'll remember every moment of it as long as I live."

He laughed abruptly. "I believe we all may, my lady."

She glanced up at him as they stepped through the door, wondering as his face went suddenly pale under his tan. This was the trip he wanted; he had the money to go now, and still he seemed on edge.

The fog was thick as they left the house; thick enough that Rosa barely recognized Wiggins as he came along behind them, walking briskly forward as Quint helped her into the coach. She didn't see Wiggins go back to the house again, but that, she supposed, was probably because she was busy settling herself into the soft seat beside Quint. This coach was lovely; very luxurious compared to the carriages they had used before.

"I do hope," she said as the coach moved smoothly away from the curb, "that the fog lifts a bit. Otherwise, it will be a slow ride and a long one."

"The driver is familiar with London streets," Quint said, staring outside at the layers of mist and smoke. "We will lose little time to the fog." He sounded as if he spoke of one thing and thought of another; while his eyes searched for someone; his head was cocked as if listening for footsteps.

"Are you looking for Wiggins?" Rosa asked, "I wondered myself when he went past us and I didn't see him go back. Likely he took the other side."

The coach gained speed, and Quint leaned over and took her hand in his, smiling. "No, he didn't go back, my sweet. Wiggins decided on having a holiday with us. He will spell the coachman on this part of the trip."

"Oh? Won't the Leightons be displeased that he left their house?"

"They won't mind." He put his arm around her and leaned toward her, burying his face in her fragrant hair. "Lovely," he murmured. "A scent of roses . . ."

His arm was warm and strong. She settled against it happily as his lips sought hers. In moments her doubts were gone, and her arms were around his neck. It was, Quint thought, a very pleasant way to stop her from wondering about the Leightons. But dangerous to his plans.

They were alone. Anna had chosen to ride with Thomas on the wagon; Rosa had examined it a day before and thought it strong and safe. There was a homemade cab of sorts built around the pillowed wagon seat that kept out the dampness and chill, and the two of them could trade off on the driving.

Now Rosa could hear the thump and rattle of the wagon, close behind. They stayed close because of the fog, which gradually grew thicker as they approached the Thames, and became as thick as pea soup as they began to cross over Westminster Bridge.

Something seemed to trouble Quint. He moved away from Rosa and began watching the few figures to be seen in the thick mist. Most of them were laborers walking toward the bridge; only a few nobles and wealthy cits appearing and disappearing in coaches and on horseback as the fog rose and drifted.

The coach was rumbling down from the bridge and onto the wide street beyond when a shot rang out, and then another, the cracking explosions muffled by the fog. In the coach, Quint's arm swept Rosa down across his thighs, while his other hand fumbled a dueling pistol from the deep pocket of his coat.

"Stay down!" His voice was low but commanding.

"Why? I—"

The shattering noise of a shot filled the coach; the air reeked of gunpowder. Outside, a clatter of hooves, a thump, a deep groan. The coach slowed and nearly halted, but Quint stuck his head through the opened window and roared, "Ranjit! That last shot was mine! Go!"

The coach jerked forward and began to sway, the horses settling into a fast trot. Tumbled half on and half off the wide seat, Rosa struggled to sit up. A hand pressed her down again on hard thighs.

"Stay down, Rosamunde!"

"But *Anna!* Quint, please."

"Anna and Thomas will not be bothered. I swear to you, they'll be all right. They are not the quarry."

Her heart clenched like a fist. Of course: Quint was the quarry, the one to be killed. *Why?* She slid the rest of the way off the seat and knelt there on the floor, trembling, folding her arms across his knees and propping her chin on them, watching his face as if she could keep him safe by her hope alone. She saw his narrowed eyes search the drifting fog. He had had a loaded gun in his pocket; he had known something like this might happen. And still he watched, though there were no more yells, no more shots. Looking up, she saw that one shot had come through the side of the coach, only inches from Quint's head.

She shuddered, and then gathered her courage. "Why?" she asked softly. "Why does someone want to kill you?"

His eyes flickered away from the slowly brightening streets outside and came down to her pale face, upturned and serious. He smiled, and smoothed back a lock of silky hair.

"They've been robbed, Rosa, and they think me the robber."

"Are you a robber?"

He shook his head, his emerald eyes hard as stones. "No. Not yet."

Chapter Seven

———— ❦ ————

$\mathcal{B}$efore they left the southernmost sections of the city, the day was clearing and the fog had drifted away. Rosa, sitting in the fresh breeze from the window and looking out as the farmland began to appear, could almost believe that the shrouded morning, the shots and the deep groan of pain had been part of a vivid nightmare.

She had asked Quint questions, but he shrugged most of them off. He said the man he had shot was an enemy who had tried to kill him many times before.

"I could have killed him long ago," Quint ended, "but why should I? He is only a pawn for another man. If he died, another would be hired—possibly a better shot."

"Do you believe you killed him this morning?"

Quint shook his head. "I doubt it. I aimed higher than his heart. Still, I may have broken his shoulder with the shot, and that will keep him disabled for a while. He is a strong man, and he was still able to make a loud noise. No, he'll not die. But perhaps he'll have to wait a bit before he takes up the chase again."

Rosa sighed with relief. "Then we'll be gone, and he'll not know where."

Quint looked away. He didn't want her to worry; but he did want her on guard. She deserved a warning. "He is a patient man, my lady, and knows his calling. He'll find us."

The certainty in his voice made Rosa shiver. "He'll find me with you, then. You must buy me a pistol."

Quint laughed. "Oh, no. The man himself is far less dangerous than an excited woman with a pistol."

"I," Rosa said flatly, "am a very good shot and I have a cool head. My mother taught me how to use a firearm."

"Your mother? Wonderful!" Quint was truly amused, laughing harder, his white teeth shining in his tanned face. "Fiery Lady Beatrice taught a girl of ten to shoot a pistol? What a pair you must have been."

"I was nine when she taught me, not ten," Rosa corrected him. Her face grew red, her blue eyes hot enough to smoke. She had to work very hard to keep her temper. "Laugh if you want to, but someday I shall prove to you that I am able to shoot."

"I look forward to it," Quint said, but he was still laughing.

That night they spent in an old farmhouse near Haslemere, the two women together in a small room; Quint, Thomas, Wiggins, and Ranjit in a loft. Earlier, as they were entering the house, Rosa saw that Ranjit was the man who'd met with Quint in the alley behind the Leighton house, and a closer look at his aquiline features told her he was of an exotic race. With that name, she supposed him a Hindu.

She glanced around at Quint, saw the hardly perceptible shake of his head, then turned, lowering her gaze, to follow Anna. He could have introduced the man, who was obviously one of their party. But her curiosity faded. The odors of food were a magnet coaxing them over to the farmhouse table, where plenty of good plain fare was spread for a meal.

At dawn they were back in the coach and heading for Portsmouth, with Thomas and Anna close behind in the wagon. By midafternoon they were making their way around the huge warehouses built near the port and toward the several tramp steamers tied up at the docks.

"Good," Quint said, looking from one steamer to another. "The haggling will be easier. Were there only a single boat, we'd have to pay twice the fair price. As it is, they'll offer to take us and our baggage across for half the usual amount."

The captains gathered around Quint as Ranjit, Thomas, and Anna begin to unload the wagon, putting the baggage and bundles on the docks. Rosa was silent, listening to the bargaining. Half the time she had no idea what was said, for the captains Quint spoke with were foreigners who had no English. But Quint had a smattering of other languages and there was no trouble.

Then for a time she just watched, approving as she saw Quint visit three of the steamers to look them over, then come back to haggle over passage on one of them and finally accept an offer. Several had bid lower, but the one he took was a clean ship, carrying mostly wool and lumber, good English oak. Another virtue was that it would weigh anchor the very next morning.

There was a large inn a street or two away from the port. They went there, hungry and tired. They ate and took rooms for the night, still maintaining the same arrangements, the two women together, and the four men.

Undressing in their room, Rosa felt her position as a virgin bride as embarrassing as ever.

"I don't understand," she blurted out, turning to face Anna. "Why does he stay with the other men at night? I am his wife! And I . . . I have good reason to know I arouse him."

"Don't bother your head. He must have good reasons too."

Rosa frowned, slipping into her lace-trimmed nightgown. "You think so? I don't. His excuses are very flimsy." She sat down, feeling a rush of new bitterness as she took the pins out of her hair and let it fall around her shoulders. "But why do I expect anything more than courtesy? After all, we both know he married me for my dowry."

"Perhaps," Anna said, coming to brush Rosa's hair, "he is not sure he will accomplish all he intends to do. Wiggins, I know, is worried. He has said more than once that he believes this time Lord Spencer has bitten off more than he can chew. And we all know someone tried to kill him yesterday morning and came close to doing it. Perhaps he feels his chances of surviving this trip are slim, and he wants you free to marry again. He is a kind man, and thoughtful. He'd not want to leave you a widow with a child."

Rosamunde was silent, feeling Anna's words slide into her heart like an icy knife. Somehow she knew it was true. He had hinted at it himself, saying what he did about being fair to her. She shuddered. There had been very few times in her life when fear had caused her real pain, and this was the worst yet. Why? And then she knew why. She reached up and took the brush from Anna's hand, swiveling around to look up at her.

"I don't want him hurt," she said, meeting Anna's

gaze. "You and Thomas must help me look after him. I —I'd want to die if anything happened to him."

Anna smiled. "I know, little one. But the man is able, both with a pistol and a sword. Thomas has seen him fencing with Wiggins. He said Lord Spencer is a master."

Rosamunde nodded. What Anna said didn't surprise her. She believed it at once. Quint usually wore a light sword, and he moved like a fencer, exuding an air of confidence at all times. But that wasn't all he would need if he was outnumbered. If an enemy hired one assassin, he could hire a half dozen. And assassins didn't fight by the rules of English gentlemen.

"Just the same, we'll look after him. He's foolish; putting adventure ahead of his life."

Rosa tossed and turned that night, though her bed was comfortable. Until now, she had enjoyed the idea of finding adventure on the sea, and in foreign lands. But the attack as they left London that morning had frightened her badly, and the conversation she had with Anna had brought an understanding. She rose at dawn and rousted out Anna for a hurried breakfast in the inn's dining hall.

"I'll find a place where they sell firearms," she told Anna. "And I'll buy a pair of dueling pistols. One for you and one for me. Thomas can handle men without a weapon."

"I know nothing of weapons, Rosa. Like Thomas, I do much better with my bare hands."

"I'll teach you."

They were gone when Quint came looking for them; he cursed under his breath and sent Thomas and Wiggins to the docks, carrying the bags they had taken to the inn.

"Don't load anything on until I get there with the women," he told Wiggins. "The captain won't wait. He has to catch the tide."

Heavy with fear for Rosamunde, Quint began searching the part of Portsmouth around the inn. He was afraid that the two women had started out for a stroll in the cool dawn and had been captured by renegades. There was no sign of them, and as the time for the ebb tide drew closer, he turned back in a panic of fear and dread, rushing toward the docks to make sure nothing of theirs had been loaded onto the ship. Then from a block away he saw the feathers and loops of ribbon on Rosa's cream-colored bonnet, and the huge woman beside her. The two were walking calmly along the pier toward the ship at the end. His fear for Rosa turned to instant fury. How dare she disobey her husband!

Lengthening his stride, he soon caught up. When he saw Wiggins glance toward him, he raised an arm and swung it down, pointing at the boxes and bundles belonging to his party and then at the ship. Wiggins jumped to obey the implicit order, sending Thomas ahead with the heaviest box, commandeering a few sailors with promises of money.

Arriving at the group, Quint gave Rosa a withering look. "You came close to ruining our plans," he said, "by your careless action. If you've left anything in your room at the inn you'll suffer the loss. There is no time to return for it."

Her welcoming smile disappeared. "I am not such a fool as that," she said, and pointed at the case in Anna's hand. "That is everything we took into the inn." And a bit more, she thought, but didn't say so. Angry as he was, she was sure he'd be even angrier if he knew there was now a brace of dueling pistols in her possessions.

The two women were taken down to their cabin by a

grinning mate who bobbed at them every time they spoke. The cabin was barely large enough to turn around in, with a bunk built onto the curved side of the ship, and another, smaller one overhead. In one corner there was a bucket with a lid.

"That," Anna said, pointing at the bucket after the mate left, "is our toilette room."

"Wonderful," Rosa said, and laughed. "All the amenities. Where do we wash?"

"In Bordeaux, once we have landed."

"Good heavens! How long will that be?"

"Two days, Thomas heard. Perhaps three or four if the weather worsens." Anna hesitated. "When we're out of port and Lord Spencer is satisfied with the arrangement of his belongings, you'd be wise to apologize for leaving the inn without permission. He was extremely worried."

"I know. He believes me to be too stupid to take care of myself. Had I even mentioned going out, he would have escorted me. But he wouldn't have let me buy the pistols. What else could I do but sneak away?"

"You could have done without the pistols, my lady. I am sure your husband is able to protect you himself."

"True," Rosa said, reddening. "But what of the dangers we may face from—well, from pirates in the Mediterranean? When they attack, should I simply scream and faint?"

Anna frowned. "You've forgotten that Lord Spencer is not one of the fancy men who hang about London declaring how brave they are. You can tell by looking at that sunburnt face that he's been in the king's service. It isn't likely that he will need your help."

"Oh." After a moment, Rosa nodded. "Just the same, the pistols may come in handy."

The trip across the channel and down to the Bay of

Biscay was uneventful. The small steamer was outclassed by huge sailing vessels that came bearing down on them, riding a strong north wind, but when the captain saw a chance of collision he used the paddlewheels, sending the steamer thrashing away from the path of danger.

"We're like a duck," Rosa said, coming up behind Quint. "A scared duck, paddling frantically to get away from a fox. Couldn't the sailing ships move over a little?"

Quint looked down at her, still irritated by the trouble that morning but amused by what she said. His gaze rested on her lively face, her smile and the deep blue of her eyes. She was wearing a simple gown; a blue linsey with a modest V-neckline trimmed with a double row of white lace, echoed by lace undersleeves at her elbows. The huge skirt blew back and fluttered in the wind, but that didn't surprise him; he had learned her dislike of the crinolines. Her color was up, her black hair glinted like silk in the sun.

He laughed, and his irritation melted. "Does a queen step aside for a scullery maid?"

She laughed with him, and leaned on the railing. "Not often," she admitted, looking behind them to see the latest queen of the ocean, a barkentine in full sail cutting a swathe in the trail of foam left by the paddlewheels. "Perhaps never. Are we making good time?"

"Yes. We should be in the Garonne River tomorrow evening. It will make little difference—we must wait to unload until the morning. After that, we will take up our journey again."

"In what conveyance, my lord?"

"We will need two, I suppose. I must find a wagon to use, and a coach."

"I am very tired of peering from those little windows.

With a wagon to carry our baggage and shelter us from rain when shelter is needed, why don't we ride?"

"You would ride a horse for ten days? It will be that long from Bordeaux to the port on the Golfe du Lion."

"Better on horseback in the fresh air than jouncing around in a coach."

"If you believe you can stand it . . ." Quint was clearly doubtful.

"I can stand it. I am a very good horsewoman. My mother taught me well."

Quint laughed. "Perhaps. You have great faith in your mother, don't you? However, you show very little talent for riding donkeys."

Rosa had to laugh with him. "It isn't the donkeys that make me nervous, m'lord. I could grow used to their comical natures. But I fear the cliffs and the rocks below."

"Then perhaps the idea has merit. We'll try it."

The Garonne River, Quint told Rosamunde, rose in the Pyrenees and swept in a huge arc toward the Atlantic, then joined the Dordogne River to form a wide estuary known as the Gironde. At their joining there was a peninsula called Entre Deux Mers thrusting out into the Gironde. The peninsula with its rich soil was famous for its grapes and wine.

Standing again at the rail, Quint pointed out the spring growth in the vineyards to Rosa as they passed the next day, thrashing through the fast-running river. The captain, his mind on a free evening, was heading upstream for Bordeaux at full speed.

"We will stay on the ship," Quint said. "The city around the docks is lawless, and not a place for strangers at night. We'll wait for dawn. Then you and I will find horses and a wagon. Until then, we will be safe aboard. The captain will set guards, for he must protect his cargo."

"And we," Rosa answered, watching his eyes, "must protect ours. I have a feeling it would cost quite a bit to replace." She was rewarded by a quick glance and a frown.

"Did you pry into my purchases, Rosa?"

She smiled. "I would never do that. But I do have a mind. We have a great deal more luggage, clothes, and incidentals than anyone could use on a trip around the Mediterranean Sea." She could see a sudden sheen of perspiration on his sun-browned forehead, though the breeze along the river was cool. Then his jaw firmed.

"You will say nothing about our luggage. If anyone asks, you will tell them the extra bundles are various goods for which we might eventually turn a profit." He hesitated. "You will not be lying, Rosa."

She looked away from him, swallowing, pretending to stare at a huge bridge that arched over the wide river ahead of them. She could feel the blood rising in her face, feel the constant regret that made her heart heavy when she thought of the past. Of course, she would do it again to save Anna, but she couldn't help thinking Quint would hate her if he knew. Well, another lie wouldn't hurt her chances at gaining heaven. Especially if it would help him stay alive.

"I will say that," she answered after a moment, "if anyone asks. I doubt that they will. When one travels with two women, one must expect too many bundles."

In the first light of dawn Quint and Rosamunde left the steamer quietly. Muffled in hooded cloaks against the inevitable fog, they walked along the deserted quay until a horse and rider came into sight. Quint hailed him, spoke a few words in French, nodded at his answer and thanked him, turning to Rosa as the man rode on.

"There is a livery stable not far from here," he said. "We'll try it."

In less than an hour they returned to the steamer, riding together on the seat of a large roofed wagon pulled by two strong horses. Four saddled horses were tied to the rear. Hurriedly, Thomas and Wiggins came down with the first of the boxes and bundles, wanting their baggage out of the way before the drays arrived for the ship's lumber and wool. Quint jumped down from the seat of the wagon and began helping, packing their load neatly into the body of the wagon, leaving room to move around amongst the various pieces.

"There are canvas sides," Rosa told Anna, who came with more bags and bundles, "that can be dropped and secured when it rains. This is a fine wagon for our purposes."

"It would seem so, my lady. That wagon will prove more useful than a coach. It's strongly made and will hold us all snugged down on a rainy night."

Rosa smiled. "Quint was delighted with it. He says we'll take it with us."

"On a ship?" Anna laughed out loud. "Our Lord Spencer has dreamed of the impossible. No captain will rope that great thing down on his deck, to break loose in a storm and roll over his sailors."

Rosa shrugged. "You may be right. But I'll not wager against him."

Anna laughed again. "Nor I, now that I think on it. Who knows what he can do?"

There was no reason to ride through the great city of Bordeaux, for it was on the west side of the Garonne, and they were going east. The new and imposing Pont de Bordeaux, a bridge fifteen hundred feet and more across and boasting seventeen arches, was between the city walls and the quay where they had docked. It was a wonderful thing to ride a willing horse across the magnificent bridge and see from its height the huge and ancient buildings inside the walls. There were more quays on the south side of the bridge, and many ships, and beyond them a great square planted with plane trees, with the city's cathedrals stabbing a cloudless sky in the distance.

Rosa drew in a deep breath, tasting the dank scent of the river, catching a faint odor of spring blossoms. The slant of sunlight touching the sides of the tall buildings made them look like gold. Rosa sighed and turned toward Quint.

"A golden city, smelling of flowers. I would love to visit here."

Quint looked at her. She had cast off her cloak, now folded neatly and strapped to the rear of her saddle. She was wearing an old gown, a plain gown, one with a fraying hem. It had been a favorite of hers because it needed no crinolines nor other fancy additions, and the color, a sky blue, was one she liked. There was no lacing nor padding used to accentuate her breasts nor to diminish her waist, nor was any needed. He thought her more beautiful than any woman he had ever seen. His body responded to his thoughts and he shifted in his saddle, turning to look forward.

"We will come here in the future, if you wish."

Rosa heard the soft note in his voice and glanced at him, surprised. She started to speak and then, seeing a muscle ripple along his jaw, thought better of it, turning to look forward as he had done.

In the future. Her throat seemed to close with fear. Did they have a future? She thought of the foggy morning when they left London, and she knew the life she wanted would take luck—good luck, and plenty of it.

* * *

In the ten days it took to cover the distance to Cette, a flourishing seaport of southern France, southwest of Montpellier and on the western Golfe du Lion, the caravan of wagon and riders found food and accommodations in several small towns. Occasionally the church spires and coal smoke of a city beckoned them in the distance, but Quint turned away. Twice they had spent warm, dry nights in the wagon on the fringes of a forest. This last, almost windless night they were camping on a lonely beach with small waves whispering to them and the towering bulk of Mont St. Clair, nearly six hundred feet high, hovering over them like a great hen protecting her chicks.

"My lord must have more than one enemy," Anna said thoughtfully. "He must have several. Otherwise, knowing that one is disabled, he would not need to take such care."

"One enemy," Rosa said, "who hires assassins."

They were together inside the wagon, making ready for sleep. Tomorrow, Quint had said, they would be at the harbor in Cette early and he cautioned them all to be ready to go aboard. Rosa had laughed and said it would be a brave captain that would take on a wagon, four men, two women, and that almighty load of baggage. Neither she nor Anna believed Quint could find a captain who would agree to it. But as Anna said, what difference could it make? The wagon and horses could be left at a livery stable and picked up again when they came back.

"I see." Anna said now, thick brows lifting. "Hired assassins. Perhaps it is good Lord Spencer's beard has grown these ten days. It changes his looks amazingly." She hesitated. "Have you been told where we're going?"

Rosa smiled without humor. "Oh, yes. Quint gave me

to understand we would sail the Mediterranean for a glorious wedding trip. And I believed him!"

Anna broke out in genuine laughter. "It's plain he doesn't intend to do that. He pulled the wool over your eyes, Rosa. It's a wonder you haven't unleashed your temper on the man. Has he given you any hints of what he plans?"

"No. But whatever it is, he feels deeply about it. I am sure there is someone involved whom he cares for very much. I—I keep wondering if it's a woman."

"It couldn't be. I've watched and learned. Unwilling though he may be—and I truly believe he is unwilling—he has passionate feelings toward you, not toward some other."

Rosamunde lay back on the makeshift bed and closed her eyes. "I'll try to believe it. And tomorrow we shall see whether we go or stay. Go to sleep, Anna. We'll need your strength."

At noon the next day they rode into Cette, passing through sunny streets to the waterfront. They found a space to stop near the quays where they could see everything and yet be out of the way. As always, Rosa and Anna drew the eyes of the curious—a young and beautiful woman on a spirited horse, a huge giantess accompanying her with a loaded wagon.

People stared, and so did Rosa. Cette was a large port, with boats of all sizes at every quay, and a forest of masts swaying back and forth in a gentle breeze. Some of the ships that rode the lapping waves were big enough to sail the Atlantic, but many more were small, like the shallow Arabian dhows with their huge triangular sails. In the midst of it all there was a quay broader and stronger than the others, used by the wagons loading the trade boats.

"You will wait here with Anna and Thomas," Quint

told Rosa. "Wiggins, Ranjit, and I will see to the ship, and later Thomas can help with the loading."

Rosa smiled at him. Black-bearded and slim, for any extra weight seemed to have melted away in the fire of his quiet determination, she found him even more attractive than before. His green eyes were like emeralds in the sunlight, the look of intensity in his hard, sun-browned face gave her a sense of excitement; of danger just ahead. He was thrilling; even dangerous . . . and she shivered with delight.

"When you are ready," she said, "we will all help. This venture is important to us, also." Her breathless voice trembled with excitement.

He gave her a puzzled glance and was gone, walking purposefully toward the south and the large warehouses that blocked a good view of larger vessels in the distance. Ranjit was beside him, silent as always, and Wiggins was at his heels. And as she watched, a handful of half-grown boys in tattered clothes came running down from the town together and fell in behind them, laughing and jostling each other. She wasn't surprised. Quint, she thought, was a man others would always follow.

After a time of waiting Rosa dismounted, tied her horse to the wagon, and climbed up to sit on the broad driver's seat with Thomas and Anna. The sun had risen enough to warm the air and a pleasant breeze had come up, riffling the water. Boats were continually leaving the docks or coming to them; men and boys worked, talked, argued, and laughed, and the fishwives—solid old women wearing fustian gowns and bloodstained aprons —quarreled loudly over whose turn it was to get the fish from the next boat. But then the odor of fish rose from the boats, hung in the warming air and drifted ashore. Rosa wrinkled her small nose and fumbled in her pocket for a scented handkerchief.

"I do hope," she said, "that my lord finds a boat owned by a man who doesn't fish."

When neither Anna nor Thomas replied, she looked up and saw they were gazing at a new kind of craft coming into the circle around the docks. Dark and sleek, narrow for its length, the ship was close to a hundred feet long. Thomas's eyes were brilliant with interest; he leaned far forward to watch, his huge hands clamped on his knees.

"A privateer," he said, and laughed with pleasure, his eyes glued to the sleek hull. "A two-masted brigantine, Ma. Look how she slides through the water, like a greased pig! An' look at the gunports! If I were a foreign merchantman with a load of goods or gold, I'd hate to see that one tippin' its bow to me."

Staring at the ship, Rosa suddenly heard in her mind the greeting Alan Ruether had given Quint: *I have heard of your exploits at sea, Lord Spencer. You are a credit to England.*

She had wondered then what favors Quinton Spencer had done for king and country while traveling the sea. Now her gaze leapt from the sleek hull of the brig and rose to the figure at the wheel. Too far away yet to see his features clearly, but the man was tall, muscular, black-bearded, and—and he was standing there with such confidence, such lazy grace. At once, everything came together in a blinding flash of insight.

"That's Quint!" she gasped, and grasped Anna's arm. "I'll wager that ship is his own, Anna! He's a *pirate!*"

Anna laughed, deep in her chest. "If so, England must know he's a loyal privateer and is happy with her share of what he takes from enemies venturing into English waters."

"I know. My solicitor, Alan Ruether, praised his

competence at sea and said he was a 'credit to England.' Now I know what he meant."

She went on staring as Quint brought the sleek ship to the dock for loading, handling it as easily as the average man handles a rowboat. The other men were with him; Ranjit like a Moor in a wrinkled white robe, Wiggins dressed in ordinary trousers and a torn shirt, all with an air of devil-may-care about them. The boys who had followed Quint from the docks were on deck and swarming aloft to tie down the sails. Wiggins caught the lines the dockhands threw to him and snugged the ship to the dock.

Rosa turned to Anna again, frowning deeply. "Still," she said, "he *is* a pirate."

Anna nodded. "Of course. He's a Marisco."

Chapter Eight

❦

On deck, Wiggins shouted orders to the scrambling youths, and Thomas leapt from deck to dock with stout lines, tying them fast to heavy wooden blocks. The ship secured to the loading dock, he stepped back aboard, but not before he looked toward his mother with a grin that split his big face.

Anna sighed. "Thomas will never be happy on land again."

Rosamunde had stiffened and gone silent. Now she looked up at Anna with a flaring blue flame in her eyes.

"Then you must tell your son good-bye, or say farewell to me. I'll not go to sea in a pirate's ship. Just look at those horrible gunports all along the side." Inside, her heart was breaking. How could Quint kill innocent people and take their money? Looking back at the ship she saw Quint leap to the dock and come toward her, his step buoyant, his grin nearly as wide as Tom's. She whirled and marched toward the wagon, head high.

"Wait!" Lengthening his stride, he grasped her elbow and swung her around. "Where do you think you're going?"

"Back to England!" she flashed, jerking her arm away from him. "I'll not be a party to piracy."

"Come, now! There will be no piracy, my lady. Those gunports will stay closed unless we are attacked, which is extremely unlikely."

"You expect me to believe that?"

"I do not lie."

"But you hold back the truth."

"Only when necessary."

She stared at him, was conscious of a great need to believe what he said. "Then . . . then why should we take a pirate's ship?"

"Because it is fast, because it is comfortable, and because it is mine."

Tears came to her eyes. "Then you really are a pirate. I had hoped you were not."

His big hands came up and clasped her shoulders, his gaze fastened on her wet eyes. For her it was like looking into sunstruck emeralds dancing in his amused but concerned face.

"You have a rare talent for jumping to conclusions, my little love. I am not a pirate. I am an English privateer. There is a difference."

She rallied once, still trying to hold her point. "What difference? You attack ships and steal their goods!"

"Precisely. We serve at sea beside our fleets of warships; the military forces fight on land. We are all patriots, helping England. We take the goods other countries carry to England's enemies, and we take no prisoners. If they wish to lay down their arms and let us have their cargo, they live to sail another day."

"Oh." She turned away, pulling a handkerchief from her ruffled cuff and wiping her eyes. "I suppose it is better than outright piracy—at least a little. And you did promise . . ."

"I did, and I'll keep to it." He took her arm and started out on the loading dock again. "Come. You'll see your home for the next month or so, weather permitting. Come along, Anna."

The wooden decks of the *Whistling Wind* had the glow and gloss of fine furniture. Rosamunde saw that much when Quint picked her up by her waist and swung her aboard, stepping down and leaving an arm about her as she regained her balance. Anna, stepping down with an armful of bundles, sighed with admiration.

"Hard wood and holystone," she said, "and the will to keep rubbing. How long since you oiled your decks, my lord?"

Quint laughed. "There are men here at the boat slips who have spent their lives on their knees, smoothing in oil. They take wonderful care of the boats entrusted to them. She'll be just as clean belowdecks and in the cabins, though we'll need new pallets brought in. Wait, you'll see. In the meantime, put your mistress's belongings in one of the stern cabins."

By the end of the long summer twilight the *Whistling Wind* was loaded. Wiggins had gone to the warehouses and brought back supplies of food, and new straw pallets for the bunks, since the old ones had gone moldy in dry dock.

Anna had found the galley and cooked a hasty meal of meat and barley mixed with herbs in a good hot soup. She made a tremendous amount, sure that the hardworking men and boys would be able to eat it all. She found hard sea biscuits in the stores and put them out with the steaming kettle so everyone could take what they wanted. The sight of the towering woman presiding over the old black iron stove silenced the boys from Cette. They scooped their portions into their dishes silently and took them up on deck to eat. Anna and Rosa looked at each other and laughed softly.

"They believe the old salts' tales of trouble at sea when you have a woman aboard," Anna said, low-voiced. "They wonder now if two women are doubling the curse."

Rosa shook her head. Looking around the low-ceilinged galley, cozy now with the smell of good food and the candles making the old wood gleam a reddish gold, she was entranced by the thought of living aboard this ship. She ladled out a share of soup for herself and sat down with Anna.

"There could be no truth in that saying," she said to Anna. "It's always the habit of men to lay blame at women's feet so they may escape it themselves. It's one of the ways we women keep our men feeling like heroes."

They were to sleep on the brigantine and leave in early morning, all of them. Even the half-grown boys who had followed Quint refused to go home, and their mothers came, smiling and chattering, to bring them clothes for the voyage. Watching from the quarterdeck, Rosa saw by the women's faces the honor it was to have a son chosen to handle the sails, especially on Capitaine Spencer's brig.

All the horses were taken in by the town's livery stable, but the wagon was on board. When it was emptied the men and boys had pulled it out the broad pier, pushed it up slanting planks, lowered it to the deck, and dragged it midships. There they took off the wheels and put them in it. Silent, Rosamunde watched and wondered. Quint would never have cluttered up the deck with that wagon if he didn't plan to use it. She sighed, but she had known for a time that this trip on the Med wasn't to be a pleasure cruise.

When she found Quint later, she confronted him. "Can you tell me now where we're going?"

His eyes, sharp as a hawk's, softened as he looked at her in the fading light. He had been working as hard as the others; his fine shirt was wet with perspiration and clung to him, showing his muscular torso. "Our first landfall is Malta, my lady, and the last Lundy Island. The ones between depend on what I learn in Egypt."

"And what do you hope to learn?" She saw by the quick shuttering of his eyes that he wouldn't tell her that.

"Perhaps nothing," he said, "or, please God, the best of news." He turned away, trying to hide the crack in his voice, the desperate hope in those last words. When she started to speak again, he held up a hand. "Wait, like the rest of us."

She watched him make his way to the open hatch, where Wiggins sat on a cask of wine, directing the boys who were storing the last of the luggage and foodstuffs in the hold. In the clear still air she heard the conversation between them.

"I'll take the first watch, Wiggins," Quint said pleasantly, "and Ranjit the next. Get some food and rest."

White-haired Wiggins frowned. "I'm able for this, my lord. The boys are doing the lifting and placing. Besides, we are nearly through." He paused, his cheeks reddening. "Aye, Captain sir," he added hastily, "I hear you."

Quint shook his head, hiding sudden amusement. "Too long away from the ship, Wiggins. You forgot who was captain. Go, and tell Thomas I'll wake him at midnight."

"Aye, Captain." Wiggins staggered as he rose from his seat on the cask but recovered quickly. "That old wound," he grumbled. "It catches me now and then. Good night, sir." He was straight as a ramrod as he headed for the galley below.

So Wiggins had never been a butler for someone called Leighton. Rosamunde sighed and turned back to the two cabins, side by side in the high half curve of the stern, below the raised quarterdeck. She had been inside them both and had found them luxurious, with windows that opened and thick rugs on the floor. The bunks, built into polished wood walls, were larger than usual, the drawers beneath them big enough for anyone's personal effects. However, her baggage and Anna's had been put in one of them; Quint's clothes and effects in the other. He was hewing to his decision, then. There would be no married bliss on this trip.

Anna had left two pails of water so each of them could wash. Rosa made up the bunks, covering the fresh pallets with linen sheets she found in a chest. Then she took off all of her clothes and scrubbed herself. She was putting on a fresh shift when Anna came in, hot and tired from the galley.

" 'Tisn't your duty to make up the bunks," Anna grumbled. "Nor to put away my clothes. Do you think me old and weak?"

"No more than you think me young and useless," Rosa said sweetly. "Would you advise me to do nothing?"

Anna's broad mouth tilted up on one side of her red, sweating face. "If I could advise you, I'd tell you to sleep in the other cabin."

Rosa sniffed. "I am not so enamored of my husband that I would force him to bed me. He had our baggage put here, and his in the other cabin. That makes his decision plain enough, I think. And if you don't mind, I'll hear no more about it." She went to her bunk and climbed in, pulling up her covers and presenting her slim back to Anna.

Rosa woke past midnight, still sleepy but feeling the rocking of the ship, which she put down to a night breeze that seemed to be strong enough to hum in the wires and lines of the rigging. Moonlight glowed hazily from the open windows, the ship creaked rhythmically, and Anna snored, a gentle humming sound that never faltered. Rosa lay still, listening to it all with a half smile and drifting off again herself, only to be jolted into wakefulness at dawn.

The sound of sails snapping as a growing wind filled them tight made her leap from the bunk and run to the stern windows. She stared out, disbelieving. There was a beautiful sky off to the east, tatters of pink clouds and long strands of burning gold reflected on the deep blue surface of the sea, but there was no land in sight.

"Anna! We're at sea!" When there was no answer she whirled and looked. Anna's bunk was empty, the covers drawn up neatly, and a bucket half filled with water sat just inside the door. Anna, no doubt, was in the galley cooking breakfast. Rosa groaned and rushed to wash and clothe herself. Quint would think Anna useful, at least, while his wife—if she could be called a wife—was a slugabed.

Bunk smoothed, the contents of the bucket thrown through the open window and into the sea, her hair woven into thick silky braids and wrapped around her small head, she put on an old gown she thought suitable for work in the galley and went out on the heeling deck, staring upward in amazement at the number and size of the sails. Four on each mast, and two jibs at the bow. One of the youngsters, lazing in a coil of rope flung on the deck, smiled at her.

"She fast, no? She has ze bone in 'er teeth, madame."

Rosa smiled, amused. "Yes. She travels well."

She had meant to head straight for the galley but the beauty of the morning grasped and held her. The sea was blue silk, and bounding along beside the thrusting bow of the ship, porpoises leapt and played in the white foam. Drawn by their grace, Rosa went forward and leaned on the railing to watch their antics. Quint found her there, laughing at them, when he came to look for her.

"You'll make a seafarer yet," he said, and put an arm across her back, his hand slanted down to clasp her small waist. "Aren't you hungry?"

"I am. But it's so beautiful here. When did we sail?"

"Before midnight. A night wind came up and from the right direction. I took it as a good portent for us and cast off. Your Anna's Thomas took over at dawn and won't let me have the wheel again."

Rosa studied him, seeing beneath his fatigue his stern purpose, his iron will. She wondered again at his control. What it was that he wanted to do was still secret, but she had learned enough about him to know he'd do it or die trying. She drew away from him and turned to go.

"I'll eat now," she said, "and see if I can be of some use to Anna."

His hand stayed her, grasping her wrist. "There is help aplenty for Anna," he said. "You needn't work on this ship. Enjoy yourself." He drew her closer, and the look on his face told her he'd make it closer yet if he could. Then he loosed her and turned away.

"Go," he said, "I'll not keep you from your meal. I know well what it is to be hungry."

* * *

The wind held, and all through the sunlit day the *Whistling Wind* bore steadily south by southeast, romping along with all sails straining, round as fat white clouds, hovering over the long, sunlit deck.

"Ten sails," Rosa marveled to Anna, "counting those two on the bow. No wonder we go so fast." It was afternoon, and they sat on pallets in the shadow of the wagon, away from the hot sunshine.

"If the wind holds," Anna began, and crossed herself for luck, "Thomas says we'll be in Alexandria in less than two weeks. But he also said Lord Spencer told him that the Mediterranean is noted for varying winds."

"I won't mind if it takes a little longer," Rosa said. "It's like a holiday." And it was, she thought. Until the ship arrived in Alexandria, there were no problems, nothing that had to be done. Nothing that could be done. She looked up, smiling as Quint stopped beside them.

"You were right to catch that night wind, Captain," she told him.

Teeth glinted in his black beard. "Pure luck, my lady. Or perhaps an answer to prayer."

Rosamunde moved a little, offering him a seat beside her on the pallet she'd thrown down, but he shook his head. "I've had my rest, thank you. I'm on my way to take the wheel from Wiggins. I'll see you at dinner."

She watched as he moved away on the slanting deck and thought he looked more at home here than ever he did on land. She sighed and looked at Anna again, who was rising, reminded of the duties she'd taken on by Quint's mention of dinner.

"This is my lord's world, Anna. He's comfortable in it."

Straightening her gown around her massive figure,

Anna nodded. "I have been thinking the same thing and wondering if your marriage to him was a mistake."

Rosa scrambled to her feet. "It was no mistake, my friend. Had I refused, you might have been hanged."

"True." Anna paused, thinking. "I suppose," she added soberly, "that I was born to the gallows. Your mother saved me once, and now you have done the same. Thank heaven Thomas hasn't inherited my disposition."

Rosa leaned on the wagon and watched Anna move away toward the galley. It was true about Thomas. He had the same enormous strength as Anna, but he was gentle-hearted and peaceable. Still, Rosa thought, he would fight if he had to—and undoubtedly he'd win. But he would never kill in a fury. Suddenly she thought of Quint, wondering how he would react if he was challenged. Then she remembered the day they'd left London and someone had tried to kill him.

It came back fresh and frightening in her mind. But Quint was calm when the assassin fired at him, and came within inches of killing him. He had stayed cool, though he'd pushed her down to keep her out of danger. And when he fired back, he tried only to injure, not to kill.

She sighed and straightened, heading aft to her cabin. Could she be brave in the face of danger? She couldn't know, for she had never been tried. She was sure she would be challenged on this trip. All she could do was hope she'd be brave enough to meet whatever came.

For three days the *Whistling Wind* plowed steadily south by southeast. Twice they overtook a dhow, the scoop-shaped Arabian craft with their huge, triangular sails like fat bellies that dragged them through the water. Aboard the dhows, dark men dressed in loose white garments and wrapped turbans flashed confident grins as the privateer slid by. Rosa was fascinated by them and amazed by their lack of fear. She questioned Wiggins.

"They don't worry," Wiggins said. "They know a privateer wouldn't bother with them. Yet at times they carry much gold for exchange. Later, you will see ships veer off when they see us." He sounded, Rosa thought, as if he'd enjoy seeing them run away himself. Wiggins, she decided, was not a gentle old man. Far from it. There was a hard streak in him.

At the end of the third day Rosa stood by Quint at the wheel, staring off to the east. The setting sun had touched the granite hills of the island called Sardinia with flaming red and gold tints. She was fascinated by the stark beauty; curious about the people who lived there. She asked questions Quint couldn't answer.

"I know little about them," Quint said at last, "that island is not one of my ports of call. It is nearly barren, or so I have heard."

"I see. Are they, like the dhows, too poor to attack?"

He looked down at her inquiring face and frowned. "Who told you that the dhows were too poor to attack?"

She looked away, unwilling to name Wiggins, and shrugged. "Does it make a difference? Or was it a lie?"

"It is unnecessary to attack them," he said stiffly. "England is not at war with Arabia. Some of my crew wish England at war with every other nation, so we could plunder wherever we wished." He glanced at her again, his stern face relaxing into a smile. "Some men are greedy; others are fond of fighting."

"I see," she said again, but warmly. Pirate or not, he didn't cheat. "What other large island will we see on this trip?"

"Sicily, likely tomorrow evening, and then a smaller one, Malta, where we will stop and replenish our stores. Malta has been under British protection some thirty odd years, and we will be greeted with pleasure."

"Wonderful! Are you often there?"

"Not often enough. I have good friends on the island."

"I see." She paused, wondering if during that first week of their marriage when he stayed alone in London he had sent word to his friends that he had married. "Do your friends know you have a wife?"

Quint laughed harshly. "They may have heard of it, but likely they thought it only a rumor."

That silenced Rosa. Her heart was heavy; her thoughts were grim. His laugh had sounded almost bitterly amused. After a moment she coolly excused herself and went below to aid Anna in making supper. She knew he wasn't trying to hurt her, but he sounded as if he'd been caught and jailed.

Waking in the middle of the night, clutching the edge of her bunk, Rosa knew the fine weather was over. The ship was tossing like a leaf in a tumbling brook, and she could hear wind shrieking in the stays and halyards. She sat up, clinging to the edge of the bunk.

"Are we going to sink?"

Anna, braced against the wall, was putting on her gown and shoes. She looked over at Rosa and grinned. "I doubt it. Lie down and try to rest. I'm going out to help the men."

Rosamunde started to protest, then lay back down. She had been going to say the men would be angry if the women came and got in the way, but with Anna's strength and knowledge of ships they would welcome her.

"Anna . . . please be careful."

Anna smiled. "That I will. I have heard of these sirocco winds and how their heat makes whirlwinds in cooler air." She went out on the deck, the wind nearly tearing the fitted door from her hand before she closed it again.

A violent night, Rosa thought, clinging to the bunk. And a hot wind. She was perspiring in the light shift she wore; the fine cotton had become damp and plastered itself to her skin. She ignored it, her mind on those in danger outside.

The wind came in powerful gusts, slowed to a puff, and then rose hot and howling again, heeling the ship over on its side. Over the sound of the wind she heard the faint shouting of the men and boys, the orders to reef the sails, the answering aye-aye sir, faint, so awfully faint. Her heart hammered, her ears strained to recognize Quint's clear voice among the others. She couldn't, and she shut her eyes and prayed. Then the cabin door opened, a gust of hot wind came in, the door closed. Rosa opened her eyes and saw Quint leaning over her, his eyes worried.

She sat up, flung her arms around his neck, and cried, her tears mingling with the salt water running down his neck. He knelt and put his arms around her. He said words, reassuring words, his warmth came through the dampness and dried her tears. She leaned back, still holding him, and looked into his green eyes.

"I was afraid. I couldn't hear your voice."

"I was above on the quarterdeck, at the wheel. Thomas took over so I could come to you. I don't want you to be frightened."

"I am not frightened now." It was true, even though the ship still leapt and rolled, the wind still howled outside, and they still had to brace themselves to keep from sliding across the cabin. Quint was there, and that was enough. She saw him looking at her breasts, visible through the damp, transparent cotton she wore. She didn't mind, not even when he muttered an anguished "Oh, Lord . . ." and closed a hand over one of them. Another kind of heat sprang from his hand and shot flame through her slim body. She sighed and leaned forward again, closing her eyes, resting a cheek on his broad shoulder. "Stay," she whispered. "Stay with me, Quint."

He made a sound that seemed to come from the deepest part of his big body; like a growl of exquisite pain; like the low thrum of his fast-beating heart. He tightened his hold on her and drew her even closer, lowering his head to her aching breasts. His mouth opened, took in the tight bud of a nipple covered by thin, wet cloth, and suckled. Rosa gasped, letting her head fall back, her breast press against his mouth. "Quint . . . oh, *Quint!* Stay! Stay with me. . . ."

He tore himself away from her and got to his feet, grasping the edge of the bunk, cracking his head on the low ceiling. "I cannot! Damn me to hell, Rosa, you know I can't. I must be fair to you. Stop tempting me!" He bolted across the rocking cabin; the door slammed hard and he was gone.

She stared after him, shocked and hurt at first, then suddenly she felt wonderful. *Stop tempting me?* She smiled and lay back in the bunk, ignoring the rolling and creaking of the ship, which seemed to be moderating now. Surely any woman could learn to tempt a man past control—once she knew he wanted her that much.

Chapter Nine

———— ❦ ————

The *Whistling Wind* lay dead in the water at dawn. There was a long, gently dipping sea running beneath her sleek shape, and the young sailors of Cette were scrambling up and down the two masts, repairing the broken lines and torn sails she'd suffered in the night's winds. Coming out on deck, Rosamunde shielded her eyes from the golden rays striking across blue water, looked up, and gasped. Quint was on the swaying mainmast, his bare feet balancing on a thin foot rope slung below the main royal, his hands busy untangling a twisted line from a clew. He looked down, grinning when he saw her. She shut her eyes and turned her back. Moments later, she heard his bare feet thump the deck and felt his hand on her shoulder.

"You have little faith in my dexterity, wife."

"And even less in your wisdom," she replied, and turned to face him, pale with fear. "You have experienced sailors on board who can do those repairs. Why risk the captain?"

"Occasionally a captain has to allow his sailors to see that he is neither lazy nor fearful of heights. Besides, that particular tangle had baffled them all, even Wiggins."

"Wiggins! You allowed that old man to climb up there?"

"He didn't ask, Rosa. He knows his responsibility. Come now, we'll have breakfast."

"Just the same—"

"Enough."

Silent, she went with him toward the companionway that led down to the galley. Her cheeks were flushed pink with embarrassment. For a woman who had sworn to herself last night that she would charm this man into her arms in less than a week, she had been extremely foolish to argue with him. Going down the steps she took his arm.

"I was afraid you'd fall." She spoke in a whisper, staring at her feet, and his, still bare. They were nicely shaped feet, she thought wildly, and quite large. The companionway was narrow, her skirts brushed his long legs, his arm brushed her breast. She was immediately reminded again of the night. She looked up as he slowed at the bottom of the steps, stopping and regarding her carefully.

"You are blushing, my lady."

"Oh . . . why, I must be," she answered, struggling with the words. "I'm very warm. Perhaps the sun, yesterday." She glanced at him again and managed a smile. "Or embarrassment. I shouldn't have argued about . . . about who climbs those poles."

"Masts."

She nodded quickly, blushing again. "Masts. Indeed."

He leaned down and kissed her, his mouth warm and lingering. She closed her eyes to dream, but the kiss was over and Quint was leading her on. Hastily.

"You needn't apologize," he said grandly, "you're learning fast."

The wind from the northwest came cool and brisk during the late morning, and stayed steady, offering rest to the sailors once the sails were set. Again the *Whistling Wind* took the bone in her teeth and ran with it. The curl of white foam at the cleaving prow looked more like a mustache than a bone to Rosa, but she knew better than to argue sailor terms with sailors. Besides, she didn't care. She stood on the leeward side of the narrow bow and watched the seabirds dart down into schools of small fish. Once she saw a sea turtle, a big one, its shell protruding from the water as it slept. And in the midafternoon, she saw what appeared to be a low white cloud on the horizon, with a wisp of trailing smoke rising from it. She pointed it out to Wiggins, who nodded, bored.

"The top of a volcano," he said. "Mount Etna, covered with snow but still putting out its warning of hellfire. The Sicilians ignore it."

"I cannot see Sicily at all. Perhaps it has sunk?"

Wiggins laughed out loud. "It is below the horizon, that is all. You'll see it before long." He went off, chuckling to himself.

She saw Sicily as she had seen Sardinia, glowing in the colors of sunset. Still she looked more at the towering snowcapped volcano than the island below it. Quint came to watch with her and show her that they were also close to Tunisia.

"Cape Bon," he said, pointing southwest to a miniature dark spot against the brilliant sky. "We would be very welcome there. Tunis is a city where everyone is your friend—if you have money."

"But we are going on to Malta?"

"Yes. We'll have an easy run of it tomorrow. We have

made excellent time. Are you ready for dinner? You've watched the sea almost all day."

"I know." She turned from the rail, smiling, her hair loosening and blowing across her face as the wind caught it. "There was always something new. But I am hungry now."

Quint scooped the shining black locks into his hand and held them, held her beside him. Her cheeks were pink from the sun; her eyes as blue as the sea, widening as she saw the look in his. Her lips parted . . .

He sighed and let the silky mass slide from his fingers as he turned away. "Didn't I tell you not to tempt me, wife? Go to your cabin and pin up that lovely hair."

She did as she was told. She swept her hair up and pinned it securely, revealing her slender white neck and her small pink and white ears, shaped like delicate seashells. From his glances during dinner Quint seemed to find her just as tempting as before. But still he slept alone again. Rosa, lying sleepless, hoped he felt as restless as she.

At dawn they could see the Maltese islands. They lay like a small gray cloud off to starboard, seeming to float just above the surface of a misty sea. The air was clear, but motionless, and heat settled on the ship like an invisible blanket.

"Pray for wind," Quint advised from the wheel. "Without it, we'll use all day and part of tomorrow making landfall. There is a current, but it's slow, and it varies." He drew a silk handkerchief from a pocket and wiped his sweating face, glancing at Rosa, who smiled at him from her place against the railing around the quarterdeck. It was truly hot now; she had dressed for it. Anna had brought out a white muslin gown and put it on her because of the heat. It was new, bought in London for the trip, and trimmed with thick white embroidery around the low neck and the cuffs of the short sleeves, and there were only two thin petticoats to fill out the wide and delicately scalloped skirt. Her hair was pinned in a fat bun on the top of her head, though some of it escaped and curled down in feathery wisps.

She looked, Quint thought, like a young, innocent girl —one he should have left in England.

He sighed and tucked his handkerchief back into his pocket. In the beginning, that had been part of his plan. Marry, collect the dowry, then take his new wife back to stay on Lundy Island while he made this trip. Somehow, once he had met and married Rosamunde, that part of the plan had faded away. She had become part of his life even in those few days, an essential part. Had he left her there, his mind would have been divided; he would have been forever worrying about her. Missing her.

Now, staring southwest at the islands he knew so well, he wondered if he should have taken another route. It was well known that he was a friend of one of the royal commissioners' in Valletta, and Malta, full of the black-clad Muslims, was a hotbed of assassins. Still, he'd left one would-be assassin wounded in London . . .

"Quint, is this a sign of wind?"

He turned and looked at Rosa, who was leaning on the rail and watching the surface of the water. He left the wheel and came to look at what she saw. A pattern of tiny, flat curves scarcely disturbed the sheen of the clear sea, but he smiled with relief. Cat's paws, a good sign of gathering wind.

"It is, indeed. On our port quarter, but wind it is, and I'm thankful. We'll be in Grand Harbour by noon."

Within an hour the ship was kicking up a trail of foam, driving hard toward the islands. Thomas was on the wheel and Quint stood with Rosa on the bow, pointing out a dot on the horizon—the island of Gozo, smaller by far than Malta, but considerably larger than tiny Comino, which lay between the two.

"We'll find a berth in Grand Harbour, and Wiggins will see to loading on the stores. You and I will stay in Valletta, the principal town, with Lord Robert Sprague and his wife," Quint told Rosa. "Lord Robert is an old friend of mine, and you'll find Mary very pleasant. But we'll make our visit brief—one night only, and we sail for Africa."

"Where in Africa?"

"Alexandria."

"Oh! Is it safe?"

Quint's serious, bearded face broke into wry laughter. "Strangely enough, I am safer in lawless Alexandria than any other place in the world. I have only one friend there, but he occupies a very high place."

Rosa drew a deep, relieved breath. "Good! Then we may spend the rest of our trip in that city. Perhaps by the time we are ready to sail home, that enemy of yours will find his real robber."

Quint was still smiling, though his brow was wrinkled in thought. "How quickly you plan for the best, Rosa. I hope it happens that way."

The city of Valletta was like an immense castle of ancient times; the high promontory on which it was built was covered with walls and walkways, with stone buildings rising on the steep streets, each row of rooftops higher than the last. Facing the Mediterranean on one side, facing Grand Harbour on another, the city seemed bounded by blue water, and as the ship sailed by, the narrow streets glistened with the sheen of polished stone walls rearing into a great expanse of blue sky. A rich town, floating between sky and sea.

"No little out-of-the-way town on a hill," Anna said, watching with Rosa, wide-eyed. "It's an important city. A trade center, I would suppose."

"And you would be right," Wiggins said behind her. "All the Mediterranean countries buy and sell here. France and England fought for the privilege of managing such a market."

"And England won," Rosa said, "naturally."

They found space at the city docks. Quint went to the dockmaster's quarters and paid for a night's mooring. When he came back to the ship, he called the crew together on deck.

"My wife and I will spend the night at Government House," he said. "Wiggins will take a sailor and buy food and other stores, including extra wine. The rest of you will guard the ship from thieves." He looked at Wiggins, who nodded and grinned. "Yes. There are many about."

Anna's eyes flicked to Rosamunde. "Will you want me with you?" She spoke softly, and Rosa used the same quiet tone.

"Why, there will be maids used to visitors there, I suppose. And, I'd rather not ask . . . I think you understand."

Anna's rare smile bloomed. "I do. And I wish you luck, child."

Her cheeks hot, Rosa left the ship on Quint's arm. He took her along a pier to a cluster of small barges tied together and stopped at a group of men talking and laughing nearby. Quint addressed them in a pidgin English mixed with what seemed to Rosa to be Arabic. A man stepped forward, his dark aquiline face pleasant, and answered him. Quint nodded and handed over coins.

"Come along," he said, and grasped Rosa's arm. "He

will take us across the harbor in his barge. There we'll find an omnibus to Government House."

The barges were all alike, with a high, curving bow and a comfortable stern, seats along the sides, and a roof like a canopy to keep off the sun. Their bargeman handled his craft with long, slender oars, standing and rowing while he faced the bow and chose their direction.

Rosa's face brightened; she smiled at Quint and whispered, "It's lovely, Quint. Like punting on the Thames."

"Or like gondolas in Venice?" He was teasing her, she knew, but she didn't mind. She trailed a hand in the water and imagined herself Cleopatra on the Nile.

The calm water of the harbor made the trip easy and fast. The bargeman poled along the stone seawall and found one of the tiers of steps that led up to a broad, tree-lined avenue circling the city. He held the barge motionless while they climbed out, thanked Quint for the fare he paid, and offered to be at these same steps in the morning for a return trip.

"Not so early," Quint said. "The afternoon ebb will suit me. Keep an eye out for us then." Taking Rosa's arm, he headed up the steps and hailed a horse-drawn omnibus rattling by. It was huge, with customers hanging on the sides and roof. Pulled by three horses in tandem, it seemed sturdy and comfortable. Quint paid for first-class seats inside and helped Rosa in.

"Government House," he told the driver, and climbed in behind her, settling down on the same seat. "This is fine," he said, taking her hand in his. "I'm looking forward to seeing my friends again, and presenting my beautiful wife. You will have a pleasant evening, my lady."

"It sounds wonderful," she said, and rested her other hand on his. "I am anxious to meet them."

Quint laughed. "They will be amazed. Lady Mary has always referred to me as Lord Robert's bachelor friend."

"Do they have children?"

"Two, both boys. The older is about ten, I would say. He was named for me."

"Ah! Then you and Lord Sprague are truly close friends."

"Since school." He settled back, still holding her hand, his strong face for once relaxed. "We are like brothers."

She thought of how serious he had been at the beginning of this trip and wondered at his relieved enjoyment now. He felt safe, perhaps, and glad of the progress. From what she had heard him tell Thomas earlier, they were almost halfway to Alexandria, and so far the trip had been an easy one.

The omnibus jolted around a corner and began to climb a steep street. The horses leaned into their harness, encouraged by the shouts of the driver, and pulled with a will. Rosa leaned forward, as if to help, and then laughed at herself and settled back again.

"Your friend must live on the highest spot on the island," she said after a quarter hour. "We've been traveling upward ever since we entered this bus."

"Yes, he does," Quint said, and took her her hand again. "On the very top of Mount Sceberras. He's one of the two Royal Commissioners appointed to rule the islands."

"Oh!"

Quint grinned at her. "He takes his title lightly, but he's serious about the work. Tonight he'll not be thinking of either one. When he plays, he is serious about enjoying himself. There, look up to your left; those are the walls around his home and the gates are standing open."

She looked. "He expects you?"

He laughed. "No. But Robert is not a fearful man. Besides, he is well liked and respected."

"I see." Her eyes moved, inspecting the other passengers. They looked foreign to her, in their black garments and the women's half veils. Their black eyes were unfathomable, full of secrets. But then, she thought, Lord Robert was used to them. Then an outside rider's dark face, suddenly seen though the window of the omnibus, glared in as if he hated her. She leaned back, jolted. "I am such a coward," she added, ashamed of sudden fear. "They are all so strange to me."

Quint smiled. "There are many kinds of people, my love. You'll meet others even stranger than these before we see England again. There, the driver is turning toward our goal."

The gates of Government House were wide, but not wide enough to allow the entry of the omnibus and the passengers who clung to its sides. The driver stopped just outside and grinned back at Quint.

"Give Lord Sprague our good wishes," he said, "may he live forever."

Helping Rosa out of the bus, Quint smiled and nodded. "I will." He waited beside the gates as the bulky vehicle moved on and then took her arm to go inside the courtyard. Amused by the native driver and his fervent wishes, Rosa turned to smile at him and make a remark. The words died in her throat. Just beyond him, creeping along the wall, was the man who had glared at her through the omnibus window. Half crouching, his eyes on Quint, he held a long, bright blade in his upraised hand poised to throw. She saw his eyes narrow on Quint's back, his arm tense.

Shrieking, grasping Quint's arm in both hands, Rosa whirled him away. The knife flashed past in the air to clatter on the courtyard stones. Screaming in rage, the man ran and flung himself on Quint's back, fastening strong, filthy fingers on his neck. Rosa leapt toward him, grabbing at his black robes, but Quint jerked the man's hands from his neck and threw him off onto the ground. The man was up in an instant and gone, rounding the corner of the high wall to disappear into the crowded streets.

Breathing hard, Quint looked at the long knife lying at his feet and then at Rosa.

"Thank you for my life."

Rosa burst into tears. "I would have wanted to die if he had killed you." She rushed into his opening arms and clung to him. "Oh, Quint, I can still smell the evil in him." There was an odor of filth and something else, a nauseatingly sweet taint that was altogether foreign to her. All she could think of was horrible death, and the odor of decay.

A half hour later, they sat together with the Spragues to retell the attack at the gate. Rosa had still been weeping when Quint took her inside Government House, and Lady Mary had instantly taken her off to comfort her and allow her to wash her hands, which she insisted were filthy from the Muslim robes. Rosa was infinitely grateful. Mary Sprague was a rounded, comfortable woman with a kind nature, and very sensible.

"We all know that Quint is in danger from a powerful source," Mary had said, "and he should thank God for your intervention. We hope very much that he will be able to clear his name soon."

Rosa had tried to find out more, but Mary shook her head. "He will tell you when he wants you to know. In the meantime, I can only assure you that he has done nothing wrong." She paused, her dark eyes serious. "You are traveling with him to Alexandria? It might be well for you to stay here, with me."

Rosa had thanked her but refused. "It may be that he will be attacked from behind again," she said. "I will be with him and watching."

Now, gathered in a corner of the huge drawing room of Government House, the four of them sipped wine and talked of the attempt on Quint's life.

Lord Sprague was worried. "Once the Muslims begin to try to kill instead of capture, it becomes a holy war. Allah against the Christians. They dose themselves with hashish and kill for their religion. I don't like it, Quint."

"Nor I. But I have no other way of resolving it than the plan I already had. And that will take time." Quint put down his wineglass and stood up, walking to a window and staring outside. "It must be done. I am not the only one in danger, as you know."

Mary answered. "We do know. I have asked Rosamunde to stay here, with me. She has refused."

Quint spun on his heel and looked at Rosa. "You refused? You should have jumped at the chance. Hasn't the attack today scared some sense into you?"

Rosa turned red. "It certainly has. Two things I have learned: One, you have no eyes in the back of your head; and two, the man did not intend to murder *me*. Therefore, I stay with you." She hesitated, suddenly meek as he glowered at her. "I . . . uh, hope."

Sprague grinned, glancing at Quint's frown. "Take heart, man. She's on your side." He glanced at Rosa. "But do remember, my lady, that 'smell of evil' you mentioned. When you smell it again, run. That was pure hashish, and a murderer under the influence of that drug will kill anyone in his way."

"And that is quite enough of that," Lady Mary said,

rising from her chair. "It is time for dinner." She looked at Quint and smiled. "I am sorry to say your namesake will not be present. He is in England with my family, preparing for his entry into Eton. But James Robert will be brought in to meet your wife and say good night to all."

At a quarter of eleven, after an excellent dinner and much talk, Marie Foussad, the housekeeper, showed Quint and Rosa to their room. The room was large, the windows open to the gentle breeze but protected by iron grilles in the Mediterranean way. There was a private bath connected by an inside door, there was a tall secretary desk and chair, with paper and envelopes should they care to write a letter. There were also two easy chairs for reading, and oil lamps beside them on small round tables. Two big bookshelves were filled with books, and soft, thick Turkish rugs covered the floor. But there was only one bed. They both saw it, and their eyes darted toward each other and then away.

Marie bustled around, lighting the lamps and turning down the covers. She went into the bath to make sure of the towels and came out again, beaming.

"Now, Lord and Lady Spencer, I wish you a good night. If there is something more you need, tell me and I bring it *tout de suite.*"

They were both silent, looking at each other. Then Quint turned to Marie and shook his head.

"Everything," he said, "seems to be in order. Good night."

Marie smiled, bobbed a curtsy, and shut the door. They stood listening to her quick footsteps until they faded away. Then Quint turned to Rosa, a silent, slender shape standing by the windows.

"It seemed a bit much to ask for an extra bed at this

time of night. But I'll make do with these two big chairs."

Rosa came to look as he moved the chairs around to face each other.

"How?"

"Well, I admit the space is rather short. Perhaps I can use another, smaller chair to bridge the middle. Bring over the one at the desk."

She brought it and placed it sideways between the others. The seat was hard and high, inches above the soft cushions of the reading chairs.

"I don't think you'll be comfortable, Quint."

"Perhaps not. Still, I've slept in places considerably worse." He hesitated. "Look, I'll take off my boots and coat and stretch out. If you wish to change to your bedgown, you can put out the lamps first, and then get into bed."

She looked at him, her eyes huge and dark in the dim light. "I thought several times," she said, "that we had forgotten something."

He stared at her. "What?"

"Our bed things. Anna should have reminded me."

Quint shrugged. "It makes no difference to me. I can sleep anywhere and in any clothes. Just get ready for bed."

"If that's what you want. Shall I put a blanket on you?"

"I'm warm enough. I'm even perspiring. Just get to bed."

She did as she was told. She folded back the bed linen and put out the lamps, finishing with the one closest to the bed. Then she undid the buttons that fastened her gown and took it off. Then a petticoat and her long drawers. She kept her loose chemise and one petticoat as a bedgown and climbed into bed, uttering a soft "Ahhhh" at the solid comfort.

"Good night, Quint."

"Good night, my love." The chairs creaked ominously, and he cursed softly in the darkness.

Rosa started to speak and then thought better of it. He was miserable enough; it would be a poor time to taunt him about his unnecessary precautions.

She dozed; sometime later she was jarred into wakefulness by a low, tortured sigh.

"Quint?"

"I am here," Quint said in measured tones. "Right here. Do not be afraid."

"I am not afraid. I—I thought I heard a moan. Is this place haunted?"

"If it isn't, it will be, my dear. I am suffering the same pangs victims felt during the Spanish Inquisition. I am, in other words, dying on the rack."

Rosa sat up in bed. "Then for heaven's sake leave those chairs and climb into your side of this bed! It's huge; you won't even know I'm in it, I promise you. And I won't try to—to change your mind. You do need your sleep."

"I can't do that."

"You can, Quint. Trust me, I meant that promise. I'll stay right over here on my side."

There was a crackling sound and a heavy thump, followed by a lurid if muffled curse. Then—"Damnation! That chair is a trap for the unwary. I think I broke one of the legs."

Rosa sighed and sat up, reaching for a lamp and lighting it. Across the expanse of bed the flickering light revealed Quint, looking twice as large as usual and very awkward. He was picking up pieces of the small chair and laying them aside. He was clearly hot and cross, and very much put out.

He squinted past the lamp and saw her watching him. She looked adorable, all soft and feminine, her hair about her shoulders, the shape of her breasts visible through the thin chemise. He roared at her, "Put out that damnable light! I'm going to take off my clothes and get into that bed. I need some sleep!"

Hurriedly, she blew out the lamp and set it back on the table beside her. In the darkness she lay back down, smiling. If she could just get him into the habit of sleeping in the same bed with her . . . She gasped as the feather mattress shifted beneath her. He was heavier than he looked.

Holding her breath, she lay absolutely still as he punched a pillow and turned on his side. He yawned, and she would have sworn she heard his jaw crack.

"You were right about this bed," Quint said after a long silence. "It is indeed extremely comfortable. I'm glad you insisted." He waited for a time and then asked, "Are you asleep?"

She held down laughter. "Yes, m'lord. I am asleep."

After a moment he chuckled. "Then I am safe, I presume."

"You are indeed. I will not seduce you. I never go back on my word."

There was another long silence following that exchange. Rosa lay absolutely still, amazed by the heat radiating from the other side of the bed. It was like a cozy furnace, except that the masculine scent tickling her nostrils was much more tantalizing than coal smoke would have been. But there was no point in trying to seduce your own husband. She sighed and gave it up, settling down on her side. It was a beginning, she thought, and maybe he . . . She smiled sleepily as she felt his muscular leg touch hers. The fine hair on his leg teased her skin.

"So you never go back on your word," Quint said into the darkness, and his deep voice shook. "A pity, that." He reached for her and dragged her into his strong arms, against his bare, aroused body. His skin was fiery hot, his grasp tight.

She didn't resist. She was amazed but cautious, feeling the growing heat of him, finding the size of his big bones and muscles astounding. She was afraid to caress him for fear of being pushed away. But he was breathing hard, trying his best to make his hoarse voice light and humorous when he spoke again.

"I'm afraid I'm more than ready to be seduced. May I kiss you?"

He was trembling. His hands were hot on her skin. He didn't wait for her answer. His mouth descended on hers and tongued it open. She didn't say anything, only gave to him, opened to him, made him welcome. She thought her heart would pound its way out of her body, and the pooling of heat that began low in her belly was amazing to her. Her hands ran over his back, and she was thrilled by the rolling muscles, the broad shoulders, the hard, flexing buttocks, and the great need he had for her. It was exactly like she had hoped it would be.

She put her arms around him and held on, dazzled by passion. He kissed her, touched her breasts with hot hands that moved to her belly, the soft skin of her inner thighs. She made sounds, breathless sounds of utter pleasure, and wanted more.

So did he. He took her almost at once, trying to be gentle, murmuring apologies, hardly knowing what he was saying. "Be easy, darling girl . . . ah, Rosa, I hate to hurt you."

"You are not hurting me. Only a little . . . I don't

mind, Quint. I don't *mind*. Oh, God . . ." Her voice shook and she clapped a hand over her mouth, mumbling incoherently. "Now, Quint, *now* . . ."

He burst in and lay still, quivering, his face against her slender neck, feeling her flesh throbbing around him, listening to her heart pound. When he managed to get his breath back, he whispered to her.

"I'm sorry, darling. So sorry. I know it was bad."

She whispered to him. "It's what I wanted, remember?" She put both of her hands on his hard buttocks, holding him there. She laughed a little, the laugh catching a sob. "I'm so happy, Quint. We're together. Now we're truly married."

"Yes." He gathered her to him and held her, her head now in the hollow of his shoulder, her slim body clinging to his. "I will take care of you, Rosa. I swear it. I love you."

She shut her eyes and touched heaven, thrilled by his words, thrilled by the slow, careful movement of his body and the heat and hardness within her, so strange; so wonderful. . . .

Quint woke her again at dawn with a questing hand cupping a breast, his aroused body pressing against her buttocks. She smiled sleepily and turned toward him, putting her arms around him, opening her thighs. He whispered to her.

"Are you sore?"

"Not too sore, darling." She winced silently as he entered, but the pain lasted less than a minute, and in another few minutes she was lost in dreamy passion, following his lead, making small, animal sounds that throbbed in her throat, her slender body moving with his as gracefully and sure as a dancer's on a stage. This time when she came to the culmination of her passion, it shook her with a stabbing pleasure, a heat that ran through her veins like a lovely bright fire.

Afterward, Quint ran a tub of warm water in the adjoining bath and invited her to share it. She watched him move around the room, stark naked and unconcerned, and thought how beautiful the human body really was. She threw back the covers and joined him.

"I'll wash you," he offered. "I'll be your Anna."

Stepping into the huge tub, she laughed out loud. "If you were Anna, there would be no room for me. But I accept your offer." She was amazed and happy with his playful foolishness; he was opening up, showing his love at last. She had never been happier in her life.

But while they were dressing, it was as if he was putting on his role of protector and leader along with his clothes. "I was wrong," he said once, "to give in to my feelings. If you find yourself with child, I will have to give some thought to sending you home. If we find a responsible couple traveling that way, you could go along."

"I will not find myself with child," Rosa said, brushing her hair vigorously. "I promise you. Our babies will all be born on Lundy Island."

He laughed and kissed her; she dropped the brush and kissed him back, her arms around his neck.

"I feel loved," she whispered. "I feel loved all over. Thank God you gave in."

His arms tightened. "I pray that you never wish I hadn't. It was selfish of me, and I well know it. I will try very hard not to put you in any danger from now on."

Rosa shut her ears to that. She was dazzled by the bright future she could see for them, the love, the adventures, the wonderful times ahead.

Chapter Ten

❦

In early afternoon the next day the bargeman rowed Quint and Rosa back across Grand Harbour to their ship. Accepting his pay, he cheerfully invited them back to Malta when their voyage ended.

"And may God be with you," he added, and smiled, his gaze running along the sleek ship, the line of ominous gunports. "Ah, yes. Very good! Fortune will smile on you, Captain."

Rosa, still in a wonderfully happy mood, ignored the bargeman's strange belief that God approved of pirates and went down to the galley, seeking food and Anna. She found both; peaches, grapes, and apricots were heaped on the table, and Anna was taking bubbling hot fruit pies from the oven. Rosa sat down and picked up a peach, biting into it.

"Delicious," she said, and reached for a napkin to wipe her chin. "And wonderfully juicy. Are the pies peach?"

"Apricot and cream. You look pleased, Rosa. Your visit was pleasant, then?"

Rosa smiled. "It was. Very pleasant." She finished the peach and picked up an apricot. "Lord Sprague and his wife were extremely hospitable. Oh!" She stood up, moving across the galley to a porthole and peering out. "We're moving away from the docks. Thank heaven we're off for Alexandria!"

Anna looked puzzled. "Naturally. We're leaving because the stores are bought and loaded and the tide is ebbing. Why are you so excited? Is there something about Alexandria that you believe you'll like more than Malta?"

"Not at all. It's just that when the *Whistling Wind* leaves Alexandria we'll be sailing for home. I truly miss England, Anna. I miss Lundy Island. It will be wonderful to be there, even though I must ride those miserable donkeys."

Anna laughed. "Perhaps they will sing to you again. But, I hadn't heard that Alexandria was our final destination. Did Lord Spencer tell you that?"

"Oh, yes." Rosa said, and then hesitated. "Or . . . well, he didn't say it in just that way. But he did say it was the safest place for him. . . ." She was suddenly pale, remembering. "I truly don't know, Anna. Perhaps I am only hoping. I was extremely frightened for him on Malta."

Anna's smile disappeared. "Why? Were you in danger?"

"Not I, but him. He could have been killed." She went on, describing the scene, the Muslim fanatic, the thrown knife and unbearable odor. Telling it brought it back, and her eyes were wet as she finished the story.

Anna clasped her shoulder, her big hand warm and strong. "Your mother would have been proud of you, Rosamunde."

"I was a fountain of tears afterward," Rosa said wryly, wiping her eyes. "I was not brave. Not brave at all."

"You saved his life. That's all that matters."

"True." Leaving the galley, Rosa sighed. She had hated those tears; both Lord and Lady Sprague had been impressed by her quick thought, both said she had saved Quint's life. But they had treated her like a frightened child, not the calm and resourceful woman she had hoped to be. She looked up and saw Quint standing at the wheel, watching other moving craft in the busy harbor as they coasted toward the open sea. He had not yet ordered a full set of sails raised, nor would he until they were out and away. She went up the steps to the quarterdeck and joined him. He had a smile and a question for her.

"Did you tell Anna to transfer your clothing and effects to the captain's quarters?"

She laughed, feeling wonderful again. He loved her. Just the sight of him now made her happy and confident. "I did not, m'lord. Anna has taken on enough duties on this ship. I'll take over that task myself."

Quint looked amused, and at the same time even more affectionate. "You treat that big woman like one of your family. Not that I mind, for I don't. I'm aware of the friendship between you."

Looking ahead, Rosa saw the open sea through the harbor entrance. There was a fair wind ruffling the surface, pushing up waves. In minutes Quint would be calling for more sail, and his mind would be on catching every breath of wind, on holding the ship to its course. She would only distract him with her chatter. She touched his arm.

"I'm going below, m'lord, to begin my invasion of your cabin."

He shook his head. "Our cabin, my darling. Always ours." There was no one paying attention to them, and he put an arm around her waist, pulling her close. "Tonight," he whispered, "will be better than last night."

Rosa laughed softly. "Then I shall explode." She kissed him quickly and moved away, straightening her gown. He looked as if he might reach for her again, and so she moved faster, heading toward the steps that led down to the main deck, turning back as she was about to step out of sight. She gave him a dazzling smile.

"There are apricot cream pies for supper, Captain."

Quint grinned, and scattered cheers came from the youngsters climbing the masts. Only Wiggins was silent, his face a study. Rosa noted it and turned away, heading for her cabin to begin her move. Wiggins was superstitious, she thought, but there was more behind that thunderous frown than just displeasure at having women aboard. Something had angered the old man. After a moment she decided it was a combination of a dislike of women aboard and, for some reason, an additional dislike of her. He never seemed to frown at Anna.

Anna came into the cabin they had shared just as Rosa finished the last of her packing. The big woman looked around at the half-empty hanging closet and chests, then laughed out loud.

"So you won him over, and you're moving in with him."

Rosa smiled. "I cannot claim the credit. There was only one bed in the room his friends gave us."

"And . . . are you all right?"

"I am happier than I have ever been in my whole life. And more frightened. I have too much to lose now."

"Because some drugged fanatic tried to kill your husband? These are foreign lands, where you can expect anything. Thank heaven you'll be back at Lundy Island before long."

"I hope so. Help me with these things, please. I want

everything neat and in order in the captain's cabin when Quint comes down."

"Yes. I'll bring water and help you bathe."

"Good. But I'm cleaner than you may think. Both Quint and I reveled in the luxury of the bath in the Royal Commissioner's guest room this morning."

Anna chuckled. "Did he help you in the tub?"

"Indeed. He was much more attentive than you ever were."

"I can well believe that."

Above them on the quarterdeck Quint could hear the murmur of their voices, the warm laughter. He thought how many years he'd kept that cabin to himself, no matter how many lovely ladies awaited his arrival on shore. He had sworn no women would ever violate his privacy aboard, and none ever had. But making love to Rosa was different. Even thinking of the way she touched him made him hot and wanting. Yet she seemed so innocent. He'd never known a woman like her.

The wind came from the northwest and blew steadily. No skill was needed to trim the sails on the *Whistling Wind*. Anyone could set the course on southeast, and the sails snapped into place, filling themselves with the strong wind.

Once away from the shipping lanes between West Africa and Malta, Quint turned the wheel over to Thomas and went looking for Rosa. He found her in her favorite spot on the bow, leaning against the port railing, watching the sea and sky. The sun had set, and though there was still enough light to see plainly, one of the hands had lit the two lanterns, one on each side of the bow, one flame behind red glass, the other behind green. In the twilight a red halo glinted on Rosa's shining black hair as she turned to smile at Quint.

"Are you ready for supper, m'lord? I believe Anna has outdone herself with all the fresh food."

He leaned on the rail and folded his arms to keep from putting them around her. He didn't want to put on a spectacle for the mast monkeys, as Wiggins called them. They were always aware of where the captain was and what he was doing.

"I'm looking forward to the apricot pie, and anything else she may have cooked. I forgot to eat at noon."

She laughed, and he wanted to grab her and kiss her open mouth. "Come, then. We'll go below before you starve."

Anna had celebrated with a roasted joint of beef, Yorkshire pudding, and fresh vegetables from the fields in Malta, followed by the apricot pie. Quint praised the food and the cook lavishly and ate enough for two. Then he went back to the wheel to let Thomas come down to eat with the rest of the crew.

Rosa went with him in the darkness, wanting the cool night air. Thomas, like a giant in the shadows, grinned at them both as he stepped away from the wheel. His big face glinted with pleasure in the dim yellow light from the binnacle.

"She's close to holdin' herself on point," he said. "Rosa could handle this wheel tonight. Look how steady she goes. An' she's flyin', sir."

"Indeed. She likes a steady wind. We'll be on the alert for smaller craft until the moon comes up. At this speed we could sink a boat we didn't see."

Thomas dipped his head in agreement. "I'll have my supper, sir, an' take over again. I can sleep tomorrow."

Quint stepped over to the wheel. "If you like. Tell Ranjit to eat and then stand lookout on the bow. Go, Tom, and take your time. Your mother has spread a real feast."

Rosa went silently to the railing as Quint settled at the wheel and stayed there, glad to be with him; glad she would always be with him now. Looking behind them, letting the wind blow back her loose hair, she saw a faint glow in the black sky that she thought might be the lights of Malta. She thought of Robert and Mary Sprague and hoped to see them again soon—surely the homeward trip would be within a month or two. She leaned on the railing, dreaming.

"Rosa."

She turned as Quint spoke, wondering at his quiet tone. "Yes?"

"Come here."

She went to him, studying his shadowed face by the dim light of the binnacle. He looked serious. "What is it?"

"Look far forward, just off the port side and nearly level with the top of the waves. Do you see anything?"

Rosa stared at the black water, the black sky. There was no moon yet, only a faint shine from the stars. She shook her head.

"I see nothing—no, wait . . . I do see something, rising and falling. It glints in the starshine like wet wood —there! For an instant I saw a mast, with a dark sail drooping."

"A dhow! Damn it all . . ." Quint swung the wheel hard to starboard, and the ship slowed. Sails rattled, losing their air, and pointing forward, Quint burst into a roar. "Somebody get on the bow down there and warn those fools off," he bellowed, "or some Arab in a dhow will die at sea!"

A single fiery projectile flew up in the air and landed on the starboard deck. It rolled, flaming, casting sparks. A man's hoarse scream vibrated in the air.

"Death to the English dogs! Burn the ship!" A chorus

followed, eerie in the darkness: "Burn them!" "Burn the infidel ship!"

Quint was down and on the deck, unsheathing his small sword, spearing the burning mass, tossing it overboard, stamping the flames and yelling back, "Rosa! Put that wheel on southeast!"

Rosa ran for the big wheel and wrestled with it, and with the burden of the huge, obstinate rudder deep in the water below. Now the ship rocked sluggishly in the trough of waves, but they'd outrun those dhows if the flapping sails could catch the wind again. Fireballs rained down, and Wiggins leapt from the galley companionway, yelling orders at the sailors, running to stamp out the next fire, and the next.

Her arms straining, Rosa threw her full weight against the wheel. She ignored the running feet and yells, the growing flames and hoarse shouts. She prayed as she watched the slow-traveling compass inch toward southeast again. It took great strength to turn to the right direction in these seas, but the compass was slowly but surely moving.

Rosa quivered at the harsh screams of pain, the strange sounds of orders shouted in Arabic, and the sudden pad and slap of bare feet on the deck. She was afraid to look.

Then, Quint's voice, thank God. "Take no prisoners," he roared. "Throw them overboard!"

That made her look below. It was a horrifying scene, lit by flames, peopled with desperate men wielding flashing knives, with screaming and thrashing bodies. Quint was hoisting a dark, bloody figure over the rail, then turning and running to huge Thomas, who was fighting two Muslims with a belaying pin and a knife. Tom's shirt was red with blood as he lifted one of the men and tossed him over the rail. The other one was on the deck, moaning. Picking him up, Quint sent him screaming and flailing into the sea.

Anna. Anna was with the young sailors, lifting a kicking, struggling Muslim high in the air, her huge hands wrapped around his skinny neck. . . .

Rosa's stomach heaved; she tasted the bitterness of gall. Setting her teeth, she swallowed and looked back at the compass.

"They have to," she whispered, trying to ignore the screams. "They must kill or be killed. God help me turn this damnable thing . . . God help us all. Please." She looked down at the spokes of the huge wheel, and stepped up on them, using the whole weight of her small body to turn the rudder.

And the southeast mark eased toward the top. She could hear the wind beginning to flap and worry the drooping sails above her. Stepping up another spoke, she listened to the noises made by the canvas, feeling in her feet the ship swinging its bow into the wind's path again. She looked up, straining to see the light patches in the dark sky; the sails began to balloon and stretch. Her heart leapt with hope. But the smell of burning oil-soaked rags grew thicker as flame flared up in the wagon on the deck. Tom rushed to put it out.

The ship moved, masts creaked, and the Muslims were gone in a flash, piling over the rails and jumping toward their boat. The young sailors of Cette were pushing the dying fireballs over with mops, pails, and anything else they could find, aiming them toward the big, barely visible dhow scraping against the starboard side. Fires were still burning on the ship, and Wiggins, with help from Anna, was dousing them with seawater pumped up from below.

"We've caught the wind!" Quint shouted, looking up, and the sails cracked like rifle shots, flinging the ship forward in an awkward rush. He ran for the quarter-deck and the wheel, ignoring his burned and bleeding hands. He took Rosa's place as she jumped down. "Bless you, my heart! You turned the battle for us! Grab me around the waist and hold on." Without waiting for a reply, he turned and yelled at the men below.

"Two dhows right in our path! Brace for collision; take no chances with your own lives!" Behind him, Rosa flung her arms tight around him, put her cheek against his broad back, and shut her eyes, expecting disaster.

Terrified shouts burst out from the black sea ahead, and then came a sudden grinding crunch. The sharp bow of the *Whistling Wind* rose high, hung for a moment, and then crashed down, swift and relentless, taking a wave over the bow before rising again. Rosa opened her eyes and looked, horror-stricken. There were pieces of a dhow floating beside them, lit by the flames. A broken mast rose along the port side, and a swimming man caught it and held on, screaming out in Arabic, whether cursing them or calling for help, she couldn't know.

Then again the ship struck the water, shuddered, and began to rise. There were hoarse, angry shouts that spun into wails of fear as the ship climbed high, higher than before, then slid forward and plunged, crushing the other dhow as it had the first. Horrified, Rosa saw the men sinking, screaming for help. One of them, thrown to the side, came hand over hand up a dangling line to get into the ship. Wiggins leaned over the gunwale and gave him a blow on his head with a marlinespike. Howling in despair the man fell, disappearing into the blackness below.

Looking back, Rosa knew the sea was clear before them, for the last dhow, the big one that had been on the starboard side, was afire, its huge sail dropping in flaming pieces, its crew diving overboard to escape.

The *Whistling Wind* settled and drew away rapidly. Still, those on deck stared behind them, for the light of the fire made the night like day, lit the surface of the water, and touched the wet heads of swimming men. The sinking pieces of the dhows were black silhouettes against the flames, smaller and smaller, and then gone.

"All those men will drown, won't they?" Rosa's voice was faint, close to a whisper.

Quint looked down at her standing beside him now, but with one small hand tucked into his belt, holding on. He put an arm around her. He knew how she felt—saddened and guilty. He had felt the same in his first battle, and he remembered it well.

"If not them, then us, my love. They were lying in wait to kill or be killed, and they knew it could happen this way. And if not for our ship's speed, it could have been their victory. Still, one or two may find wreckage to float on and another dhow may pick them up. But by then we'll be in Alexandria."

She let out her breath. "And safe. Your friend there will see to that, I hope."

Quint laughed without humor. "He will. He has only to speak in Egypt and Arabia, and he is obeyed by every Muslim. Unfortunately, that doesn't hold true on the open sea."

"This will change," Rosa said, suddenly determined. "That enemy who believes you a thief will learn you are not and call off the men. It's a stupid thing for him to be doing, and he will see it. Killing you will not return what someone else has stolen."

Quint's serious expression lightened. "For a youngster of eighteen years, you have a deal of common sense; I wish my enemy had half as much. Thomas is coming up to take the wheel again, and you need rest. Go to bed. Go to sleep if you can. I'll have Anna bandage the burns on my hands."

"I could bandage your hands," Rosa said, "but I know Anna is better at it." She paused. "Are you sure Thomas can take the wheel? I know he is walking around, but when I saw him last he was red with blood."

Quint smiled wryly. "I know. But that was Muslim blood, not his. Tom has scratches and burns, but so do we all. Thank God those Muslims were young fanatics, not experienced fighters."

"Are you coming to bed soon?"

"I cannot. There may be another attack in the dark from my enemies. I'll wait until after moonrise, when Tom and Ranjit can see." He leaned down in the darkness and kissed her. "Go along, my darling. You've been shocked and frightened, and I want you to rest."

Rosa was conscious of great fatigue as she went down the steps and turned to the cabins built beneath the quarterdeck. She took a candle, lighting it with a match from the cache outside the two doors, and stepped inside. With the lit candle to help her, she found and lit the gimbaled oil lamp on the table. The paneled walls took on a golden glow from the steady flame, and she paused to admire the luxury of the cushioned chair and the double bunk built into the gentle curve of the ship's hull and decorated with bands of beautifully carved ebony and gold.

Hot wax dripped on her hand. Startled, she hastily blew out the flame and put the candle down. She went to the hanging closet beside the door and took off her gown, hanging it up neatly. Then her chemise and petticoats; her long, ruffled drawers. She washed, and then, naked, stood on the dipping and rising floor of the cabin and combed out the wind snarls in her hair, brushed it to make it shine, and then shook it loose to lie on her shoulders. She would look her best when her husband came into the cabin and saw her there. Perhaps he would need her affection after this horrible night, if he wasn't too tired.

She was in the big bed when he came in, snugged into the covers and sound asleep.

Chapter Eleven

In the morning Rosa woke to bright sunlight. She was alone, but a lingering warmth and a dented pillow proved she'd had a companion in the night. She hugged Quint's pillow, breathing in his scent. He had been with her, at least.

Sliding out of the double bunk, she pulled a sheet around her for modesty and went to the windows to look out. The sun, rising directly on her right, was blinding. It shone on a fresh white spanker sail attached to a pole over the stern and tied to the sternpost. They were no longer heading with the wind, they were going directly south; they had made the sweeping turn toward Alexandria. Suddenly excited, Rosa decided she would put on her best gown for the occasion, a light blue silk with a cool, billowing skirt trimmed with thickly embroidered lace.

Nearly dressed, she heard the door open. Quint, dressed to the nines; he was even wearing his doeskin gloves. He looked wonderful, except for a bruised cheekbone and a small gash on his neck, half hidden by his collar. She laughed and went on brushing her thick hair.

"Were you bored by your sleepyhead wife, my lord? You never woke me."

He cupped her face in his hands and kissed her, then held her away from him and looked her up and down admiringly.

"You needed your rest, my love. You worked like a Trojan on that wheel. When I came down you were like a beautiful angel in my bed, fast asleep. How could I bear to wake you?"

She blushed and smiled, warmed by his praise. "I was bound I'd help in any way I could. And proud to be of use. But I did very little, at that. Show me your burned hands."

"They are fine, there is nothing to do for them but wait until they heal. I'll show you tonight; the work of getting these gloves on and off is tiresome, and I must wear them to greet the great pasha, Mohammed Ali."

She drew her breath in, startled. "Mohammed Ali? I have heard the old tyrant hates the English."

"Not now. He is grateful to us, along with others who aided him in his war against the Arabs of the Hauran. He is old, but he's still an arrogant man who feels all men should bow to him. And you, like all women, must wear a veil in his presence and be silent."

Rosamunde gave him an incredulous look. "If that is true, I shall remain on board with Anna while you make your visit."

Quint laughed and took her hand, drawing it through his arm and opening the cabin door. "Then come out on the deck, and look at the city you intend to ignore. You'll change your mind."

She laughed and changed her mind in a second. She would go with him. "Is the city in sight?"

"Indeed. Look! We will be in the harbor in less than an hour."

"But not before you've eaten," Anna said from the companionway. "I'll bring up fruit and meat. It's calm enough to sit on deck at breakfast and look while you eat."

"Too calm for speed," Quint said, "but we'll not worry about that. We had our wind when we needed it."

Anna grinned. "Yes, m'lord. We ran and lived to fight another day. I've looked the mast monkeys over; they complain of their burns, but they're all on their feet." She went below to bring up their food, and Rosa, reminded of the night, looked at the charred places on the once shining decks and wondered if any of the swimmers had been rescued.

Across a clear blue sea the ancient city of Alexandria shimmered in a blaze of slanting gold, made brighter by the deep purple shadows in the narrow streets. It was pleasant to sit in the sun and have breakfast while they watched the space between them and the city grow narrower. Huge stone buildings hovered over those shadowed streets, denying the sun entrance.

Then the ship changed course and they were approaching the city from due north, and Rosa's eye was caught and held by a glittering, turreted palace built on a promontory that pushed high to the west from the main city. Quint saw her interest and laughed.

"You have an instinct for royalty, wife. You are staring at the home of Mohammed Ali himself."

Rosa shrugged. "Then since I have no veil, I must look elsewhere, or I may catch his eye and offend him. I see large ships beyond that palace, Quint. Is that where we will dock the ship?"

"It is. There are two harbors, one on each side of the city, but the eastern one is shallow, and used mostly for fishing boats. We could use either, I suppose, but this one is more convenient."

"In what way?"

He was silent for a moment, staring at the city, now growing even more detailed as they entered the wide harbor. There were men on the docks carrying boxes, trundling wheelbarrows full of merchandise. He turned and answered her.

"I have a permanent berth in this harbor," he said, "and I need pay no fee to use it. It's a gift from Ali."

"Oh." Suddenly somber, she stood with her face turned away from Quint, her whole young body tense with a foreboding of trouble ahead. "I am beginning to see. This Ottoman despot is your friend, isn't he? The friend who keeps you safe."

Frowning, Quint nodded. "Yes, he is. There is no one else in Egypt or Arabia powerful enough to guarantee my safety."

She turned and looked up at him. "Quint, what is it that your enemy thinks you stole from him? Surely no man would hire so many assassins to kill you unless he thought you'd taken away everything he held dear."

"Precisely, Rosa. That is what he believes, and it's up to me to prove him wrong. But at this moment I'd better see to the docking. We'll talk later, after I present you to the Pasha Mohammed Ali." It was strange, Rosa thought, that Quint seemed almost to mock the grand title.

The settling in was carried on by the dockmaster, a small thin man who was flustered by the quick arrival of one of the pasha's most trusted men, Kai Ibn Bey, who came in haste to the dock where the *Whistling Wind* lay.

"Lord Spencer!" The dockmaster and your fine crew can dock your ship without you," he said in excellent English. "The pasha recognized it entering the harbor and is now awaiting you." He extended a hand to help Quint step up onto the dock.

Quint grasped the hand but only shook it. "I am honored, Kai Bey. But I ask permission to bring my wife. And she must be provided with a robe and veil for a presentation. Can you solve that problem?"

"So you are wed, my lord? I am amazed! The lady who tempted our footloose adventurer into marriage must be an irresistibly beautiful woman. And yes, I can solve the problem. There are many robes and veils in the seraglio; we could ask for and receive a dozen if necessary."

"Good." Still standing on the deck, Quint turned and motioned to Rosamunde, who was nearly hidden behind the wagon, listening carefully. When she came to his side he picked her up and swung her onto the dock beside the darkly handsome Kai Ibn Bey. Stepping up himself, he seemed perfectly at ease, looking from one astonished face to another.

"As you know," he said to Bey, "the women of England do not hide their beauty as they do here. But my wife will follow the custom when she is presented to Mohammed Ali, do not worry."

Kai Bey came out of his semitrance, laughing awkwardly. "If all English women were as beautiful as your wife," he said, bowing to Rosa, "other countries would war on England constantly for the chance of taking one home as a prize."

"The English," Quint said, taking Rosa's arm and going along with Kai Bey toward the city streets, "are famous for keeping their own treasures well guarded while seeking diligently for other treasure abroad. Keep that in mind, Kai."

Kai laughed and agreed. And Rosamunde pondered that remark as they climbed into a small but luxurious carriage with a silent driver. As they drove through the line of warehouses that lined the east shore of the port, she decided it was true. The English *were* marauders; if not, how had they taken over the seas, and India?

Rosamunde wished to learn all she could by paying attention to the city and its inhabitants, and so she was as quiet as the driver, who seemed intent on every word that passed between Kai Bey and Quint. They drove through the narrow streets she had seen from the ship. The houses were crowded together, the shops were many, some of them advertised large, gloriously beautiful handmade rugs by stringing them up like awnings, allowing them to cast shade on the walkers below. There was much pottery displayed for sale, many small rugs and bolts of silk. And there were many green silk banners with the crescent moon and three stars embroidered on them in silver.

The men on the street wore a great variety of garments: suits such as English businessmen wore, robes like priests', rags that hung from their bony frames. All wore turbans; some silk, some tattered cotton. She saw but one woman—she supposed it was a woman—looking much like a small bundle of black robes, walking swiftly along a street, one graceful brown hand holding a fold of her headdress across her face just below a pair of ebony eyes. The eyes widened as the open carriage came along beside her and the woman saw the Englishwoman in it. Rosa smiled, and instantly surprise turned to a frown and the black eyes looked away. Rosa sighed.

"It is good that you have a friend in Alexandria," she said to Quint, "for I would have none."

Kai Bey's large dark eyes had seen the exchange. He smiled, showing beautiful white teeth. "That is not dislike, my lady. That is jealousy. You have freedom; they do not."

Rosa wanted to say it was a pity they didn't, but Quint's glance was a warning. She sat back and watched the street before them. They were approaching the wall that circled the large palace, and she could see there were several gates into the grounds, all wrought iron and wide enough to admit two carriages much larger than the one they rode in. Kai Bey spoke to the driver, who was slowing, and pointed to another entrance farther on.

"There, Hassan. We must borrow a veil from the seraglio for the Englishwoman."

The driver bent his head in agreement and stopped at the gate Kai had pointed out. Kai swung down from the seat and the gate opened for him. He went in and across a tiled courtyard to an elaborate stone archway that shadowed carved wooden doors. The building itself was part of the huge palace but had its own guards, huge men lazing on a nearby bench. They both came to their feet as Kai went toward them. He stopped and spoke to them at length, and after a few moments one of the men went through the carved doors and disappeared.

Rosa looked at Quint curiously. "Kai Bey is not trusted to enter the seraglio?"

"Kai Bey would not want to earn that privilege," Quint said, looking amused.

"Why not?"

Quint glanced at the glowering driver and shook his head. "I will explain later, my lady."

They sat in silence until the huge man reappeared, a cotton sack in his arms. He handed it to Kai Bey, who brought it through the gate and stepped into the carriage, smiling.

"Not only a veil, my dear Lady Spencer, but a robe

also, both of them made of the finest China silk. The first wife gives it to you as a gift to a friend, and asks you to remember her in your prayers."

"How very nice of her," Rosa said, overwhelmed. She opened the sack and touched the dark material, cool and soft as a bird's breast feathers. "Should I put them on now, Quint?"

Quint nodded. "Certainly, if you wish. Can you manage?"

"Yes, of course. Like this." She stood, shook out the soft material, and swept the robe around her, tying it at the waist. Then the long veil, settling like a breath of air around her shining hair, covering her head and upper body. She sat down again on the seat and took one side of the veil in her hand, pulling it across the lower part of her face. "Now, does this seem right to you, Quint?"

"You have it exactly right," Kai Bey said, surprised. "If it weren't for your blue eyes and such white skin, no one would dream you were other than a Muslim wife."

"Or a pasha's favorite," Quint said, fingering the cloth. "A fine silk, my lady, and, if you look closely, not black. It's a deep purple, the color of royalty."

"I am very grateful," Rosa said softly. "It is a lovely gift." She looked up at Kai Bey. "Please send word to the first wife that I shall treasure it and keep it forever."

Returning to the first gate and entering another courtyard, of blue and white tile, red granite obelisks, and statuary, they left the carriage and went toward an immense entrance guarded by a group of eight soldiers. One drew his sword and stepped forward, assuming a warlike stance and blocking their path.

Kai Ibn Bey stopped and stood silent and waiting, and Quint did the same, holding Rosa close to his side. After a moment the soldier bowed, stepped back, and slapped the sword back into its scabbard. Still silent, they passed on.

"Pomp," breathed Rosa, looking around at the ornate hall they entered into, "and power. How wonderful."

"Shh. No ridicule," Quint whispered very softly.

"Wasn't."

"Good."

They came to a small but very comfortable anteroom, furnished with soft couches and chairs; there were small tables with wine and comfits set out, and mirrors everywhere. A middle-aged woman in white robes approached them, bowing and smiling. She spoke to Kai Bey and he nodded, turning to bow to Rosa.

"You will remain here with Maru until the time of your presentation, Lady Spencer. Lord Spencer and I will attend the Pasha Ali now, on matters of state."

Rosa inclined her head, accepting the decision, knowing there was no choice. She watched the two men leave through a door in the far wall and disappear without a word. She looked at Maru and smiled. Maru smiled back.

"Wine, Lady Spencer?" The woman too spoke excellent English.

"No, thank you."

"Sit here. The breeze likes this small window best. May I bring you tea then, Lady Spencer? Perhaps some fruit?"

"I am not at all thirsty or hungry, Maru. Sit down and tell me about Alexandria and the people here."

"That is not allowed, Lady Spencer."

Rosa sighed. "In that case, I shall simply sit."

It was over an hour before the door opened and Quint appeared, beckoning to her. With a surge of relief she rose, smiling, and went to him, taking his arm.

"At last! I am willing to give up being presented at court if you promise me we will soon be going to sea again. Was the news you received to your liking? You—you look renewed, as if you'd been holding your breath and have finally taken in some fresh air."

He laughed, holding up a hand to stop her flow of words. Then he turned and began leading her into the space beyond, a large room with red granite pillars stretching upward to a ceiling twenty feet or more above their heads. The colorful tiled floor was bare except for a wide path in the center of thick Turkish rugs in red, blue, and gold wool. "Shh," he cautioned under his breath. "Keep your head down and speak only when spoken to, my lady. This meeting is of the utmost importance."

Rosa opened her mouth and shut it again, lowering her head but looking through her thick eyelashes toward the end of the long chamber. There, undoubtedly, was the great Pasha Muhammed Ali, sitting on an immense carved and gilded throne. He was old, she thought, and not particularly handsome.

Her first impression was that the old man was dressed for a charade, for he wore a long gown of golden silk, heavily embroidered, and a sleeveless robe of shining lavender satin. His turban was of striped silk, with a jeweled emblem above his forehead. Her hidden gaze swept from his turban to his face, noting the closely trimmed black beard streaked with gray, and the long sideburns that swept down to join it. His jutting black eyebrows shadowed jet black eyes, which were watching her. She lowered her own eyes and watched the toes of her shoes appear and disappear beneath the edge of the deep purple robe. Quint had said this was of the utmost importance; she must be on her very best behavior.

Quint stopped her at the foot of the dais and bowed. "My wife," he said, "Lady Rosamunde Gilbert Spencer of London. She wishes to have me say she is honored far above other women by being allowed into your royal presence."

Rosa quivered. Then, her head still lowered, she shrank toward Quint bashfully. Her full skirts swung to cover the toe of his left boot, and she stepped on it, hard. That, she hoped, would teach him not to present her to anyone as if she were an inferior. Quint was still smiling but it was not a happy smile.

"Tell your wife I would see her face," Ali said abruptly. "I have heard she is very beautiful."

Rosa felt the shock run through Quint's arm and glanced up again. He was suddenly very pale. She squeezed his arm and gave a tiny nod to show she didn't mind. He faced her and spoke quietly—too quietly for his words to reach the pasha's ears.

"You don't have to, Rosa. You may decline."

The look on his face told Rosa that he'd lose the pasha's favor if he allowed her to refuse. Yet he had. She smiled at him with full forgiveness and turned confidently to face Mohammed Ali.

"For an Englishwoman, Your Majesty, that is an easy thing to do. We hide our faces from you only because we feel that when we are in your country, we should honor your rules. However, if you are curious, I will be glad to show you my face and hope it is not found wanting." She reached up and took the large veil off, draping it over one arm. She faced the pasha and smiled, looking directly into his startled eyes.

Ali stared, silent. Blood came up in his dark cheeks; he shifted his weight twice in the huge chair and finally clasped his hands closely in his lap and looked at Quint.

"Lady Spencer is indeed beautiful, my friend. And

young. If her body matches her face, she will be worth a fortune when you need more gold."

Rosa gasped and flung the veil over her head again, wrapping it across so that only her furious eyes could be seen. She would have answered for Quint gladly, but the only words that came into her mind would have been greatly insulting to the all-powerful Ali.

Quint spoke seriously. "The time will never come for me to consider selling my wife, great Pasha, not even if I starve. She is the mate of my soul."

Ali shrugged. "A woman is only a woman, Lord Spencer, born only to give a man sons and pleasure. But I have seen that other Englishmen are like you in protecting their wives. Since it is an English custom, I take no offense at your refusal."

Behind the veil, Rosa gasped again. That had been an *offer?* She moved closer to Quint and felt his arm slide across her back. "Bow," he whispered, and bowed with her. Straightening again, he spoke calmly.

"Thank you, Pasha Ali, for your great favors and your priceless friendship. We will never forget our debt to you."

Ali smiled, pleased. "You have earned my trust, Lord Spencer. Go in peace."

Kai Bey, who had come in from a rear door and had stood silently behind the pasha during the presentation, now motioned Quint and Rosa to follow him through another, smaller passage that led to the outside courtyard. He led them briskly around a wing of the palace and into the area where the carriage waited. Helping Rosamunde into her seat, he laughed aloud in relief.

"I will never forget your face, Lady Spencer, when you realized our pasha had become an admirer."

Rosa felt the heat of blood in her cheeks. "I had no idea," she said, "that he would think me desirable. I am not of his kind. And, besides . . ." She caught Quint's glance and was quiet, hastening to remove her veil and throw back the robe from her slim shoulders. Gathering them together, she placed them in the cotton sack and settled herself in the seat.

"The whole thing was lamentable," she said after a few moments, "and I will not speak of it again. I am anxious to be on the ship and on our way."

There was a dead silence, broken only by the clopping of the horse's hooves on the stone streets and the calls of an occasional street vendor hawking his wares.

"There are many things to be done before we set sail again, my dear," Quint said finally. "You will have time enough to see the sights of Alexandria and buy to your heart's content. Kai Bey's mother will be happy to accompany you, with a brace of servants to carry your purchases."

"But I need nothing."

"You will."

She started to deny it, but Quint gave her an impatient look. She was silent. It would be better to wait until they were alone. There were quite a few things she thought she should tell him before he became too secretive. A man should share his every thought with his wife.

"Here we are," Kai Bey said, waving a hand at a large gate set in a high wall. "My mother will be delighted to have you as a guest again, Lord Spencer, and doubly pleased to have your lovely wife. She has been looking forward to this for weeks." He leaned from the carriage and motioned to an old man peering through the iron gate. "Let us in, Abdul." The man nodded and disappeared.

Studying Quint's impassive face, Rosa suddenly felt cold and withdrawn. Again she had been kept ignorant of his plans. Perhaps he had never been truly honest with her. She settled back and turned her head away, asking in a cool tone, "How many more surprises have you planned for me, Lord Spencer?"

Quint frowned. "I cannot say precisely what I am planning, my lady. By the pasha's order, Kai Bey is taking care of my needs, and while he does so, I shall see to the ship's repairs. But I am sorry you aren't delighted with the chance to go shopping in Alexandria with a knowledgeable woman."

Rosa relented. Quint did look puzzled, even hurt. She supposed he felt he'd offered her a pleasant day and she hadn't appreciated it. She touched his hand and smiled as the carriage rolled on again, through the opening gate and to the ornate front of the big house. There, Kai Bey leapt down from his seat and left them, wisely giving them time to finish the argument without an audience. Rosa flushed, aware of his sudden escape.

"Perhaps I will like it very much," she said. "Thank you."

"I hope so," Quint said, and stepped down onto the courtyard tiles, offering her a hand to help her out. "There is much to see, and you need different clothes than those you are wearing now. I am beginning to realize I should have told you more—"

"Quint! There is a wagon behind you—look! It's exactly like the one we have on our ship." She stepped down and pointed. "Isn't that amazing?"

He didn't bother to look. "It is ours, my love. We, ah, need it. We are going traveling again."

She drew in her breath, thoroughly shocked. The sudden guilt on his face was very clear. Here was another case of his keeping her in the dark.

"Oh? Where are we going in it, Quint? There's nothing around here to see but the Nile, and after that nothing but desert. . . . We are going traveling in a *desert*?"

Red crept up under his tanned skin. "Yes. But not very far. Only to the Red Sea."

That connected the puzzle. She stared at him, and all at once tears of anger and disappointment came to her eyes and overflowed onto her cheeks.

"We aren't going home, are we? We're going to India, and we may never see Lundy Island again! India is thousands and thousands of miles from England, and—and I'm *homesick*!" She burst into angry tears and flung herself into his opening arms. "Please, Quint . . . take me home!"

He caught her and held her, smoothing her hair. "I will, I promise you. But there is something I have to do first. You will understand when you hear of it. I know you will."

"What? What impossible thing could be important enough to make you face the dangers you are facing now?"

Quint sighed. "I see I must tell you everything. I will do so tonight."

Chapter Twelve

$\mathcal{A}$marna Bey, once a first wife and now a widow, came from the entrance of her home to take Rosa's hand and lead her in. A small middle-aged woman, Madame Bey still retained the large, liquid eyes and fine features of an aristocratic family. In somewhat broken English, she gave Rosa to know she understood homesickness, having come from Malta to marry Nehmet Bey some forty years ago.

"Oh, I was so sad, so *distraite*. Then I have babies and no time to cry. Now I like this birthplace of my children. I have learned to like Alexandria and Egypt very much, because my children are at home here. So, I forget Malta."

It seemed to Rosa that she could never forget England, but she nodded and tried to smile. The woman was trying to make her feel better, and was succeeding.

"I think I am only overtired, Madame Bey. Perhaps a nap?"

"Very wise. Follow me." She led the way up red granite steps to the next level of the house and showed Rosa into a large, airy bedroom that opened onto a wonderful balcony overlooking a flower garden. The huge bed, made up with a thick duvet of goose down, looked like heaven.

"Wait," Amarna said. "Your maid is here. I call her to assist you." She started for the door and turned back, her brow wrinkling. "You are not afraid, I hope? Your woman is very large. Does she . . . ah, watch and report to your husband?"

Startled, Rosa realized that Madame Bey was asking her if Anna was a spy who reported her actions to Quint. "Oh, no. Anna has been with me since I was a child, Madame Bey. She is completely faithful to me."

Amarna nodded, looking only somewhat reassured. "I am happy to hear it. But the woman has new knife wounds on her arms."

And those who put them there died of broken necks. Rosa felt the sting of tears in her eyes again and turned away. "I know. But you may still trust her."

"That is good, Lady Spencer."

As Amarna hurried out, Rosa sat down on the edge of the bed and wiped her tears away. It wasn't all homesickness, after all. It was partly because of the fight on the ship; that moment of seeing Anna with a skinny Muslim struggling and dying in her powerful grip. It had brought back a memory she couldn't face. She had thought that awful night was gone, buried with Cedric Brownley under a garden wall in Devon. But it wasn't gone. It had come back twice to haunt her, to twist her soul, to remind her that she had condoned a murder— and, God help her, would do it again if she had to.

That night, after refreshing baths in an outside bathhouse and a dinner fit for the table of Mohammed Ali, Quint excused himself and Rosa with a plea of exhaustion. He had told the story of the fight with the fanatics to Madame Bey and Kai, her son, who were amazed by the tale and ready to believe Lord and Lady Spencer must be in great need of rest.

As Rosa left the table, Madame Bey caught her arm and whispered, "Now I see how the big Anna is cut! She fought hard for you. She is a brave woman."

Rosa nodded. "Always," she said, "she protects me. I am not sure I deserve it." She went out, her hand tucked through Quint's arm, her face pale and thoughtful.

Upstairs, the Bey housekeeper had turned down the bed and left a small oil lamp burning. But Quint turned Rosa toward the balcony and a bench in the open air. In silent agreement, they sat down in a cool breeze.

"We must talk, Rosamunde. I had hoped to keep my deepest worries to myself, but I was wrong. You have every right to question me. You are my wife, and your money is making this trip possible."

She made a gesture with one small hand, as if to say that wasn't a problem. "That is not true. The money you have was the dowry you received for marrying me, and is yours only. And I only want to know where we are going, and why. I much prefer England in summer to this deadening heat, and I am sure you do too. Besides, you are putting yourself in grave danger when you go to India, for your enemy can follow, and you'll be without Mohammed Ali to protect you."

Quint sat beside her with his head down, his hands clasped loosely between his knees. He did not look at her. "Unfortunately," he said after a pause, "that is all true. And I have put you in grave danger also."

Stung, she struggled to find words. "It is not my safety that worries me. It's your skin they want, not mine. And—oh, I don't want to lose you! *Why* are you putting yourself in such danger? There must be a reason, for you are no fool."

Quint sighed and sat back, staring out into the darkness. "I said I would tell you everything, but it's hard to begin. Do you remember Porter Ogilvie?"

"Yes, of course. Your cousin with the friendly smile and the icy eyes who met us on the dock as we left Lundy Island. I'm afraid I didn't much care for him."

A corner of Quint's wide mouth flicked up. "You are a discerning woman, my love. Do you also remember him asking about 'young Jon'?"

"I do. And I remember you brushing off the question with only a careless word or two."

Quint took a deep breath. "Ogilvie meant to worry me, and I hated to give him satisfaction. Jon is Jonathan, my younger brother, much given to getting into scrapes." He hesitated, swallowing, staring off into the darkness once more. "At the moment," he added abruptly, "Jon is imprisoned in the dungeons of the maharajah of Burawanda, accused of stealing a quarter million pounds' worth of uncut jewels from the maharajah's collection. His life is in grave danger."

"Good heavens!" The words came from Rosa in a breathless squeak. "Surely he didn't do such a dangerous thing!"

Quint shook his head. "He didn't, of course. Jon can be foolish, reckless, and at times stupid. But he is never a thief. The jewels belong to an Arabian chieftain who wanted to turn them into gold. He entrusted them to us —Jon and me—and told us to sell them for him and share the profit. They are all uncut jewels of the finest kind, Ceylon rubies and emeralds, all clear and beautiful, worth more than a half million if they are properly cut." He stopped, his face changing, his eyes growing as hard as the rough emeralds he spoke of.

"But while I was in England searching for new buyers, Jon went against my orders. He took the jewels to the palace of Burawanda to sell them. Someone had told him the maharajah there was an ardent collector of jewelry and other art, and he hoped, I suppose, to show me what a smart trader he had become. Undoubtedly, he thought the maharajah was honest. He was wrong."

"I see. He should have made inquiries, then?"

Quint shrugged. "He may have tried. Few men would name a powerful maharajah a thief, especially to a young man who might repeat it and name the source. No matter, for as soon as he showed the jewels to the maharajah, the maharajah claimed Jon had stolen them from his collection. From what I've been able to find out, he had Jon given thirty lashes and thrown into his dungeon. His usual procedure, I'm told, is to keep a criminal there in cruel conditions until he confesses the crime—and then kill him."

The last sentence came out in a hot rush of words snapped off at the end, and when Quint turned and looked at Rosa she felt his repressed fury, and she heard it in his next, half-whispered words:

"If my brother dies before I can rescue him, the maharajah will die also. I swear it."

There was a long silence, finally broken by a strained question from Rosa.

"Why haven't the English authorities stepped in? He is an English subject, is he not?"

When he spoke, Quint sounded more contained, in control. "The English rule India in trade and have taken over the cities and countryside. But they quite carefully leave the maharajahs alone. I have had only one secret report from the governor general's headquarters. I was given it in London, right after our marriage. It said Jon is alive, and that he is confident I'll get him out. I hope to God I can live up to the trust he has in me."

After a moment, Rosa stood up and went to the balcony railing, looking out at the scimitar shape of a new moon rising. "I see," she said. "The English rulers must turn their heads and pretend nothing is wrong. So we will rescue Jon ourselves, either by stealth or bargaining."

Quint stared at her. Her face showed anger and excitement, and beneath the excitement, a firm resolve.

"Did you say 'we,' Rosa? Do you think I'll let you in on something so dangerous? I will want Thomas along, with Wiggins and Ranjit, but you and Anna will be safe in an English household in Simla." He stood and reached for her, drawing her into his arms. "I'll not risk you, my dear love."

Her eyes were soft as she gazed at him. "No one," she said, "has tried to hurt me. It's you they are after. I would be a help to you, not a responsibility. Surely the maharajah wouldn't give orders to shoot a woman."

Quint shook his head. "You have jumped to a conclusion, Rosa. The maharajah has no quarrel with me, though he may have heard that Jon has an older brother and expects a visit. In short, my love, the maharajah is not the man who hires trained assassins. That man is Fedruis Murad, an Arabian chieftain, who firmly believes I took his jewels, sold them for a fortune to the maharajah of Burawanda, and kept the money. When I sent word and informed him about the theft of the jewels, Murad put a guard together and traveled to India. He questioned the maharajah, who of course said he had paid well for them; that he had traded them to another collector, and that I still had the money. Murad believed his lies instead of me."

"How could he? Doesn't he know you're an honest man?"

Quint gave her a twisted smile. "He must have trusted me when he handed the jewels over to be sold. But there are many races who are suspicious of the English. There is an understandable distrust in every native when the English move into their country and take over. Therefore, the Arabian believed the Indian because of his own prejudice."

Rosa was silent, her cheek resting against Quint's shoulder, her arms around him. It sounded such a desperate thing, to rescue a man from a maharajah's dungeon while dodging the bullets of an assassin hired by another powerful ruler. It sounded, in fact, impossible. But it was the right thing to do. That, she decided, was enough to balance the scale.

"It will happen," she said slowly. "We will rescue your brother. I know we will. But it will be very difficult." She reached up and pulled his head down, kissing him slowly and lovingly with a soft, open mouth. He kissed her in return, taking her mouth with a gasp and a hungry thrust of his tongue. She could feel the whole length of his strong body, tense and hot against her, and knew the frustrated strength in it, the sadness and passion that racked him. His emotions would burn him up if he let them, would send him racing toward a meeting with his enemies, perhaps half prepared; perhaps alone. She wouldn't let that happen to him.

"Come to bed," she whispered, sliding her hands down from his shoulders, beginning carefully to remove his cotton jacket. "We need each other, Quint."

All at once, he let go of his thoughts of vengeance. "Ah, Rosa, my darling girl, my wife. I thank God for you." He swung her up and carried her into the dark room, to the pale square of the big bed, and sat down, still holding her tightly. His mouth fastened on her slim neck, one hand burrowing beneath her skirts, sliding up her soft thighs, finding the top of her long, loose drawers, then pulling them down, tossing them aside, pushing her skirts up to her waist and fondling her secret places until she gasped and rose under his hand, wanting more, much more. She spoke, frantically.

"Wait, darling, I'll take off my clothes . . . oh! Oh, yes, Quint . . . yes! *Yes,* my love, my dear love. . . ." He was inside her, and instinctively she locked her slim legs around his loins and arched against him, knowing that this time there was no pain for her to fear, no reason for Quint to hold back. She felt his fierce passion and reveled in it; reveled in her own sudden, tumultuous desire. She wanted to ask him if everyone who loved felt the same, had this same wonderful feeling—but she suddenly knew they couldn't. In all the world no one else had ever felt a love like this. It was only for them.

And it was such a wonderful way to make love, trusting each other, giving as much as getting . . . oh now, now she felt him beginning to tremble, to thrust faster, and knew she was trembling, too, and cried out softly when her inner flesh convulsed around him. Waves of vivid sensation rippled through her; she moaned with eagerness and felt him thrust deep, deep inside and go rigid, throwing back his head and making a guttural sound of intense pleasure deep in his chest. Then he slowly collapsed into her arms, his face turned into her tangle of silky hair.

"I love you," he said, his voice muffled, "I always will. I never thought I'd find a woman like you. I feel—I really feel so damnably *lucky*. Never leave me, Rosa."

"I won't. I wouldn't dream of leaving you. I—I can't tell you how I felt this time. So wonderful, my darling. I'm still . . . oh, how can I say it? Still hugging you inside me."

He laughed breathlessly. "I know, I feel it, and it's wonderful for me. But we'd better take off the rest of our clothes and get into bed properly, don't you think?"

Rosa's smile faltered and she was glad of the darkness. She wanted more. But she had to be sensible, to impress Quint with her new responsibility. Certainly she shouldn't insist on more lovemaking if he didn't want it too. "Yes, of course. This is lovely, but we have much to do tomorrow, I know. I haven't been much help. And we should get our rest."

His teeth closed gently on her ear and worried it a little. He licked the bite carefully, feeling the shudder that went through her. "We will get our rest," he said, "but not quite yet. I need more loving . . . if you don't mind?"

It was midnight before they drifted off, replete with lovemaking and feeling safe for the first time since the fight on the ship. They slept well and woke feeling wonderful, a state that lasted only an hour or so, for a slender man in a white robe wearing a white headcloth with a colorful twist of brocade to keep it on his head came bringing a message. Questioned by Madame Bey's houseman, the stranger said that an older well-dressed man had given him a gold piece to bring a note to this house and to give it only into the hands of a man named Lord Spencer.

Quint was sitting in the rear garden with Rosa at a small table, finishing a big breakfast. He watched the man, who held a folded white paper in his left hand. As he came up to them, the man smiled, but only with his mouth. His eyes were those of a wary wolf.

"You are Lord Spencer?"

"I am."

"Then this is for you." He thrust the paper toward him, and with lightning swiftness, a long, glittering blade appeared in the other hand, flashing in the sunlight.

Instantly Quint had the wiry arm clamped in his fist.

The man shrieked and let go of the knife, which he had kept hidden in the folds of his robe. Rosa was on her feet, frightened but steady, swooping down and picking up the knife as it fell into the grass. Quint rose, dragged the man to the gate, opened it, and kicked him out, sending him sprawling.

"Tell Fedruis Murad to send a man to fight me," he called after the running, stumbling native, "not some squealing boy. Better yet, tell the coward to stop risking other men's lives and come to fight me himself!"

Leaning on the gate, Quint watched the frightened man scramble toward the main part of town, hidden almost at once by the tall buildings there. That one, he thought, will not be back. But another will come. . . .

The long knife clutched in her hand, Rosa picked up the folded paper the thin man had dropped. She opened it and handed it to Kai Bey, who had run from the house half dressed when he saw what was going on. He looked at the message written in Arabic symbols and shook his head.

" 'Death to all thieves,' " he translated, frowning. "Mohammed Ali must see this. He will track down this fool."

"The man is only a pawn," Quint said, coming back to the table. "And Murad would be hard to find if he heard of a search for him. No, Kai. You can't reason with a snake."

"But—" Rosa broke in, but Quint cut her off with a shake of his head.

"No matter, Rosa. Murad will expect a search and reprimand from Ali. He will be even more cautious if it doesn't happen soon. That will give us a chance to get to India while he's still expecting trouble. Get your shopping done today."

Bewildered, Rosa stared at him. "But I need nothing, Quint."

Quint frowned. "I should have told you earlier, I suppose. You do need other clothes, my love. Native clothes that blend in, which cannot be bought in England or France. Take Anna along, and Madame Bey to guide you. Have you money?"

"Of course. More than enough." She said it calmly, seeing how on edge Quint was. "I am ready to go when Madame Bey is ready to take me."

He smiled, raising her hand to his lips, kissing her slender fingers. "Then be off with you, and buy whatever Madame Bey suggests. I will see to loading the wagon."

Rosa gasped. "We leave today?"

"Tonight, my love." He glanced at Kai, who nodded. "It is all arranged. We travel in darkness until we've left the city behind. Then we join a caravan Kai has found for us, travel to Cairo with them, and then across a narrow band of desert down to Suez on the Red Sea. There will be a ship there ready for us."

"And after that?"

"Bombay."

She inclined her head, accepting the one word. She had known they were going to India but now it became real. Turning away, she saw Madame Bey beckoning to her from the open hallway of her home. She went toward the small but dignified woman feeling as if she walked in a dream—no, a nightmare. *Bombay.* A great city, filled with people she would never understand. And if she remembered the stories rightly, after Bombay came a long and arduous trail across a sweltering land where graven stone gods with rings in their noses and eight arms were worshiped by dark and secretive people in long, flowing garments.

And then there were also strange tribesmen who prided themselves on murder because they worshipped a demon goddess named Kali. Thinking back on things her mother had said, she remembered Lady Beatrice telling her that none of them liked the English, that they only waited in patience for a chance to throw them out. Her steps slowed as she thought about it, and she jumped as Madame Bey called to her.

"Hurry, Rosa. I've sent the houseman to bring a carriage. This will take much of the day."

Anna went along. Quint had decreed it. First, he wanted to make sure that Anna had the same kind of clothes that he had told Madame Bey to find for Rosa, which turned out to be clothes worn by middle-class Arabs. Madame Bey was at first dismayed, for none of the shops had clothes of Anna's size. But a merchant looked at Anna, laughed, and went to his men's clothes, bringing back a long, voluminous burnoose that suited her well, but without the wrapped garment inside that covered a man's loins beneath. There was little difference between it and an Arab woman's attire except for the head covering and veil, which could be added.

But Anna shook her head at a veil and bought a turban for herself. "All the better if strangers think me a man," she said to Rosa. "They are much less apt to attack."

Rosa winced. "In our disguises perhaps no one will attack any of us. Please, don't dwell on it. I've seen all the fighting I wish to see in my whole lifetime."

Anna looked incredulous. "That little spat on the ship? Why, there was nothing to that."

"Enough, Anna." It annoyed Rosa to be teased about a serious subject.

Anna laughed and moved away toward the carriage,

carrying their purchases, and Madame Bey, coming up beside Rosa, touched her arm.

"Anna means no harm. The woman would die for you."

Rosa nodded and then laughed herself. "And I for her, Amarna. Which she knows. We are the closest of friends."

Quint had also instructed Rosa to purchase two saris. Rosa spent time with an Indian employee, learning how to wrap the sari about her and leave enough of the sheer, softly printed silk for the headdress and veil.

"It's like trying on costumes for a charade," she said to Anna as the carriage turned toward the Bey house. "No matter how hard I try, I'll never fool anyone into thinking I'm an Arab or a Hindu."

"I agree, if by anyone you mean someone who comes near to you and looks into your face. But from a distance—and I understand there is much distance in deserts and along mountains—no one will suspect you of being an Englishwoman."

"You may be right. But what of the wagon?"

Anna looked perplexed. "That is different. I have wondered myself about dragging a heavy wagon through desert sand. I'm not sure it can be done."

Madame Bey laughed outright. "I too wondered. But Kai said to me there is a good road to Cairo, and then the things in the wagon will be hung on camels, and the wagon pulled along light and empty to Suez. The ship captain there has agreed to carry it to Bombay."

"I see." Rosa said. "At least, I think I do. I . . ."

No, she thought, I'll not question Quint's plans behind his back. He may have good reason to take it along.

Chapter Thirteen

———— ❧ ————

They left Alexandria at first dark. Kai and Ranjit went with them, and Wiggins, who came up from the ship to tell Quint he'd managed to find a large dhow going to Cette and had sent the young boys home with their pockets filled. Quint, Rosa, Kai, and Ranjit rode, Anna, Tom, and Wiggins preferring the wagon to the spirited Arabian horses. They came into Khirbata by noon of the next day, stopped for an afternoon rest in the shade, and started out again that night. The next night they came into the ancient city of Cairo and went directly to the large and luxurious home of Kai Bey's brother Nehmet, named for their father, a trader who had arranged for the ship at Suez.

Nehmet Bey was older than Kai, but no less friendly. His wife was shy but smiling, showing everyone to a comfortable room, offering sweetmeats and fruit.

Like many of the homes of the wealthy, the house had a small outside pool used as a bath, with high walls for privacy. After everyone else had gone to bed, Quint and Rosa went there and bathed, enjoying the cool water.

"This is the last night for you to be an English lady," Quint said, lolling back in the water and watching Rosa soap her hair. "Tomorrow you become an Arabian wife, in white robes and a half veil. And I become an Arab."

Rosa laughed. The water was like cool silk against her bare skin, and she was luxuriating in it, her whole body feeling free and supple. She looked at him in the dim light and thought his tanned, black-bearded face would suit the disguise perfectly—and perhaps his nature would too.

"A sheik of Araby?"

He laughed, hearing the subtle flirtation. "Indeed. Does the thought excite you?"

She came closer to him. "Of course. They are supposedly very romantic. However, I have very little knowledge of such things." Dipping down into the water, she rinsed her hair and then flung it back, her hands smoothing and squeezing the water from it, smiling at him, her soft lips parted. From the look in his green eyes she could see she was successful in arousing his interest. "But," she added, "I am learning. I have an excellent teacher."

Her breasts shimmered just below the surface of the water, the nipples tight and pink, the curves irresistible. Without thought he reached out and pulled her to him, wrapping his arms around her bare body, catching her warmth and the silky smoothness, so different from his own hard physique.

"I'll teach you more," he said in a hoarse whisper, "once we're home again."

"Yes," she murmured, "yes, my dear love." Her hands smoothed up his wet, hairy chest and locked behind his strong neck. She kissed him, loving the feeling of cool wet beard against her face, tasting the male flavor inside his mouth, the taste that sent ripples of desire through her. Then she laughed, a small, surprised laugh full of excitement, and moved her body seductively against his hardening erection.

"Why wait? You could teach me more right now." Her soft voice trembled, her hands stroked down and took him in her palms. "Oh, Quint, I want you inside me. Can we? Can we do it right here?"

Her hands were driving him wild. Every time they were together lately he had been in a state of semierection, alive and aching for release. It was as if he had never gotten as much as he wanted in their encounters in bed, as if he had to have more, or go on aching. He reached down and cupped her buttocks in his big hands, raising her up, settling her down on his erection, pressing into her. It felt like heaven; like a small, warm heaven that closed around him and wriggled. He let out his breath in a low, growling sound of pure lust and gently bit the side of her neck.

"Come with me," he whispered, "and be my love. . . ."

Later, in the room the shy hostess had given them, Quint lectured Rosa in the dark. He sounded very dignified. It made her want to laugh.

"I realize you're very young, compared to me. But surely you aren't too young to understand the dangers and problems we're about to face. Just remember that I find you hard to resist, and you—well, you must stop tempting me and help me to leave you alone. If you become pregnant . . ."

"I won't, darling. Not now."

"It's ridiculous for you to say that, you know."

"Perhaps. But I do say it." She rolled over and raised herself on her elbows to look down at his shadowed face. "So, believe me, m'lord. You'll feel much better."

Quint laughed and pulled her into his arms. "I'll try,

my angel. And you try to sleep; the trip that begins tomorrow is extremely tiring, and we must be alert."

They set out at dawn. From even a short distance, they were well-to-do Arabs with one Hindu, traveling with burdened camels and saddle horses. There was also a team of dray horses pulling a rattling wagon with two large servants on the driving seat and an old servant inside—Wiggins.

"We are moving into the fertile Nile valley," Kai Bey told Rosa. "Those who see the wagon will believe it is filled with bags of wheat, barley, and beans, and that we are headed for our home in the desert." He laughed. "Not that the people here are curious. They see so many kinds of travelers going to India that they've become bored."

Rosa nodded and adjusted her headdress, pulling the edge of the soft cloth forward to shade her eyes. The bottom half of her face was hidden behind a gauzy veil, the lines of her young body obliterated by the many folds of her robe. Anna had proposed that Rosa should ride in the wagon, for her weight would never matter, but Rosa had declined. A saddle, she thought, was more comfortable than the bumping wagon. Besides, if she sat in the wagon, all she would see would be the solid, wide backs of Anna and Tom, and Wiggins's disapproving face. It seemed to her that Wiggins's dislike of her grew every day.

Putting that thought away, she glanced up, looking for the dark gray Arabian horse that Quint rode. He was leading, which didn't surprise her. Quint was always eager. He wore a white burnoose that covered him from head to heel. Red and gold bands held the hood snug to his head, and beneath it he wore a white shirt with loose sleeves and a pair of white riding pants stuffed into knee-length, shining black boots. His open robe streamed back over the Arabian's sleek hide. With his black curling beard and sun-browned face he looked, she thought, exactly the way a sheik should look, though few did. Most of the ones she had seen in Alexandria and Cairo were fat and lumpy.

They crossed the many fingers of the Nile, some small enough to step over, others spanned by makeshift bridges, and kept going for miles in the fertile green valley. They spoke little; the way was plain and well used, for the travelers to India had beaten it down. It wandered, veering off soggy ground, but continued on toward Suez and the Red Sea. They had traveled for hours before they could see the desert in the distance. The green of the valley stopped abruptly and the pale sand began, as if some Egyptian god had leaned down and drawn a line with his finger.

Here, and no farther. Not one blade of green grass will mar our desert.

Kai Bey rode back to Rosa and pointed ahead at the sand. "It will be hot, Lady Spencer. You might prefer the wagon for a time."

She smiled. "I would still be hot, and bored. I'll stay with my horse. He is easy-gaited."

"He is an Arabian," Kai said, as if that explained it all, and rode back up to the front beside Quint.

Rosa looked after him. Kai Bey, she thought, was not only pleasant and attractive, he was also strong and very able. Quint had a good friend in Kai. Perhaps she did, also. He had become very attentive to her comfort.

The wind was light but blowing from the southeast; they felt the hot, dry breath of the desert long before their horses stepped into the sand. After a quarter hour every face was wet with sweat, and all were silent. At midafternoon Quint left the van and dropped back to speak to Rosa.

"Are you feeling faint, my dear? You are rather pale."

"I'm fine, Quint. No dizziness. These clothes seem to protect me from the sun."

"Good." He glanced back at the wagon, which kept to the rear to avoid throwing sand at the riders with its wide wheels. "The wagon top would protect you better."

She shook her head, smiling. By now she knew she would be less affected by the heat in the wagon, but she needed no black looks or bitter advice. Wiggins was Quint's friend; she wouldn't complain about him. It was his right to dislike her, and she'd not cause trouble between Quint and his sailmaster.

Late that night they camped at a water hole, resting the horses and giving them grain. They were on the way again at two in the morning and entered the desert town of Suez at noon, exhausted but laughing, making jokes, feeling a great relief, and the sight of the Red Sea on the eastern boundary of the town heightened the mood. They would soon be away, for there was the steamer they had been promised, waiting for them.

Riding near the wagon, Rosa was limp with the heat, limp from near exhaustion, but a feeling of triumph rose in her chest. There had been hours when she was afraid she wouldn't stand up to the trip, but here she was. She caught Quint's gaze as he turned and looked for her. Laughing with relief, she urged her horse into a trot to catch up with him.

He slowed and waited until she was beside him; then he smiled, teeth glinting in what now seemed a forest of beard. "I'm proud of you, Rosamunde. I thought you'd be in the wagon after an hour of desert travel. But you didn't give in."

She blushed, partly with pride, partly with shame: she

would have been in the wagon if Wiggins had stayed in Alexandria. But she couldn't tell Quint that.

"Thank you, m'lord. When do we board the ship?"

"Immediately. You and Anna may go aboard at once. Its cabins are more comfortable than the accommodations in town."

"Wonderful! But will you have time to load everything? Even the wagon?"

"Indeed. The ship doesn't sail until tomorrow night. That gives us time to rest today and see to the heavy loading in the morning. Tell Anna to sort out your luggage and hers, and I'll have a word with the captain."

In less than an hour Rosa was settled in a sparsely furnished cabin on the port side of the steamer *Eastern Star*. She was able to have a sponge bath and change into English clothes, but she didn't lie down to rest. She was worried about the bunk in her cabin. Clean and dressed, she went looking for Quint amongst the thick crowds on the docks and in the streets. Anna followed her off the boat, growling under her breath.

"If I hadn't seen you leaving, you'd be walking around alone in this unholy place. Can't you smell the hashish?"

Rosa hesitated, looking around the docks, sniffing the air. "Why, yes. Now I do. I'm glad you came. I have to find Quint."

Anna looked pained. "He's on the ship, Rosa. I saw him sitting in the captain's lookout, or whatever that strange little building is on the bow. He and the captain were having a drink."

"Oh." Slowly, Rosa retraced her steps, with Anna beside her. Quint would hate having her burst into his conversation with the captain, she knew that. But this was serious.

"They've given me the wrong cabin," she said to

Anna. "There is only one bunk, and it is small. Quint and I could never fit into it together." She looked up at the ship and saw Quint striding down the gangway, frowning.

"There he is," she said, and smiled. "I'm sure we have time to see that it's changed, and—"

Anna grasped her arm. "He may have chosen it purposely, Rosa. Be careful." She moved away rapidly as Quint approached, giving him a respectful nod.

Purposely. Rosa had no more than an instant to think about that, but an instant was enough. He would never do that. At least, she was reasonably sure that he wouldn't. She opened her mouth to ask, but he took her arm and spoke before she could.

"Can't I trust you to keep yourself safe? One of the ship's officers came to tell me you'd left the ship, and that your big maid had followed you. Certainly if you had looked around you'd know better than to walk out alone."

She was red-faced, shamed by her stupidity. "I'm sorry, Quint. It was just . . . I needed badly to see you. There's been a mistake, and you'll want to change it."

He was leading her firmly up the gangway and toward the door of the cabin she had just left, still in a hurry, still frowning, but the anger leaving his eyes, his mouth softening into a smile. "What mistake, Rosa? I haven't had time to make many."

"Here, darling," she said, seeing the door before them. "Come in and I'll show you."

He opened the door but didn't go in. He only looked. "What is it, my love?"

She laughed. "I didn't see it at first, either. But just look at the size of that tiny bunk. We'll never manage to get both of us into it."

Quint stepped inside, taking her with him, and closed

the door. His face was pale. "Damn it, Rosa, I thought you'd understand. You know how hard it is for me to resist making love to you. I asked for this single cabin, so I wouldn't be tempted. I'm bunking in with Tom, Ranjit, and Wiggins."

She stared at him, her expression slowly changing from amazement to understanding and then, as she realized exactly what he meant, to a hurt acceptance. "I see," she said, and turned away. "You're still afraid I might begin a child. Why, Quint? I'm no weakling. I'd never hold you back from saving your brother."

He came to her, clasping her slim shoulders, looking down into her eyes, his own eyes worried. "It isn't that, darling. You don't know how hard it would be for you. Even the trip across India is too much for a woman in that condition. If you were with child now you'd have to stay with my friends in Bombay until I returned."

Her gaze flickered, moving away from his intent eyes. "Oh? I'm . . . really quite strong, Quint."

"You've just proved that. But I'll take no chances. I've been extremely selfish until now. And if we shared a cabin, I'm afraid I'd be selfish again. You tempt me much too much."

Rosa sighed and moved away, going to the porthole and looking out at the blue water below. "All right. I see that nothing I can say will change your mind. Therefore, I won't try." She looked back at him and smiled crookedly. "We will resume our marriage, I suppose, when this is over."

Quint frowned. He wasn't at all sure that Rosa's new mood suited him. She seemed different; as if his ultimatum had changed her sweet nature. But he was damned if he'd give in. It was for her own good, and she would see that in time.

"Our marriage, dear wife, is still intact. Never think

otherwise. Not even if you wish it." He turned on his heel and left the small room, heading for the gangway.

The next day all the small bags and boxes were loaded into the ship's hold, and the wagon tied down on the deck, its wheels taken off and stowed inside it, as they had been before. And another band of travelers had arrived, Englishmen, heading out to India just as they were, but none with wives or children. Rosa and Anna were the only women aboard. Except for Quint, Kai, and the old man who brought their food and water, no one spoke to them. Quint's size and his frowning bearded face kept even the friendliest man away from Rosa; Anna's huge figure and suspicious expression put a damper on any admiring glances from the strangers when Quint was absent from his wife's side. Rosa was relieved when the ship left the docks and headed down the Red Sea, bound for the Gulf of Aden and the seas beyond.

"How many weeks?" she asked Quint one morning, finding him leaning on the rail and looking morose. "Or months?"

He shrugged. His temper was uneven; changeable. But she paid no attention to it, for he seemed to be the same with everyone else.

"Weeks, of course. Three or four, depending on the weather. But it will seem like months. What were you and Kai talking about last evening, when I saw you together?"

"His mother."

"His *mother?*"

"Yes. He was telling me how hard she worked on her English when she knew you were coming to her house and bringing your bride. He said she thinks of you as another son."

Quint's expression softened. "She's a maternal woman. Is that all you talked about?"

Rosa shook her head. "No. We talked about India for a time. I'm trying to learn all I can, and Kai is wonderfully patient. He answers all my questions."

"If you have questions, ask me." He was frowning again, and Rosa looked away, her small face thoughtful and quiet.

"I would like to, Quint. But you're always with the captain."

Quint moved closer, his muscular, tall figure for once seeming awkward and graceless, his resonant voice dropping to a near whisper. "Rosa. You know why I avoid you. I want you too much."

She shook her head, refusing to meet his eyes. She still thought he was being ridiculously dramatic. "I won't argue with you," she said, and left him, going toward her cabin, going in, shutting the door.

Anna was now Rosa's only confidant, and she advised patience. "He loves you," she said. "He wants to protect you. Why don't you tell him you think you've already conceived? That should end his misery, if not his worry."

"No! I'm not sure, and I won't lie to him. Besides, I'd be worse off. If he thought it was true he'd leave me in Bombay. He thinks the trip across India is too hard for a pregnant woman."

Anna shrugged her heavy shoulders. "Then leave it alone. It will all work out."

The Arabian Sea was hot, the few winds sighing and then dropping, good weather for a steamer. The *Eastern Star* came in sight of Bombay at the end of seventeen days, leaving a trail of dark smoke between the burning blue of the sky and the darker blue of the calm water.

With no wind, the smoke was like a black ominous arrow pointing the way to India.

The cry from one of the Englishmen rang out with exuberance: "Bombay is in sight!"

There was a rush to the foredeck, excited laughter, a joy that spilled over onto the weary and bored travelers. Among the crowd that rushed forward were Anna, Rosa, and Kai Bey, standing together and watching the great port of Bombay spread itself before them, as if preening in the mirror of its bay.

This port, though not as busy as Calcutta, was by far the more beautiful. The harbor curved into the land gently, and above it small foothills leaned toward it, green and softly rounded. And the new buildings that circled below the hills were clean and beautiful, in a European style. As they drew closer, the passengers were congratulating themselves for the weather and for the early arrival.

"Rosa."

She turned, startled. Quint was there, speaking to her across Anna's shoulders. She was shocked by the strain in his face. Kai stood behind her, calm and listening.

"Yes?"

"Is your packing done?"

"Almost. A few minutes' work."

He nodded, glancing at Kai, seeing Ranjit elbowing into the group and joining them. He waited a moment and then began again in a low tone.

"We will be a split group in this port," he said. "Our friends here have small houses. You and I, Rosa, along with Anna and Ranjit, will stay the night at the home of Ranjit's mother and sister. Kai, Thomas, and Wiggins will be with Kai's friend, a Christian from Alexandria. We will leave Bombay either tomorrow morning or, if the plans are not complete, tomorrow night." He looked at Ranjit, who nodded.

"I will escort the women to my mother's home," he said. "When they are settled I will come back to help. The wagon will be loaded in time."

"Good." Quint was strung tight, abrupt. "Get your baggage ready, Rosa. Don't delay us with more problems."

Rosa turned red. "I am not a fool, Quint. Anna and I can be off in seconds. We had anticipated the day."

He looked at her, surprised. "Good," he said again, and then added almost humbly, "I meant no insult, my lady." Then he was gone, striding toward the companionway that led down to the hold.

Kai looked after him and then turned to Rosa. "He's on a narrow edge, Rosa."

She nodded, her eyes stinging, already sorry she'd been so quick to take his words as criticism. "I know. His mind and heart are far ahead of him. I wish I could help."

"You do," Kai said. "You're his wife and he's very much in love with you. You and his brother are the only family he has."

She couldn't answer. She nodded and turned away, going to the cabin to help Anna finish the packing. If only it were true, what Kai had said. But perhaps it was.

An hour later Anna and Rosa joined Ranjit in an open carriage and went rattling through the streets that led away from the harbor and into the section of the city where Ranjit's family lived. Rosa was fascinated by the thick crowds that filled the narrow streets; the constant noise of yelling, jabbering people that filled the air, and the tall color-washed houses crammed together, the vivid trees, the huge cows that wandered everywhere. Parrots flew overhead like pigeons in London, and there were ancient, jingling victorias and rumbling bullock carts vying for space.

At Rosa's request they stopped at a huge open market full of strange foods and the heavy scent of spices. They bought a basket of vegetables, sweets, and a bouquet of roses and jasmine for Ranjit's sister. Ranjit laughed.

"Shulbita will be embarrassed by such riches. But she loves company. She is also a good cook."

Shulbita, very small and slender, came to them as Ranjit led them into his mother's small house. She bowed and welcomed them in her soft voice, smiling happily.

"You go," she said to Ranjit. "We will talk. Then I will let them rest in their cool beds until Lord Spencer comes." There was awe in her dark eyes as she gazed up at Anna. Later, Anna laughed when she saw the thin pieces of wood that held the pallet intended for her.

"I'll not break their bed for them," she said, and moved the pallet to the floor. "I've slept on much worse."

The two men came in late, but satisfied that they could leave in the early morning. They had found good horses to ride and a team to draw the wagon. When they went outside to wash themselves before eating and sleeping, the women could hear Ranjit laughing and joking. A sign of confidence, Rosa thought, and wished she could hear Quint's laughter break out. She listened, but it never came.

They all ate together, a spicy meal of strange vegetables, goat meat, and barley, satisfying and very good. Afterward, Shulbita brought out her zither, draped a beautiful gauze shawl over her head and shoulders, and sat on the floor to play and sing the haunting love songs of India. Her voice was soft, each note clear, her dark eyes deep with feeling.

Quint sprawled on the floor, his broad back slumped against a wall, and in the dim room he allowed his eyes to rest on Rosa. This time, she saw his love for her written plainly on his tired face, the painful desire and frustration. If only, she thought, I could hold him in my arms. . . . But since they had been apart and she had seen the enormous task that lay before them, she understood his fear for her at last.

Then the songs were done and everyone was rising and heading toward their beds. Quint was the slowest to move. He had started to rise, but Rosa came and knelt beside him, touching his face with a soft palm, smoothing the lines on his forehead. She kissed him, stroking back his black hair with both of her hands, burying her fingers in his crisp, curly beard and kissing him again.

"I love you," she whispered, "and want you, so much. But now I understand. I will be only your friend until Jonathan is free. Then, my dearest, darling Quint, I shall be your ardent lover forever."

When he got to his feet she was gone; he could hear her speaking to Shulbita in the next room, complimenting her on her songs. He stood for a minute, listening to her voice, then turned and went to the bed assigned to him. It was going to be all right. She understood, and he was happier than he had ever been in his life; even happier than when he was a child, and life had been spread like a feast before him.

Chapter Fourteen

— ❦ —

*F*ollowing Quint's plans, the caravan left Bombay early in the morning. The men and the two women who rode with them were all Arabs—from a distance. The white robes had proven their worth in the desert near Suez and were now preferred as cooler and less confining than English clothing. Besides, it seemed to all of them that it was wise. Very few roving thieves took on the fierce knife-wielding horsemen of Arabia.

They had met earlier at Ranjit's home and had sat together to hear Quint describe the route they would take. He was full of confidence; the strain and worry of the last weeks had disappeared. He appeared strong and rested, his gaze clear, resting often on Rosa's calm and attentive face.

"We strike north and then northeast," he had said. "We follow the Narmada River to Manahata, cross it there and seek to the east for the Yamuna, an offshoot of the Ganges. From there, on to Gwalior, Agra, and the Punjab before the worst of the heat sets in. Our goal, the palace of Burawanda, is in the Punjab, close to Simla, where we will visit friends."

This time, Quint hadn't mentioned leaving the

women in Simla, but Rosa supposed he still meant to leave her and Anna there with his friends. While he was talking, she worried that in her mind. She had promised to be his friend while this trip was made and his brother rescued. Friends didn't necessarily take advice from another friend if they disagreed. Naturally, he wanted to protect her, but she felt the same way about him. He took great chances, and she wanted to help if she could. She thought of the pistols in her baggage and decided that she and Anna could make a difference.

As they finally left behind the northern part of the great, crowded city of Bombay, Rosa rode in the middle of the column, between Thomas, who had decided to ride after all, and Kai Bey. She looked ahead, past Quint's tall figure, and saw that this road was not crowded like the others. There were few travelers on it. She mentioned it to Kai, and he nodded.

"Most of the traders and traffic come to Bombay from the south. This part of our journey will be longer but perhaps easier than some of the trials behind us."

"How long will it take?" She had been reluctant to ask that of Quint, for it would sound impatient to him. But Kai only shook his head.

"So much depends on good fortune. With no trouble, perhaps as few as twenty days. With trouble . . ." He shrugged wide shoulders. "Who knows? We must take what Allah sends."

"Thank you, Kai. I'll remember that." In her mind, Rosa settled firmly on twenty days. In the wagon there were two tents, blankets and cots. There was grain for the animals and stores of fruit, loaves, and vegetables for the people. There was also water, sloshing in great clay pots, and three extra horses, tied to the wagon and coming along willingly. Quint had done well, providing for problems yet not overloading the wagon. Twenty days. She sighed and settled herself in the saddle. Why in the world would neat little England want to manage such a huge, brawling, sprawling land like India? Once the millions of tribes and the various warring maharajahs got together, they could throw out the few Englishmen and take over their own destiny.

On the twenty-first day the caravan left hot Rajasthan, passing the great city of Delhi at a respectful distance, and, steadily climbing amongst the growing hills, came into the Punjab a day later. They camped that evening in a cool, secluded valley with a clear running brook, and in the morning, protected by the thick trees, Rosa and Anna washed thoroughly, trying to contain their shrieks as they splashed in the cold water. Then they changed into their English clothes; Quint had suggested it the night before.

"Too confining," Rosa said, buttoning tiny buttons, shaking out wrinkles from a layered riding skirt. "I'm going to miss my Arabian robes. But how welcome the cool air."

Anna studied her. "You've changed in other ways, Rosa. You no longer remind me of a child playing the role of a grown woman."

Rosa smiled. "You say that, but I doubt you, Anna. You still treat me like the child you took over when my mother fell ill. I will always be ten years old in your mind."

"You may be right. Old habits die hard. Come, I smell that spicy hot porridge of Ranjit's that we both like."

By midday they came across a small Hindu village and Ranjit went amongst the farmers and traders, seeking a place, he told them, to store a wagon they had brought along and would need again, soon. They would pay a man well to keep it safe in a dry place until then. A man with a small barn and no cows came forward and promised to take good care of the wagon and the dray horses for the price of a cow. The bargain was struck, the wagon, holding the tents and all the bundles and boxes for camping, was wheeled into the barn, and the party was on the way again.

Shimmering in the distance were the Himalayas, the unbelievably high snow-covered peaks piercing a gray sky and disappearing in a mass of clouds, sending down the frigid air that wreathed their summits and upper valleys with ice. Simla, the refuge of the English government in India's hot season, was now only a day's ride.

Because of the narrowing roads, which at times gave sudden, frightening views of deep gorges and sheer rock walls, they went up the hills in single file; first the riders and then the extra horses, pressed into service as bearers of bundled clothes and other essentials. Occasionally they came to a resting place where the narrow way widened into a large flat area, and at one of them Quint gathered them around for a rest and to talk of plans.

"There is an inn at Simla, the Peleti, which will take us all. It's extremely comfortable, and the food is good. We have enough friends here to put us up, one or two at each home, but I have decided that I want us together. We'll not stay long. All I need is an hour or two of talk with Sir George Eden, the governor general, to work out a sensible agreement. He will do what he can to help us."

Rosa's heart jumped. One of her problems had just been solved. If she and Anna were left with Quint's friends, there would be a search made if they were missing. At an inn, all she would need to do would be to hand over a key, pay the bill, and walk out. A plot sprang to life in her mind. She looked away from the others, caught her bottom lip between her teeth, and began to plan, feeling excitement taking her over. If things went wrong and the men were captured and imprisoned, as Jonathan had been, she and Anna could at least try to get them out. They would need a native gun bearer in case of tigers, another horse—no, two horses, since they must carry supplies. Yes, it would be expensive, but there was that gold sewn into the hem of Anna's old cloak. . . .

"I have also decided," Quint said, glancing at Rosa, "that when we leave Simla we will set up a well-hidden camp near the palace of Burawanda, and we will keep the women with us." There was a glint of amusement in his green eyes, and, she noted, a distinct warning. She and Anna would be near, but there would be no feminine forays. She sighed and turned her horse as Quint motioned them on. It would be the same as it had been all throughout history—the men would go out and do what must be done, and the women would sit and wait.

The hill station of Simla, draped over the top of a high hill like a lumpy but colorful shawl, came into sight gradually as the party came on, passing small cottages, one very large three-story residence overlooking a cliff, and then the town itself, a livery stable and small tavern on its outskirts. They went on, gathering curious glances from passersby, to the Peleti, where they dismounted and turned over their horses to a dark-skinned Santal man who took the animals to the stables behind the inn.

A Hindu took their baggage and bundles to their rooms, returning later to collect soiled clothes for the launderers. He engaged Quint in conversation; pleased when he found the Englishman spoke his language. After he left, Quint told Thomas, Wiggins, Ranjit, and Kai to load their guns before they left Simla.

"An old tiger," he said, "ranging the land north of us. He has killed five people in the last two weeks, more than he needs for food. An old tiger that kills for the sake of killing is much more dangerous than a prime young male."

"That is Burawanda territory," Ranjit said, frowning. "I am suddenly less afraid of the tiger than of being noticed by the maharajah's men who must be looking for him."

"We will be well armed," Quint said, unsmiling, "for either the tiger or the maharajah's men. I came here to fight for my brother's life."

After two days they were ready to leave. The governor general, after pointing out his own neutrality, had given Quint full permission to do anything short of murder to rescue his brother and regain the jewels the maharajah claimed as his own. Rested and well fed on the Peleti cuisine, the party of five men and two women rode down the steep trail to the valley, paid what was owed on the wagon, and continued their journey, turning north, toward the Burawanda, a fertile section along the Beas River valley, near a day's ride from Simla. It was a clear day, the light reflected from the glaciers and snow of the Himalayas seeming to be bright enough to blind unprotected eyes. Anna was driving the wagon, a look of contentment on her broad face.

They were all silent. They watched not only the road and the few travelers on it, but also the thickets and reeds along the way. From the latest report, the tiger was still on the prowl.

In midafternoon the road they traveled was empty of any other humans. However, there was a dome of blazing white off to the north; a great wall with carved towers enclosing the dome and what appeared to be dozens of large trees, their crowns barely topping the wall. Outside the wall men worked in a field, plowing with oxen.

"Clearly," Kai Bey said, breaking the tense silence, "the farmers are not afraid of the tiger. Or is it that they are more afraid of the maharajah?"

Quint shrugged his broad shoulders. "The tiger kills more quickly. I have heard the workers here fear the dungeons more than any other death." He slowed, raising an arm and pointing north. "We will continue," he said to Kai Bey, "so that to watchers on the walls it will seem that we are only passing through."

Rosa hardly heard the men talking. When she saw the walls and dome she knew what it was. She stared at the walls as if she could see through them; in her mind she could see a young man who looked like Quint, who had Quint's green eyes, lying hopeless in a cell of iron bars, starving and beaten, wondering if he had been forgotten . . .

She looked forward again and started to call out a question, but then there was the sharp report of a rifle and a flurry of shouts, followed by an enraged roar and the terrified squeal of an elephant.

Rosa gasped and kicked her horse into a gallop, for the men were already charging around a curve ahead and off the road into a meadow of crazed sheep running in all directions. And there was the elephant, a dozen men with beaters, and a huge, wounded tiger in a monumental rage, climbing up the flank of the elephant, snarling and slapping at the rider, a young boy, who was valiantly trying to fend him off with an elephant prod. Below the boy, a half-naked old man with his turban askew was struggling to rise from the ground, yelling, "Akbar!" Then the tiger was up, crouching on the gray quivering back of the frightened elephant, his snarl rising to a roar.

Quint's horse shot across in front of Rosa, swung to the side, and stopped; Quint's rifle was in his hands, leveled on the tiger's head. The air cracked with a loud report. The snarling roar coughed into silence and the great yellow and black striped body slid from the padded back of the elephant, shaking the ground when it hit.

It was suddenly quiet. The boy turned, showing a bloody stripe from the tiger's paw on his cheek, and looked at Quint with enormous black eyes. The old man picked up his empty gun and stared at the strangers.

The boy swallowed and spoke, shakily. "You're English, aren't you? Only the English shoot that well. You saved my life."

Quint inclined his head. "I was glad to do it." He dismounted and walked over to the elephant, peering up at the boy's bloody cheek. "Well, he almost missed you. That scratch isn't deep, but you should have it cared for."

The boy swallowed once more. "I will. And if you come to my father's house, he will reward you for killing the tiger. I am Akbar, son of the maharajah."

The old man said something in another tongue, hung his gun on his shoulder, and grasped the elephant prod that had fallen at his feet. He picked it up and hooked it in the edge of one of the elephant's ears. The elephant knelt with a long-drawn-out groan and the old man climbed onto his neck, waving the prod and yelling at the beaters. Four of them ran up with a long pole and ropes, tied the legs of the tiger to the pole, and started out with their heavy load toward the white walls. The rest of the party turned and followed. Akbar swung around on his padded seat on the elephant's back and waved.

"I am in your debt, Englishman!"

Rosa turned to Quint. "That was a wonderful shot,

Quint. Perfect! And perhaps a good omen. But how did that Indian boy learn English out here in the wilds?"

"It is the custom. All high-class Indians speak English, some have three to four languages. The families hire teachers." Quint said the words absentmindedly, still looking after Akbar. Then he looked back at Rosa, frowning.

"I shot the tiger to keep him from killing the boy," he said, "and I'm glad I succeeded. On the other hand, if it had been his father . . ."

"You would have helped the tiger?" She asked the question innocently enough, but her eyes gave her away. He laughed, for the first time in weeks. Then he got back on his horse, looked around at the group and motioned them on.

"We'll need to find a good hiding place," he said as they started away. "There will be men looking for us, if Akbar tells the story about an Englishman."

"I am not sure you should hide," Kai Bey said. "Perhaps the maharajah will be grateful enough for the life of his son that he'll free your brother and give back the jewels."

Quint shook his head. "I cannot risk it. I talked to the governor general about him. It seems he has episodes of mental illness, when he believes everyone wishes to kill him. He is a strong man, and when he's in one of his fits he has to be controlled with bars or chains. Even his family is afraid of him then."

Everyone stared at him, but no one spoke. They set off again. The valley widened, and Quint sent Kai exploring on one side of the road and Thomas on the other, in search of hidden campsites near water. Before dark, they found a place: a thicket of large trees on the edge of the Beas River, with a tangle of underbrush and saplings that would hide the wagon and horses from passersby.

They went on until they came to a part of the road that was full of small river stones, where there were no wagon tracks or hoofprints. There they rode into the icy river and, staying along the shore, went back to the thicket and entered it.

"The gods are on our side," Quint said, dismounting. "We met no one on the road who could tell of what we did or where we stopped. Tomorrow we will put our plans into action."

Waking the next morning, Rosa was stiff with cold. She had removed her outer clothing; now she hurried to put it back on. Stepping out of the tent that had been put up for Anna and her, she froze, standing silent and still, watching a tall, white-robed Arab opening Quint's baggage under the trees. She slipped back into the tent, holding a finger over her lips as Anna glanced at her, and opened her own bag, taking out one of the dueling pistols. She loaded it, crept again to the flap of woolen cloth, and went out, pointing the pistol at the Arab, who now held a flat, square box in one hand.

"Don't move," she said in a hoarse whisper, "or I'll shoot!"

"Good heavens," Quint said, turning his head to stare at her from the depths of his hood, "put that pistol down, will you? It could go off and hurt someone."

He didn't laugh, but she could see he wanted to. She turned and went back into the tent, put the gun away, and came back. She remembered that Kai and Thomas were guarding the place and felt like a fool.

"Why did you change back into an Arab? I thought you were going to be English."

"Kai said I look too much like Jon, and the maharajah could be suspicious. We talked it over, and I decided to be a friend of Fedruis Murad's with a few jewels to sell."

"Jewels?"

He opened the flat box and showed her a collection of rubies and sapphires: rough, uncut stones. He tilted the box toward the light and gleams of red and blue sprang to life. "Once they are cut, they'll be beauties. At this point, they are only bait."

"Oh. . . . But what if he puts you in the dungeons?"

"He won't. He'll be afraid Murad would object."

"You can't be sure. He's not a sane man."

Quint suddenly looked uncertain. "Stop pushing up problems, Rosa. This is something I have to do."

"Quint!" Rushing up, Thomas looked huge and disturbed, his broad, honest face sweating. "There is a woman wearin' jewels comin' this way. Ranjit says the men with her are a troop of Gurkhas. They're searchin' the sides of the road inch by inch, an' takin' their time about it. They're bound to find us."

"Good God!" Quint shoved the box of jewels back into his baggage, tore off the white robes and headdress, and reached for his trousers and English boots. "Gurkhas! This calls for diplomacy. Watch, Tom, while I think." He looked at Rosa. "You'd better come out with me. A man with a wife along is often considered harmless."

Rosa's eyes were wide and curious. "All right. But what's a Gurkha?"

"Only the best fighting man in India."

"Including the English?"

"Indeed. Including everyone."

Thomas came crashing back into the camp. "They're almost here, Lord Spencer."

"Thank you, Tom. Come along, Rosa." Offering her

his arm, he smiled. "Look calm, my dear. Dignified, if you can manage it."

They came from the thicket as if from an English garden, arm in arm and smiling politely at the advancing troop of hard-faced Gurkhas and the small, exotic woman riding a Thoroughbred horse in their midst.

At sight of them, the men who were walking and peering behind thickets and trees on either side of the road stopped immediately and climbed back on their mounts, taking their places again in the group. They came on, slowing and stopping as the woman drew near the English couple. She watched gravely as Quint bowed, pressing Rosa into joining him. Then the woman smiled. The smile lit up a small but beautiful face with large gray eyes tipped upward at the temples. She wore a round, jeweled medallion on the center of her forehead, its gold chain woven into her hair, and a dark red silk gown, topped by a cape of silver-tipped furs. A shawl made of gold and silver threads was draped over her head and fell gracefully onto her shoulders.

"You," she said in perfect English, "are the man who saved the life of my son. He described you well." She looked at Rosa and her smile widened. "And you must be his wife. Am I right?"

Quint bowed again, relieved. "Yes, Maharani. You are right on both counts."

She bowed to him in return. "Then I owe you my greatest debt. The life of my son is more important to me than anything else in the world. I have come to reward you."

"That is not necessary," Quint said. "I was there, and my gun loaded. Anyone else would have done the same thing."

The maharani shook her head. "But no one else did.

My son himself has told me that the beaters and old Sundhu were too frightened to act. Without you, he said, the tiger would have killed him."

Quint suddenly smiled. "Akbar had nothing but a broken elephant prod, but he hit the tiger with it and kept it at bay long enough for me to shoot. He is as brave as one of your Gurkhas."

Not one Gurkha smiled, but a wave rippled over the whole guard, straightening already straight backs. The maharani nodded.

"You know soldiers, then. And boys. Akbar told you his name. He seldom does that. Now, make my task light. I want to give you the boon you want most. Only tell me what it is."

Quint stopped smiling and took a deep breath. He had to try. "I'm afraid that is impossible, Maharani. Only your husband, the maharajah, could give me what I came for. I have a foolish young brother who has spent the last four months in your husband's dungeons for a crime he didn't commit. I want him freed."

The maharani was silent. At the mention of her husband's dungeons she had stopped looking at Quint and began examining the Himalayas in the distance. She finally spoke. "What is his name?"

"Jonathan Spencer."

"And what is he accused of doing?"

"Stealing jewels from your husband's collection and trying to sell them back to him."

Pain tightened the maharani's forehead. "I see. That is his obsession. He'll not willingly let him go, then." After a moment she turned to the Gurkha who rode at her right.

"Leave me, Stani. Take the men and go. You have heard the name of the prisoner. Tell my husband that the Englishman is holding me for ransom, and only his brother's freedom will pay it. Now listen to the Englishman." She turned back to Quint. "What are the conditions?"

Quint looked down to hide his excitement. "My wife and my traveling companions will follow the Gurkhas and wait outside your gate with a wagon. I will wait here, with you. When they come back with Jonathan, the Gurkhas will travel with them and return as your guards again. Is that agreeable?"

The maharani blushed like a young girl. "Not entirely. It is a good plan, but you must send only your men to get your brother. I cannot stay with you without your wife present."

"It will be as you say, Maharani." Quint said, and turned toward the thicket. "Anna! Come here."

Anna emerged from the underbrush, slapping dead leaves from her full skirts, and advanced on the scene.

"Yes, m'lord?"

"You, Thomas, and Kai will take the wagon back to the palace and wait outside the gates for Jon to be brought out. Take along bedding and water, a little food. He may be ill or very weak. Bring him back here."

Anna's heavy face brightened into a wide grin. "Now, that makes sense! I'll load up and get the team." She was gone, her long strides carrying her into the thicket again.

"What an enormous woman," the maharani said, and dismounted, handing her reins to Quint. Turning to Rosa, she smiled. "Now, where do you keep your captives?"

Rosa returned the smile, took her hand, and led her toward the shelter in the thicket.

The hours of waiting were hard on Quint. If he was to succeed in the rest of his plan—to steal back the jewels that had been stolen from Jon—he couldn't risk being seen by the maharajah. He had known that from the beginning. But it was hard to send some one else to rescue his brother. He did a good deal of pacing back and forth on the riverbank before they finally heard the wagon creaking toward them.

By then, the maharani and Rosa had become friends. They had drunk tea together and eaten fruit, small cakes, and the sweetmeats of nuts and butter melded with ground grain. They had talked, each interested in the other's life. But they too listened with one ear for the wagon, and when it came they were out along the road, waiting with Quint.

As the first of the Gurkhas passed and gave a good view of the wagon traveling in the middle, Quint groaned.

"He's not in the wagon." His eyes met Rosa's, and in them was the fear of Jon's death. He reached for her hand, and she gave it to him, words rushing from her.

"Don't think it! He may be ill, and lying down. Go and see."

He whirled and went, striding through the riders and leaping onto the wagon step, hesitating as he looked inside, then turning to throw a hand up and nod, his face grim. Then he was gone, disappearing into the back of the wagon. When it stopped at the thicket Rosa, Ranjit, and Wiggins rushed to climb up and look in. Staring, Ranjit and Wiggins cursed under their breath, and Rosa's eyes filled with tears. The maharani mounted her horse and came to look, crowding close to the others.

Quint sat on the floor of the wagon, his young brother lying in his arms. Jon was emaciated, a skeleton with pale skin, long, tangled black hair, and huge green eyes that looked at them with frightened reverence, as if he thought angels had come for him. He was clothed in ragged pants torn off halfway down his thighs, and a singlet full of holes hung from his bony shoulders.

Quint's face was iron as he looked at Kai Bey. "The lying thief will pay for this," he said softly. "Long and painfully." His eyes swept the circle and came to a stop on the maharani's shocked face.

"Warn him if you wish, Maharani. Neither you nor Akbar will be hurt, but your husband has a debt to pay."

The maharani lowered her gaze. "He owes many," she said softly. "More than you can imagine. His Karma will punish him for centuries."

Chapter Fifteen

———— ❦ ————

"You will not be disturbed here," the maharani said before she left. "No one will know where you are."

Quint frowned. "The Gurkhas know."

"Yes. But the Gurkhas answer only to me and give no information to any other." She hesitated. "You don't understand, I see. I am from Nepal, a daughter of a ruling family. The Gurkhas are supplied to me from that family and have no allegiance to my husband." She paused. "It is also true, and perhaps shameful, that none of them wishes to be in his service."

"But your husband will ask you."

The maharani did not smile. "True. It is a sad thing, a woman's fear. I shall have to tell him I was so frightened I had no idea where I was or even which road we took. He will believe it, for he thinks of women as foolish children. But I will remember to say that I was treated as a queen and never touched by another man. That is important to him."

Quint's frown left. "You are more than fair, Maharani. Let me warn you: I intend to retrieve the gems my brother brought here. They belong to Fedruis Murad, an Arab. Your husband has told Murad he bought them from me at a good price and that I had been given all of the money. Murad believes him and thinks me the thief. I must have the jewels to prove that I didn't lie, or someday my luck will run out and his assassins will kill me."

"I am sorry, and I wish you well." The small woman turned and put out her hands to Rosa, who took them, then dropped them with a quick sigh and hugged the small figure.

"You will never know how much you've helped us, Maharani. You were a gift from heaven."

The maharani, blushing and warmed by Rosa's embrace, bowed to them both. "I am glad to help. My debt to you, Lord Spencer, can never be fully paid, for I know that my son lives only because of you." She turned and mounted her tall horse with a quick leap, settled her skirts around her, and rode out of the camp. By the time her horse gained the road the Gurkha escort had formed a square around her.

"Now," Quint said, expelling a held breath, "we move. Not because I don't trust her, but because we have to take Jon to Simla. There is no time to waste. He will die without proper care."

They took a circuitous route, passing the palace at a distance, then heading straight to Simla. Jon, who went in and out of consciousness, was placed on a thick pad in the wagon, given water and soup, and tended by Rosa and by Anna, who picked him up like a baby when it was needed.

At the village where they had left the wagon, they left it again, hiring two bearers who often aided the elderly by taking them up the mountain in a litter like a woven canoe fastened to long poles. Jon was made comfortable in it with quilts and slept almost all the way up.

That evening the governor general, Sir George Eden,

brought his own physician to the Peleti to care for Jon. He went red with anger when he saw how starved and frail he was. He offered to send a message to Burawanda, complaining about the treatment given a British subject, but Quint waved it off.

"I will do my own complaining," he said, "in my own way. I doubt our Queen Victoria would approve of my methods. Only ask your doctor to repair what has been done to my brother, and I will be satisfied."

Lord Eden nodded. "You can be sure of that."

On the third morning Rosa went to Jon's room to take over from Anna, who had watched over him during the night. She came in to find a startling change, for Anna was laughing and Jon was sitting up, propped with pillows, looking puzzled but wonderfully normal, though terribly thin. Quint was sitting beside the bed, his bearded face serene and happy. He reached out and swung an arm around Rosa's slender waist and brought her down to sit on his knees. He kissed her cheek and turned back to Jon.

"I am sorry to tell you, little brother, that the angel of mercy you have set your heart on is not available for you to marry. This beautiful, kind lady is your sister-in-law."

Jonathan changed color; good red blood ran up in his thin cheeks. "Good Lord, Quint! She's entirely too young for you. You have silver threads in your beard. Besides, you always said you'd never marry. Give over, now; she didn't really marry you, did she?"

"I did," Rosa said, suddenly enjoying herself, "and I'd do it again. But you do have an argument there, Jon. He truly is a bit old."

Quint laughed and brought her closer, tight against his broad chest. "I see you mean to insult me, my dear.

However, I have business to attend to in town. Can we make time for our quarreling this evening?"

Rosa smiled and leaned against him. "Certainly, we can try. I'll do my best to cooperate."

"And so will I. I'll have a quick breakfast and be on my way." He was up and gone, pausing to ruffle Jonathan's silky black hair. "Glad you're back with us, Jon. Next time, not so rash, please."

"Never again, Quint. Sorry I acted without permission."

"It's not such a bad thing you did. You couldn't know the maharajah was a madman. Now, sleep and eat, and you'll be on your feet again soon."

That evening Quint asked that dinner for all of them be served in Jon's room.

"A family gathering," he said, and meant it. Not just he, Rosa, and Jonathan were to attend but all of them: Anna and Thomas, Wiggins and Ranjit and Kai Bey. They were like family to him now, and he wanted Jon to know how close they had all become in the quest to rescue him.

Jon was still trying to take in the wonderful fact that he was free; that the lash marks on his back were healing fast and no one could wake him up from this dream of freedom and start lashing him again.

"I knew you'd come," he said to Quint, "but I didn't know when—or whether I would still be alive. I was tempted once or twice to lie, to confess to stealing those damn rocks, but the other prisoners told me that was what the maharajah wanted: he kills everyone who confesses. And some did, wanting peace and knowing there was no one to rescue them. They had had enough of torture. But I knew I had someone working to free me. Some of them had no one who even cared."

Listening, Quint's face was grim. "Then there are others in the dungeon? How many?"

"A dozen, perhaps. They die off, but new ones are brought in."

"I see." Quint dropped the subject as the waiters arrived with trays of redolent meat and bowls of vegetables. He rose then and pulled the corks from bottles of chilled wine, serving it around, proposing toasts. Rosa watched, wishing she could change the way he felt. He was playing the genial host; he was acting as if the whole thing were over, but she could see the strain beneath his mask of hospitality. He wanted those uncut jewels. Or, she thought, perhaps the money Murad had expected to get for them.

Later, as they climbed up to the next floor of the inn, where their rooms were, she asked if Murad had ever mentioned the sum of money he expected from the sale of the uncut jewels.

"Yes. Like all men who collect jewels, he thought he'd make twice as much as the jewels were worth. In any event, I suppose he'd take a thousand English pounds for his share."

"Why, then, that's wonderful! We can easily pay him, Quint, and you'll be safe."

"No, my love. The maharajah needs to learn he cannot get away with thievery, torture, and murder."

She slowed, reaching the door of her room, feeling tears spring to her eyes. She had suspected that Quint wasn't satisfied with Jon's rescue. He wanted the stolen jewels too. And she had seen his face when he learned there were more men imprisoned and beaten in the maharajah's dungeons. She had known at once that Quint would do something to help them—and that truly frightened her. She put her hand on the doorknob and looked up at him, gazing at his strong, sun-browned face, the gleaming black beard, the green eyes, soft and shadowed, looking at her with love.

"When will it be over, Quint? *I* need you, too." There was a break in her soft voice, a note of hopelessness.

Suddenly he reached past her and opened her bedroom door. Then he picked her up in his arms and went in, turning to kick the door shut. He carried her to the bed and fell into it with her, covering her with his body, crushing her into the soft duvet and kissing her thoroughly, kissing her breathless. When he had her gasping, he answered her question.

"Soon. Soon it will all be over, and we'll be heading back to Lundy Island. I thought I should wait, but I cannot. I want my wife *now*. Let me undress you, my darling. . . ."

She pulled away from him, half exultant, half angry. "So you can break our covenant, but I can't? How do you know I want this sort of—of celebration? Have I said so?"

He paused in the act of unbuttoning her blouse, pushed his bearded face into the opening and found a warm mound, a thrusting nipple. The hot mouth, the soft beard, the active tongue took over, lavishing her breasts with heat and caresses. She was pushing him away, panting, pulling him back again with her slender fingers clutching his beard, holding him to her breasts as if she would never let him go. She tried to be sensible, to use words, futile, gasping words.

"Let me get these clothes off, Quint . . . oh, please, help me take—what in the world are you doing? *Again?* Are you always so—so sudden? Oh . . . oh, yes . . . yes, my darling." Her slender hips rose to take him in, to cherish him, to give, to get, to love. Rhythmically, she rose and fell with waves of ecstasy, purring.

Afterward they lay together in silence until they caught their breath. Then Quint sat up and turned to her, pulling her into his arms.

"Now," he said as he finished unbuttoning her blouse, "I want us naked together, like Adam and Eve. Like the whole world is ours, forever and ever. Like there is no evil, not even a serpent to bring it. Just us."

She stood still while he removed her clothes, while he caressed her with his hands and mouth, while he told her how beautiful she was. How soft and luminous she was, even more so than he remembered, that she was wonderful, as pure as an angel.

"No, I am not. I have done things in my life I wouldn't want you to know. Crazy things, bad things. I am no angel."

He only laughed, and pulled her closer. "Whatever you've done, you're still my angel."

"And you are mine. Take me to heaven again, my love. My body aches for you." Her eyes were huge and soft, full of love, full of admiration, full of trust. Quint felt a twinge of guilt, quickly gone. There were things he had to do, things that were not a matter of choice but of honor. She would understand, in time.

The next morning, when Rosa came down to breakfast in the Peloti's dining room, she discovered that Quint, Wiggins, and Ranjit were missing. For a moment she thought she would faint. She knew, and she blamed herself for not insisting that Quint ask the governor general for help. She went at once to Kai.

"I won't ask you where Quint is," she said, "because I am sure I know. I intend to take Anna and Thomas and go after him. He is dealing with a madman, and we should all be there, solidly behind him. If you like, you can go with us."

Kai was pale and nervous. "He would rather we stay here, my lady. He left me with you in case he . . . that is, if you and Jon needed someone to help you get back to England. He particularly told me to say that he expected you to stay in Simla and wait for him."

"That," Rosa said, "is a blatant lie."

Kai drew himself up. "Rosamunde! I do not lie."

"Not your lie, Kai, his. He certainly did not expect me to do any such thing. He knows very well that I won't sit here and worry until he gets back. We'll be leaving in an hour. If you'd like to come along, you'll be welcome."

Kai was helplessly fascinated by the determination of such a small and feminine woman. "Then I will. That was the rest of his instruction. I was to join you if you insisted on following him."

After much thought, Rosa left the wagon where it was, hired a camel, and saw to it that the tents and blankets, clothes and various foods were distributed into the panniers and across the animal's back. Camels were the favored beast of burden for the British when they moved in this area of India; and she thought and hoped that having a camel instead of the wagon constituted a sort of disguise. Then, as a final effort to confuse the enemy, she put on her Arabian robes. It had taken three hours; not one.

"You, Anna," she said as they started out, "are the only problem. The palace guards saw you when you helped with Jon. And you aren't easy to forget."

"I will stay in the background unless I am needed. But they must have seen Kai."

"There were sentries on the wall," Kai said, "but they were never close to us. Anna they might remember, but not me."

* * *

At midmorning Quint, also wearing his Arabian robes, had appeared at the gates of Burawanda's palace with Ranjit. They were playing the parts of an itinerant Arab hawking uncut jewels and a Hindu associate. A turbaned dark-skinned man with aquiline features and quick eyes spoke to them from the top of the gates in an Arabic dialect.

"This is a bad day to try to sell anything to the maharajah, my brother," the gatekeeper said, speaking low and fast. "He is not in the best of tempers. Come back tomorrow."

Quint shook his head. "I have no tomorrow, gatekeeper. I must leave here tonight. I have uncut jewels, and I hear the maharajah often buys such gems. Perhaps seeing the jewels will sooth his temper."

"*Jewels?* Then you're as crazy as he is! Begone!"

Quint grinned, white teeth flashing in his black beard. "You amaze me, friend. I understood the ruler here loves jewels."

The gatekeeper's eyes narrowed as he leaned closer. "Do you love dungeons? That's where you'll be if you offer to sell jewels to our maharajah."

"I'll take that risk," Quint said. "Let us in."

"Then I will. But remember, your fate is on your own head, brother. I have warned you."

"And I thank you for it."

The gates, thick, solid planks fastened together with iron bands, swung open. Ranjit's dark eyes met Quint's green ones.

"Slowly," Ranjit cautioned under his breath. "Calmly. Be like Buddha." Sweat gleamed on his brow, but he followed Quint without hesitation. They emerged into a wide courtyard paved with colorfully enameled tiles and were met by silent servants who grasped the reins of their horses while they dismounted. As the horses were led away Ranjit went with them, insisting that he must see where the animals would be housed.

Quint waited. He used the time to examine his surroundings; his gaze took in the huge palace and the many exits and entrances he could see. He studied them, trying to fix them in his memory.

There were formal gardens that stretched from the courtyard to the south walls, with pools and statuary, ranks of roses, lilies, and jasmine, and an immense green hedge winding down from the palace to the wall like a wall itself, with tiny close-set leaves and long, pink thorns. He wondered about it, but then he heard feminine laughter on the other side and understood. Glancing up, he saw the usual wrought iron cage built onto the high palace wall; women could sit behind the decorative bars of black iron and the panes of glass, enjoying the view in rainy or cold weather.

So behind the hedge was the fair-weather garden given to the members of the maharajah's zenana; a place a man must stay away from, unless he wished to lose his manhood to a sharp knife. These were the other wives; wives without power. Dutiful wives. Not, Quint thought, like the maharani. More like slaves.

Ranjit appeared again, accompanied by a servant, and walked briskly toward him.

"There are two other gates in the outside wall," he said in English. "One behind the stables, where we put the animals, and one on the west. The one behind the stables is not locked. I don't know about the other."

Quint answered him in Hindi. "I am sure they will treat our animals well. There is no reason to worry about it. We'll not be here more than an hour."

Ranjit shrugged. "Then I worried for nothing," he said, also using Hindi. "Shall we go in?"

"Yes. We may have a wait, but we may have good fortune also."

Both of the servants entered the formal hall with them, walking together, murmuring about the visitors. The one who had taken the animals to the stables looked insulted. "Do these foreign fools think we would hurt their beasts?" he asked the other man, and then lowered his voice. "They will not be treated as well as their horses, once the maharajah has them in his power."

Quint's full attention was on the servants, though he appeared to be staring around at the statues, the thick, beautiful rugs, the tinsel and gold leaf trim spiraling up the pink marble columns that marched the length of the room. At the far end was the usual gold-and-jewel-encrusted throne. As the servants fell silent, he addressed them.

"Where shall we wait? Is there a place with chairs?"

"No. You must stand. No one is allowed to sit for an audience with the maharajah of Burawanda."

"Then we will wait outside. There we can sit on the steps. You may tell us when he arrives."

The servant stared at him. "If you are not waiting in the durbar when the maharajah comes in, he will not see you."

"Oh? Let it be, then. There are other and more courteous men who buy jewels." Wrapping his robes around him, fastening his sword belt, Quint went out. Ranjit followed closely, pale and bewildered.

"You would make a madman angry? What do you hope to get from this rudeness?"

"Knowledge."

Without asking, Quint led the way to the stables. A man there brought out their horses; they mounted and rode back to the gate. The Arab gatekeeper grinned as he opened it and let them out, nodding at Quint.

"My friend, you have saved yourself misery. Allah be with you."

Quint stopped as the gates closed and looked up at the gatekeeper. "Is it true that at times your maharajah is possessed by a demon?"

The gatekeeper gave a swift look around. Then kept his voice low. "Yes," he said, lowering his voice, "and a time of possession is near. He is in the first of it now. He had a servant lashed yesterday for nothing and flung into the dungeon, to be lashed daily. Soon the demon will take over."

Shading his eyes from the rising sun, Quint stared at the gatekeeper's suddenly fearful face. "What happens then?"

"He becomes like an old tiger and kills for no reason. He would as soon kill me as you. The only one who can stop him is the maharani. She and her Gurkhas are our protection."

"Ah. Perhaps I have gained by leaving, then. And I thank you for telling me. Allah be praised."

Riding away, continuing toward the thicket where they had left Wiggins, Quint was deep in thought. Gradually, Ranjit lost his paleness and became cheerful, opening a conversation again.

"Perhaps we can stay in the river thicket until the maharajah regains his senses and then approach him, sahib."

The use of the word that meant *master* brought Quint's gaze to Ranjit's face. Ranjit hadn't called him sahib for several years, and his doing so now meant the

Hindu was truly afraid and asking for guidance. And that meant, in Quint's decisive mind, that Ranjit could not take part in the foray. He had learned long ago that fear loses fights.

On the other hand, Ranjit often saw things that he missed on reconnaissance. He turned to him now.

"When we went for our horses, I noticed that the northwest wall of the palace had high windows covered with wrought iron grilles. I thought perhaps it was part of the dungeons. Did you notice it?"

Ranjit nodded. "Yes, sahib. When I went with the servants to find out where the horses would be, I heard the cries of a man being lashed. One of the maharajah's men remarked on it, saying I might be next to give the maharajah pleasure."

"I see." He also saw where Ranjit's fear had come from. He would have to depend on old Wiggins. He cursed himself silently for leaving Thomas in Simla. But if the worst came to worst, Rosa would need both Thomas and Anna to get Jon home—and, he thought with a start, she would also need Wiggins. Wiggins was the only master sailer in the bunch.

He rode on, his brow furrowed with thought. He would have to go alone to the maharajah's palace, and perhaps he should do so now, in the middle of the day. The element of surprise might see him through. He sat straight and looked over at Ranjit.

"You go on," he said, slowing his horse. "There is something I want to see more clearly about the palace."

Ranjit reined in. "I'll go with you, then."

"No. One rider is more easily hidden amongst the trees. You report to Wiggins."

Ranjit's dark eyes were worried and fearful. "What shall I say?"

"Tell him to wait. If I'm not back in two days, notify the governor general in Simla."

"Yes, sahib." Ranjit watched him out of sight, then turned to the west again, traveling fast.

After the big noon meal that was always served in the Burawanda palace there was an air of sleepy contentment over the whole establishment; both the sunny courtyard and the fair-weather garden were deserted as both women and servants sought their couches for a nap. Quint, noting the absence of noise, went quietly to the door behind the stables that Ranjit had said was unlocked and went in, sword drawn. There was no one there, not even a groom. He tied his horse in the stable with the others and sauntered along to the palace wall itself, trying every door and window, looking for a way in. He stayed near the northwest end of the palace, near to the stables, near to the dungeons. He had reasoned that here, where the walls were thicker and the windows smaller and higher, there would be one room put aside for treasures.

Finally, as he put his hand on a latch, the door opened. A man stared at him, eyes widening. It was the taller of the two guards who had ushered them into the durbar earlier, and the guard recognized him at once. He opened his mouth to yell, but the sound fluttered away as Quint grabbed him, holding his sword blade to the guard's throat.

"Make a noise and die," Quint whispered in Hindi, "or show me where the maharajah keeps his jewels."

The man agreed quickly. "I'll take you there. I have no love for that cruel man." His whisper contained fear but also truth. Two, Quint thought, this man and the gatekeeper. He wondered if there were any servants who were truly loyal to the maharajah.

"Then go. If you lead me into trouble my sword will be in your back."

"I'll not cause you trouble, sahib, I swear it. Down this way, to the last door. Someone must have told you where the treasure room is. You were close to finding it yourself."

Their boots echoed hollowly on the split stone paving, and then they were at the door, a door inches thick, bound across with iron bands. The servant looked around at Quint.

"I have no key. No one has a key except for the maharajah and his first wife."

"Give me your weapon," Quint said. He had looked the servant over on the way down the hall and had seen the shape of a long knife bulging in the side of his boot. He tensed as the man pulled the knife and straightened with it in his hand—if he wanted to challenge, this would be the time. But the man only reversed the knife, holding the blade and offering the chased silver handle to Quint.

He took it. "If I manage to escape after this," he said, "I will leave the knife just outside the gate. It's a remarkably beautiful weapon."

"Use it," the man said, "if you need it. It throws well."

"At this moment," Quint answered, bending to his task, "I am more interested in how well it slides a bolt."

Minutes later they were in the treasure room, the unlocked door pulled shut behind them.

"Truly, sahib, you are a master thief." There was a great deal of admiration in the servant's voice.

Quint ignored the praise. He was busy looking around in the dim light of two small windows high above. The whole room gleamed with silver and gold figurines, with jewelry, with gold cups and silver platters, with supple chains of gold and necklaces of gold links set with precious stones. On one wall there were shelves holding a matched set of silver serving dishes, the goblets set with emeralds. He saw no small caskets or bowls and wondered where to look for the uncut jewels that had brought him here. He knew only too well that they could have been sent to a jeweler months ago and be unrecognizable now.

A gleam in the dimness beckoned; a small chest, tucked beneath the shelves, had brass fittings that caught the light. He went to it, pulling it out to lift the lid. Inside there were pouches and bags, boxes and more boxes. Quint's heartbeat jumped. The fine maroon leather bag in one corner of the chest was familiar. He pulled it out and loosened the tie to open it. The dull gleam of uncut gems struck his eye. He poured a few out on his palm and saw that they were all rubies and emeralds: Fedruis Murad's fortune in gems. He shut the chest and shoved it back into place, then stuffed the maroon leather bag into a hidden pocket in his robes. Standing up, he felt seven foot tall and blessed by good fortune.

"I have found what I was looking for," he said to the watching servant. "I'll leave now. Walk with me to the stables."

The servant looked amazed. He waved an arm at the rest of the treasures. "You are leaving all these things here?"

Quint smiled. "The bag I took is mine; those are not. Hurry, friend. I should be gone."

They made it all the way to the open gate behind the stables. Quint was on his horse; the servant walking beside him, when three armed men rushed them. In the fight, Quint managed to drop the bag of jewels into the thick shrubbery along the wall, and then he was down, knocked from his horse by heavy lances, wounded by someone's knife. He felt the blade thrust into his ribs, inches from his heart, and then came a hard blow to his head, and then nothing.

Chapter Sixteen

Rosa's party left Simla before daylight. Kai and Thomas led the train, with Kai leading the camel behind his horse and Thomas keeping an eye out for trouble. Anna, mounted on a horse big enough to pull a wagon, brought up the rear. Rosa, her small curved figure draped in white robes, felt stifled amongst so many big, anxious, and protective bodies. She had hated saying good-bye to Jonathan. He had begged to be allowed to come with them, but she was sure he was too weak— and sure that if she allowed him to join the train Quint would be furious. Even more furious than he was going to be just to see her.

"I can leave Thomas with you," she had offered, but Jon refused.

"You may need him, Rosa. I don't. The people here are spoiling me with attention." He smiled, forgiving her, and added, "I'll be on my feet when you return, ready to start for England."

Ready to start for England. Mounting her horse in the small courtyard of the inn, Rosa agreed wholeheartedly. She felt the same as he and perhaps even more so. She yearned for England, thirsted for England; the bottoms of her feet ached for English soil. India was not home, nor anything like home.

"I would take the smallest, coldest hovel England could offer and live in it gladly," she said to Anna as they started off. Anna only laughed.

"We've had troubles on this journey, I know," Anna said, "but I've loved every bit of it. I never thought I would travel, but I've always wished to see other lands, and the people who live in them. Now I have, and I think England is dull. I'd like to stay in India, at least for a time." She was silent a minute, and then glanced at Rosa, adding, "Also, there are good reasons for me to stay away from England."

Rosa nodded, her heart contracting in pain as she agreed. "I'd hate to lose you, Anna. But it might be best. We'll talk about it later." She rode on, saddened. She kept her mind away from Quint as well as she could—every time she thought of him she saw him injured, bleeding, in some dark, dirty hole with bars. Why did she see something so awful and grim happening to him? And why did he have to be so determined to do everything himself? He could have told his story to Lord Eden and perhaps—

"Daydreaming?" Kai spoke to her bent head and smiled as she looked up, his eyes soft. "Where are we headed?"

She looked at Thomas, who spoke thoughtfully. "The best place is that thicket where we stayed afore. Our friends know where 'tis, an' our enemies don't. What could be better?"

They all laughed. Not because it was humorous, but because they were worried and didn't want it to show. Nothing seemed right without Quint.

With the thicket by the river as a goal, they rode faster, urging the stubborn camel along. By early afternoon they had again passed the palace of Burawanda and were bearing down along the river when they saw Wiggins come riding toward them. They stopped and waited, hoping for good news.

Wiggins was upset; his first words were a curse, followed by several more as he hauled back on his nervous horse.

"By God, we have trouble enough without women sticking their noses into this business. Why in hell did you bring them here, Kai?"

Kai frowned. "Where is Lord Spencer?"

"I'm damned if I know. He and Ranjit went to see the maharajah, and Ranjit came back alone. Lord Spencer hasn't shown up. He must have been caught."

Rosa turned away, breathing deeply, terrified. Quint in the dungeons? Had her terrible vision come true? The insane maharajah killed on whim, and he had reason to hate Quint. She turned back as Wiggins spoke again.

"Maybe Ranjit could tell you more, if he gets over his fright. He got scared this morning, listening to some fool getting lashed in the dungeon. Anyway, I'm on my way to Simla and then the Red Sea. This is no place for me."

Rosa gasped. "Wiggins! Are you deserting Quint?"

Wiggins gave her a look of intense dislike. "I am, if you want to call it that. From what I've heard of the Burawanda durbar, he's dead. I won't waste my time waiting for a dead man to get up and walk home."

Thomas turned and put a hamlike hand on Wiggins's shoulder. "Then go, Mr. Wiggins. Take your poison somewhere else. We'll be better off without you." He gave him a openhanded slap that made the older man's teeth rattle and followed it with a crack of his whip across the flank of Wiggins's horse, which sent him tearing and bouncing down the road, with Wiggins hanging on desperately, cursing at the top of his voice.

"There," Thomas said, looking at Kai, who was pale with anger. "We're rid of one problem. Let's talk to Ranjit."

Anna glanced over at Rosa as they started off again, and reached out to touch her arm. "Wiggins is full of hate, Rosa. He said those things as much to hurt you as he did to explain his own cowardice. Forget what he said."

White-faced with fear, Rosa nodded. She knew Anna was right, but still she saw .Quint in a dim, horrible place, bloody and unconscious. Her hands were shaking as she took up the reins. What they needed was a miracle, and as they rode on, she prayed for one.

An hour later they saw the grove of trees along the river, but there was an added problem. There were riders ahead of them, and they seemed to slow as they neared the thicket. The brown and gold of Burawanda uniforms was easy to spot on two of the men, with the rider of the other horse small and unidentifiable between them. Rosa looked at Thomas.

"Should we stay out of sight until they leave, Tom?"

Thomas shrugged. "They know we're here, Lady Spencer. Those are Gurkha soldiers, an' Lord Spencer said they've eyes in the back of their heads. Besides, they may come as friends."

"Yes. It's possible. I'm not thinking very well." She shook her head, clearing her blurring eyes, and tried to smile. "The maharani may have sent them."

"I think," Anna said, staring through narrowed eyes, "that Akbar brought them. That middle rider is even smaller than the maharani. Let's pick up the pace."

"It's true," Akbar said when they all dismounted to talk, "that there is a tall, black-bearded Englishman in my father's dungeon. My mother and I are not allowed to see him. The Gurkhas also have been forbidden to enter. Because of this, we are all positive that the man must be Lord Spencer." He hesitated. "It is said he is wounded."

Kai spoke up. "What crime has the man committed?"

"We have been told he took a bag of uncut jewels from the treasure room, though none were found on him."

"Then how could they charge him with the theft?"

Akbar cast his eyes down. "One of the palace guards confessed under torture that he had helped the man find the treasure room. The guard is dead now. My father had him executed." Akbar's head came up, his black eyes swept the group around him. "My father," he said, "is possessed by a bonga spirit sent by a Santal witch. The bonga dreams murder and fire. We must get Lord Spencer to safety before the bonga dreams again."

"Then we must do it by stealth," Kai said slowly, "and you and your mother must help us."

"We will. My mother has already sent a physician to bind up the prisoner's wounds, and she is willing to do much more. So are the Gurkhas. Neither they nor we will be in danger of losing our lives, for the Gurkhas will keep us safe. When will you come?"

"As soon as we can, but after dark. Can we signal?"

Akbar brooded over the question, black eyes huge. Then he nodded, his young face serious.

"Fire. It will draw my father to it, for fire excites him beyond any other thing. The Gurkhas and I will build it and light it after dark, inside the wall of the Garden of Delights. Men are allowed in there at night to keep watch. Everyone will rush as if to put it out, but we will feed it instead. Then, you will come in at the opposite wall, through the door near the stables, close to the dungeons and far from the fire. The gate will be unlocked."

Kai nodded but frowned. "Is the door hard to find?"

Ranjit broke in. "I can lead the rest, for I know the place. And with all of you here, I am willing, even anxious to help. I must redeem myself."

"Then it is planned," Kai said, and his dark eyes moved to Rosa's frightened face. "Pray for our success."

It was hard to wait for the rest of the day to pass. Rosa and Anna made a stew from the stores of grain, spices, and salt meat; Ranjit brewed coffee. After they ate, they rested for a time.

Then they went over their weapons. The men had two rifles amongst them; Anna and Rosa decided not to mention their pistols, which were loaded and ready. All of the men had knives, and Kai was known to throw accurately. Thomas had never felt a need for weapons other than his hands, and he didn't now.

The sunset was red. Like blood, Rosa thought but didn't say it. Anna spoke of it cheerfully. "Red sky at night, a sailor's delight. A good omen, Rosa. It's a fine sailor we've come to rescue."

Rosa managed a smile but was silent, waiting and watching the shadows lengthen, the dark come sliding down from the great peaks off to the northwest. And when it was truly night, it was the blackest night she had ever seen. It was like a midnight of the soul, a dread and terror in her heart. But when Kai spoke to her her faltering courage sprang up again.

"It will be easier for us to find and transport Quint away from the maharajah's palace if we have nothing else to worry about," he said. "I'm not speaking for anyone except myself, but I say it is not a place for women. You, Rosa, and you, Anna, will be more help staying here, ready to bind up wounds."

"No."

"But you are not fit—"

"Perhaps we are wrong," Rosa said, and because she had talked it over with Anna she let him know they were in agreement. "But we feel the chances of success are stronger if we are with you. Even if the maharajah's men loved him, still they would be loath to shoot a woman. Since they do not, they may refuse to fight us at all. Some men think it cowardice to fight a woman."

Kai shook his head. "Still, it seems wrong."

"If necessary," Rosa said tightly, "Anna can pick up Quint and carry him all the way back to this camp. Can you?"

Kai stared at Anna, who stared back. Finally Kai shook his head. "I doubt it, though I know I'd try hard. Perhaps you are right. Will you promise to keep out of it as much as you're able?"

"All I want is to be with Quint."

"Then I agree. But Quint will kill me for this."

"No, he won't. You'll see. We'll help you."

They formed a marching order: Ranjit in the lead, because he'd been there before, and Thomas bulking behind him as a protector. Then Kai, and then together Anna and Rosa.

They went along the edges of fields, through the clumps of trees near the palace wall, and thanked the night wind for the constant flutter and stir of leaves and rattling shrubs that covered their stealthy movements. They were all in dark clothes, faces shadowed by hoods. Cautiously, they approached the high wall, recognizable in the dark because of its light color; turning to the north, they went along it, moving out and around the patches of wavering light from torchieres flickering in iron cages. There were very few of the lights, for the palace of Burawanda was avoided by thieves. The harshness of the maharajah's rule was well known.

The door in the northern wall was easy to find; someone had opened it just enough to leave a streak of dull light in the shadow of the wall. They stood outside in silence, waiting for the signal of a blazing fire. Rosa was conscious of the rising wind that soughed through the tops of the trees, ready to fan the coming flames. Her heart lifted with it. Perhaps, she thought, the wind came to bring good luck to an imprisoned sailor.

There, a few faint cries. Then a growing sound of shouts and screamed orders, and the southern sky was red, with tongues of flame shooting upward from the Garden of Delights. Thomas reached over Ranjit's shoulder and pushed the door open; they were all inside with the door closed in seconds. They followed Thomas around the stables and saw another door open and close as a man leapt from a hidden entry in front of them. He ran toward the fire without looking around.

"Try that door!" Kai whispered, and Thomas ran to it, pulled it open, and went in. Ranjit, pale with fright, followed, and after him Kai. Anna took Rosa's arm and hurried her through the opening and into a narrow passage that seemed to lead nowhere.

Inside, solid blackness. A fitful gleam from a tallow lamp showed Thomas tying a man's hands behind his back, pressing a trembling finger against his lips to warn him not to make a noise. The man nodded frantically as Thomas finished and stepped away, rising to his full stature.

"Good luck," Kai breathed, his face close to the damp wall, "very good luck. This man is a prison guard, and alone. They watch the prisoners from here through this peephole. See if you can find a door along here, Thomas."

"Here," Thomas said. "Right here. There's an odor of dead air, smellin' of sweat an' rotten food." He reached out a hand and pushed. The section of wall opened, creaking eerily. He took a candle and went in.

Anna followed her son, her long arm reaching out for a ring of big keys that hung on the wall beside the door, and Rosa, trembling with hope and fear, was right behind her.

Kai followed, grabbing up the tallow lamp. "Careful," he warned Ranjit, who was watching through a crack in the outside door. "Don't show your face. You've been seen here before, and you were with a man they think is a thief."

Ranjit nodded, his dark, liquid eyes huge in his set face. "If they capture me," he said, "I'll not betray you. Go, and help the others—watch out! Someone is coming this way."

Kai inched along the wall toward Ranjit and the door, holding the tallow lamp in one hand. It was the other prison guard, coming back from the fire. Kai put the lamp down and fumbled for his knife.

"Step back," he said, his voice low. "Let me take him."

The man stopped a yard from the door. "Akbar sent me. I am to help you."

They let him in. "What of the maharajah? Has he gathered his soldiers together? What does he plan to do?" asked Kai.

The guard shrugged. "I do not know, sahib. Only Akbar spoke. But be quick if you can. The old man is a devil from hell."

Kai nodded and turned, going quickly down the passage and through the open door into the prison itself. Rosa whirled from the group and came to him.

"Oh, Kai! He is not here, and no one knows where he is! Where is Ranjit? We need someone to ask the other prisoners, and they are all Hindu."

"I am here," Ranjit said, coming in. "I will talk to them."

"And I," Kai said, "will talk to the guards." He went back to the passage and untied the first man, then asked the two guards if there was another way into the cells. They nodded.

"There are stairs," one of them said, "that go up to the durbar. They bring prisoners down those stairs after their trials. But no one tries to escape that way. There are many guards up there."

Kai nodded and turned to go back. He had been in tight spots with Quint before, and he knew the man would try. And likely Quint would escape if he could walk. Or crawl. They would have to find the stairs and go looking.

At the inner door, he stepped aside to let a thin, ragged man pass him, wavering but heading for fresh air. Then more emaciated prisoners came staggering through the passage, pushing for the outside door and freedom. Kai saw Anna unlocking the last of the cell doors. He looked back at the guards. "Aren't you going to stop them?"

The older guard shook his head. "No. The poor devils have had enough, may God show mercy to them. We'll be able to say with truth that someone released them during the fire."

Kai didn't answer. He was already through the door into the prison and following the others, who were rapidly disappearing through another door, one hidden away behind the row of cells, leading to a dark, steep flight of stairs. He ran to join them, seeing them mounting the steps, seeing the flicker of candles, one in Thomas's big hand as he led the way, and one showing Rosa's white, frightened face in the middle of the group. Kai took a deep breath of relief and followed.

Rosa had never imagined a fear as strong as she felt now. *Where was he?* Hidden away from his tormentors, dying in a dark corner alone. . . . Trembling, she dragged her thoughts away from horror. She turned at the sound of hurried footsteps, her heart leaping, hoping to see him coming up after them, but of course it was only Kai, who had been questioning the guards. They went on, emerging in the huge, pillared room where Ranjit told them he and Quint had been the day before. There was the grandeur of pink marble columns wearing foolish friezes of silver tinsel and looping gold chains about them, and an air of cold disdain that seemed to emanate from the only chair in the immense room, a chair so bedizened with jewels and gold and embroidered satin pillows that it reminded Rosa of an old but very successful whore.

"This is the judgment room," Ranjit said in a low tone. "Only the maharajah sits, here. Others must either kneel or stand."

"Was Quint here long enough to examine this room?" Rosa asked. "Would he know where to hide here, and how to leave?"

"Yes, of course. Lord Spencer has a talent for that. Come this way, it leads out to the grounds."

"But would he leave?" Kai asked. "I doubt it. He came here for a reason; I think he would still want to find those jewels."

"He did," Thomas said, impatient. "Don't you remember? The jewels are missin'. An' he was caught outside. Perhaps some other thief grabbed them, or he could have hidden them somehow, in the courtyard. We'd best look there."

Ranjit looked fearful again. "But they—the maharajah's men—may find *us*."

Anna laughed. "We will say we were just passing by and came in to help put out the fire. Try to look innocent, Ranjit. Thomas is right. Lord Spencer wouldn't stay in the palace a moment longer than he had to. If he were able he'd be out and away, but if he knew where the jewels were, he'd stop long enough to get them before he left."

"Then," Ranjit said, "he will be between here and the door behind the stables, or at our camp. That is the door he came in, and he'd know it would likely be open. We will search for him."

The fire was still roaring, sending up high flames; the figures on top of the south wall were still dashing water on it from buckets handed along from those below. Hurriedly, Kai gave orders to spread out and look among the shrubbery and the many small houses built near the stables, houses for chickens, for laundry, for pigs, for coal.

They all searched, but it was Rosa who found Quint. He was lying unconscious behind the heavy shrubbery along the back wall, the maroon leather pouch under his hands. A flicker of light from the fire shone through the branches and touched his tousled black hair. That was enough for Rosa, who felt her heart leap in recognition, her courage return to full strength. She took a deep breath and dropped to her knees to push her way into the tangled branches.

But he was still—was he too still? Dreading what she might find, she crawled in farther and put her arms around him, felt his heart thumping hard beneath her breasts and knew he was alive. Weeping for joy, she crawled out again and ran for Anna.

Anna came, took the pouch and handed it to Rosa; then she crawled in and dragged Quint out, picking him up and cradling him in her strong arms. The others ran to them and gathered around Anna. They left the courtyard, shutting the door behind them, and struck off toward the river and the thicket, saying nothing but not bothering to be quiet, for the roar and crackle of flames with a counterpoint of hysterical screams from the maharajah, who danced in frenzied circles and rushed back and forth on the top of the wall, hid the noise of their going.

Chapter Seventeen

❦

*A*t the thicket, Thomas and Kai sectioned off a corner of the bigger tent and laid a foundation of small, springy limbs. Putting a thick pad over them, they stretched Quint's long body on it. Kai helped Rosa to take off his shirt and removed the makeshift bandage over the knife wound in his side. He washed the wound and watched while Rosa bound another bandage over it. It was swollen and blue, but Kai told her that was normal.

"The fever is because he's pushed himself too hard," Kai told her. "He always has. He thinks he's immortal." Kai's tired face gave Rosa confidence; he looked relieved, triumphant. She smiled, knowing he was a true friend. Not a Wiggins.

"Perhaps he is," she said. "I hope so. Go to bed, Kai. I'll wake you if I need you."

Kai looked at her questioningly. "But you need rest, Rosa. Let me take the first hours."

"Oh, no, Kai. You are much too large to fit on this pad with him. I am not. If he stirs or moans, I'll wake. If not, I'll have as much sleep as you. Now, be off."

Kai nodded and was gone. Rosa took off her outer clothes and stretched out on Quint's right side, pulling a blanket over them both. With an arm over him, her hand against his neck, she slept most of the night, waking twice to his mumbling in her ear. She gave him water, spoonful by spoonful, and when he went back to sleep, so did she. It was not until daybreak that he opened his eyes and looked at her, unaware of where he was but recognizing her. He tried to struggle to a sitting position but fell back.

"Tell me who put you in this dungeon!" he roared at her. "I'll have his head, damn him! Why aren't you at Simla?"

She blinked, smiled, and put a hand to his cheek. "Oh, good. Your fever is abating. We brought you here last night, my love. You aren't in that dungeon anymore. Stop yelling, and I'll give you water. Kai says you must have water."

Quint closed his eyes and groaned. "I'm hallucinating. I know I am. You aren't really here. I love you, my Rosamunde, loveliest rose of all the world."

"And I love you, my darling Quint. Now, open your mouth. There. Swallow, and you can have more."

"Kiss me."

Rosa braced herself on an elbow and leaned over to kiss him. When her mouth touched his he grabbed her and held her tight against him. She relaxed, smoothing back his hair, kissing his fevered lips, his closed eyes. "My darling, my love . . . oh, Quint, I am so glad we found you."

He opened his eyes and stared into the pure English blue eyes looking into his. "You—you're really here, then. Oh, God, they'll torture you, my love."

She sat up, frightened by his fear. "Oh, no, Quint! We're in the thicket. And our friends are here, too. Wait, I'll call Kai and you can see. Kai! Come in here, please."

Kai lifted the flap of the tent and came in, averting his

gaze from her in her thin chemise, coming to the side of the makeshift bed.

"I heard all that," he said, "I guess he really is hallucinating. Or," he went on, staring down into confused green eyes, "he's crazy. Which is it, Quint?"

Gradually, the look in Quint's eyes cleared. "Crazy," He said finally. "I admit it. I was stupid to try it alone. If it wasn't for a knife slipping off a rib the right way, I would be dead. And"—he reached a hand to Rosa, who took it and held the rough palm to her cheek—"I had such a wonderful world to lose. We're going to pay off old Fedruis Murad in our own money, my darling, and let it go at that."

Kai and Rosa looked at each other, mouths open. Then Kai laughed. And laughed. And went back into the main tent and brought in a maroon leather pouch.

"This," he said, showing it to Quint, "is what you had clutched to your bosom behind a bunch of shrubbery. Does it have any meaning to you?"

Quint reached out for it, then dropped his hand. "I'll not touch the damned thing. You, Kai, shall carry it until we meet its owner. I've learned its lesson: Never deal with a man who doesn't trust you."

In late morning they were visited at their camp. Both the maharani and Akbar arrived, bringing a physician to attend to Quint, who was still running a fever. The mother and son were tired and pale themselves and said little in the presence of the physician. But after he had given healing herbs and drugs to Quint and advice to Rosa, the physician left, and the maharani spoke intimately to Rosa.

"The maharajah is dead. With my help and the counsel of older men, Akbar will now begin to learn the responsibilities he will bear as the maharajah of Burawanda."

A picture flashed before Rosa's eyes: the ornately dressed maharajah screaming and whirling on the top of the wall, sending out waves of evil fury, yelling orders that could not be obeyed. She was suddenly sure of what had happened: he had danced too close to the flames and had fallen into their embrace. Had the Santal bonga spirit dreamed of fire? Chilled and uneasy, she put the horrible scene out of her mind as quickly as she could.

"I am very sorry, Maharani."

"It is for the best, Lady Spencer. For all of us. Even for him. In a short time he would have been put in a cell and kept there forever, in the grip of an evil spirit. And so we are beginning a new life, and we want you and your husband, and all of your faithful friends, to come to the palace and be our guests until Lord Spencer is able to travel."

Rosa smiled. "You are wonderfully generous, Maharani. But my husband's brother awaits us in Simla, and—"

The maharani took her hand, smiling. "This morning I have sent my Gurkha captain to bring Jonathan Spencer here. I believe he can persuade him."

Rosa turned and looked at Quint. He was still flushed with fever, but his grin glinted through the black beard. "I would like to hear that conversation," he said, "and see Jon's face. But he will come. It's a family trait to take the off chance in the far corners of the world."

The maharani's slanted eyes shone with amusement. "Good. Then we're in agreement. Akbar and I shall go home and see that rooms are prepared. Then I will send a litter and bearers for Lord Spencer, and a wagon for your goods. Have you enough horses?"

"We do, Maharani. We also have a camel that carries all we have. We will come at the hour you say."

"Come as soon as the bearers arrive with the litter," the maharani said. "There are empty rooms in our palace that have waited for years for pleasant company."

The maharani sent not only the bearers and the litter but also a brace of Gurkhas and a half dozen other servants wearing cotton dhotis and the long, flapping shirts that hung to the calves of their thin legs, and each a decorated woolen turban, woven in colorful stripes. They grabbed up boxes and bundles and helped to take down the tent inside the thicket. Four of them, using the utmost care, lifted Quint carefully into the woven litter, and they began the exodus.

Following the edge of the fast-flowing river, they circled around the soot-blackened top of the palace wall on the south and, expected guests instead of thieves, went in by the huge eastern gates. The Arab gatekeeper, who ran to open the gates when he saw the crowd and the Gurkhas with it, grinned at Quint on his litter and then bowed.

"You return in triumph, Englishman. May your wounds heal quickly."

Quint grinned. "I thank you for your good wishes, gatekeeper. I should have listened to your warnings."

The gatekeeper went a few steps beside the litter to answer in a whisper, "If you had, we would still be in thrall to a madman. You and your friends have changed Burawanda for all time, and all within these walls are grateful."

Quint was taken inside on his litter, up a broad marble staircase that served the upstairs rooms, and down a long hallway carpeted with thick, colorful rugs. He and Rosa had been given a large room overlooking gardens below; but on the south side the view, seen through billows of mal mal, a curtain material so fine as to be almost invisible, was of the Garden of Delights, seared and blackened by the fire. The scene made Rosa's heart heavy.

It was, Rosa thought after a moment, a thing better ignored. She moved to those windows and pulled the heavier side draperies across the view. As she finished pulling the last one closed the maharani came to the open door, wearing a wonderfully draped and tied sari in flame-colored silk trimmed with gold, and over her head and shoulders a shawl of matching silk so fine it was nearly transparent, its border thick with gold thread and tiny beads.

"I greet you, my friends. If there is anything you need or want, come to the door and clap your hands. A servant will hear you."

Rosa came to her and curtsied. "We thank you for your generosity, Maharani. Once all the baggage is put away, my husband will want a bath and clean clothes. Is there a tub?"

"There are bathing pools below, but with Lord Spencer's weakness I would say a tub would be best. We have one large enough for him. I will have it delivered and filled when you want it." Smiling, the maharani looked across the room at Quint and added, "I am sorry to say that the young women of the zenana have already left the palace, en route to Agra and Gwalior, and likely to another wealthy rajah who pines for variety. They were quite practiced at bathing a man."

"I'm sure I'll not need help," Rosa said hastily. "However if I do, I'll send a servant to find one of Lord Spencer's men."

"Very good." Still smiling, the maharani drifted away soundlessly toward the wide marble staircase. When she disappeared down it, Rosa quietly closed the door.

Behind her, Quint struggled with a laugh. "So, you

wouldn't have trusted me with the ladies of the Garden of Delights?"

"You flatter yourself." Pink-faced, Rosa made a small fuss over the boxes already in the room, taking things out, shaking them, hanging them up in the wardrobe or simply folding them again and putting them on hidden shelves. She discovered more and more shelves behind the heavy wall hangings, and she went back and forth, hiding the empty crates and bags, busily putting their clothes and personal effects on the shelves. Quint watched and finally spoke.

"We aren't going to stay here the rest of our lives, Rosa. Leave some of those things in their boxes."

She stopped immediately and sat down. "You're quite right. We'll be leaving as soon as you can travel, won't we?"

"Yes. We'll arrange a meeting with Fedruis Murad and return his uncut jewels. Then we'll be gone, back to England. Back to little Lundy Island. Does that make you happy?"

Seeing her eyelids drop, her lips press together, he was silent. His tone had been teasing, but an odd bitterness had crept in, almost as if he was making fun of her, as if he knew her hidden desire to go home and was letting her know he didn't like it. She rose from her seat and came to the side of his bed, kneeling and threading her slim fingers into his thick black beard, holding his cheeks, looking into his eyes as she spoke.

"I love you," she said, and kissed him gently. "I will go wherever you go for all the rest of our lives. But I have to admit my heart is sore. Even with the wonderful friends we have here—and I have none at all in England—I cannot help dreaming of home. Of Lundy. Of small green hills, and English gardens."

He put his right arm around her and held her close.

"Then I will take you home. And I'll stay there for a time. But I'll not promise to stay for the rest of my life."

She laughed, her eyes as soft as if he had given her diamonds. "That will do nicely for the present."

"Fine. When do I get my bath?"

Rosa jumped up, still smiling. "Now, m'lord. Right now."

As it turned out, she needed no help except from the men who brought the tub and the water. One of them helped Quint into the metal tub before they left, and when they came back to remove the water and tub, the man got him out again and over to his bed without any trouble. After they had disposed of the water and came back to take the tub away, Rosa shut the door and locked it.

"We need to rest," she said, taking off her simple gown. "We need to know it's over." Her soft voice eased to a stop as she looked at Quint, half smiling, half asleep. She crawled into the bed with him, pulled a pillow under her cheek, and put an arm over him. He was cool, his fever gone. Safe, she thought as she drifted off. All of us . . . safe at last.

Quint woke first. The windows to the west had only the billowing mal mal curtains over them; the filmy cloth that let in the colors and shapes of the world outside. The sky was a brilliant red streaked with purple-blue and a wreath of gold that marked the spot where the sun had dropped below the horizon. He watched it for a time, still resting, knowing he was healing as he lay there. Rosa's small body lay against his right side, clinging protectively to his chest, her face neatly fit against the side of his neck, and her black, fragrant hair was draped over his chest and shoulder. He had never felt as comfortable with a woman as he did with her. She seemed always to conform to his desires, even to conform to his body. She stirred, and then yawned, opening her eyes.

"Of course," Quint said to the air, "I wanted her to wake, and she did. Am I not a great magician?"

Rosa sat up, looked at the windows and slid from the bed. "How beautiful, Quint. Look at those colors." She went to the windows, wearing only her loose chemise and her gauzy petticoat, and stood there in the brilliant light, the outline of her figure drawn with gold and red, her mass of shining black hair tipped with jewels of color. Quint stared at her, at the clear lines and shape of her body inside the transparent muslin, the look of wonder on her face when she turned and looked back at him.

" 'Red sky at night, sailor's delight.' Anna said that last night, and it proved true. Perhaps it will again." She came back across the room and leaned over to put her hand on his brow. "Why, Quint, I believe you've beaten the infection. You're cool."

"Come back to bed." He could hardly get the words out of a thickening throat. He had never wanted a woman as much as he wanted her now. Right now. She drew away, intrigued but unsure.

"Your wound might open again, darling. It wouldn't be worth it."

"Yes it would. God Almighty, Rosa, I'm the judge of that. Get into bed."

"No. I'd love it, Quint, but I'm sure you shouldn't."

"I'll burst if I don't! Look." He threw back the covers and Rosa's eyes widened.

"Oh." Pink ran up in her cheeks. "Well, I . . . do you think we could manage some other way? Some way that's easier for you?"

"Yes! Yes, we can." He moved, sliding into the middle of the bed. "Now, take off the rest of your clothes and I'll show you what I want."

She smiled slowly, feeling the heat of desire gathering low in her belly. "I think I know, darling. I think I really do know. . . . But you may instruct me."

He let out his breath and smiled, reaching for her. "The first thing to do is to remove the rest of your clothes."

"I can do that myself."

"But I wish to help you, my love." His hands seemed as strong as ever, fastening on her waist, dragging her onto the bed, pulling the chemise off, untying the strings of the petticoat. She laughed with excitement, giving in, taking off the last of the clothes herself and leaning down to kiss him, her skin like shining, pearly silk in the last of the sunset light.

"Now, Quint?" Her soft voice was husky, ripe with wanting. "Now?"

"God, yes. Be slow, my love. Put a knee there. And there, over me. And . . ." His rough hands stroked her inner thighs, the hot, damp center of her body, then moved to the flare of her small hips, grasping, pressing her down, down and onto the quivering, stone-hard proof of his passion. She let out her breath as she enclosed him, took him in, settling across his muscular loins. She whispered to him breathlessly, still afraid of hurting him.

"Are you sure this will be all right, Quint? Does it bother your wound?"

He gasped with low laughter. "No, not at all . . . I feel wonderful. Magical. Taken by a hot little angel." He put his hands on her hips again and began showing her what he wanted, the slow, smooth motion, the heat, the tightness as her flesh swelled around him. And then they were gone, lost in the rhythm, the giving and get-

ting, the caressing hands, the low, sweet words . . .
and he eased her down onto his body, feeling her breasts
nestling against the soft mat of hair on his chest, feeling
her inner flesh lock around him and throb, coaxing for
his seed. Then came the muffled cries, one after another,
half from the pure joy of sensation, half from the prime-
val triumph of mating that comes from the deepest well
of instinct.

Afterward she slid down to lie on the rumpled bed,
tight against his right side, her hand on his chest, her
cheek on his shoulder. And from somewhere there was a
scent of spices, of a roast of lamb, of fruit and curry. She
roused herself, pushing herself up and looking down at
his dark face, barely visible in the twilight.

"Are you hungry? I think someone has left a tray of
food outside our door. Shall I bring it in?"

"Yes. Light the small lamp first and put on a robe."

"Of course. I do have some sense of propriety."

"Indeed? I hope it isn't catching."

Laughter rose in her throat as she wrapped a robe
about her. "You needn't worry. I am sure you are immune to such things."

She lit the lamp, pulled a table to the side of his bed,
and went out to get the tray. It was heavy enough to
make her cautious, but she managed it.

Quint smiled as she put the tray on the table beside
him. "Either there's a backsliding Muslim here or perhaps a lone Christian. Either way, I am grateful for the
jug of wine. Are you going to feed me?"

"Of course." She sat on the edge of the bed and arranged his pillows, packing them behind him. "There.
Pretend I'm your handmaiden, your willing slave."

"Pretend?" He looked offended.

She laughed, a soft sound full of pure amusement, warm laughter that was celestial music to his ears. "Oh, but you are healing fast, my love. Yes, pretend only. I will not always be your slave. Here, open your mouth."

Chapter Eighteen

———— ❦ ————

It was after dark when the Gurkha captain brought the Honorable Jonathan Spencer to the Burawanda palace, and to the attention of the maharani, who greeted him courteously and informed him that his brother, Lord Spencer, was resting and would see him in the morning. Jon looked at the maharani's firmly decisive face and accepted that as an ultimatum. Not even his brother would be allowed to see Lord Spencer until Lord Spencer awoke and made his wants known.

Jon thanked her, bowed to kiss her hand, and expressed his joy in being asked to be her houseguest while his brother regained his health. He thought but did not say that he had been a houseguest here for some little time during the past year, and that the accommodations then were not quite up to snuff. He felt that the maharani's sense of humor might not be keen enough to appreciate the joke.

Once shown to his room and provided with a tray of food, he realized he was exceptionally tired from his first trip since his rescue, and that bed was where he should be. He got into it and slept dreamlessly all night. Awakened by a knock at his door, he yawned, stretched, grabbed his greatcoat as the nearest thing to a dressing robe, and went to the door, opening it and looking down at the new maharajah.

"I came to welcome you," Akbar said stiffly, "and tell you I intend to make up for your months in our dungeon in the only way I can. The maharani agrees that we will give you a cup of jewels from my father's collection for every month you were held in the dungeon. If you feel that is not enough, you must say so now."

Jon stared down at him, amazed. Then he thought about it, and decided the boy must be speaking of inferior jewels. But even so, the offer was more than handsome. He bowed politely, pulling his greatcoat close around him.

"I have no objection to your plan, Your Royal Highness. It seems very fair to me."

Akbar grinned, his teeth white in his dark face, the look in his eyes firm and satisfied. "And to me. We shall leave it at that." He turned and started for the center stairs, looking back once to add, "It's just 'Your Highness,' Spencer. 'Royal' is an English affectation."

Startled, Jon nodded. "Uh . . . thank you, Your Highness." He watched the boy as he joined the two Gurkha soldiers at the head of the stairs and started down between them. Then Jon stepped back into the bedroom and closed the door. Four months. *A quart of jewels!* He grabbed up his clothes and rapidly put them on. Quint would be beside himself.

Quint and Rosa were finishing breakfast when Jonathan, shown the way by household servants, knocked and asked to come in. Rosa slid from her chair and went quickly to the door and opened it, giving Jon a warm hug.

"You look wonderful, Jon! How quickly you've regained your health. Come, are you hungry?"

"I could eat a horse. Quint!" He was across the big room, grabbing Quint's shoulder, staring at him with a frown. "You've got one hell of a bandage there—was it a deep wound?"

Quint shook his head, smiling. "Not deep, Jon. Just too close to vital parts. I was lucky. Rosa is right—you look like yourself, ready to go. Ready to take a chance again. But sit down, have some of this fruit and grilled meat. You need to build up your strength."

It took some time to tell Jon what had happened, and how it was that now, with the maharajah gone, the Burawanda palace, its soldiers and servants, along with the population of miners and farmers in the valley, were under the benevolent rule of the maharani and her son, Akbar.

"Then the old man was truly possessed by evil spirits?" Jonathan asked, "Or was it, as I truly believe, a case of virulent hate and unlimited power?"

Quint gave him a faint smile. "There are no spirits as evil as virulent hate and unlimited power, I agree. But it helps his wife and son to believe his actions were not his fault, that he was taken over and couldn't stop himself when he was in a rage. I would not tell them otherwise. They have suffered enough."

Jon grinned. "And so did I, and I am rich beyond belief. I have been promised a cup of uncut jewels for every month I lay in the Burawanda dungeon. I have never held a whole quart of jewels, have you?"

Quint drew in his breath and then laughed, letting it all out. "My brother," he said, turning to Rosa, "fell into a mud puddle at the age of two and came out with a gold sovereign stuck to his chin. Clearly, good luck still sticks to him." He looked at Jon, grinning. "Who offered you that?"

"The maharajah himself. May he reign forever."

They were still amazed and laughing as Kai opened the door and came in, dressed for riding. Quint's laughter died away. He stood, though the effort drained the color from his face, and extended a hand.

"You're leaving, Kai? I suspected as much when you sent me that note. Why? All of us will be going soon."

"I know." Kai's handsome, sensitive face reflected a half dozen regrets. "But there is one thing that must be done before you sail up the Red Sea to Egypt. It is a safe thing for me to do—and could be fatal for you. I am going to see Fedruis Murad and explain to him that you have taken his jewels from the lying maharajah of Burawanda and will be returning them to him on your way to Alexandria. And since Murad and I are friendly, I will wait there for you at Jidda, so there will be no mistake."

Quint grinned without humor. "Have I acquired a nursemaid to keep the naughty boys away? Or have you lost faith in me, Kai? I can take care of myself."

Kai met his angry gaze steadily. "That is most likely true. However, there is more to be considered now. You are not alone. You have a family."

Rosa gasped soundlessly, staring at Kai from her seat just behind Quint. What else would Kai say? She shook her head, a tiny, negative movement no one but Kai seemed to notice. And, she thought, thank God he did. He smiled and moved closer to Quint, putting a hand on his shoulder.

"Sit down, friend. You'll be fine in another week, and a few weeks after that I will be watching for you from Jidda's tower. For you, your lovely wife, and your extremely wealthy brother, the Honorable Jonathan Spencer."

Jon got to his feet, bowed left and right, and sat down

again, beaming. "At last," he said, "my talents are recognized."

Easing himself back down into his chair, Quint gave Jon a critical look. "What talents?"

Jon gave him a wide smile. "My foremost talent is acquiring wealth without working. Believe me, I will be envied all over the world. Now, tell me what you want done, Quint, and I'll do it. I feel fine."

After a moment of doubt, Quint gave in. "It's true that there's a lot of ground to be covered in the next few weeks, and I need a majordomo. Wiggins was always the man for getting things organized, and he's gone. Start with the animals, Jon. And the wagon. Thomas knows where it is. All of us will help, but you will organize. Will you take it on?"

"Of course. It's as good as done. Don't give it another thought." Jon stood and shook Kai's hand in turn. "And you don't have to worry about him, Kai Bey. I grew up a bit while vegetating in a dungeon."

Kai nodded. "A lesson in survival is a useful thing. You came through it nicely, Jon. I have an hour before I leave; I'll give you a hand with beginning your lists if you like. You've a number of people and animals to plan for."

"Good. Come, we'll go to my room where we can talk, and where I can ask a servant to bring me something to eat. One of the things I learned in the dungeon was that when food was offered you ate it; when it was gone you asked for more. I am now about to enjoy my second breakfast."

Two weeks later the train was assembled in the courtyard of the Burawanda palace. The camel had been sold in the village below, and the wagon, with Thomas as driver, was loaded with food, clothing, grain, and dried dates, and the huge clay pots of water. There were dray horses to pull the laden wagon, two riding horses tied on behind as extras, and five saddled horses waiting to be ridden.

Inside the palace, Rosa and Anna were alone in the room Anna had been given. It was a spacious, airy room with a huge bed and soft rugs underfoot. Anna stood at a window, looking down at the train of people and horses and the loaded wagon that would set out in minutes. Rosa was pale, her eyes wet, and Anna's heavy face was lined with sorrow. But when she spoke, she managed a smile.

"You will say I am dead, my lady, and my sins forgiven. And I will say penance for forcing you to lie again."

"You never forced me, Anna, nor did you need to. I would lie fifty times over to save your life, and you well know it. I am going to miss you as much as I miss my mother, and I loved her well." She went to the huge woman and hugged Anna hard. "You are in the right place. The maharani will be more than kind; and you will look after her, along with her Gurkhas. This is an excellent arrangement for everyone. And now I—I must go, for the train is waiting." She turned toward the door and then turned back again, flinging her arms around Anna once more. "I will never forget you, my dear friend. Never!" Rosa hurried away, wiping her eyes.

Coming out into the bright sunlight, Quint squinted at the train, counted horses, looked around and nodded at Jon, standing with the gatekeeper. "Fine, Jonathan. Couldn't be better. Where are the others?"

"Minding their manners," Jon said. "Saying their good-byes. It's a long way home from here, and they may never see each other again. I feel a bit sentimental myself." He paused. "Ah, did you know that Anna is staying here?"

"What! Anna Castner is part of the family, just like Thomas. We can't go home without her."

Thomas turned on the wagon seat and looked at Quint. "She knows what she wants, Lord Spencer. Let her be. My mother is respected here an' will have a good life."

"But Rosa loves her, Tom."

"And so do I. Enough to let her live where she's happy."

Quint turned and strode rapidly toward the palace, slowing as he saw Rosa coming out, head bent, fastening her riding gloves securely. When she looked up, she smiled at Quint, but he saw the tears on her cheeks. He went to her and took hold of a slender wrist.

"What in hell is this balderdash about Anna? She's your bond servant, isn't she?"

"Not now. I have given her her freedom." Rosa's eyes came up to him, a burning blue. "Don't question me, Quint. I do not wish to speak of it."

He opened his mouth and shut it again. Indeed she was not always the devoted handmaiden, the willing slave. Sometimes she was a woman he didn't know. He took her arm and walked with her to the horses. Jonathan and Ranjit were already mounted, riding slowly toward the gate, and when Quint gave Rosa a leg up and mounted his own horse, they followed in silence, leaving the big horse intended for Anna. Behind them, they heard Thomas slap the reins and call to the dray horses, and then the squeak and rub as the wagon began rolling.

The gates opened wide. The gatekeeper, standing on the wall, grinned at them and waved them on. He called out to Quint, "You have an audience, Englishman! Look!"

Quint did and grinned himself. Akbar was leaning

out the window of the gatekeeper's lookout, waving good-bye as they passed beneath him.

"May you live forever, Lord Spencer!"

Quint made him a sweeping bow from his saddle. "And you, Maharajah, may you live to become the greatest ruler of all time, so that all praise you."

Akbar's smiling face was suddenly determined. "I shall try, my friend. I shall try!"

They made no stop at Simla. During the past week Quint and Jonathan had gone there, had made their formal visit to Lord Eden, and had reported the death of the maharajah of Burawanda. When Eden questioned the ability of the new ruler, ten-year-old Akbar, they had hastened to say that his mother, a Nepalese princess, had all in control. They mentioned the Gurkhas, and Eden had stopped questioning them. His last remark was that they'd picked a poor time to travel, considering the southwest monsoon.

"We'll have a week or two of dry desert heat in Rajasthan," Quint had answered. "After that, the rains will be welcome. We do have an enclosed wagon and tents."

Now, looking around at the train, Quint was satisfied. Rosa would have to take care of herself on this trip, with no maid to brush her hair or to shake out her wrinkled clothes. But as they left, he saw her face gradually lose the sadness of leaving Anna and begin to brighten. And as they passed the road up to Simla and turned down into the foothills, she looked at him and smiled. There were no tears in her eyes; they were brilliant with happiness.

"We're on our way," she said, "we're headed home. If I complain, remind me of that."

Through Rajasthan they wore the loose white garments again, against the hot breath of the desert just north of them. Then they changed as the rains began.

The days grew longer and longer; the pace slow in the deep mud. Camping was miserable. When the chance came to stay at any kind of inn, they took it. But no one complained, least of all Rosa. And finally, after five miserable weeks, they came through the last of the small passes to the narrow coastal plain and saw the Vindhya mountains looming to the east, which proved they were no more than hours from the sight of the Gulf of Khambhat and the Arabian Sea, and perhaps a day and a half from Bombay. Jonathan set up a cheer, which the rest of them echoed.

"If we ever get back to true civilization," Jon said afterward, "I am going to luxuriate in it. I'll roll in it, like a cat in catnip." He reached over and rumpled Rosa's long hair. "What about you, pretty lady?"

She only smiled, her eyes on Quint. He had turned to look when Jon spoke and frowned when he saw him rumple her hair. But he said nothing, turning back and going on in the lead. It was late that night when they found a place to stay, a place that offered baths and spicy foods as well as decent beds. Tired as they were, they set up a ragged cheer when Quint came out and told them the place was clean and had empty beds.

"And we," he told Rosa, "have a room to ourselves."

"Wonderful!" She was tired enough to sleep on a floor, but having a room of their own with a bed was amazing luck. All of the other places had rooms full of pallets, and one slept in a sort of exhausted daze, trying not to listen to the snores, the arguments, the sounds of awkward lovemaking.

Inside, a Maratha woman, tall, sweet-faced, well versed in welcoming confused Englishwomen, assisted Rosa in her bath. She put aside her shawl of thin red silk bordered with stripes of deep purple and gold, washed Rosa's long, thick hair, and rinsed it twice. Wrapping the wet hair in a towel, she offered to continue with her back. Rosa smiled but refused.

"I can do it, thank you."

The woman nodded and left, coming back as Rosa stepped from the tub and picked up a towel. The woman smiled, put a hand on her own belly and pointed at Rosa's gently curving one.

"Baby?" she asked, and added, "I, too."

Stunned, Rosa stared at her. "No baby," she said, shaking her head. "Don't say it to others, please."

Later, in bed, she wondered if any of the men in their party had noted that small bulge and decided they wouldn't. Her waist was still small, and her wide gathered skirts concealed her lower belly perfectly. Then, when Quint got in with her and put his arms around her she forgot it. She could forget anything in his arms.

"It's been so long." She sighed, and held him tight. "I love you, Quint. Are you awfully tired?"

She felt his cheek move against hers and knew he was smiling. "Not that tired. Are you?"

"I'm tired of no privacy, no chance even to talk without others hearing. But I'm not too tired for love."

"Nor I," he said, and turned toward her, wrapping her tight. "In fact, I am in dire need of it. I am foolish enough with desire to resent my own brother. When he touched your hair today, I was ready to call him out."

"Oh, Quint. He's only a boy."

"Is that so? He's three years older than you, wife."

"Well, he certainly doesn't act like it. Anyway, he means no . . . no harm, Quint. Quint? What are you *doing?*"

He laughed, his voice muffled in her hair. "I should think you'd know by now, my love, my little love. Give to me, my darling, let me in. Let me have all of you."

"Yes, darling. But you must give to me, first." Her

hands moved over him, pushing him gently onto his back, her fingers smoothing down his muscle-ridged belly, finding huge heat and quivering hardness, moving over it, circling it with her fingers, soft and teasing, then leaving it to stroke the inside muscles of his thighs, slowly, slowly . . . knowing what he wanted, not giving it but teasing, teasing . . .

"Rosa." His voice was shaky, "Rosa? What are *you* doing?"

She laughed and rolled up over him, her small face filled with joy, her black hair making a fragrant tent over their faces. "I should think you'd know by now— oh! Oh, *Quint* . . ."

It was the first good night's rest they'd had for weeks, but all of them were up at dawn, packing their bundles on their horses and laughing, making jokes, clapping each other on the back in the sheer happiness of being closer to home. And they rode hard all day, coming into the streets of Bombay at dusk. They went first to the port and called on the dockmaster to inquire about the next steamer out. The dockmaster, a heavy Englishman with a cheerful grin, laughed at the question.

"There she is," he said, pointing at a steamer vaguely seen through the darkening twilight. "She leaves at noon tomorrow. Better see the captain now. He's aboard."

Tired as he was, Quint nodded. "I will. We are anxious to leave as soon as we can. If he hasn't enough cabins, when will the next one be coming in?"

"Two weeks."

Quint looked around at the rest of them. "Pray," he said, only half in jest. "Are you coming with us, Ranjit?"

Ranjit's white teeth flashed in a grin. "Not this time, my lord. I must gather courage again."

"Then we only need two double cabins. Wait here. We'll see how our run of luck holds." He strode toward the ship.

They waited, Thomas sitting on the wagon seat, the rest of them still on their horses, with Jon holding the reins of Quint's stallion. Tired to the point of exhaustion, they were quiet, staring at the white shape of the ship. Finally, the dockmaster spoke.

"Aren't you the group that came in here close to four months ago? You had a great big woman with you. Biggest woman I ever saw, bar none. What happened to her?"

Everyone looked at Thomas. He answered after a moment. "That was my mother. She . . . died on the trip, sir."

"Oh! Say, I'm sorry I spoke. Didn't intend to cause pain. Must have been a terrible shock. She looked well, I thought."

"Yes," Rosa said, "it was very sudden." She lapsed into silence again as Quint appeared out of the darkness, smiling.

"We've got our cabins. Now we'll see about dinner."

Ranjit, confused by what Thomas and Rosa had said, spoke up quickly to end the tension. "We'll stop at the city market and buy some food. Shulbita will cook for all of us. She'll be happy to do it."

It was like a meeting of lifelong friends. Having seen Shulbita's delight in the flowers she took to her home the first time they went there, Rosa took her a great bouquet of pure white jasmine and roses like red velvet, along with fresh food from the city market. The dinner was delicious, Shulbita was happier than ever. Having Ranjit back to stay made her glow.

"Our mother," she said to Rosa, "misses her son. She will be happier, knowing he is safe. And so will I."

There was no privacy at the small home; no way to sleep apart from the others, but neither Quint nor Rosa mentioned the cabins waiting on the ship. They stayed and listened to Shulbita's songs of love, and when they were over they lay on pallets among the others, feeling companionship and trust and a pang for the uncertain future. Leaving Ranjit was almost as hard as leaving Anna, Rosa thought, yet they were both in their right places, safe and happy.

The ones leaving were up early, when the mists from the great harbor were still thick enough to send drops rolling down the sleep-warm skin of their cheeks. Ranjit came to Rosa when Thomas, Jon, and Quint went to saddle the horses. He stood close, speaking softly.

"If someone came to me and asked for the big woman, what should I say?"

"Say that you heard she died, Ranjit. She wants it so. She is happy where she is. And safe. The maharani values her."

"That is all I need to know. I will do as you say."

"Good. You are a real friend, Ranjit. Will you come to England again?"

"When Lord Spencer sends for me, I will be there."

It took time to unload the wagon, but it was done and the wagon lifted aboard the steamer in time to sail. When the engine rumbled and let off steam in the three blasts that meant the ship was leaving, Rosa went to the rail and waved to Ranjit and Shulbita. Quint joined her, browned again and healthy after the long trip, his tall, muscular body clothed in thin cotton trousers and shirt. She envied him his comfort.

"Late June on the Arabian Sea is like floating on boiling water in a cookpot," Jonathan said, coming to rest his arms on the rail and smile at Rosa. "We'll be bouncing up and down in this west wind until we make the turn to the Red Sea. We'll be glad to get to England's cool shore."

"I dream of it," Rosa said. "I hunger for it. But first we have to get past Fedruis Murad. I hope Kai Bey has calmed the bloodthirsty animal."

"That maroon leather pouch will make him purr like a kitten," Quint said, and laughed. "He will probably tell me to take the stones along and find an honest buyer. But I'm through with him. He has no faith in my word."

"Now that is true," Jon said, straightening, "of both Arabs and Indians. Their friends lie to them, counting on their distrust of the English. My jewels will be sold in Europe." He strolled off, looking for more company.

Rosa sighed, watching him go and then turning back to Quint. "It will be wonderful to know that no one is lurking about and trying to kill you. But I am not looking forward to plodding through the desert to Murad's home."

"Nor I. But let's not cross the burning sands until we come to them. Kai Bey is to meet us at the Arabian port of Jidda. He may have some other solution for us."

Rosa looked out over the water. "Kai," she said, thinking of him and how kind he had been to her. "I have missed him awfully. He is a wonderful friend, both to you and to me." After a long moment of silence, she looked up at Quint and saw that his face was as still as a bronze mask. Only the green eyes, squinted against the sun, moved. They cut over to her face and narrowed.

"Kai is in love with you," Quint said with coolly cynical humor. "That pleases you, doesn't it? That's why he left early. He couldn't stand being around you any longer, unable to declare himself."

Rosa turned and looked at him in sudden anger. "Quint! You have to stop thinking that every other man in the world is out to deprive you of your wife. Kai was lovely to me, but he never did or said anything the least bit improper! He treated me like a sister."

"I know he did. He would. He also put himself in this tangle because of you. He was afraid Murad would find out I was in India and take advantage of the possibilities. Murad could have hired twenty assassins in Bombay for the price of one in England. And one of them might shoot you while aiming at me. Kai wanted to prevent that."

"That's insane! Besides, if any of that is true, Kai would do it for you alone."

"He would not. He would trust me to save myself."

"This," Rosa said stiffly, "is a stupid argument. I'll not listen to any more ridiculous opinions." She left the rail, walking rapidly to the companionway that led down to the saloon. There were wicker chairs there, and a few well-worn books. She sat down, picked up a book with a clean cover, and held it up in front of her face. Minutes later Quint's big hand closed over it, took it, turned it right side up and handed it back.

"I was not insulting you."

"Then you were insulting Kai. I don't like that, either."

"I was not insulting Kai. I think he has marvelous taste in women."

She wanted to yell at him, but there were others coming into the saloon, looking around and chatting. She lowered her voice.

"Are you going to stay in this place?"

"I am if you are."

"Then I'm going up to the deck again."

"All right." He stepped aside to let her lead the way.

She went, every inch of her back stiff as a board, angrily conscious of his sizable body lounging along behind her. "You could find another place," she said without turning, "and I could have a few moments alone. I . . . would like that."

"I wouldn't. I may have to be away from you often; this is my chance to make up for my absences."

"I will not dignify that ridiculous statement by arguing about it. Do what you will." Flushed and angry, she went to the rail again and leaned on it, keeping her eyes on the water and saying nothing. He settled beside her, his forearms resting on the rail, his expression amiable. She waited, knowing he would begin another argument soon. A quarter hour later, he took her arm in his big hand, turned her around, and walked her along the plunging deck to their cabin. She went with him without protest, conscious of the other passengers walking on the deck, but when they were inside their cabin she pulled away from his grasp and sat down on the edge of the bed.

"Why did you bring me here?"

"To show you something."

"What?"

"That." He pointed upward. She followed his finger with her eyes and saw a small version of one of the big reed fans used in India to keep the rooms cool. Such a fan hung from the ceiling in almost every room, and a small Hindu boy often took on the duty of pulling it up and letting it swing back for hours. Her eyes came back to his.

"A punkah fan? What good is it, without someone to pull it back and forth?"

Quint grinned, opened the curtains that covered the cabin window, then reached up and unhooked the fan, letting it drop down halfway to the bed. Slowly, it began to wave back and forth, creating quite a breeze. She watched it, her eyes wide.

"How does it do that?"

Quint laughed aloud. "It doesn't. The waves do it, rising and falling, making the ship rise and fall. And the waves never tire, as small boys do. Simple but effective."

"Indeed. Why, it's already cooler in here than it is out in the sun."

"My thought exactly." His eyes met hers, and in them she saw his intention. She jumped up from the bed, furious.

"So that's what you're thinking! First you accuse me of flirting with Kai, and now—" She gasped as his hand closed around her arm and held her still.

"I did not accuse you of anything, Rosa. I only told you what I knew and you didn't. You will be in Kai's company often before we leave Alexandria, and I thought you should be warned. Kai is a good friend of mine, and so far he has acted honorably. But any man can be pushed into rashness when he is in love."

Rosa's eyes filled with tears. "I hate this," she said brokenly, "I really do."

Quint smiled without humor. "Usually," he said, letting her go, "a woman is thrilled to know some man is wildly in love with her, whether she loves him or not."

"I am *not* thrilled," Rosa said, wiping her eyes and steadying her voice. "I like Kai far too well to want him to wish for more from me and know he cannot have it. And I am sure if ever he did feel an interest, he's over it." Thinking back to the day when Kai said he was leaving for Arabia and a parley with Murad, she heard his deep voice saying to Quint *There is more to be considered now. You have a family.* Thinking of that, she was suddenly sure it was all right.

Quint was simply wrong. A single man, she was sure, wouldn't find a pregnant woman desirable. Even if Kai was attracted before, he wasn't now. He was just more thoughtful than most men. And more discerning. Kai knew she was pregnant when no one else had noticed it. Rosa turned and left the cabin, heartsore from Quint's cynical remarks. How could he think she was secretly enjoying attention from another man?

Chapter Nineteen

❀

*I*t was evening before they spoke together again. The saloon, like the first-class cabins, was built above deck, and its windows were open to the wind. Meals were served there, for the heat made it impossible to eat in an enclosed space. Thomas and Jonathan had found a table with four empty chairs and were sitting there when Quint found Rosa on deck and brought her in. The two men motioned them over and Jon, who made friends immediately in any company, introduced them to the English couples going home from Bombay. One of the men recognized the name of Viscount Quinton Spencer, remembered his exploits at sea, and kept a conversation going on the art of privateering during the whole meal.

Rosa listened but said nothing, only watched Thomas drinking in the tales of chase and danger and remembered what Anna had said when Thomas, looking like a child at Christmas, first stood on the deck of the *Whistling Wind*. Anna had sighed and said, "Thomas will never be happy on land again." Excusing herself, Rosa left the table and went to their cabin. It had occurred to her that very possibly Lord Spencer would never be happy on land either.

A scant half hour later Quint entered the dimly lit cabin and found Rosa in the double bed, her small figure gowned in thin white muslin, her silky black hair loose and covering her pillow. Her eyes were shut, her breathing even, and with the punkah loose and swishing back and forth, she looked cool. But there was a tension that showed itself in the way she lay there, rigid as a statue. She was not asleep, but he knew she wanted him to think she was.

He sighed soundlessly, angry at himself for the quarrel about Kai. It was true enough; he'd known Kai Bey for years and he had seen the shock of discovery in Kai's eyes when he first saw Rosamunde. It was like his own feeling when, reluctantly, he had come for an unknown bride and had seen that lovely face, that small but perfect body. He thought as he took off his shirt and dropped it over a chair that it must have been a miserable situation for Kai during the past months. But he had acted honorably. And you, Quint told himself, have been unbelievably jealous for no reason.

Once naked, he slid onto the bed and gave himself up to the soothing rhythm of the long, easy waves rocking the ship. His eyes closed, he felt the sweep of breeze as the punkah passed over them, swung back and passed over again, cooling his hot skin. Beside him, he felt Rosa move, careful and slow, and opened his eyes. She had turned her back to him, and he didn't blame her. But he had no intention of allowing her to go on separating herself from him, creating the silent, unending war he had seen between other couples. Battles were inevitable, he thought, but constant, undeclared war poisoned a marriage. That was *not* going to happen to them. He turned and reached a long arm across the space she had created and dragged her back against him. She flashed up, trying to push away, struggling ineffectually with his muscle-knotted arm.

"Damnation, Quint! Can't I have a moment's peace?"

"You have had a half hour of peace at least, and I three hours of remorse."

She moved away and sat up, peering down at him in the half darkness of a moonlit night. "Remorse?"

"Indeed. I made a fool of myself, talking about faithful Kai. I was jealous. I kept thinking of him taking care of you while I was in the dungeon."

Rosa eased down again, facing him. "Anna took care of me, Quint, as always. Kai was never more than friendly and cheerful. Please believe that."

"I do." He pulled her closer, his hands hot through the thin muslin, his body hotter as he embraced her. He was suddenly thoroughly aroused, trembling with passion. "Ahh, Rosa, how I want you. Touch me, darling, let me know you want me."

Totally relieved, sure that he had finally understood that Kai was only a friend, had never wanted to be anything more, Rosa soared, filled with excitement. She laughed, a low, sweet sound that bubbled up from her throat. "Then I will, my love, my darling, sweet Quint." She knelt beside him and pulled her gown up and off, flinging it to the end of the bed.

"Now, where should I start?" She was leaning over him, whispering, her soft hands smoothing back his black hair, her fingers burrowing into his beard, holding him while her lips moved against his, her tongue licking inside, tasting, soothing. She felt the heat rising, felt his hands tremble and reach for her breasts as she straightened. She pretended to ignore his hot palms against her and leaned down again, searching through the dark curls on his chest, finding his flat nipples, grazing them with her teeth.

"There," she said softly, "we aren't so different, are we?" and her lips went to his flat belly, his muscled thighs. Her mouth was open and hot, moving over him slowly.

Minutes later his big body rose beneath her, flipping them both over so she lay beneath him. Laughing with excitement, she pulled him into her arms. He was panting, struggling to gain the mastery of her and himself, and doing rather well at it. In an instant he was between her thighs and pressing, huge and hard, pushing slowly into her tight heat.

"Witch," he said, breathless and tender. "Lovely, lovely witch. Love me, Rosa. Let me in."

"Yes, my darling, ahhh, yes . . ." Minutes later, she thought she might die of sheer pleasure—and believed it would be worth it, even so.

It took time to cross the Arabian Sea, for the southwest monsoon winds blew against them all the way and the steamer, even though the power was steady, had to battle its way to the Gulf of Aden and the sharp turn into the Red Sea. Then they traveled faster, but in solid, unrelenting heat day and night. After all the extremes of weather in India and Egypt, Rosa had given up complaining about it. It seemed better to dress in the lightest clothing possible, stay out of the sun, and never mention it.

Leaning against the starboard rail with Quint, watching the monotonous stretch of deep blue water sliding by, she asked when it would be that the ship would stop at the Arabian city called Jidda.

"Tomorrow," Quint said. "And we will be there all day. Not all of the ships that ply these waters stop at

Jidda." He straightened and looked down at her. "Could I persuade you to stay on the ship, my love?"

Her eyes looked into his, searching for meaning. "Why would you want me to?"

He smiled. "I feel protective, darling. There are all sorts of diseases in these crowded cities. I wouldn't want you amongst the people around the port."

Did he wonder if she were pregnant? No, for he'd ask if he did. She looked away, realizing for the first time that her health was important to someone besides herself. And not just Quint, another someone who depended on her completely. She smoothed her billowing skirt and thought of Quint's child growing inside her. It still seemed impossible. It could, she thought suddenly, *be* impossible. She had been frightened, worried, half crazy with fear. Anna had told her fear and anxiety could stop a woman's monthlies. And as for that little bulge in front, that could be the rich Indian food.

"In that case," she said, finally, "I'll stay on board. But you must promise me something, too."

"I will if I can."

"Be safe. Take Thomas with you to guard your back. I still don't trust Fedruis Murad."

He laughed and put an arm around her. "Wait and see. Kai will have him sweet as honey."

Fedruis Murad, sheikh of his own Nejd tribe, did not wait for Lord Spencer and the Honorable Jonathan Spencer to seek him out. He came, accompanied by Kai Bey, to board the steamer as soon as it made port at Jidda. He marched up the gangplank in flowing snowy robes, sleek black boots, and a white cloth held on his leonine head by a band of supple leather covered with jewels. More jewels sparkled on his broad chest and dangled from his belt on gold chains.

Quint saw the one-man parade as he stepped from his

cabin and let out his breath in a long sigh of relief. He turned and went back inside.

"Come," he said to Rosa, and took out the maroon leather pouch concealed in his luggage. "I will present you to our Arabian friend. He is on board."

"What? Are you sure he won't try to kill you?"

"I'm sure." Quint laughed at her expression. "Remember, he doesn't do his own killing. Come along."

She went with him, dressed as she was in a cool white morning gown with no embellishment but a line of lace around the low neckline and short puffed sleeves. Her black hair was drawn back and hanging in satiny curls on her nape. The gown was very high-waisted and the skirt very full, concealing the growing curve below. She clung to Quint's arm as they crossed the deck, her eyes wide as she saw the huge white-robed Arab waiting there with Kai Bey. She smiled at Kai, happy to see him again. And then the sheikh was bowing to Quint, shaking his hand, and then bowing deeply to her, his dark eyes assessing her, running over her like little black mice. She could feel his hot gaze on her skin; it brought color to her face and neck.

"Ah, Lord Spencer, your friend Kai Bey has told me of your recent marriage." The sheikh spoke excellent English. "I congratulate you sincerely. Your bride is beautiful and young. Surely your tribe will increase."

Frowning and puzzled, Quint looked from the sheikh to Rosa and back again. Kai spoke hurriedly.

"I have told Sheikh Murad that you believe you have all of his uncut jewels, Lord Spencer. Is that the pouch in your hand?"

"Oh." Quint's expression eased. "Indeed. Here it is, and I am glad to hand it over, Fedruis. A treasure that causes bad blood between friends is no treasure to me.

Has Kai told you the maharajah of Burawanda is dead?"

Murad nodded, hefting the pouch in a powerful hand, his dark face serious and sad. "It is true, Lord Spencer, that he who steals from a friend draws the evil eye to wreak his own destruction. Will you and your lovely wife honor me with a visit to my home? I have perhaps another venture that may interest you."

Quint tried to hide his true thoughts. "I am flattered by your invitation, Fedruis, but I must go on. Perhaps another time? And if you are ever in England, we will welcome you on Lundy Island." He held out a hand, ending the conversation.

Murad hesitated, then took the hand, smiling wryly. "You do not forgive easily, Lord Spencer."

Quint laughed and relaxed. "You are right, indeed. But I do forgive eventually. It depends on the damage done. Your assassins gave me a few problems, but thank God, they were all poor shots."

The sheikh's dark face was suddenly lit by a wide grin. "Except in one case, Quint. The man at Malta was undone by your lovely and courageous wife. He is an excellent knife thrower and is still grieving about being thwarted by a mere woman."

He stepped back, turned and bowed deeply to Rosa, nodded to Quint, shook hands with Kai, and without another word paraded back down the gangplank to join a clutch of white-robed attendants and stride away.

Silently, Quint, Kai, and Rosa watched the group move through the busy street lined with wharves and huge warehouses and disappear toward the city. Finally Kai broke the silence.

"I'll speak to the captain," he said, "and if there's an empty bunk, I'll get my bags and board now. I am extremely tired of hot sand."

Quint turned and slapped him on the back. "Kai, I owe you much. Not only for your help on our trip, and in the dangerous corners, but you also saved us from a week spent traveling on that hot sand. And it could have been a very dangerous week if Murad had doubted me. So I will reward you by giving you whatever you ask for, if I have it in my power."

"You have it," Kai said, and hesitated only a moment. "I want to see England. Is it possible?"

Quint's green eyes sharpened, staring at Kai's darkly handsome face. "Indeed, yes," he said slowly, "nothing easier. We're heading there at once. My wife is homesick." There was a subtle accent on the word *wife*, and a definite air of ownership as he put an arm around Rosa's waist. "Aren't you, my darling?"

"Indeed," Rosa answered, smiling at them both. "I look forward to it more every day." Now that she saw Kai again, she was sure Quint was wrong. Kai had hardly given her a glance, except for a smile and a nod when they had first gathered around the sheikh. She had put it right out of her mind and proceeded to dream. She felt wonderful to be on the way home, knowing there would be no assassins hunting for Quint, no insane rulers to capture him and put him in a dungeon. She sighed and then laughed out of pure pleasure. "Yes, Kai, you will like England. It's cool and beautiful, full of lovely gardens."

"And lovely women," Quint said, and laughed, slapping Kai again on the shoulder. "You may never want to go home."

The rest of the trip was miserably hot but thankfully short. This time, leaving Suez, staring out across the burning sands of the desert, Rosa chose to ride in the wagon, taking advantage of the thick canvas roof that kept off the direct rays of the sun. No sour, irritable

Wiggins was along, and Thomas kept an eye on her, glancing back from his seat as he drove to make sure she was as comfortable as anyone could be.

In the evening she rode beside Tom, on the wide seat. They were close in their loneliness for Anna; they often spoke of things that had happened to the three of them and laughed, or felt tears spring to their eyes.

"She did the right thing," Thomas said, late on the last day of rumbling along in the sand. "She's safe at last. No one would look for her there. But, I miss her a great deal. There is no one like her."

"I agree. And I will always remember her." Staring across the great expanse of glaring white, Rosa saw a line of brilliant green and pointed. "Look! We are nearing the fields of the Nile. Soon we'll be in Cairo. And then Alexandria and Malta, and—oh, Tom, perhaps we'll be heading for England within a week!"

That night they went again to the home of Kai's brother Nehmet Bey and after a good dinner retired to lavish rooms with soft beds and rich linens. Undressing, Rosa found fine desert sand clinging to her skin and clothes.

"Quint? Wouldn't it be better if we bathed before we slept? I remember a pool of running water here."

He laughed and swept her into his arms. "I too remember that pool, for good reason. Come, we'll use it again."

It was the first time for a long while that they had bathed together, and Rosa was sure Quint would discover her different figure even in the fast-falling twilight. The curve of her belly was hardly to be noticed, but her small breasts were no longer small, they had bloomed into creamy mounds with stiffened, dark rose nipples that caused a delicious pain when touched or rubbed. She waited, half excited and half afraid, for

Quint to ask the inevitable question. Undressing quickly, she got into the pool, standing in the deepest part with her breasts barely breaking the surface of the water.

Stripping off his clothes, Quint grinned at her, looking like a boy given a wonderful present. "Is it cold?"

"Cool. Just right, I think," she said, and smiled, thinking how happy he was. Rosa held out her arms as he plunged in and came to her, wrapping her close against his already aroused body. She kissed him, exploring the hot mouth inside the wet, curly beard, tasted him and found again the essence of this man she loved. She felt his hands stroking her round buttocks, sliding up to her waist, moving from her back to her breasts, cupping them in his big palms, hefting them, taking the hard tips into his mouth to roll and nibble.

"You are becoming more lushly feminine every day," he murmured in her ear, "more tempting than ever." He pressed against her, pushing her tight against the smooth wall of the pool, and when she understood what he wanted, she tilted her hips to his thrust and wrapped her slender legs around his waist. He entered her with a rush and a satisfied growl, deep in his chest.

"Be gentle, my love," she whispered, and instantly he slowed the movement.

"Always tell me if I am too rough," he said, rocking slowly, easing his thrusts. "I would hate myself if I hurt you now."

She had closed her eyes, wanting to forget everything but the motion, the possession, the way he felt inside her. She thought of the baby growing in there. "Oh, yes," she said softly, "yes. I would tell you, but, oh, *Quint!* Oh, my darling . . ."

He wanted to speak, to promise her the world, but her body had him in thrall. They clung together as passion swept them, making the water around them swirl, filling the dark air with soft cries of pleasure and a low, satisfied growl. Later they wandered back to their bedroom, naked in the moonlit garden, carrying their clothes, and fell into bed together, reaching for each other, moving close.

"Tomorrow," Rosa said into the warm darkness around them, "we'll be in Alexandria again, and Kai's mother will be glad to see us. There will be no men with knives up their sleeves, no dhows setting sail to burn the *Whistling Wind*. It's over, Quint. Our troubles are all behind us."

"Don't say that, darling. You're asking for more."

She sat up and looked at him through shadows and faint moonlight and saw the white grin in the black beard. "And you're teasing me! Admit it, now."

He pulled her down into his arms, fit her into the hard planes and angles of his masculine body, and stroked her hair, pushing it back from her face, smoothing it over his arm. "I'm not teasing you, my darling. I'm holding my breath. Things are too perfect."

The next evening they rode into Alexandria, made their way through the busy city, and arrived at the Bey home at sundown. Amarna Bey rushed out into the courtyard and hugged them all, tears in her eyes.

"The man Wiggins came here weeks ago and told me you had all been captured by a maharajah who caught you stealing his jewels. He had very little hope that any of you could get away. I thank God you did!"

"Kai will set you straight on that," Quint answered. His face was hard, his eyes narrowed with suspicion. "It's a tall tale, most of it. Where is Wiggins now?"

"I don't know. I haven't seen him again."

Quint went to his horse and remounted. "I'll take a

look around the port," he said, and looked down at Rosa. "Wait here with Amarna. I'll be back soon."

Kai and Thomas both remounted as well and went with him, silent and tired, full of suspicion. Their last meeting with Wiggins had given them a clear view of the man's character and his lack of loyalty. Wiggins had changed in India. That sultry and lawless country had burnt away his mask of goodwill for others and revealed an ugly, mean-tempered coward.

Amarna put an arm around Rosa's waist and led her back into the house. "And you are carrying a child, my dear! How wonderful that even in that hostile land you were able to conceive. Is Lord Spencer pleased?"

Rosa looked back and realized the men were too far away to have heard Amarna. She relaxed. "He doesn't know, Amarna. I haven't told him."

"Ah! And why not?"

"For one thing, I was not sure until yesterday. For another, I thought it might worry him. He thinks of me as a person he must guard at all times. I thought myself he might notice it, but so far he hasn't. I've decided to leave it at that. When he asks, I'll tell him."

Amarna smiled approvingly. "Very good. A woman knows these things. It is not necessary for him to hear it yet."

It was over an hour before the men came back to the house. Rosa, in the same room she had had before, heard Quint's boots on the stairs and came to the door to greet him.

"Is the ship still in good shape?"

His head came up, and the expression on his strong face frightened her. She went to him, catching at his sleeve. "Tell me, Quint. I see something is wrong."

"That old fool! I'll kill him if I catch him. The ship is *gone*. With Wiggins at the wheel, it's impossible to know where he is or what he's doing. Piracy is frowned on in these close waters."

"Wiggins took the *Whistling Wind* away?"

"So the dockmaster said. He described him well. He said a small, elderly man came to him and said the man who owned the ship had died in India, and that he was looking for a crew to help him take the ship back to England."

"That's easy to believe," Rosa said. "He was very upset and frightened when he left us there in Burawanda. And Thomas sent him flying."

"Thomas did? Wiggins must have acted strangely. Thomas admired the old man's skill."

"As did we all. But that afternoon Wiggins had changed. I think he was terrified. And I do know he was sure you were either dead or dying. India frightened him, Quint."

Quint put his arms around her and held her tight against him. "I suppose it did. God, I wish I knew which way he would travel."

"Toward England."

He drew back and looked at her. "Why did you say that? Did he mention wanting to be there?"

"No. He only said he was heading for the Red Sea. He hated India, and he wouldn't dare stay here amongst your friends after he took the ship. Maybe Malta."

"Malta! Yes, he'd feel at home there. He's too old to go privateering without a full crew, but he could make money running goods from the African shore and trading in various ports. All right. That's where we'll start our search."

"How? You must be out of money." She wondered if she should dig out her share of those gold pieces. Anna's share was still sewn into Anna's cloak, something the big woman could depend on.

Quint laughed. "One chip from a small stone in those cupfuls of jewels Akbar gave to Jon will pay our fares on any ship traveling from here to Malta, and with plenty left over. Come, let's talk with the others."

Chapter Twenty

———— 🌹 ————

$\mathcal{T}$wo days later, midmorning of the second day, they entered Malta's Grand Harbour again. The sun was behind them, shining across small sparkling waves to the docks ahead. The *Whistling Wind* lay there, sails drooping, her black sides dull, the lines tied to the dock hung with rotting seaweed. Rosa turned and grasped Quint's hand, looking up at his sun-browned face as he studied his ship. On one hand, he looked tremendously relieved; on the other, he obviously wanted to kill.

She turned and looked behind them at Thomas and Kai. Thomas looked as if his prayers had been answered, no matter the shape the ship was in; but Kai was utterly disgusted. He broke the silence.

"We'll be days just cleaning her up," he said, "and if he's left those sails to flap and tear, we'll have to have them patched or new ones made. Wiggins should be hanged from a yardarm."

Quint was silent, staring as they drew closer. "I don't understand," he said finally. "Wiggins isn't a man who would let a ship go like that." He turned and looked at Thomas. "You know how he is, Tom. What do you think?"

Thomas turned his broad face to Quint and nodded. "Yes, I know how he is. He has more affection an' thought for a ship than he has for a human. I think he must be ill or hurt to let her go like that. When we land, I'll find out."

"We all will." Quint turned to Rosa. "All but you, my love. I'll take you up to the Spragues. Mary will be delighted to see you, and I will bring Lord Sprague down to see my pirated ship. He may be able to throw some light on what happened."

Rosa inclined her head. She knew she hadn't a chance of winning any argument, and she didn't care. It would be delightful to see Lady Sprague again. Perhaps, she thought, she could apologize for the broken chair. Neither of them had mentioned it before they left.

The ship they were on unloaded at a bigger dock, far from the *Whistling Wind*. Quint left Thomas and Kai to take care of the rest of the baggage and took Rosa's bags and boxes along to Government House. Again Quint waved down a horse-drawn omnibus and they rode up the ever-rising, winding streets. Rosa looked at the wide gates of Government House and shuddered, thinking of that knife clattering to the stone pavement. Then they were there and climbing out, and the gatemen came running to help with the bags and boxes.

"I'll come in with you," Quint said, striding along the walk. "Robert may know something of this puzzle. He would recognize the ship."

Mary Sprague met them at the door, pushing past the butler to take Rosa in her arms and lead her into the foyer, talking rapidly and with a great deal of emotion.

"Oh thank God we were mistaken! We thought everyone had drowned! How were you two saved?"

"Why, we are fine, Lady Mary. We came in on one of

Malta's own ships this time and had a lovely trip. No trouble at all."

Quint spoke behind her. "What trouble did you think we had, Mary?"

"But Quint, didn't you know? One of the big fishing boats found your ship empty and drifting at sea. They brought it in, and Robert inspected it. There was blood on the deck, and the gunports were open, as if you had battled some enemy. We—we thought you all drowned or killed! Oh, it's such a relief to know you're all right. What did happen?"

"We'll never know. The ship was stolen while we were in India. This is wonderful luck, getting it back again. We'll be here some few days while we get it in shape to leave. Can you put us up?"

"Of course! I'll be delighted to have your charming wife for company." She turned to Rosa again, hugged her, and then stood back and looked her up and down. "She looks wonderfully well considering her condition, don't you think?"

Quint smiled at Rosa. "She always looks wonderfully well, Mary. Even in the heat in India she—" He stopped suddenly, looking from one smiling face to the other. "What do you mean, Mary? What condition? She looks fine to me."

Lady Sprague laughed. "And to me, also. But she is increasing, is she not? In a short time you'll be a father, Quint. I hope you aren't frightened at the prospect."

Quint turned and stared at Rosa, his puzzled expression fading. "Is that true, Rosa?"

He had that domineering look on his face again. Rosa straightened and spoke clearly.

"Yes, it is." She knew by his sudden stiff-legged posture that he was furious. It did *not* matter. He could rave all he wanted; there was nothing that could be done about it.

"Then, madam," Quint said, barely holding on to his temper, "why haven't you mentioned it before?"

Across the room, Mary Sprague was slipping through a door and closing it quietly. She knew Quint. He'd not hurt his young wife, but he was in a real temper and he would give her a dressing-down. Mary didn't want to hear it. But she did want to stay reasonably close; Rosa, she thought, would need a shoulder to weep on. Even as she slipped into the dining room across the hall and started to close the door, she heard Quint's voice rising into a sustained roar.

"You knew very well that I had decided to leave you in Bombay if you conceived!"

"But, Quint, I wasn't pregnant then! No, thinking back, I must have been. But I wasn't sure."

"When were you sure? And who did you tell? Don't lie, now."

"I don't lie! And—and I'm not exactly sure when I decided I must be. And I didn't tell anyone but Anna."

Quint drew in a deep breath, his face scarlet with anger. "But Kai knew, didn't he? He said something once that sounded as if he did, but I thought him wrong. You told him, didn't you? Were you bragging, or looking for his sympathy? Damn it all! You'll lie and say he guessed it, won't you? Didn't you realize you were putting the life of a child in danger? *My* child? How could you be so careless?"

Rosa gasped. "A liar, and careless? *Me?* I am no liar! And what about yourself, Quint? You could have been killed, and our child would be fatherless!"

"Not for long, by God!" Quint said, lashing out in a fury. "You would marry again—and in a hurry—if anything happened to me! You've got Kai Bey waiting in the wings, and he's nearly as wealthy as you are. Now go wipe off those damn bloody tears. You look awful."

Rosa drew herself up, so angry she felt at least six foot tall. "You are a damned bully, Quinton Spencer! In the last five minutes you have accused me of being a liar, a flirt, and a fool! Do not speak to me ever again unless you want to apologize. I will not listen to any more of your insults."

She whirled and left, slamming the door into the hall hard enough to make the paintings on the foyer wall rattle against the paneling.

Mary Sprague rushed from the dining room door and put an arm around Rosa. "Come with me, dear. You must be worn out."

Rosa burst into tears. "He hates me, Mary! He *hates* me."

"Now, now." Her gentle face full of sympathy, Mary led her toward the stairs. Behind them, Quint left the study and strode toward the front door. He turned there and spoke to Mary, carefully keeping his voice down.

"I will stay aboard my ship, Mary. I think it best."

Mary nodded and kept on going toward the stairs, her arm around Rosa's waist. The front door slammed, and Quint's boots cracked down the steps like a fusillade of rifle shots.

"What a temper he has," Mary said, almost admiringly. "He is a roaring lion when something makes him mad."

Rosa wiped her red face and nodded, trying hard to regain her poise. "He is. And I . . . well, I can lose my temper too. After all, the fire-breathing Beatrice Gilbert was my mother, and I came by it naturally." She winced at her own words. As an excuse for what Mary had heard, the statement was entirely too weak.

"Ah, so that explains it. Here, my dear, is a nice, cool room. I'll have the maid draw you a bath if you like."

"Oh, I'd love it! How wonderful."

Mary smiled. "You'll soon be sweet again, Rosamunde. I'll send up your bags." She started for the door, and turned back. "Who, if I may ask, is Kai Bey?"

Rosa sighed. Of course Lady Mary had heard the whole quarrel. How could she help it? It was likely the neighbors on either side could recount it word by word. "Kai Bey is an Egyptian, Lady Mary. Part of Muhammad Ali's court. And a wonderful friend, both to Quint and to me. We stayed with Kai and his mother Amarna Bey when we were in Alexandria, and he went with us to India. He was extremely helpful to us."

"And, I gather from Quint's unwise remarks, this Kai Bey is attracted to you?"

"He's just a close friend, Mary."

Mary sighed. "I'll wager you'll have a difficult time making Quint believe that, my dear."

Rosa stiffened and turned away. "I have no intention of trying. If Quint cannot believe I love him and am faithful to him, then so be it. I admit I was wrong to keep him in the dark about my condition, but he was so involved in his dangerous mission that I hated to add to his problems."

"Then he has been successful?"

"Yes. I am sure you and your husband knew all about it, though few others did. He rescued Jonathan first, then risked his life to retrieve the jewels stolen by the maharajah. Kai returned them to Fedruis Murad, and Quint's life is no longer in danger. It all turned out well —except for me. I am not the kind of woman he needs."

"Never say that, Rosa. He adores you."

Rosa gave Mary a small, bitter smile. "No, he doesn't. He doesn't even trust me with one of his friends. And he never will. This isn't the first time he's thought I lied to him. He keeps trying to believe me, but he can't. And I can't—I will *not* live with a man who thinks me a flirt and a liar."

Mary sat down on a chair, folded her hands, and looked at her admiringly. "Tell me, what can I do to help?"

Rosa gazed down at her, realizing what she had just said, and thinking suddenly that the wife of one of the two governors who ran Malta must have knowledge and power.

"I don't know," she said slowly. "I don't know what to do. It would be wonderful if I could just leave. If I could wake up tomorrow and find myself in London, I'd be fine. Once there, I can draw money on my mother's estate, which is mine, of course. Then I'd find a place to live, and hire a staff."

"Is your mother's estate large?"

"Very large."

"Isn't it under Lord Spencer's control?"

"No. My dragon mother did not believe in allowing husbands to take the reins of a woman's estate."

"Then who manages it, my dear?"

"Plimpton and Ruether."

"Aha! Then it is in good hands." Mary's soft brown eyes studied Rosa's pale, tear-stained face. "Then you would be in their hands, also, would you not?"

"Do you mean would I take their advice? Of course I would. Alan Ruether is like an uncle to me."

Mary stood up. "Then if you like you can be in England in less than a month, and the trip will be comfortable. There is a big full-rigged barkentine leaving the end of next week for the new Saint Katherine's Docks, and two friends of mine, both matrons, are traveling with it to see their grown children who live in London. They will be happy to take you under their wing."

Rosa clasped her hands and breathed deeply. "Then I am going! I will set Quint free to do as he likes, and I know he'll thank me for it. But I'll never marry again. I could never love anyone else the way I love him, and I won't settle for less. But you needn't tell him that. I suspect he knows it."

"But if you love him, why leave him?" Mary asked, puzzled, her whole round face a question. "He'll come around."

"Has Robert ever accused you of lying?"

"Heavens, no!"

"Of telling secrets to another man? Making overtures to one of his friends?"

"He knows I'd never do that."

"There," Rosa said, and sat down again. "There's the difference. Robert trusts you. Now tell me how to get in touch with these two ladies."

Mary shook her head. "I will take care of everything. Don't worry a minute. I know exactly what to do."

Every tap on the door for the next four days brought Rosa to her feet, wondering if Quint had come to visit her. Then the time to board the barkentine came, and Mary ordered out the carriage. They stood on the steps and hugged each other, their eyes wet.

"You can still change your mind," Mary told Rosa. "I know this is hard on you. Do you want to give him another chance?"

Rosa shook her head. "He has had more than enough time to cool down," she said, "and yet he has made no move to talk to me. I believe he bitterly regrets our marriage."

Even saying the words twisted her heart. But outwardly she remained calm and entered the carriage for the ride to the docks. Boarding the big vessel, she went right to her cabin and stayed inside, watching from the porthole as the ship coasted out of Grand Harbour.

The *Whistling Wind* looked like new. Her pock-marked dull black hull was again a shining ebony, her sails were clean and patched, the brightwork on her rails and mast shone like gold. There was no sign of Quint, but she saw Thomas on his knees, holystone in hand, rubbing oil on the new boards. It made her think of Anna, and tears came to her eyes. She dashed them away. Anna was free, and happy. She felt a stricken pride in that. At least she had done what she had started out to do—she had saved Anna from the gallows.

She took one last look at the sleek little ship and turned away, her heart plummeting down into dark depths, twisted and aching. It was like losing half of herself to leave Quint, but she must do it. What they had had was wonderful, but now everything was soured and spoiled between them, threatening to ruin even the good memories.

She walked forward as they cleared the inlet, seeing her two new friends, Lady Evelyn Killian and Lady Barbara Knowlton, both in their fifties and both delighted to meet a young woman just back from India.

"Do come sit down, Lady Spencer, and tell us of your adventures. Neither of us has ever been to that most enchanting bit of England's possessions."

With a soundless sigh, Rosa sat down. There was so little she could tell them, but she began. She told them of Simla, of course, with its cool height and cold aristocrats, and then the great palace of Burawanda—but never of the real things, the fear, the danger. No, no, only the splendor, the gorgeous gowns and jewels, the dazzling Himalayan peaks. . . .

Chapter Twenty-one

*N*ot quite four weeks later, heavily veiled and wearing a fluttering gown meant to hide her now burgeoning pregnancy, Rosa dismounted from a hired carriage and entered the waiting room at Plimpton & Ruether, solicitors. She sent in her name, and the office clerk came back immediately to usher her in to Alan Ruether's office. She put back her veil and went with him, her small body erect, her smile bright and confident, her heart aching at what she knew lay ahead.

Ruether met her at the door and put an arm around her shoulders to lead her to a chair. "You look in good health, my child!" His wise eyes ran over the arranged folds and layers of her garments and his smile widened.

"So, you've begun a family. I approve! Beatrice's courage and intelligence should not be lost for want of descendants. I imagine Lord Spencer is hoping for a son."

Taking a seat, Rosa breathed deeply and came out with it. "I'd like to keep this cheerful, Uncle Alan, but I cannot. I am here with more than one purpose, and one of them, I fear, will scandalize you. I want an agreement of separation between my husband and myself. We are no longer living together."

Alan Ruether was silent for a moment. Looking at him, Rosa wondered if the news had indeed scandalized him. She didn't think so, but with him it was hard to tell. He answered her calmly.

"You can't mean that, Rosa. I never saw two people more suited to each other, and so clearly in love. What has come between you?"

"Many things," Rosa said, and sighed. "No, I shouldn't say that. There is only one thing, but it ruins our life together. He cannot trust me. He believes that I lie; he has accused me of an affection for another man who is no more than a friend. I cannot live with that."

Ruether sat back and laced his long fingers together. "You sound like your mother, Rosamunde. Why can't you be like other young women, sweet and simple?"

"Because, dear Uncle Alan, I am neither. But I am in need of a place to live. Preferably in London until my child is born. Can we manage that?"

"Yes, of course. And a staff?"

"A small staff, yes. A cook, a maid, a footman. I'll need no more, since under these circumstances I will not be entertaining."

Alan Ruether took off his spectacles and polished them with his silk handkerchief. His jaw was set firmly, the creases between his eyebrows were deep. Disapproval was written all over his kind face.

"Perhaps you should find someone else to locate a house for you to live in, Rosamunde. If your husband asks me where you are living, I will feel that I must tell him."

"Yes, I know." There was a wry amusement in her suddenly unhappy face. "Men always stick together. If he asks, by all means tell him. He won't visit me, I'm sure. I hadn't seen him in over a week when I finally decided to come home alone."

"He deserted you?"

"No, I can hardly say that. He left me with Lady Sprague on Malta but refused to stay with me after a quarrel. I am sure he would have brought me home in his ship, but after an embarrassing week of waiting alone in the home of the Royal Commissioner, I—I wanted it over with." She wiped her eyes with quick, angry dabs. "I do wish, Uncle Alan, that you would take my word for this and ask me no more questions. I am quite undone by it all."

"I see." Ruether sat forward. "I'll not add to your sorrow, then. We'll simply proceed. Where are you staying now?"

"In Mayfair, as a guest of Lady Evelyn, widow of the late Lord Robert Killian of Oxford. She was one of the ladies I accompanied on the trip from Malta."

"I know the place, of course." Ruether made a notation on a desk pad. "I will begin the search for a house for you, Rosamunde. I should have several in hand by tomorrow afternoon. Come then, and we'll go through them."

She waved a hand, dismissing care, and stood up. "If a house is clean and in a good neighborhood, Uncle Alan, I will take it. It need not be charming or fashionable. All I need is a safe place of my own, and a staff." She hesitated, and then went around the desk and gave him a quick hug. "Thank heaven my mother had you for a friend! I don't know how I could have managed alone."

Alan Ruether smiled. "You would have managed, Rosa. I know you. You're just like Beatrice."

For the first time, Rosa heard a wry note in that kind voice. And as she left the building and climbed into the hired carriage waiting for her, she seemed to hear again Porter Ogilvie's sardonic advice to Quint. It had been something about not allowing her to turn out like her mother. She frowned, wondering if perhaps she had jumped to conclusions about Quint. Her mother had often jumped to conclusions and regretted it later. . . .

Riding back to Evelyn Killian's place in Mayfair, she kept thinking about those first weeks of marriage to Quint, about how the two of them had been with each other. Both hiding their secrets, afraid to be honest with a stranger, yet gradually falling in love, learning to trust, beginning to tell each other their problems. But, she thought for the first time, not every problem of hers had been unfolded and seen. She hadn't told Quint about Anna committing murder. She hadn't dared. Had he sensed that she was holding something back, and had he then jumped to his own conclusion? Had he wondered and then become suspicious? It was possible—yet surely he must have known he was the only man she cared for.

The very next day Alan Ruether came for her to take her to see a house he thought she would like. It was small for a Mayfair house, with only four bedrooms on the second floor and four on the third floor, where the servants slept. A tall, narrow house with a carved and arched and embellished entrance, it had a small garden in the rear and hedges in the front, with topiary figures of ladies in full skirts at each corner. The house was furnished, and a lease, Alan said, was available. Inside the floors were covered with the best of oriental rugs, and the tables and bookcases abounded with Indian brasswork. On the hearth there were three *surahis*, brass containers with long necks for carrying the sacred water of the Ganges, and on the mantelpiece were two temple hand lamps with their dippers. Rosa examined them closely and then, without speaking of India, went through the rest of the house without comment. When she returned to the foyer where Alan had waited, she asked only one question.

"Who owns this house?"

"As a matter of fact," Alan said, pinkening, "I do. At present I own several places in Mayfair. Some of them come to us from people who have, ah, suffered a reversal of fortune. Do you mind?"

"Not at all. I only wondered. It's a bit large, but it's quite comfortable. I'll take it."

"Very well. Are you still set on having only a cook, a lady's maid, and a footman?"

"For this house, I'll also need a downstairs maid. And I suppose I'll have to have a boy about to see to the coal and run to the livery stable when we need a carriage." She frowned. "A lot of bother, I think. But necessary."

"It'll take a week or so to settle, Rosa."

"I know. First, I'll hire a maid. Oh, but I do miss Anna."

"You won't find one like her."

"I know," Rosa said again, and turned away, feeling tears blur her eyes and not wanting Alan Ruether to see her feelings. She felt as if she had lost everyone she cared for. Quint, and Anna and Thomas. And Jonathan, who had won a part of her heart and was gone with the rest. "Lady Killian says," she added as they left the house, "that everyone is moving to the countryside since the smoke from the railroads has become so thick. Keep an eye out for a country place for me, please. I will have little use for the city once my child is born."

Helping her into the curricle he had rented, Alan patted her hand. "No worrying, my dear. I'll find a good place for you away from the city. But it will take time."

* * *

In ten days Rosa was settled in, and she thought herself as happy as possible under the circumstances. Her maid, Dorothy, was very young, but well trained and, more important to Rosa, intelligent. The cook, Cora, was fond of her work and very good at it. The house shone. Jobs in London were scarce with the social season over, and Betty, the housemaid, and Terence, the footman, made sure of keeping theirs by working hard. The errand boy, Billy, was Terence's young brother and was kept busy by both the cook and Terence.

On one of Alan Ruether's frequent visits he noticed a book of Spanish grammar on a table beside Rosa's chair. "What is this?"

Rosa smiled. "That is my daily dose of education, Uncle Alan. I write in my journal in the morning, walk in the park in early afternoon, and after dinner, I spend a time educating myself."

"Good." Alan Ruether's eyes were the same silver-gray as his hair, but today they seemed dark and uncertain. "Keeping both body and mind healthy is important. But what of your heart? Have you made friends?"

"You are my friend."

"You need more than one, my dear. I am an old man, and you need life and youth around you."

"When young Quint is born, I will have both!" Rosa's face lit up for a minute; she laughed softly. "He will keep me busy, I am sure of that."

"But you need more. Have you heard any news of Lord Spencer?"

"Uncle Alan! Don't remind me of my loss, please. I want to be happy with what I can have. Tell me, have you found a place in the country for me?"

"Not yet. But I will, I promise you." He hesitated. "I do have another question, and I'm afraid you won't like it. Lord Spencer is in London, and he has asked me to say that he wishes to meet with you. He is willing to agree to any terms.''

"No!"

"Don't be unfair, Rosa. It's his child as well as yours."

Suddenly pale, Rosa stood up and went to the window, staring out at the small garden behind the house.

"Later," she said finally. "After the child is born. Then he can see him—or her—in the presence of a nurse. I would not keep his child from him."

"Rosa, listen to me. He is anxious to see *you.*"

Tears came to her eyes. "No, Uncle Alan. I cannot. I will not. It is . . . it is just too hard! I was so in love with him."

"And you still are."

She looked at him in silence, knowing he was right. "Yes," she said finally, letting out her caught breath. "I am. And that's why I don't want to see him. I have to get over it. Past it. I must learn to live without him."

"Why?"

"Because I cannot live with him. He will never have faith in me. I've thought it all out. We had a wonderful, marvelous love together, and still he thought I kept secrets from him and told them to others. He loved me and then he hated me. He gave me the only love I've ever had except for my mother's and Anna's, and then . . . and then, he called me a liar and turned his back."

"He was a fool, then." Alan Ruether's sympathy was suddenly with Rosa. "You aren't the kind to tease other men."

She returned to the window and stood there looking out. "In one way, he was right. I did hide things from him. Perhaps he sensed that, and feared that the hidden things concerned him. But there were problems that were not all mine, things I kept secret to protect others, not myself. I could never be false to Quint, nor could I live with him if he doubted me."

She turned and came back to Alan, taking his hand in both of hers and looking at him directly. "Make him understand, please. If he wants a divorce, he may have it."

"Do you want a divorce?"

"It makes no difference to me. I'll not marry again. But he may want to. Or perhaps he will simply want to be free of any tie."

"I will tell him what you said."

Two days later, Betty answered the door, told the gentleman to wait, and went in search of her mistress, whom she found in the small library.

"A gentleman to see you, Lady Spencer."

Rosa's heart turned over, her hands trembled so that her heavy book slipped and fell from them. She bent and picked it up, opening it again and placing it on her lap, searching for a calmness she couldn't find. "I see no gentlemen except for Solicitor Ruether, Betty. You know that."

"This man said you would see him. His name is Thomas Castner."

"Oh!" Rosa threw the book on a table, leapt up, and ran down the hall, her full skirts flying. She swung open the door and held out her arms.

"Thomas! How wonderful to see you!"

Tom stepped in, shutting the door. He bent down and hugged her briefly. He was grinning all over his big face. "I had to come, Miss Rosa. I heard from Ma. You'll want to read the letter yourself. Here 'tis."

"Oh! Oh, Tom, how nice of you! Is she all right?"

"Never better. Read it, you'll see."

"Then come with me and sit awhile. I've tears in my eyes to get rid of."

They sat in the library, Tom on the edge of a big chair, still grinning, and Rosa alternately laughing and weeping, wiping her eyes and reading Anna's letter, written for her by the maharani. There had been a position created for her, Noble Protector of both the maharani and Akbar. At the end Anna said:

> *Since no one wants to threaten either Akbar or the maharani, I have little to do but enjoy myself. I wear silks and embroidered satin and have handmade shoes. When durbar is held, I am on duty in the hall to take convicted thieves and murderers down to the dungeon there. However, the dungeon is clean and the food brought in is good. And there is very little crime amongst the villagers, and none at all, I will tell you, against the maharani. Her subjects, including myself, think her a minor goddess. Continue to be worthy of your position with Lord Spencer, Tom, and be sure to show this letter to my dearly beloved little friend, Rosamunde. My love and thoughts are with you both.*

Beneath that, still in the Maharani's delicate script, was another sentence: *You have blessed me with a wonderful friend, Rosamunde. I thank you.*

"Oh, Thomas, I am so happy for Anna! I thank you so much for coming and bringing her letter. How was it sent?"

" 'Twas sent to Lundy, my lady, an' on to London by the staff there. She supposed all of us were there, since she had no way of knowin' you had left Lord Spencer. He gave me permission to bring the letter to you, so you could see for yourself that Anna is happy an' well."

"Then you must give him my thanks," Rosa said stiffly. "It was . . . kind of him."

"I will," Tom said, and unfolded himself from the chair, taking back the letter from her extended hand. He looked at her doubtfully as he pocketed the letter. "Is there any other message you'd like delivered?"

"None, thank you."

"Then I'll be goin'."

She walked down the hall with him and out onto the small marble floor of the outside entrance. There she took his hand and thanked him again. Thomas colored up and started down the steps, turning at the bottom to look at her.

"We'd all be a lot happier," he said awkwardly, "if you got over your mad an' came home. I wish you would, Miss Rosa."

From anyone else, the remark would have angered her. But this was Thomas.

"It isn't that simple, Tom," she said gently, and went back into the house. Sitting down again, she felt entirely different than she had before Tom came. She felt warm, connected again to Anna, to Thomas, even to Lundy Island. But thinking any further made her throat tight. She felt no closer to Quint. All she could see was that hard, furious look that came over his face when he found out she was carrying his baby.

No, she thought suddenly, he had been angry, yes, but the furious look came later, when he suddenly realized that Kai had known. He'd accused her of telling Kai and told her not to lie about it, which infuriated her. Then he had said it wouldn't have mattered if he died, for she'd marry again, and most likely she'd marry Kai —and then *she* lost her temper. She had called him a damned bully. She had told him never to speak to her again unless it was to apologize. And then—and then, she'd slammed the door in his face!

She stood up from her chair and went to the window

that looked out on the small garden in back and stood there thinking of her own hot temper.

"Perhaps," she said, half whispering, "I should have explained things better. Neither of us made much sense."

In the days following, Rosa entertained Lady Evelyn Killian and Lady Barbara Knowlton at tea and attended gatherings at their homes in return. She was thoroughly bored with the senseless talk of fashions and social events, though she managed to hide it and to pretend a gaiety she didn't feel. She yearned for the day when her baby would be born and she could leave the city and find an ideal place in the country. She often asked Alan Ruether if he had found a place, and his answer was always the same:

"There will be no problem in finding what you want, my dear. There are so many lovely spots available to a person like yourself, who has money to spend."

At times she felt that Alan thought of her as a spoiled child, but she also knew his affection for her never wavered. Then a day came when she saw pure horror in his eyes when he looked at her.

He had come to report a terrible, shocking crime, bringing the news himself rather than allow her to hear it from someone else. He was pale and shaken as he gave the footman his hat and cane, and he took Rosa's arm almost as if he needed steadying himself.

"Come," he said to her, glancing at the footman and the maid, who was dusting in the hall. "I must speak to you alone."

She was instantly terrified by his expression and his words. She put her cold hand on his where he clutched her arm. "It . . . it isn't Quint, is it? Nor Thomas?"

"Oh, no. But an awful scandal, my dear. A murder has been discovered."

Murder. Her throat closed up. "Oh, God . . . whose?"

"Wait. Let me find a chair."

For the first time, Alan Ruether looked his age. Rosa took him into the small library and made him sit down in a big leather chair. Then she got out a decanter of brandy, poured him a measure, and put it into his hand.

"There," she said, "drink it down. I can wait to hear the rest of it." She was shaking inside; she thought she knew what he was going to say. She could still see it. *Anna's strong hands, squeezing without mercy*. . . . She poured another glass of brandy and drank it herself, barely conscious of her burning throat. Then she sat down, her stomach on fire, and took Alan's hand.

"I am listening, Uncle Alan."

"You must be brave, Rosa. This . . . this atrocity is connected with your family—closely connected. Now, don't faint, for heaven's sake. It is bad for your baby if you become too upset."

She nodded, speechless. She was beginning to feel the brandy. It did seem to give her courage. She got up again and took down the decanter, filling his glass and then her own. They drank slowly and in silence, then set their glasses down.

"The body," Alan began, and belched. "Pardon me. The body, as I was saying, is that of your stepfather, Squire Brownley, duly identified by a gold ring on his left hand that had his name engraved inside. Also by his remaining teeth. There is no doubt of his identity. Besides, the body was found in the squire's garden, buried beside a wall."

"I see." She barely got the words out. She was shaking in spite of the brandy. "Was . . . was someone searching for him?"

"Naturally. *I* was. I had waited months for him to

write and give me a new address, and finally I sent a man to query the neighbors and others who might know, so I could send him his quarterly stipend. Then the constable at Bideford became interested. He wrote to tell me that the squire's brother had taken over the squire's house in lieu of debts the squire owed him. The constable had questioned the brother, who swore he had tried hard to find the squire but had found no trace of him. After that, I went to Sir Robert Peel for help. He was good enough to send two of his best men from Scotland Yard to investigate, only as a favor to me, for it was out of his jurisdiction. They turned up the body."

In spite of the warming brandy, Rosa was freezing. "I see. But you've mentioned nothing about the, uh, murderer, Uncle Alan. Haven't they begun to search?"

Alan Ruether looked at her with admiration. "Child, you are a marvel. Just like Beatrice. You haven't turned a hair or shed a tear. What courage!"

Rosa looked away. Inside her rounded belly her baby kicked and swam, bringing her back to reality. "I take no pride in that," she said. "Squire Brownley was not a lovable man, and I feel no great sorrow. However, the thing is shocking, as you say. Do the police plan a search for the killer?"

"Why no, my dear. The whole situation pointed to his brother as his murderer. The men from Scotland Yard arrested him when he couldn't show a will or a deed for the house. It was clear that he'd murdered for profit and hid the crime on the grounds. Undoubtedly he'll hang after the next assizes."

Alan paused, his attention caught by Rosa's expression of horror. He reached over and patted her clenched hands.

"I know how you must feel. To think that a man would kill his own brother is loathsome. No matter the bad blood between them, there is still the blood of brotherhood. But you must put it out of your mind, Rosa. You have a child to think of."

"Yes," she said, "yes, I do." She stood up and went quickly to the window, staring out and wincing as she realized what she had to ask of him. "Alan," she said, and this time she did not sound like a young girl, "I know Lionel Brownley. He is a wretch, but he would not kill his brother. He cannot be allowed to die for it."

Ruether shot to his feet. "What? What? Why, the bluecoats say it's a clear case. The two men hated each other."

Rosa nodded, her face pale and grim as she looked around. "They did. But Lionel didn't commit murder, no matter what the bluecoats said."

Wiping his forehead with a handkerchief, Ruether shook his gray head. "Rosa, leave this to the authorities. They know what they are doing."

"No. Will you do something for me? Will you send word to Lord Spencer that I wish to see him on a matter of great importance?"

Ruether let out a great sigh of relief. "Yes, I will. I certainly will! But Rosa, please say nothing about this to any casual acquaintance."

"God forbid," Rosa said. "Be at rest. I'll talk to no one other than Quint."

Chapter Twenty-two

❦

At breakfast the following morning, Rosa's footman brought in a note from Alan Ruether along with two invitations to tea on separate days, one from Lady Killian and one from Lady Knowlton. Rosa set the invitations aside and opened the note with trembling fingers.

> *Lord Spencer will attend you today at one o'clock. I have told him the story of what has occurred, and he is aware of your feelings in the matter. I will leave the rest of it to you. I hope you will come to a conclusion satisfactory to you both.*

Determined to remain cool, Rosa picked up and read the invitations. When she finished her fruit and a dish of porridge, she took her note and invitations to the library and painstakingly wrote out polite regrets for the teas. These she gave to the footman to post. Then and only then did she turn and run up the stairs to her room, where she spent the rest of the morning hours trying on her best gowns and asking Dorothy which one was most appropriate and dignified for a woman soon to give birth. Dorothy, young and full of dreams, was amazed by the change in her mistress.

"You look beautiful in any one of them, my lady. Perhaps more glowing in the dark red. We've time to wash and dress your hair, if you like."

"I haven't a thought of attracting Lord Spencer, Dorothy. He is my estranged husband, not a suitor. But still, perhaps I should let you wash my hair. The smoky air dulls it, don't you think?"

"Indeed. And your hair is so thick and springing. I'll brush it into shape while it's damp. Excuse me while I heat some water."

At precisely one o'clock Rosa paraded down the curved staircase in the dark red silk faille held out by hoops and petticoats and trimmed with matching silk ruffles. The loose dark red sleeves were complemented by huge billowing undersleeves of white silk that banded around her wrists and made her small hands look even more delicate. Her hair was knotted high on the back of her head, and long, shining black tresses fell to lie against her white neck. She looked utterly beautiful—and exceedingly frightened.

Lord Quinton Spencer, handing his top hat and cane to the footman, was also at the peak of fashion. Clean shaven now, he was wearing cream-colored doeskin trousers, fitted to his long, muscular legs, and over them a cutaway coat of brown velvet that accentuated his taut waist and wide shoulders. Waist-length in front, the coat dropped in lavish pleats on sides and back. Stripping off his gloves, he stepped forward to take her hand and bring it to his lips. Her hand was cold and trembling. Surprised, for he had expected a confident and self-assured woman, he tucked the small hand through his arm and felt hope leap into his heart. Until this moment, he had been extremely upset himself. He had supposed the visit was partly for arranging a divorce. And, he thought, it still could be. But perhaps a small chance still lingered. . . .

"Where shall we talk?"

"Oh. Why, down this hall there's a small library. Would that be a good place?" She hated the way her voice sounded. Half muted, half shaky. He looked so sure of himself. So handsome. And virile. The suit was new, and extremely becoming.

"That will be fine." He led her down the hall and stopped at the library door. Opening it, he ushered her inside and then closed it after them. Turning back to her, he smiled.

"You are at the peak of beauty, Rosamunde. Are you well?"

She managed a small nod. "Indeed. Very well. And you?"

He shrugged. "Aside from a twinge now and then from an old wound, I have no complaints."

She put out a tentative hand toward his ribs and snatched it back quickly. "That last wound . . . did it ever heal properly?"

"Yes. From the beginning, I had a very good nurse."

His green eyes, hopeful, met hers. Her face was sad, her lips trembled as she turned away.

"I suppose," she said, "that I'd better get on with my confession. You'll be glad enough for your freedom from me when you hear what I have to say."

He moved around in front of her, wondering, wanting to understand what she meant. "I doubt that. I have found our separation extremely lonely. I've missed you very much."

"Stop," she said fiercely, moving away, twisting her hands, "Just stop! This isn't a comedy, Quint, it's a tragedy. My sins have caught up with me. Sit down in that chair and let me talk."

He sat, wondering. So small, so belligerent. What sins could she have to confess? "Talk, then, my love. I promise to listen."

She paused, and then blurted out, "Will you promise not to yell at me?"

"I do so promise." He was suddenly amused in the middle of his misery, yet hopeful. Somehow he would find a compromise of sorts. He couldn't see life without her.

"Did Alan tell you about the murder of Squire Brownley?"

Quint's brows went up. It wasn't possible that Rosa was upset by the death of her stepfather, considering her opinion of the squire. "Why, yes, he did. In fact, I had already heard it. It's all over London. I understand his brother was the culprit. No one will miss either of them, I say."

"Lionel Brownley did not kill his brother. Anna did."

"What?"

Tears came to her eyes and overflowed, running down her pale cheeks. "I'll tell you again. Please listen. Lionel is innocent. Anna killed the squire."

Quint sprang to his feet. "What are you saying, Rosa? That's impossible! Anna never left your side after we married. She had no opportunity . . ."

She looked at him, straight into his face, and her wet blue eyes were dark with agony and regret. Quint read her feelings at last. He was white and silent as she went on.

"Cedric Brownley was killed and buried in the garden the night before we married, Quint. When I spoke of him then, telling you he'd been called away, I—I lied. If you'll settle down I'll tell you all that happened, and why it happened. Then you must tell me what to do."

"I do agree to that," Quint said somberly, and noticing how pale she was and fearing she might faint, he took her hand and led her to a small sofa. "I will sit, and you will sit with me while you tell me what happened."

She sat beside him, and he'd never seemed as big and powerful as he did this day. It was like sitting with a god who held life and death in his hands. She told him the whole story, from the moment she woke to find Cedric trying to rape her in her bed to the moment they had discovered the marriage contract and the gold pieces.

"I was frantic with worry because of Anna," she said, "for she had barely escaped hanging before, when she killed a man who tried to drag my mother into his carriage to abduct her. And I had no idea who you were. I pictured an old man who would raise a hunt for the squire and his gold pieces if I refused to marry him, so I put on the wedding gown and sent for a license."

She stopped and took several deep breaths, afraid herself that she might faint. But she made herself go on. "Anna and I divided the gold pieces and planned to make a run for it as soon as we could get away from the elderly bridegroom we believed would be coming for his young bride. We had no idea what to do or where to go, but I was determined to save Anna, and she was determined to keep me safe from scandal and out of an old man's clutches. But as soon as we saw you, we knew our scheme could never work. You were young, strong, and intelligent."

"Did you realize at the time that you would become hunted criminals if the story got out?" Quint's voice didn't rise; his face was still calm, but there was a deep concern in his eyes. "It could still be a scandal, my lady. We must be careful with this knowledge."

"I know. That is why I asked for you to come. It is your good name that could be sullied."

"And yours. You are my wife."

"That," Rosa said, summoning every ounce of her courage and sense of fairness, "will be rectified. You must put me away from you. You had nothing to do with the crime, and I want you to know I will not fight a bill of divorcement."

Quint leaned toward her, grasping her shoulders and looking straight into her eyes. "And I want you to know I will never divorce you, nor would I if you had killed the man yourself. You are the true love of my life, and I have been in my own bit of hell ever since I left. I will never again give you cause to leave me."

"Oh, *Quint!*" She burst into tears and fell into his arms, sobbing. She was so relieved, so hungry for his embrace, his healing kisses. She put up her face and when he kissed her she cried more, happy for the thrust of his tongue, for the taste of the man she loved. He lifted her into his lap and held her tight, conscious of the new weight in her small body, the bulge beneath the thin layers of silk. He put his hand there, and felt the bump and turn as the baby kicked and rolled. Then finally he pulled away from her kisses and settled her firmly in his lap, his hand on the peak of her abdomen.

"I'm moving in," he said, "and I want no argument. I've already missed part of this business; I will miss no more. My son is sending me messages of welcome."

"And so is your wife," Rosa said, sniffling, and tightened her arms around his neck. "I have decided that part of that silly quarrel was my fault, after all. I should have told you when I knew that I might be with child. But I was so afraid you'd leave me behind."

"I wanted you safe."

She smiled. "I am safe. And so is this energetic baby. Kiss me."

"So all of this is why Anna stayed in India," Quint said after long moments of heartfelt kissing. "Isn't it?"

"Yes, of course. She is safe there." Rosa's face was pink, washed clean of strain and worry. "I know she can be dangerous; her temper is quick and hard, her strength immense. But I love her, and she loves me."

"I know." He was silent for a moment, and then nodded abruptly. "I think I still have some little persuasion I can use on Robert Peel and his bluecoats. If it doesn't work, then we will have to go higher. But I promise you, no one will hunt down Anna, and the squire's distasteful but innocent brother will not be hanged."

"I knew you could figure it out," Rosa said, relaxing into his arms. "Poor Alan Ruether! He was shaking like a leaf. He looked so relieved when I said I wanted to talk to you."

Quint grinned. "He has his uses, Rosa. I asked his advice on disposing of the uncut jewels Akbar gave to Jon, and he said he'd take care of it. He sold them last week for four times the best offer we had received from the London jewelers. Jon and I are now gentlemen of leisure."

"Oh? Jonathan shared with you?"

"Gladly. He insisted. After the problems he caused by disobeying my orders, he felt he should. And so do I. That trip to rescue him had some harrowing moments."

She laughed and slid from his lap, standing and stretching, taking a deep breath. "Will you bring Jon to stay with us?"

"No. Only Thomas. We will remain in London until my son is born. Then we go back to Lundy Island."

She laughed again and whirled to a window, looking

out to the west. "Lundy! I dream of that place. When I first thought I might be with child, I thought I would have my baby there. But I suppose it will be safer here, in case of complications."

He came up behind her, resting his chin on her shining hair, clasping her in his arms, his hands cupping her swollen breasts. "Do you still want to have the baby on Lundy, darling?" He felt her head move as she nodded, and then she sighed.

"It's probably ridiculous, though. All that climb, on a donkey. And no doctor in case of trouble."

"There is an excellent midwife in the village." He felt her turning in his arms and smiled as she looked up at him, hope dawning in her eyes.

"Quint. Do you really think we could? I would love having the next Lord Spencer of Lundy Island born on his own estate!"

"Then the noble lying-in will be in the castle keep, as it should be."

She laughed and flung her arms around his neck to kiss him. "How marvelously suitable, my lord. How long will it take to move? I am eager to be a wife again."

"We'll not wait for the move, my darling. I'll not be parted from you, not even for a day."

"Wonderful! What about Thomas?"

"I'll leave Thomas in charge of packing and making arrangements for our trip to Lundy. And I'll send him to an appropriate doctor for a list of things needed for the lying-in. He won't mind the work as long as he knows we're returning to Lundy together."

"Where is he living?"

"We have both been living aboard the *Whistling Wind*, tied up at Saint Katherine's Docks."

Her eyes widened. "Our ship is here in London?"

Quint laughed. "We were here a day and a half before

you arrived, my love. We followed your great fat barkentine within one hour of your departure from Malta and passed it within two."

Her face lit up with excitement. "Oh! Can we go home to Lundy in our own ship?"

"Yes, and comfortably. We restored her well."

She hugged him, her cheek against his, clean-shaven again. "Ah, Quint, I'll remember this as a perfect day. I have been so lonely."

"And I. Thank God it's over."

Later Quint insisted on her having a nap. Then he went down into the cellars and came back with a cobwebby bottle of champagne. He put it to cool and prowled the kitchen, looking for red meat and oysters; when he found none he sent the footman for both, saying it was to be a celebration for two but to get enough for the staff to enjoy also. He was clearly walking on air, and the footman took the cook and rushed to do his bidding, hiring a horse and a cart to take them to market.

According to Rosa, the dinner was by far the best she'd had in England. And the wine—oh, the wine! Clear and crisp, with a wonderful aftertaste, and a lingering sense of pure gaiety. She was only a trifle dizzy when she went up the stairs with Quint, smiling with him as they spoke of Shulbita's dinners and Ranjit's gentle nature and wished them both there to have had this dinner with them. It was only later, when she dismissed Dorothy and said she could take down her own hair, that she became conscious of how she would look to Quint. That enormous, bulging belly, those heavy breasts—how could he think her body wasn't ruined for all time? She stood, hesitating and wondering if she shouldn't blow out the candles. . . .

"Quint?"

He turned toward her, his body the same as ever; smooth, with taut skin and rolling muscles, perfect except for scars. He had his coat, waistcoat and shirt off, and his boots, but his tight trousers gave away his thoughts. The doeskin strained around a tremendous erection.

"Yes, my love?"

Even his condition didn't make her feel less ugly. She put it down to his memories of her months before. She looked down at herself now and shook her head.

"I think," she said, turning her back to him, "that it would be better for me to take off my clothes in the dark. Otherwise you may find me repellent."

He came close to her back and put his arms around her as he had earlier. His hands again cupped her heavy breasts, and she felt the hands tremble. He kissed the side of her neck, his breath hot, his lips sucking her soft skin. "You," he said hoarsely, "are anything but repellent. You are like a goddess of love, so damnably erotic with my baby in there that I had to struggle to keep my hands off you in front of the servants. All I want is to be part of this. Now get ready for bed before I go crazy, will you?"

She hurried. Clothes flew, dropped, were thrown aside. Pins and ribbons came out of her hair; she shook it loose in a mass that spread over her shoulders and down her back. Then she wriggled out of her ruffled drawers and was naked, her body proudly erect, the swollen breasts tight and shining, dark rose nipples thrusting, and just below, the rounded, contained cradle of her belly that held his child. Quint drew in his breath and, to her amazement, tears sprang to his green eyes.

"I never realized how miraculous it is to see a new life growing," he said. "It's beautiful beyond words. Come, let me touch you, darling, for it's my miracle, too. That's my son you're making in there."

She went to him, amazed and happy, moving without hiding, and knowing at last that he truly loved her. And still wanted her! His arms closed around her; he picked her up and took her to their bed, his eyes still wet with tears, his love surrounding her, his passion rising hot and wildly sweet. . . .

It was perfect, she thought later, drifting off dreamily toward sleep. All three times.

Within a week Lionel Brownley was released from prison because of a lack of evidence against him. Sir Robert Peel put the story out to be published. It seemed that the old squire was living alone after his stepdaughter had married and had taken her bond servants away with her. And since he was killed and buried in his nightshirt, it seemed likely that he had surprised a thief in his house at night, and the thief had buried him to hide the evidence. It was known, Peel added, that the squire had a hoard of gold coins, which disappeared at the same time. Peel's written account ended with advice to readers with substantial hoards of money. He said they should invest their money in the Bank of England instead of keeping it at home, where it would be a sure temptation to thieves.

Alan Ruether breathed a great sigh of relief when his partner, Richard Plimpton, brought the news in and laid it on his desk. He read it and immediately put on his hat and coat, picked up the paper, and headed for Mayfair. He found Lord and Lady Spencer at breakfast, and the servants rushing about, packing Lady Spencer's clothes and effects. After hasty greetings, he sat down with them and accepted a cup of tea.

"I am filled with admiration, my dear little Rosa! Very few women would have had the courage to push an investigation of a suspected murderer. It is true, evidently, that this ill-favored and annoying little man was actually innocent, just as you said! You have saved his life, useless though it may be." He blushed suddenly. "Actually, I didn't intend those last words. It is not up to me to say Lionel Brownley is useless. He still deserves to live out his life." He looked around, hunting another topic. "What is all the turmoil this morning about?"

"We are removing to Lundy Island," Rosa said, and smiled. "Don't look so upset, Uncle Alan. I fully intend to honor my lease here."

"Oh. Why . . . no need for that, is there, Lord Spencer?"

Quint laughed, looking at Rosa. "None. It's our house, my love. Since I have paid off the loan at last, the house now belongs to me again. We will use it quite often, Ruether. But my wife has chosen to have our son born on Lundy Island, and we shall travel there tomorrow."

"Good heavens!" Ruether looked pale again. "Don't tell me you will risk the lives of your wife and child for a whim!"

"Lundy Island," Quint said calmly, "has a good midwife and nurses, and I have reason to believe my wife is extremely healthy. Besides, she has nerves of steel. Don't let it worry you, my dear sir. She asked to go, but I wouldn't have agreed to take her there unless it was safe."

"Nerves of steel?" Rosa turned to Quint, amused, as the heavy front door closed behind Reuther, "what makes you believe *I* have nerves of steel? You are the one with the colossal nerve. How dare you lease your own house to me?"

Quint laughed. "I didn't, of course. That was Ruether's idea, not mine. I borrowed against it two years ago, and he collected the rents to pay off the loan. Do you like it, my love?"

"I do. It will be a place to spend some time in London when we wish for a change of scene."

"Yes. Porter Ogilvie will have to find another rental for the London season. He has usually asked for it during the spring and early summer months, though as far as I know, he has yet to capture a young and wealthy wife. No doubt that is due to his lack of a title."

"Or lack of charm," Rosa put in, wrinkling her nose. "He seemed irritating to me. Do you suppose he's still on Lundy?"

"I certainly hope not. I sent Jonathan to Lundy as soon as we tied up, and I imagine Jon would get rid of Porter as quickly as possible. However, if he is still there, I'll run him off. Leave it to me."

Rosa smiled. Leaving it to Quint seemed to bring success in many problems. "Thank you, my lord. I'll see to the packing now. Has Thomas begun on his errands?"

"Indeed. We'll set sail day after tomorrow."

Chapter Twenty-three

❦

The evening of the fourth day the *Whistling Wind* nosed into the harbor of Lundy Island, dropped her sails, and coasted toward the docks. Fishermen on the smaller boats rushed to help secure the ship, laughing, calling greetings, pulling the barkentine into safe harbor. Watching from the quarterdeck, bundled against the sharp winds, Rosa looked up at the shining black rock wall that wrapped halfway around them. It was strange, she thought, that she felt at home here, felt to her own amazement as if she were safer here than anywhere else in the world.

Looking back, she realized just how little time she had spent on this small island before they left for their "wedding trip," that odyssey of high adventure and dangers she had never dreamed of. Yet over the months Lundy had become her cherished goal, her home—her den, where she would birth her cub. She laughed at that fancy, and Quint turned to her, an eyebrow rising, giving his sun-browned face a humorous cast.

"You are pleased to be here, then?"

"Very. I am even resigned to riding a donkey, m'lord.

But consider the added weight I'm carrying, and make sure the donkey is strong."

He laughed, putting an arm around her to help her onto the dock. "One of those donkeys carried Anna, my love. The smallest would be strong enough for you."

From the top of the cliff came a shout. "Need help, Quint?"

They both looked up. The face peering down at them was only a blur in the gathering darkness, but the voice was unmistakably Jonathan's. Quint waved him off.

"Stay where you are, youngster. We'll be there shortly."

Rosa had been sure that after the past few months of danger and real difficulties she would be immune to the hazards of the narrow trail up Lundy Island, the complaining, stumbling donkeys, the ominous rumble of surf on the rocky shore below. It was not true. Her eyes squeezed shut at the same dizzying spot she had closed them before, and her prayers were very like the simple prayers she had said on that first trip.

After all, she reasoned, they had proven to be effective. She hadn't fallen; she hadn't been killed. And this time she opened her eyes as soon as the donkey gained level ground and began to trot. Then she laughed, pulled up on the reins, and slid off to hug Jonathan, who hugged her back enthusiastically.

"What a wonderful woman you are, Rosa! Nothing frightens you, does it? Have you come to Lundy to show the villagers that they'll soon have another rascal with Marisco blood in the castle?"

She laughed. "Perhaps. And a touch of the dragon blood of Lady Beatrice Gilbert with it." She looked around, seeing the young maid Dorothy, pale-faced and dazed, sliding from the back of a donkey into Thomas's supporting arms. She smiled at them.

"Take her inside, Thomas, and see that Henry Trask receives her as my maid but his responsibility. As I remember, he prefers it that way."

Thomas grinned. "I also remember. But Ma wasn't an ordinary servant. M'lord was right to keep her separate from the others. Dorothy here will be well liked by all. With Ma, some always thought her dangerous. 'Twas better to keep them apart."

And then as they walked on, there was the lovely old keep. At the end of summer, the shadowy ruins of the courtyard were beautiful, with emerald moss between the paving stones, late lilies in the corners, and climbing roses blooming on the tumbled walls, sending their scent all about them. And just as they had been on the first trip, the wide doors of the keep were thrown open, the candelabra inside sent forth a blaze of light, and the staff was standing there to greet them. Rosa caught up to Quint, who was waiting for her, took his arm and went in. She was home.

They passed down the row of servants, nodding, smiling, saying a word here and there. Rosa stopped long enough to smooth back the unruly hair that hung down over young Robert Brooks's excited face and smile at him. As they came to the great hall and the dinner table, Kai Bey appeared suddenly from the shadows of a corner, came to her, and kissed her hand.

Straightening, he smiled at her, his dark, handsome face glowing with admiration.

"You look wonderfully well, Lady Rosamunde. Your stay in London has rested you, I am sure."

Rosa smiled and agreed. "And do you like England as much as you thought you might?"

"Indeed. I intend to live here, at least for a while, and see what I might learn to improve my understanding of the English peoples."

"I see. That seems wise before you make a decision. And your presence is a pleasure for m'lord. He will have another good friend nearby. That is fine, Kai Ibn Bey." She called him by his full name, formally, as she would always do in the future. That, she felt, would be best.

That night, lying together in the big bed where she had lain alone those first nights of their marriage, Quint spoke to her of his hopes and plans for the village people.

"The people of Lundy have made a lean living from fishing for many years. I hope to help them find other ways to add to their incomes. There is hardly enough pasturage for large herds of sheep, but the animals here are known for their excellent wool. In fact, the men tell me the women are expert at embroidery and knitting in the village, and that could easily be an industry in the future."

"Why, yes! I can see to it that they have customers," Rosa said into the dark. "Lady Killian is very fond of embroideries, and Lady Knowlton adores soft knitted shawls. They will know other women who will want the same."

"That's true," Quint said, and yawned. "Also, men like knitted mufflers in the cold weather ahead."

She sat up, excited. "Why, Quint, that is true! With the fall season coming on apace, there could be many orders. The islanders could become rich!"

"Good." He reached for her, lifting her over him. "Now that you've solved their problem, help me with mine. I'll never get to sleep in this condition."

She swallowed a laugh. His "condition" was throbbing against her slender thighs, hot enough to warm her with sweet anticipation. She slid upward and kissed his parted mouth, holding his flat cheeks in her soft palms while she explored his face with her lips, moving from his mouth to his closed eyes, his sensitive ears, smiling as he quivered, biting him gently on the neck and then soothing the bite with her velvety tongue. He tasted of salt and aroused man. Delicious.

"Is your condition improving, m'lord?"

"I am slipping over the edge of madness," he muttered, clutching her closer. "You are only making it worse. Or do I mean better?"

Her soft laugh turned into a seductive moan. His strong hands had lifted her hips, had managed to pin her neatly in place on his "condition." "There," he said, and blew out his strangled breath. "That's better. Now do try to remember . . . oh, my darling, my little love . . . do that again."

She did it again. And again. And then they lay in a murmurous heap, half gasping for air, half laughing.

"I love you," Quint said as the laughter stopped, "more than anything else in the world. And I have no doubts about you at all. I truly believe I sensed that secret worry you kept from me and knew you were hiding something. Now my faith in you is perfect. Never leave me, my lovely Rosa. Never."

The next day, Rosa visited the village midwife, Jane Byrd. Mistress Byrd, her dark hair going silver, was in her fifties but looked much younger. She took Rosa into a room she kept apart from her family and told her to lie down on the clean, high bed. Then she examined her, brows knitted in thought, pushing aside clothing and laying her hands on Rosa's bare belly. She closed her eyes, saying she could feel the position and movement of the baby better when she couldn't see.

"I, too," Rosa said, surprised. "When I waken in the dark and feel for movement, it is always clearer to me. It is as if your fingertips can see."

"This is a strong one," Jane said after a few minutes,

and opened her eyes, smiling. "We'll have no trouble with him. He kicks like a donkey."

Rosa laughed, adjusting her clothing. "How can you tell it will be a boy?"

"I am wrong at times. But you are carrying it all in front. From the back, no one would think you pregnant. That is often the sign of a male child. And you're young. A young mother is more likely to have a boy."

"I hope so. My husband is counting on it. He speaks often of 'his son,' as if he knew."

"Perhaps he does."

They talked. They counted up the weeks since her last flow, and decided that she would deliver within the period between the full moon of the coming week and the following full moon, twenty-eight days later.

"It is hard to wait," Rosa said, and Jane Byrd laughed.

"I hear that often, Lady Spencer. However, the time will pass. Send someone for me at the first solid pain. I will come to you immediately."

"What should we have ready?"

"Leave that to Lillian Brooks. She knows. She helps me often."

Walking back up to the ruined castle, Rosa felt surrounded by gentle women wiser than she. It was a good feeling. At the keep, she went in search of Lillian and told her what Jane Byrd had said. Lillian nodded and smiled.

"We'll have no trouble, Lady Spencer. You are young and strong and in good spirits. The birth should be easy."

"I feel sure you are right, Lillian. And I am glad to have two experienced women to help me." She turned away, and then turned back.

"Do you happen to know whether Lord Spencer is in the keep or has gone to the village?"

"Yes, he is in the keep. Where, I do not know. But he came in only a few minutes ago with his cousin, Porter Ogilvie."

"Oh." Rosa felt her heart drop as she nodded and left. Porter Ogilvie, he of the bright smile, the icy eyes. The cousin who wished himself the lord of Lundy Island. Why was he here? It was certain that he had no love for either Quint or Jonathan, so it had to be that he was looking for a favor. Or for an opportunity.

At the sound of boots in the gallery overhead, she looked up and saw the two men, neither of them smiling, coming toward the stairs. Porter eyed her from above, and coming down the steps, he was the first to speak.

"Ah, Quint, your lovely lady is as lovely as ever, and she is bearing you a child. How terribly delightful. Another Marisco pirate, I suppose." Stepping down from the stairs with a swagger, he came to Rosa and lifted her hand to his lips. "So, Lady Rosa, you are doing your duty—providing another lord of Lundy to take over after your husband. You look marvelously well."

There was nothing wrong with his words, but his tone and his eyes both betrayed his real feelings. There was venom in every syllable, and a look of cold dislike on his arrogant face. Quint moved in and took Rosa's arm, turning her so that he stood between them.

"I'll let you see yourself out, Port. Are you staying in the village?"

Startled, Ogilvie laughed harshly. "Indeed, if the keep is filled by your growing staff and family, perhaps I must, at least for a day or so. I will see you again before I leave." He left, letting himself out the big doors. Quint breathed a sigh of relief and looked down at Rosa's pale face.

"Ignore him, my darling. He has another spot he insists on digging up. He cannot forget that old story of the hidden gold."

Rosa's face was suddenly full of amusement. "There is hardly a manor house in England that hasn't its secret cache of gold and jewels, according to the legends. However, I would hate to base my future on finding any of them. But I see no reason why we should forbid him the chance. Work in the open air and sunshine may improve his disposition."

That evening, when Quint, Rosa, and friends came together at the dining table, Kai Bey and Jonathan told of watching Ogilvie from a distance as he dug around the crumbling walls.

"He is very serious," Kai said, amused but puzzled. "He attacks the wall with all his strength. I believe he is sure of eventual success. However, it seems hardly likely to me that your long-ago ancestors would bury treasure in the outer walls of the courtyard. Wouldn't a man hide his gold in the walls of his own room, so as to protect it?"

Quint looked at him and laughed. "Indeed. However, please refrain from mentioning that to Cousin Porter. In a word, I'd like to keep the keep. His dashing holes in the walls of our rooms might make the place rather drafty."

Kai nodded. "I understand."

There was a silence while they all ate and drank, searching without success for another topic. Gradually, their food disappeared from their plates; the dinner was over. They all rose, knowing that the staff was also hungry and waiting their turn.

Then Jonathan sighed, throwing down his napkin.

"To be truthful," he said, "Porter embarrasses me. Like a family ne'er-do-well, he demeans us all."

A door closed, and a tall form emerged from the shadows. "I suppose, dear Jonathan, that while it's you who speak of me, you are likely giving the same opinion the rest of the family has. None of you has ever given me a kind thought."

Jon turned and faced Porter Ogilvie, his color draining away, whether from embarrassment or anger, it was hard to tell, but he wasn't shy about answering.

"Nor have you ever blessed one of us with affection, Porter, since we left childhood. Only sarcasm, jealousy, and dislike. How could you expect warm family feelings?"

"You and Quint fell heir to every acre of this land," Porter said. "An angel would be angry at something so unfair. I may not be Marisco, but I'm part of your family, and I should have had a share."

"You always knew that only those with Marisco blood could share in Lundy, Porter." That came, calm and cool, from Quint.

Porter came closer, his face red with anger. "You could change that, Quint! But you won't, will you? You'd leave me to starve before you'd share the profits from your lands." His eyes flicked to Jon. "And you, Jon. You've been in enough scrapes yourself to understand why I've nothing left of the miserable pittance my father left me. Have you no generosity either?"

Quint gave a short laugh. "That 'miserable pittance' your father left you was twice the amount our family left to the two of us. You spent it, cuz, on fine clothes and worldly pleasures. I suggest you find work."

"What kind of work, Quint? Piracy?" Ogilvie sneered. "I'd rather try your second line—wedding an heiress."

Behind Quint, Rosa gathered her skirts and slipped past him through the door and across the great hall to the stone steps that went up to their room. She was trembling, hating the sound of the quarreling men, the bitterness that had seized them. Just looking into Porter Ogilvie's face, she had seen the kind of man he was. It was there in his eyes: hatred, jealousy, anger. It was as if men who looked at him became infected with the same feelings, and she was even more afraid of the thought that now came into her mind—would this end in bitter fighting?

She ran up the stairs, still agile in spite of her burdened body, and picked up a candle from a table nearby; lighting it from the lamp near the door, she went into their room and closed the door behind her. There were two other candles in their stands, and she lit them both before she blew out the one she carried. Better, she quoted to herself, to light a candle than to curse the darkness. But still her heart was heavy. She had never had a sister or brother, nor even a cousin, but she had heard it said that no other enmity could match the murderous rages that erupted in quarreling families.

After she removed her clothes and put on her nightgown, Rosa took one candle to the wardrobe and knelt to open the bag tucked in back on the floor. She took out of it the dueling pistol she had never used and brought out with it the box of powder, the lead balls, and a greased square of cloth. After she had poured in the powder and tamped down the ball in its cloth, she pulled back the trigger to half cocked, brought out the explosive caps, and put one in place. Then she put everything back except for the loaded pistol, which she put in the top drawer of her dresser. There was no real reason in her mind for any of what she did. It just seemed to be a thing she should do. Hate was gathering like dark clouds around Lundy Island. Around Quint.

Rosa was asleep when Quint came to bed, and he was careful not to waken her. In the early morning she wakened just enough to mumble to him as he got out of bed, then turned and went back to sleep. Something told her to rest, and she obeyed. She slept until almost noon, and then, waking and seeing how far the day had progressed, she was ashamed of her laziness. But she felt wonderful.

The door opened, and Lillian Brooks poked her head around the edge. "Are you all right, Lady Spencer?"

"Oh, yes, I'm fine." Rosa swung her legs out of the bed and stood, stretching her arms above her head, arching her back. "I overslept, didn't I? So lazy! I'm hungry, though. I'll dress and be right down. Where is Lord Spencer?"

Lillian frowned. "He left for the village early and hasn't returned. No one is here except for Porter Ogilvie, who is banging away at the old walls again." She came in, shutting the heavy door behind her and looked directly at Rosa, speaking softly now. "Why does he do that, m'lady? He knows as well as anyone that there are no hollows or crevices in that tumbledown wall. Most all the servants think him crazy."

"As I do," Rosa said, and shrugged, turning away to find a gown. "Perhaps he does it hoping for sympathy, or hoping Lord Spencer will give him the money to leave. He's—very peculiar, I say. Will you send Dorothy to me, Lillian?"

"I will, m'lady. No pains this morning?"

Rosa smiled, liking the thought. "Not yet. He's stubborn, Lillian. Perhaps he prefers his warm quarters."

Lillian laughed. "Robby talks constantly of the baby. He is hoping it will be a boy he can play with. I've told

him babies can't play with ten-year-olds, but he says
he'll wait."

"I hope my son will be as charming and good-natured
as yours. Robby is a wonderful child."

"I thank you for that, m'lady. And I'll see to Dorothy." Lillian left, closing the door, going quickly down
the steps, calling for the maid.

It was a strange day. While Dorothy helped Rosa
dress, the air was cool, almost cold, but the sun was
bright and there was no wind. The noise of Ogilvie's
pounding echoed and reechoed in the crisp air when
they went down to the kitchen. Taking pity on him,
Rosa had Robby take out a bowl of soup and a chunk of
homemade bread with butter.

"At least," she said to Lillian, watching from the window as Porter ate ravenously. "He won't starve. But he
must be cold."

"Not if he keeps on splitting stone," Lillian said.
"He'll be warm enough from the effort."

"Perhaps." Rosa fought a feeling of guilt. The man
must have a place in England that would be warmer
than Lundy—and certainly he would have a warmer
welcome there. "Has he family, Lillian?"

"None, or so he says. One of the fishermen said he
had a woman with him when he came down to the
Clovelly wharf one day, but not the kind of woman a
man marries."

"I see."

"My lady, he is not worth your thought. He used to
come to see Lord Spencer and his brother years back,
when he had his portion from his family. He was
dressed fine and wore jeweled rings. And a braggart he
was, lording it over the Spencers, who were struggling
to keep the village going and themselves, too. And never

a penny did he offer for his lodging and food. Don't waste pity on him."

"Then I won't. He doesn't deserve it." Rosa shut the window and pulled the heavy drapery across it, muffling the sounds of Ogilvie's pounding. She decided that the sooner Porter Ogilvie realized that no one on Lundy was going to help him, the sooner he would leave. He must know by now that the legend of hidden Marisco gold was only a fairy tale, a tale of wondrous treasure tucked away in the walls of the ancient castle by men who had made the seas their own and exacted payment from the others who plowed their waves. A flamboyant tale, perhaps once true, but surely the gold was gone. Only the legend remained, passed down from Marisco to Marisco to keep the old, resonant name alive.

Chapter Twenty-four

———— ❧ ————

*I*n the afternoon Quint, Jonathan and Kai Bey came home from the village, having spent nearly the whole morning talking to the villagers. Quint sought out Rosa in their room, where she sat reading. He was excited, walking back and forth as he told her of the day. Plans had been made; land that had long lain fallow would be planted again, and the sheep would not all be killed for meat. Half of them would be sheared and the wool spun and made into fabrics.

"The villagers had fallen into a hopeless life," Quint said to Rosa, "for they lacked leadership. The old men had died. Now they want to make their lives better. We will help them."

Rosa nodded. "We will. They are good people. Your son will grow up here and know them." She hesitated, wondering if she wanted to hear his answer when she asked, "That is, will we be here most of the time, or will we be sailing?"

Quint laughed. "How did I know you were going to ask that question? I must have, for I have an answer ready. We will do both, but as my son grows old enough for school, we will stay here from fall to spring. Summer winds will find us gone."

Rosa went to him and put her arms around his neck, her eyes soft. "I will like that. Summer winds . . . Ah, but that does sound lovely. My heart yearns for the blue Mediterranean. But not, if you don't mind, for the hot desert sands."

He laughed again and hugged her. "Nor do I yearn for desert heat and long treks, my dear love. But still we may visit India again. We both have friends to see there."

"True. We will go. We will see Shulbita and Ranjit again, and visit Anna and the maharani. Thank heaven the threat of Murad's assassins is gone."

There was a knock on the door of their room. Quint's eyebrows rose at the interruption. He went to the door and opened it, frowning. Henry Trask was there, looking at Quint apologetically.

"Mr. Ogilvie is here, Lord Spencer. He insists on seeing you. Something to do with the walls, I believe."

Quint's frown deepened. "The walls?"

"Yes, m'lord. The walls of the keep."

"Good God! The man is crazy." Quint pushed past Henry and headed toward the steps down into the great hall. His bootheels rang a resounding cadence. His voice came back to Rosa's ears, flaring with anger.

"What in the name of God gives you the right to burst into my home, Ogilvie? You've been creating a nuisance outside for days—can't you see you aren't welcome here?"

"Now listen, Quint. Be reasonable. The gold we sought must be in these walls, not those crumbling bits outside. And I want my share."

"Your share, Port? Your share of what? The Marisco legend? There is no fortune in gold here."

Rosa, coming to the thick balustrade that ran around the gallery above the great hall, looked down at them, amazed at the change in cool and fashionable Porter Ogilvie. He was sweating and red-faced, his fine clothes stained and dusty, his boots rubbed dull from particles of smashed rock. He looked a different man, his lips trembling, his eyes wild and reddened. He still carried his sledgehammer in one hand, as if he'd forgotten he had it. But when he spoke again, his voice was different —not pleading, now. Telling.

"I suppose you know where it is, Quint. You're just waiting for me to leave so you can have it all. But I won't leave. I've nothing to go back to. No house, no money. Not even a horse." He laughed harshly. "Not even a whore. She left when the money was gone. I've thought of flinging myself over the cliff out there, but I haven't the courage." He shifted the sledgehammer to his other hand and wiped his face with his filthy neckcloth. "And that," he said, "is all your doing. If you'd have taken me in on your deals abroad, I'd be in clover, just like you. Like Jonathan. Riding high."

Quint hadn't moved. Now he did. He came down the other three steps and put a hand on Ogilvie's shoulder. "I'll give you a hundred pounds, Porter, as a gift. That will get you home and keep you until you can find something to do. You've been educated; you can find a position. But there is nothing on Lundy that belongs to you. You must accept that."

Watching from above, Rosa saw Ogilvie's face go pale, his brown eyes darkening to near black. But he lowered his face too quickly for her to decide whether he was angry or pleased by Quint's offer. Staring down at the sledgehammer, shifting it again to his right hand, Porter Ogilvie nodded.

"I'll take it, of course. At this point in time, I would

have taken half of that and left the island. I'm glad to get the hundred."

"Fine," Quint said, and turned to go back up the steps. "I'll get it, and you'll be ready to leave on the tide."

Motionless on the gallery, half hidden by the railing and the shadows, Rosa saw Porter raise his head and stare after Quint. There was a look of pure hatred on his arrogant face; a look that sent shudders through her, squeezed her heart with fear. She turned and went quickly into their room, where Quint was counting out the money he meant to give his cousin. She shut the door behind her and went close to him.

"He hates you, Quint! I saw the look on his face as you left. He truly hates you. Be careful."

Quint smiled grimly. "With Port, I am always careful. But he'll not hurt me while I'm handing him money."

"Still, my love, be alert. Both Jonathan and Kai have left the hall, and the servants are busy with dinner. Who knows what he may do."

She watched him leave the room, and her heart was still cold. A pulse beat heavily in her throat. Quint hadn't seen that look, didn't fear the man. But she did. That sledgehammer was a terrible weapon. A blow could split a skull. . . .

Turning, she went swiftly to the drawer where she had put the dueling pistol. She took it and went out again on the gallery, holding the pistol by her side, hidden by her skirts. The two men were standing as they had before, alone in the great hall, and Quint was counting out the money again, into Porter's outstretched hand.

"There," Quint said, giving him the last of it, "you're on your way, Port. And I wish you luck."

Porter Ogilvie put the money in his pocket. He stepped back and smiled, hatred in his eyes.

"And you," he said, taking the handle of the sledgehammer in both hands, "are on your way to hell!" He swung the weapon with all his strength, aiming at Quint's head. But Quint, seeing his intention at last, threw up an arm and leapt toward him. Still the thick handle hit his shoulder and he went down, headfirst, slamming onto the stone floor, sliding away from Porter. His body jerked once and was motionless.

Rosa cried out, and Porter looked up and laughed with breathless surprise. "How dramatic! You will see your husband die, Lady Spencer. Even his hard head will be crushed like the stones outside when I hit him with this!"

Rosa took a deep breath. Then her hand came up, the pistol fully cocked. Her other hand joined it, and she leveled the pistol at Ogilvie. "No! I will shoot you if you step one foot toward him."

For an instant, Porter hesitated. Then the wild hatred showed again. He took a step and raised his weapon. "You're shaking like a leaf, my lady. You'll miss your mark—but I won't. I'll have my revenge. Your husband dies, now!"

"My husband lives!" Rosa cried fiercely, and pulled the trigger. The shot shook the air, echoing and re-echoing from the stone walls. Across the great hall, Lillian Brooks screamed once and rushed forward. Porter, dazed and bleeding heavily from a wound in his shoulder, dropped the sledgehammer and staggered outside through the open door, howling hoarsely, falling on the stone steps. He struggled up, crying out like a child, and ran, wobbling and screaming, toward the path down to the ships. Rosa heard his cries as from a long distance. She was running down the steps to the great hall, dropping the pistol and going to her knees beside Quint. Lillian joined her, and together they lifted his head, feeling for blood.

"No blood," Lillian gasped, and felt further. "Only a swelling!" She took a deep breath and sat back as Quint opened his eyes and pushed himself up, blinking, coming to his senses, looking from one to the other, shaking his head and then holding it, rubbing the swelling on one side.

"What in hell happened here?"

Rosa sat back and wept with relief, covering her face with her hands. Quint turned to Lillian, who looked as if she too might cry. More of the staff had gathered, Henry and Evaline Trask, shocked and silent, and young Dorothy, who came to stand trembling at Rosa's side.

"Brace up," Quint said, staring at Lillian and Rosa. "Stop weeping, for God's sake. Who's dead?"

"Your lady has just saved your life!" Lillian squawked at him. "She shot Mr. Ogilvie. He was going to smash your skull." She pointed a shaking hand at the sledgehammer. "With that!"

Quint looked at the sledgehammer and then at Rosa.

"That's right, I remember now. He swung on me and knocked me down. *You* shot him, m'lady? With what?"

"My d-d-dueling pistol, m'lord. I have it . . ." She reached behind her fluff of skirts and found it where she'd dropped it. "Here. You keep it. I don't want it anymore. I don't ever want to shoot anyone again. It—it was awful, even though I had to do it. I h-h-hated it!"

Quint looked at her pale face, at the tears running down it, at the sad, drooping corners of her lovely mouth. He winced.

"I'll make sure you won't have to, my darling. That's my duty, not yours. But I have to admit I'm glad you took it on today." He waited for her answer, but she said nothing. She had ceased to weep. She panted, and her eyes widened, amazed.

"Quint?" She said his name on a gasping breath, and then "Quint!" It sounded demanding. He stared at her. She had never been demanding before. She was looking right at him with those wide eyes and not seeing him at all; whatever she did see with that intense look had awed her into silence. He was suddenly frightened for her.

"What is it, my love? Are you all right?"

She took a deep breath, looked at him directly, and smiled. "Yes. I am all right. A little shaky, but I am fine." She took a handkerchief from her sleeve and mopped her eyes. "Help me up."

Quint was up and pulling her up beside him, putting an arm around her. "A thing like this," he said, trying to ease her mind, "would make anyone shaky. I am shaky myself, I think. But you needn't fear Porter now—he'll stay away from here. He's not a brave man."

Lillian got to her feet, staring at Rosa, watching her closely. When Rosa winced and spread her hands beneath her belly, Lillian stepped over beside her, taking her other arm.

Rosa looked at Lillian and nodded. Then she turned back to Quint, her wide eyes a brilliant blue, excited and amazed. "I do believe, m'lord, that our son has decided this day will be his birthday."

"Oh my God," Quint breathed, and gripped her tightly. "What shall we do? Let me carry you upstairs."

"I have her, m'lord," Lillian said, half laughing and trying not to, "and she needs to walk. You'd best send Robby for Jane Byrd."

Quint turned and stared at the shocked gathering of servants.

"Why in hell aren't the rest of you doing something?

Didn't you hear? Get Robby and send him down for Jane Byrd, and—never mind! I'll go myself!" He shot through the door, leapt down the short flight of steps, and headed toward the village, disappearing rapidly in the gathering shadows.

"Well," Lillian said, helping Rosa up the stairs, "that bump on his head certainly didn't slow down Lord Spencer. Let's get you ready for Jane, and then we'll walk. The walking helps."

An hour later Jane Byrd arrived, breathless and still wearing the kitchen apron she'd had on when Lord Spencer appeared at her house. However, the few things she needed were always packed and ready. She had grabbed her case as he pulled her through her front door.

Jane looked up at Lillian and Lady Spencer strolling back and forth on the gallery and smiled, relieved. They smiled back at her.

"Now, Lord Spencer," she said, turning to him, "you may leave us and find your dinner. All is in order."

"Thank God for that," Quint said, letting out his breath. "Remember, my wife is not to suffer at all. I'll not have it. She is extremely nervous today. She shot my cousin."

He turned and went rapidly toward the other end of the great hall, where a subdued Jonathan and Kai were waiting in front of the fireplace, nervously looking toward the shadowy figures pacing back and forth and not wanting to intrude. Quint stopped and looked at them.

"Did you hear? All is in order now. Break out some brandy, Jon. I need a tot."

Jon cleared his throat. "Did I hear you say that Rosa killed Ogilvie?"

"No, of course not. She merely shot him through the shoulder, and he ran off. Or so I am told."

"Why?"

Quint took the brandy Kai offered him and drank it down. "There. That helped, Kai. Very warming, brandy is. Have some. You look a bit pale."

Jon reached out and gripped Quint's arm. "Listen, damn you! Is she hurt?"

"Oh, no. She's having the baby, that's all." Quint's tall form wavered and Jon eased him into a cushioned armchair.

"Quint? Buck up, brother. Are *you* hurt, then?"

"I may be a bit dizzy, Jon. Ogilvie attacked me with his sledgehammer, and I have a knot on my head."

"Good God! He actually hit you with his sledge-hammer?"

"Oh, no. He hit me with the floor. Then Rosa shot him so he couldn't do it again."

Walking past, Lillian Brooks stopped and looked at Jonathan. "I can explain, sir. Let Lord Spencer rest."

Quint leaned back in his chair and closed his eyes. "Yes. Thank you, Lillian. I am a bit confused. Is the baby here?"

"No, m'lord. It will be hours yet. But your wife is fine. She said I was to tell you not to worry."

Quint visibly relaxed. "Then that's all that matters. She knows, I'm sure. I'll just sleep here, in this chair. If my wife needs me, you know where I am."

At midnight, there was a knock at the front doors. Jon, who had thrown a pallet on the floor before the fireplace and slept on it in case Quint needed him, got up and went across the great hall to answer the knock. John Slater came in, carrying a canvas bag. He set it down and spoke in hushed tones.

"Your cousin Ogilvie has been found dead at the bottom of the cliff, with a gunshot wound in his shoulder. The wound was not serious, but evidently he fell over the cliff and broke his neck. There was a hundred pounds weighing down his pockets, and I thought perhaps he had, ah, stolen it. I brought it along, and there it is, in that bag."

Jonathan nodded. "Indeed, and you are quite right. Ogilvie went crazy when he couldn't find the hoard of gold he thought was hidden in the castle walls. He knocked Lord Spencer down with that great sledgehammer of his and took the money. It was Lady Spencer who winged him with a shot, but we would appreciate your silence on that part."

John Slater stared at him, his mouth open. "Indeed, I'll not mention that! Good God, and her in a delicate condition! The poor woman must have been horribly frightened."

Jon nodded. "Again you are correct. It saved my brother's life but shocked m'lady right into labor. We are waiting now to hear what the midwife will say. She is with her now."

"Ah, the pity of it. Our poor lady. She's a brave one, sir. Listen, I and my men will dispose of Ogilvie's body. We'll give him a Christian burial at sea, and I'll report the death to the Clovelly justice as accidental. I'll not be lying, either, for it was the fall that did him in."

"True." Jon clapped Slater on the shoulder. "You're a real gentleman, Captain. No one outside the family needs to know the poor unfortunate man's greed and lack of morals. I know Lord Spencer will be shocked and sorry, but he will also be glad not to be a subject of undue gossip. He'll be down to thank you when he's on his feet again."

"Then I'll be on my way. You can promise the family there will be no talk of this at all."

"Thank you, Captain." Closing the door, Jonathan felt close to righteous. That, he thought, went very well. Making his way back to the still smoldering fire, he saw the small licks of flame glinting in Quint's open eyes.

"Ah!" Jon said, grinning widely. "You're awake. Did you hear that?"

"I did."

"And what did you think of it?"

"I was greatly relieved. However, it taught me something."

"What, Quint?"

"It taught me to look behind your friendly talk and find what you are really saying. You have a real talent there—you could be a solicitor."

Jon's face fell. "You have no gratitude," he grumbled, and flung himself down again on the pallet. "Go to sleep."

"That is not all it taught me, Jon. It also taught me that you have grown up. And that your affection and loyalty to me and to Rosa are very valuable assets. I won't forget."

Jon chuckled. "That's better. You are thinking clearly again. Good night, Quint."

"Good night."

An hour later, both were wakened by a feeble cry. By instinct alone, Quint knew at once who had made the sound. He leapt to his feet and rushed toward the gallery stairs. Another, stronger cry followed, and he took the stairs two at a time. Trying to waken, Jon shambled along behind him in time to see him stop at an opening door, through which a soft light gleamed. Standing in the opening, Lillian beamed at Quint.

"That was a boy you heard, Lord Spencer, and a beautiful, strong baby he is."

"But my wife?" Quint asked shakily, "Is she all right?"

Rosa's voice answered him laughingly from beyond the door. "I'm fine, m'lord. Everything is fine. Just give us a few moments to make ourselves presentable and you can see for yourself."

Quint sagged against the doorway and nodded at Jon, a foolish smile settling on his haggard face. "My wife is fine. My son is fine. Everything is fine. It's over."

Jon laughed out loud, full of joy and relief. "Over? I think this part of your life is just beginning, Quint."

Quint's smile widened. "If I live with that woman in there for a hundred years more, it won't be long enough for me. I only hope you do half as well, little brother, when you choose your destiny."

Jon laughed and then sobered, leaning on the wall beside him. "I, too. She's a wonder, Quint. So young, so brave and resourceful." He sighed. "And so beautiful." He straightened and gave Quint a slap on his sagging shoulder. "I'll not intrude on the three of you, big brother. I'll see the baby later." He left, yawning, heading around the gallery toward his own room and disappearing within.

Minutes later Jane Byrd came to the door and motioned Quint in, leaving the room herself. She was smiling, pink with pleasure.

"They are waiting for you, Lord Spencer. You may stay for a while."

"Thank you, Jane. I won't tire her." He stepped inside, closing the door. The room was glowing with candlelight; candles were everywhere, in sconces on the wall, in candlesticks on the tables, the dresser, the wardrobe, and the tall chests on either side of the bed. None were as bright as Rosa's eyes, blue stars in a flushed face, her smile greeting him.

He came to the edge of the bed, his eyes on her, soft, searching, intent.

"Are you really all right?"

"I'm fine, Quint. Really fine. Jane says I'm one of the naturals. No problems at all. And just look at your son."

She pulled back a corner of blanket from the small bundle in her arm and showed him the red, sleeping face, the round head, the small hand. She took Quint's hand and brought it down to the baby's, and the baby grasped the big forefinger and wouldn't let go. She laughed and Quint smiled, dazed and unbelieving, looking from the baby to her.

Then, without removing his finger he reached behind him and pulled up a chair. Sitting, he examined the baby minutely, touching the fuzz of black hair, opening the blanket with his free hand, going over the small body delicately, then pulling the soft cover closed again. The baby opened his eyes and blinked, letting go of the finger and making a small cry.

"Shhh," Quint whispered. "Don't make a fuss. You and I have the best of all worlds. Let's not ever complain."

Rosa broke into soft laughter. Pushing herself up on the pile of pillows, she exposed a tight, shining breast and held the baby close. He mouthed the nipple and then took it greedily.

"Oh, good!" Rosa exclaimed. "He does know how. I offered before, but he didn't take it. That's wonderful, isn't it? He's already learned."

Quint stood up, wavered, and caught his balance, still exhausted, still feeling wonderful. He beamed down on his glorious family.

"But that was to be expected, m'lady. After all, he's

my child. His instincts are finely honed. Wouldn't surprise me a bit to learn he was reading my mind."

Rosa gave him a startled look and then hid her expression by looking down at the baby. Still, Quint could see the corners of her mouth curling upward.

"Quint," she said, "I want you to get some rest. I'm worried about that big bump on your head. Everything is fine now, and we can all sleep safely in our home."

"Wonderful," he said, and leaned down to kiss her softly on her parted, smiling lips. "I love you, my darling girl. I'll love you forever."

She felt tears well up in her eyes. She reached up and touched his bristly cheek. "And I love you, dearest Quint. You fill my heart."

Quint's mouth curved in a faint smile; his finger touched the small, fuzzy head at her breast. "Make space for this one, too, my love. I won't mind sharing with him."

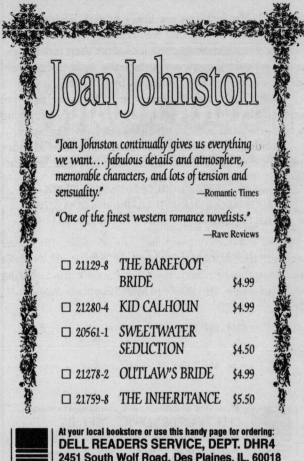